Smash all the Windows

JANE DAVIS

This book is a love letter to everyone who is trying to make a life out of whatever they've been left with.

It is also in memory of Les Moriarty, whose morning missives always raised a smile, and who was so generous with kind words and encouragement.

PRAISE FOR THE AUTHOR

'Davis is a phenomenal writer, whose ability to create well rounded characters that are easy to relate to feels effortless'.

Compulsion Reads

'Jane Davis is an extraordinary writer, whose deft blend of polished prose and imaginative intelligence makes you feel in the safest of hands'.

J.J. Marsh, author and founder of Triskele Books

CHAPTER ONE

Gina, 2016

As the court steward opens the door, Gina's scalp prickles. It's as if an electrical charge has entered the air. She gives the framed photograph of her son – her Ollie – one final look. Her hope has been that, held upright in her lap throughout the second inquest, it would remind both witnesses and jury that her son was a person with a life every bit as vivid and complex as theirs – just how complex, she'd had little appreciation of. But it has become more. Something to sing her silent lullaby to when she could no longer bear listening to the witness testimonies. *Hush Ollie, hush Ollie, hush Ollie.* When, at last, she was forced to confront the moment of his death. *Hush Ollie.* Now, Gina is jolted by stark realisation: *had he lived, he would turn twenty-nine next Thursday.*

It seems impossible.

A second jolt. Her forearm is grabbed. "Mum!" Tamsin's breath brushes her cheek. "It's time."

Not impossible, she reminds herself as she squeezes her daughter's hand. Two years and three months separated Ollie and Tamsin. Unbridgeable then, now the gap would seem insignificant. Tamsin might even have gained the upper hand.

Gina rallies because she must. She slots the photograph inside her handbag, which she stows under her seat.

Just in time.

Here they come. The members of the jury. Feet shuffling. Eyes purposefully downcast. Expressions impenetrable. Not a glance towards the families. Acutely aware that Tamsin is looking to her for reassurance, Gina reaches again for her daughter's hand.

Damn you, Bill! You should be here.

Though her ex-husband began the drawn-out process of leaving on the day Ollie died, he's still Tamsin's father. But Bill wanted nothing to do with the second inquest. The failure of the class action finished it for him.

"Even if we finally get to the bottom of what went wrong, unless someone's brought to task, it won't change a bloody thing."

Gina couldn't allow herself to believe that.

Get over yourself, Bill. You can't continue to hide behind Jackie and the baby. Even now, at this defining moment, bloody Jackie is in their midst. The last person Gina wants to think about. She pushes her aside, reminding herself why they're here: to erase injustices, to clear the names of their loved ones, please God. The point isn't blame. It's the reverse.

With a scrape of chair legs, the jury sits. A second hush falls, deeper than the first. As Gina inhales, doubt fills her lungs. For over thirteen years the search for truth – for the undoing of injustice – has eaten up everything. Marriage, friendships, family, health, career, finances. Now she isn't sure she can bear to listen to the jury's interpretation of how hundreds of almost indistinguishable elements collided and went tumbling, tumbling, down. She's afraid of what comes next; afraid of what Tamsin is about to hear. Already, images will be imprinted on her retinae that no sister should ever have to see. But Gina can't waver, not now. Everything she was, she has invested in this.

She risks a sideways glance at the Chapples. A combination of determination and vulnerability, Maggie Chapple has made the journey each excruciating day of the eighteen-month inquest. At the start, her curls were sleek chestnut, and soft. Now her hair is wire wool.

"*Look, there she is, all on her own.*"

"*Who?*"

Gina had given a slow, measured nod in the direction of the woman wearing the smart suit. "*I'll just go over and pay my respects.*"

"*Why the hell would you do that?*" How quick Bill was to write Maggie off.

"*Because she's lost a child, like us –*"

"*She's nothing like us! She's got a bloody nerve showing her face!*"

This version of her husband was a stranger, his anger new and startling, but Bill wasn't alone in his thinking. When Maggie took a seat that first day in the row reserved for family members, resistance was tangible. Maggie must have felt it, must have been wounded. At times, given the revelations about Ollie, Gina has wondered if anyone else would want to sit next to *her*. It was Maggie who made sure she never had to find out. Gina draws strength from this unlikely friendship of theirs.

The way Maggie's face moves suggests she's chewing the soft inside of her cheek. She's gripping the hand of her husband, Alan – a quiet man who radiates quiet strength in a way Bill never could. She's holding on for dear life. Gina reaches for her right hand and feels a twitch of surprise before Maggie glances up. In a moment's eye contact, Gina offers her a silent promise. To see this through together.

As Gina turns back towards her daughter, Donovan acknowledges her with a nod. *You aren't the only one without a partner here to support you.* In all this time, she has never met Donovan's wife. Quite why is never spoken of, but the fact that it's not a subject for discussion is an understanding of sorts. Donovan raises the hand in which he has Tamsin's right hand. *I've got her.* A swell of gratitude washes through Gina. She hopes something of it is transmitted through the chain they've formed. The rows of bereaved, devastated, wrecked family members.

Movement. All eyes turn as the spokesperson for the jury stands. Nobody dares breathe.

The Coroner clears his throat before addressing her: "I'm going to go through each of the fourteen questions in turn, and you will answer with a simple yes or no. Do you understand?"

The poor woman wets her lips, nods. It isn't a role Gina would wish on anybody.

"Do you agree with the following statement, intended to summarise the basic facts of the incident? On 22 August 2003, following the admission of a large number of passengers, fifty-eight people died in the disaster at St Botolph and Old Billingsgate stations after falling on or from the escalators."

The spokesperson's voice quivers. "Yes."

Though Gina's limbs are perfectly still, her blood is restless.

"Was there any error or omission on the part of station management or staff, for any reason whatsoever, on 22 August 2003, which caused or contributed to the dangerous situation that developed?"

"Yes."

Several rows behind Gina, someone is already weeping. Whatever Gina has to endure, it will be ten times worse for the Chapples. Whatever Ollie was or was not, unlike Rosie Chapple, he wasn't supposed to have been in charge.

Around her, an eruption of wonder, joy, tears. As the spontaneous applause directed at the jurors peters out, the families turn to one another. "We did it!" they repeat in disbelieving voices, and, "Finally." Words spool without registering. *The crowd was not responsible!* Gina repeats this to herself, clasping one hand to her mouth. She'd always hoped, of course she had, but this is a moment she has barely allowed herself to imagine.

"What just happened?" Beside her, Tamsin sits back down and grips the edge of her seat as if she risks falling off. Her head drops forward and hair curtains her face.

Gina squeezes her daughter's shoulder but struggles to remember anything after the Coroner's third question. The isolated phrase *unwiped truth* swims towards her, unmoored from its context. "We won," she says with a swirling eddy of emotions. "I can't quite believe it." But a shadow passes through Gina as Ollie looks up from somewhere deep within Tamsin's dark eyes. He shouldn't have been one of the fifty-eight. *Why, oh why, did you have to try and be a hero?* "Take all the time you need," she manages.

It's not just Gina who has received what others will call good news. Behind her, Alan is murmuring to Maggie. *I should say something.* But Gina must wait for Alan to release his wife from his embrace. He gives the slightest nod over Maggie's shoulder and steers her around.

Disorientated, Maggie reaches out her arms. "Gina. My God. I never thought I'd be so glad to hear Rosie called a victim… This is…" Her unlikely friend falters.

The victims have been referred to as the fifty-eight for so long, it will be tough for Gina to adjust her thinking. The corners of her mouth twitch into a lopsided smile. At a loss for something appropriate to say, the idea that anyone would want this… She goes to hug Maggie, who claims the words for the first time.

"Rosemary Chapple. Victim fifty-nine."

CHAPTER TWO

Gina, 2016

Through the double doors, release. One hand on her daughter's arm, it's unclear who's steering who. Outside, a surreal ambush. Flashing bulbs, camera crews, lorries topped with satellite dishes. Gina shields her eyes against the sensory onslaught, narrowing the view through her fingers to a slatted-blind arrangement.

"Delivering up to the minute breaking news, we bring you the reactions, live, from outside the court."

Penned in on the courtroom steps, a growing atmosphere of expectation has turned her insides to liquid. If only the rest of her body could complete the process, pooling onto the granite step and trickling between the polished shoes of those standing in front. Instead, every tortured smile, every anguished frown, will be transmitted into living rooms the length and breadth of Britain. This knowledge magnifies each tiny tremor at the corner of Gina's mouth, each blink, each pore. Just as their loved ones were declared the property of the Coroner, just as politicians and priests laid claim to the disaster, the press believe the public is entitled to the families' churned-up emotions. Thirteen years ago, it had been just the same.

"You have to expect it."

"Expect it? What we need right now is privacy. Privacy to grieve."

Though she'd thought his anger justified, Gina held Bill back. Second only to grief, hatred of the press is the thing that unites the families. What journalists do, what they've done in the name of 'truth', is indefensible. It would take little to convince Gina that their own Chuck Tatum had constantly dreamt up new ways to prolong their ordeal in order to come up with tomorrow's feelgood headlines. Triumph over adversity sells newspapers.

Someone stumbles into the narrow space Gina had deliberately left between herself and the next person. As an elbow scrapes Gina's arm, she looks accusingly at a jacket sleeve.

"Merde." Unmistakable. A Gallic growl, only one syllable but not a letter wasted, the final emphasis on the 'd', a springboard. It's Jules Roche, unwitting poster boy for the disaster, then a young man cradling the head of his infant son. Reluctant to embrace the success that came about as a result of the disaster, he gained a reputation as something of an *enfant terrible.* "Forgive me, Gina," he says. "It is so crowded."

"Don't worry." She forces the smile that's expected, at the same time reassuring herself that the toes of her shoes haven't strayed too close to the edge of the step; that she's in no danger of falling and pulling Tamsin with her. But it's Tamsin who tugs on Gina's arm, her expression bewildered.

"They won't expect us to say something, will they?" Mascara has left a slight smudge under her right eye.

Gina's only certainty is that her need to break free of the crush is rising. "Just let one of them try and shove a microphone at me," she erupts.

"Look at them." Jules nods. "Each after his pound of flesh."

Just then, amplified words in a familiar voice: *"They say that anything is true if enough people believe it. And why wouldn't people believe what so many newspapers printed as 'fact'?"*

Gina squints as she looks about for the speaker, locating the back of Sorrel Carwood's head. Their solicitor has positioned herself between the families and television crews, a welcome buffer.

"Pound of flesh. *Pfff!*" Jules adds with ruffled intensity. "What kind of saying is that?"

"But repetition alone doesn't make lies true. Today, the families have been vindicated."

These words demand that Gina stands to attention. As Tamsin hisses, *"Merchant of Venice,"* she turns to hush her daughter. Again it hits home. Tamsin is a grown woman, more than capable of deciding for herself what is and isn't appropriate. As for Jules, he's an artist; immune to what others think. And his son, that small child whose head he was cradling in the shot that appeared on all those front pages – the enduring image of the tragedy – he must have reached Ollie's age... Ollie's age when...

She brushes the corner of her eye. It will always be like this, see-sawing between pride in her daughter and profound sadness at her son's absence. There cannot be one without the other.

"Always it is Shakespeare or the bible." Jules speaks across Gina. "My Evelyn would tell me off for not remembering. She try her best to educate me."

How casually he mentions his wife. As if she's just stepped out for a few moments.

"Thirteen years after the 2003 tragedy, the jurors have contradicted previous findings, deciding that the behaviour of commuters did not contribute to the disaster."

A cheer goes up. Eric's face stands out among the cameras and sound-recording equipment. The real hero of the hour. This result is the culmination of his years of research, his burnout, his breakdown. His mouth is moving, as if he's transmitting words to his wife.

"Though it wasn't on the scale of Bethnal Green, Aberfan or Hillsborough, the St Botolph and Old Billingsgate disaster will form part of the nation's collective memory."

It moves Gina to know that they rehearsed for success. But there was never any doubt in Eric's mind. Today's verdict was another of his inevitable outcomes.

Someone who's aware of the connection between Eric and the families' solicitor comments on how refreshing it is to see a man who's happy to let his wife take the limelight. The record will show that today's victory was Sorrel's. Gina is among those who will remember it differently.

"No single community had to absorb the shockwaves. The families – those you see here today –" briefly, Sorrel's serious profile comes into view, *"were spread out all over London, its suburbs and beyond. Some of the victims were tourists, simply passing through. Thirteen years later and the identity of one man has yet to be discovered. He is known only as Victim Thirty-four."*

Time for reflection. Insulated inside the head-bowed silence, Gina recalls how Eric first turned up on her doorstep, barely able to make eye contact, fiddling with the file he held in front of him, nails bitten to the quick. Six years later he still resembles the fidgety youth who begged for fifteen minutes of her time, but he, too, is changed.

"That lack of community has been particularly tough on the families. They haven't had the kind of support that comes from knowing your neighbours have been through the same as you."

Desperate to convey something of what she feels – overwhelming gratitude mixed with something bordering on maternal pride – Gina wills Eric, *Look at me for just one moment.* But he doesn't, and that's fine. He has a mother of his own.

"Nonetheless, the families are members of a club they can never leave. Today's outcome was the result of their dogged

persistence. A refusal to be dismissed and ignored, a refusal for their loved ones to be vilified." Sorrel punches the air. *"The crowd was not responsible!"*

A roar of approval goes up. Sharp bursts of "Come on!" Though her firm might have preferred a verdict of unlawful killing, Sorrel represented the families' wishes. Integrity like that will bolster her reputation. It saddens Gina to think that it should have bolstered Eric's.

"We should feel ashamed that people who had already lost so much have been put through this further unnecessary ordeal. How many more times must someone stand here and say, 'Justice delayed is justice denied'?"

Cheers erupt. From Gina's vantage point, she spies a trestle table, on it a dozen green glass bottles. Champagne. Now that the journalists with their lenses and recording equipment part to let them pass, Gina desperately wants to stay put. The sight of Tamsin in high heels, striding down into her own shadow, makes her uneasy. She finds herself falling into step with Jules, but the mechanics of walking feel unnatural, as if dictated by the ranks of cameras massed before them. "Champagne! Can you believe it?" she says.

"You prefer gin?"

Should she tell him? *'I'm an alcoholic.'* He'd be the last to judge. But he's only teasing. She tempers her reply with sarcasm. "It's not from you, is it?"

"You think *I* have a crystal ball? No, Gina. The champagne, it is from one of the big newspapers." He raises his eyebrows as if shrugging the journalists off. "They want their photo. They want to make loose our tongues," Jules continues. "But I have other plans."

"Are you heading straight back to Paris?"

"Not for a few days, *non.* I have business over here."

Gina struggles to think of sculpting as a business. Though outdated, her image of a solitary craftsman chipping away at a block of white marble stubbornly persists. "Anything interesting?"

"I have a piece being shown at the Whitechapel Gallery but," he pauses and gives an awkward smile, "there is another possibility."

"Oh?"

"I cannot say anything yet. Perhaps it come to nothing."

The pounding of feet. *"Jules! Jules Roche!"*

"They have found me out." He gives her a gentle push. "I think you will want to go ahead."

"You don't have to talk to them, you know."

He shrugs. "I could stay away but I choose not to. Go! I will find you."

She agrees readily, then stops. It's as if she's gone upstairs to fetch something and can't remember for the life of her what it was. Tamsin. She scans the scene, looking for her daughter.

"Champagne?"

Already, a scattering of people are clutching the stems of champagne flutes. God knows, Tamsin could murder a drink. She imagines knocking back the first one and holding out her glass for a refill. But she won't accept a thing from the bastards who printed those lies. She has other plans.

As she waits in line, a television reporter close by speaks into a microphone: "The families and survivors were systematically bullied, intimidated, manipulated or used for personal and political gain."

Impatience clogs Tamsin's throat. *You've changed your tune. Bloody hypocrites, the lot of you.*

"Here we are," the waitress says, sounding a little too pleased with herself.

Mum constantly tries to impress on Tamsin how much she adored Ollie, dismissing their teenage spats as a phase that would have quickly resolved itself. But it's as if the data has been wiped from her hard drive, and each reminder of this failing produces fresh agony. Not today. Today, she has the opportunity to make up for it.

A final glance at the camera crew, Tamsin stages herself as she would a prop. Her chin is high as she takes the delicate stem of the glass. (It's a good weight; the waitress hasn't skimped.) She turns and, as she knew she would, finds several lenses trained on her. The same camera crew who, if the families had lost today, would have recorded that arrogant bastard saying, 'There comes a time when you have to accept that, no matter how many different ways you find to ask the same question, the answer will still be no.' Well, he's just had a few of his assumptions turned inside out. Tamsin smiles directly into a camera lens and raises her glass. What she's about to do requires no script. She won't give the fuckers words.

Fill your boots, Ollie, this is for you. She tips her champagne flute. The balance shifts. From behind Tamsin comes a collective intake of breath. Conversations halt. The sound of champagne hitting tarmac is deeply satisfying. 'Like someone having a wazz,' she imagines Ollie saying and, for the briefest of moments, he's here with her. They aren't at each other's throats, Mum isn't having to say, 'I don't care who started it, I'll finish it!' They are simply sharing the moment.

Liquid pools near her high-heeled patent-leather shoes.

'New shoes, sis?'

'Clarks – but don't tell anyone.'

'The shame!'

'I know.'

'Remember how we –?'

The reduced weight, the twist of her wrist, tells Tamsin her glass is empty. When she staged this moment in her mind, others joined her in one united gesture. Dangling the upside down champagne flute in one hand, Tamsin watches the last few drips with a kind of fascination, hoping that a camera will capture them, glistening and jewel-like. Ollie is gone. They are back to not talking to each other. Headphones on. The Keep Out sign on his bedroom door. And she is back in the real world.

From between the shoulders of the camera crew, observing her daughter's performance, it's as if Gina has been looking through the wrong end of a pair of binoculars. How did Gina miss Tamsin's transformation into this marvellous defiant creature? I mean, she always *was* defiant. But that was before.

Tamsin has sought out Gina's gaze, seems to be seeking her approval. Gina tightens her mouth, nods. *Yes, I saw. Everything.* Their exchange doesn't go unnoticed. A camera is turned on Gina. "No, thank you." She shields her face from the lens, irritated by her own politeness as she sidles out of the way.

Would Jules call her daughter's lone protest 'art'? And where's Maggie? Did *she* see? Gina weaves backwards. Lord only knows where all these extras have appeared from. The press corps have multiplied. She spots Crisanto, one of the so-called 'fortunate ones' who took the witness stand to have all those memories dredged up. The twenty minutes or so when he waited to be pulled from the pile of bodies, head locked, chest pinned, desperate sounds all around. Someone praying. *Someone praying Lord, kumbaya.* It was begging really, begging to some unseen force. *You will not fear the terror of night, nor the arrow that flies by day, nor the pestilence that stalks in the darkness, nor the plague that destroys at midday.* He didn't seek comfort in the psalms. Into Crisanto's mind drifted his grandmother's voice, bringing tales from a distant childhood. Aponibolinayen, a mortal who marries Ini-Innit, the Sun. Aponibolinayen, wrapped in the vine and the vine carrying her upwards until she reaches the sky. But Crisanto wasn't wrapped in vine. He was wrapped in tangled limbs and, as time went on and people ran out of air, they grew quieter, deathly quiet. He saw bodies that would later be marked 'not to be viewed', where identification had to be made through the contents of wallets and handbags, dental records, fingerprints; in one case, a helium balloon tied to a broken wrist. "It's something you never escape from," he told the courtroom, close to breaking. "That, and the fact that you lived, while they..."

Again, Gina is struck by how irrevocably affected he is by the suffering he witnessed. Other survivors told of chaos, confusion, things done in moments of panic, things that would have been unrepeatable were they not under oath. But no one else spoke of blackened and swollen tongues, faces such a deep shade of purple that you could barely tell black skin from white. Even now, Gina shudders at the sight of Crisanto's raw, slightly manic look.

"All these years, I've lived with the idea that the behaviour of 'the herd' – yes, that's what they called us." He folds one arm across his body and supports it, as if it's in need of a sling. "They made it *our* fault. I heard it repeated so often I came to believe it."

They *must* see he's in no state to go on. But the ringmasters want his distress; the tremor of his chin as he struggles to retain dignity. These are the kind of wankers they've been forced to deal with over the years. *Yes, I do mean wankers,* she answers the critic inside her head. *That's* exactly *what I mean.*

"It's not as if I told them anything different this time round. Shame on them for refusing to listen all those years ago!"

Speedily convened, speedily concluded, that's what Sorrel said about the public enquiry in her summing up. Not that Gina thought so at the time. All she remembers is the overpowering sense of betrayal. Now Crisanto is backed up against a broadcast van, microphones thrust at him like blunt weapons. While her thoughts are changing from *someone should rescue Crisanto* to *I should rescue Crisanto,* her mobile buzzes. She twists to sift through the contents of her handbag. "Hello?"

"I take back everything I said. They actually did it." In the midst of this madness, the familiarity of Bill's voice offers comfort.

She reminds herself that she's supposed to be angry with him. "I tried to tell you. Conviction like Eric's goes a long way." At the time, shining through the paper-thin casing of his nervous exterior, it meant everything to Gina.

"I was so mad at you for going against me. I thought he was looking for something to beef up his CV."

"He's never taken the least credit."

"I know that now."

Gina's emotions shift. On top of everything else, what is as close to an apology as she's likely to get is too much to bear. She has no idea how to hold herself, how to stand, how to breathe.

"Are you still there?"

"I'm here. I just… I don't know." She turns on the spot. "It doesn't feel the way I thought it would."

"You can't rehearse for something like this. You feel the way you feel. That's it."

Irritation creeps under her skin. *Now you find the right thing to say.* There's no way to rewind the clock and Gina doesn't want Bill to try. The need to finish this conversation transforms itself into an urge to move. "I'm… I have to go now." She begins to walk. "I'm wanted."

"Wait! Is Tamsin with you?"

"Not right this minute, no."

"Tell her I saw her on television… Tell her I'm proud of her, will you?"

"She should hear that from you, Bill. Just swallow your pride and call her!"

Gina spots Maggie. More accurately, she spots Maggie's hair. She feels the need to vent: *Bloody Bill never thinks of anyone but bloody Jackie and the bloody baby.* But that will have to wait. Maggie is standing beside Alan as he reads to camera from a sheet of paper. Never having heard him say more than the odd sentence before, Gina weaves closer.

"Time and time again, we've been asked, 'Why are you here? This isn't your daughter's inquest.'"

Echoes of Bill's words. He wasn't the only person to voice them but unlike the others he isn't here to take them back.

Suddenly Eric is by Gina's side, serious, nodding. She says his name, "Eric," condensing such feeling into that one word. She cannot help glancing at him from time to time as Alan continues.

"No, it wasn't our daughter's inquest. At the start, based on what the families of the fifty-eight had been told – the lies they'd been fed – we understood only too well that we were the *last* people they wanted to see. People were angry, rightly so, but Rosie became the focus of that anger. We received hate mail. Hate mail. After losing our daughter."

Unable to help herself, Gina gasps. She looks at her friend in a new light. Her head may be high but her mouth is quivering. Gina holds Maggie in her gaze. It's all she can offer, as one mother to another.

"We risked causing offence because we always believed that when the full facts came out, as they eventually had to, people would understand that Rosie was a victim too.

"Today, we've had that belief confirmed. Brand new to the job, she should *never* have been left in charge. The risk assessments, oh, there were plenty of them, but management only ever considered the possibility that *one* thing might go wrong at any one time." Maggie's nostrils flare. "The whole system was bursting at the seams. Four hundred thousand more passengers a day than in the mid-eighties. *Years* of underinvestment. Jobs automated, so when an emergency happened there weren't enough staff to cope. Recommendations made in the aftermath of King's Cross still hadn't been implemented." Anger clouds Alan's features. There's a sharp crack as he flicks the page in front of him. "The list goes on! And the thing, the truly awful thing is, even after today's verdict, I honestly believe it could happen again tomorrow."

"There," Eric says, his voice low. "That's the soundbite the journalists have been waiting for. Tomorrow's headlines."

CHAPTER THREE

Eric, 2008

E ric untangles himself from Sorrel's arms.

"Do you have to go?"

"Duty calls."

The last thing he'd expected was to find himself in bed with the smartest – not to mention the most attractive – girl on his law degree course. Least of all after an afternoon lecture, both of them perfectly sober. Though Eric has been naked in front of several women before – hell, he posed for an art class when he fell behind with the bills – he's embarrassed by his pale limbs as they emerge from under the duvet. Aware that Sorrel is observing him (she's someone who never just watches), he can imagine what she must be thinking.

"You have very pale skin." See. The girl's a mind-reader.

"I'm blue-blooded." Still perching on the mattress, Eric steps into his underpants. Already, the magic is fading. He's served his purpose. Tomorrow, when they bump into each other in the library, they'll pretend to be casual, conversation strictly limited to case law, names, dates. But how is it possible to be so awkward with someone when you've just…?

"I can see your veins."

As he pulls his underpants over his thighs, Eric feels the

lightest touch. Sorrel must have reached out to trail a fingertip down the length of one of his blue veins just as he pushed himself to standing. He steadies himself from the thought, decides he must have imagined it. With no time to shower, he dresses – undies, jeans and a jumper – then kneels to drag the musty-smelling costume out of his kitbag.

By the time he's hauled it clumsily over his head, Sorrel is up on one elbow, tousled. "Is that what you're wearing?" She gives a lazy half-smile.

He holds out his arms in their ridiculous sleeves. "Don't you think it suits me?" Formerly a costume monk's habit, a packet of black dye has given it a new lease of life.

"But you walk to work, wearing *that?*"

He pulls the hood over his head. "I like to get into character."

"As Obi-Wan Kenobi?"

"Close." He holds up one finger, a kind of *wait for it.* Then Eric kneels with as little grace as someone who's accidentally knelt on a piece of Lego, takes some lengths of plastic from his kitbag and assembles a scythe.

She laughs. "I don't know what to say. What does that make me?" Her next thought follows swiftly behind. "Does guiding pay well?"

"No."

"Oh," she says, clearly disappointed.

"They don't *have* to pay well because tourists tend to tip. Americans are the most generous. I lie awake at night praying for Americans." Then it strikes Eric. "Shit. Can I ask a small favour?"

She purses her lips. "You can ask," she says, in a way that suggests the answer will be no.

"Could I leave my bag here? I can't really take it with me."

"No problem. I'll bring it in tomorrow."

"I don't want to put you out. I'll drop round later and pick it up." *Idiot.* Of course she doesn't want him to call round later. Why would she?

Her eyes widen. "Are you *worried* people will think we *know* each other?" She lies back on her pillow, staring at the ceiling.

He's so obviously blown it.

"Pick it up next time if you prefer."

"OK." Eric suppresses the fizz in his stomach, not wanting to question his understanding of what's just been implied. "I'll, uh –" He points at the door, looks at Sorrel as if he's checking it's the way out. "I'll see you tomorrow, then?"

She clears her throat, points to her cheek. "Don't I get a kiss goodbye?"

He almost stumbles in his rush to lean over. She turns her head so that her lips meet his. To be fair, it's not a bad effort.

"The Grim Reaper." She sighs. "That was certainly a first for me."

Eric closes Sorrel's front door. His self-image has just undergone a dramatic transformation. He walks into the waiting dusk with a spring in his step not usually expected from Death personified. *Next time.*

By far the most effective approach when dressed for the part is to stand stock still until the last possible moment, like the out-of-work actors who dress as statues at Covent Garden. A small group of tourists has gathered by the south-eastern entrance of Bethnal Green station. A couple of Americans, judging by the way they're dressed. And here's Eric's number fourteen. "Is everyone here who's coming, Ladles and Jellysp–?"

A middle-aged Japanese woman visibly startles. One hand is high on her breastbone, fingers splayed. Several large plastic rings adorn her small bony fingers.

"I'm sorry, I was going to ask if we're all ready. You know it's odd," Eric muses out loud. "People happily hand over their hard-earned cash, but apparently it doesn't occur to them that their tour guide might speak." The truth is that tourists embarking on a ghost tour often tend towards jumpiness. "You don't mind if I…?"

"No, no." Her voice is staccato. She leans backwards, away from Eric. "You took me by surprise, that is all."

"Yes." He elongates the word and gives her a look of mock condescension. "Then I'll start by letting you into a little secret. Not all of you. Just you." The hand he extends is naturally pale and bony. It helps. "The young lady in the fetching glittery scarf."

The shortest of the group and hanging back, the girl glances uncertainly at her mother, then touches one hand to her chest. *Me?*

"Yes, you." He beckons. "Over he-ere."

The balance between embarrassment and curiosity tips. Having decided to play along, she now looks rather flattered to have been singled out.

"You see, I'm not really the Grim Reaper." Eric rolls his 'r's and pulls back his hood to reveal a shock of red hair, then bends down to exaggerate a whisper, close but not too close, loud enough for most of the gathering. "I'm actually Eric the Viking."

This raises a small polite laugh. "You don't believe me? It matters not. And I'm here to tell you that ghosts don't care whether you believe in them either." He nods. "They're too busy. Existing."

The thing that's made the greatest impression on Eric since he started guiding for Ghost Tours of London is this: people *want* to go along with whatever you tell them. He's just a facilitator. Now he draws them in, lowers his voice and confides: "London, as any fool will tell you, is the most haunted city on this planet. Every street corner, every alleyway, has its own ghost. But tonight we're going deep down into the bowels of the earth."

Unlike Ghost Tours' average guide, Eric isn't an out-of-work actor. Though his stage will be a courtroom rather than Shakespeare's Globe, he must be every inch as convincing as any Hamlet. Ham it up though he may, his intent is deadly serious. "Imagine you're working late at night in an under-world station. My apologies, did I say underworld? Slip of the tongue. I meant under*ground*. *Under*ground," he repeats to himself, as if trying to make the revision stick. "You've just turned off the platform lights and you're heading back to the cramped, white-tiled staffroom, when a noise stops you in your tracks." He cups one ear. "It sounds like children sobbing." Shakes his head. "You dismiss it. After all, you just watched the last train leave. There are no children here, not at this time of night. But now there's a sound that's impossible to ignore: women screaming in panic. Terrified, you run towards exit three. Oh, look!" He feigns surprise as he looks up at the sign for the station. "This *is* exit three. Shall we?" Eric steps as lightly as Gene Kelly (punters expect a little showmanship), then gives an impatient backwards glance. "Come along, gather round!" He shines a torch on a small plaque on the wall.

The site of the worst civilian disaster of the Second World War.
In memory of 173 men, women and children who
lost their lives on the evening of Wednesday 3 March 1943
descending these stairs.

Eric, who has climbed several mountains, recalls his Scout-master's words: "Ninety-nine per cent of accidents happen on the way down."

"'Why were they in such a hurry?' you ask. Good question. Construction of the Central Line's eastern extension began in the thirties. At the outbreak of the Second World War, tunnelling was complete but rails had yet to be laid. *Voilà,* your perfect bomb shelter!" He extends an arm, his robes swirl. But wait: he detects a doubter. "Oh, yes! Entire families would sleep on what would later become platforms. Instead of cocoa in front of the living room fire, your average evening routine involved sending a responsible adult to the Bundle Shop – a left luggage room full of bedding – and from there to bag one of five thousand bunk beds, while someone else gathered up kids, toys and rations. Meanwhile two thousand hardy folk would grab a space on the floor.

"This particular Wednesday evening happened to fall just two days after the RAF began to bomb Berlin. The good British public had been warned to expect retaliation from the Luftwaffe. It was pitch black. Much darker than it is tonight. For starters it was early March. Still a hint of winter. No street lights, no house lights – because that would have shown the Germans the way. People were feeling their way down the blacked-out staircase, everything nice and orderly – because, after all, queuing is what us Brits do best." A few nervous giggles, but he had their attention. "If anything, they were going slower than usual because it had been raining. I don't know if you've heard, but very occasionally it does that in London!" Right now, it's drizzling, but soon that won't matter. They'll be underground. "And the steps were a little slippery. At twenty seventeen – that's military speak for seventeen minutes past eight – the air raid siren went off. Still nice and orderly. All terribly British. But then there was a noise like nothing anyone had ever heard before. And it was coming from very close by."

No jokes now, no more camp impressions. The Grim Reaper becomes still and sombre. Eric wants his audience to feel the change. He meets a smile from the girl he singled out earlier with a shake of his head. Recent ghosts deserve respect. "We know that a woman with a small child fell, but she was already near the bottom of the steps." He points downwards. "We know that an elderly gent walking close behind her also tripped. Remember how dark it was? People had to *feel* where they were putting their feet. They couldn't see what was happening in front of their faces, let alone what was down there at the bottom of the stairs. They kept on coming. After all, the Germans were getting closer by the minute and parents were desperate to get their children to safety." Eric pauses, draws a deep breath. "Lifted off their feet by the force of people behind them, they toppled like dominoes." Conscious of the young girl, he holds back on the detail. Silence and imagination are a powerful enough combination. Tangled in an immovable mass, twenty-seven men, eighty-four women and sixty-two children were crushed and asphyxiated.

With a stern look he silences a couple who have bent their heads and are whispering. Looking up to the right, he pretends to listen. "I can't hear them tonight. We're safe to go lower. Follow me." At the bottom of the run of steps they cluster once more, closer this time because space is limited. "Police Constable Thomas Penn arrived at the shelter with his wife. Right away, he knew something was terribly wrong, so he told her to stay where she was. To get to the place we're standing now, he had to crawl over the bodies. Twice he fainted as the horror of what he was doing dawned. After he found all those people trapped, he then crawled back out to send for help.

"Miraculously, the woman who'd been at the front of the group survived. Sadly, her child didn't. The youngest to be killed was Carol Geary. She was five months old."

Not one of his party speaks now. A few steps further on, Eric ushers them to one side of the tiled ticket hall. Rush hour is supposedly over, but a steady trickle of passengers gives the group a wide berth. Having brought the mood down, Eric must now perk it back up. "A brief history lesson! In 1860, a Dr Cumming announced that construction of the Underground would disturb the devil, thus precipitating the end of the world. Well, it opened in 1883 and," he pinches himself, "I'm still here. Would you like me to –?" He goes to pinch the nearest man, who jerks away his arm and cradles it protectively. "Have it your way. Now, I'll be honest with you. It's been a while since the devil and I had one of our *soirées*." Eric's image of the devil is the South Park cartoon version. A sympathetic character, frequently misunderstood, yearning for a glimpse of sky. "But," Eric smiles ruefully, "the construction most certainly disturbed the dead.

"Tunnelling for the Victoria Line ran into trouble when they drilled straight into a forgotten plague pit." He holds his nose with one hand and wafts away an imagined stench, then waits for the groans to subside. He indicates a map of the Underground on the wall. "Makes the tracks look straight, doesn't it?" A slow headshake. "Mm-mm. In the dark ages, summers in the City weren't what they are today. People were terrified of the plague, and rightly so. To prevent the spread of infection, pits were dug deep in the earth where they buried their dead. When the plans for the Underground were drawn up, no one knew just how many pits there were – or where they were located. Excavations for the Piccadilly Line unearthed one that was so dense with skeletons, workers had to go around it."

He's about to remark that, to the construction workers, it must have seemed as if the whole of London was a graveyard, when the girl with the glittery scarf pipes up, "They should have asked you!"

"Well, yes, now you come to mention it, that would have been the sensible thing to do," he uses the point of his plastic scythe to scratch delicately at his chin, "I can't imagine why they didn't. My hourly consultation fee is most reasonable. But *they* always think they know best. *Now* they know better. One of the pits was under Green Park, right next to Buckingham Palace. 'Was' being the operative word. And, as the network expands, more and more forgotten graves are being unearthed. So, really, it should come as no surprise that, in the most haunted city on the planet, the Underground is the most haunted place of all. Tickets please!" While he glides over to the barrier, a drawn-out screech jars his bones. "Worse than nails being dragged down a blackboard! Nothing to worry about. Not yet, anyway." He pretends to inspect his party's tickets before directing them through. "If you could wait for me at the top of the miraculous moving staircase. Oh, you know what it's called! You have them too? Well, in that case you probably know that when escalators were introduced, the Underground had to employ staff to demonstrate their use before they could convince the public that they were safe." He grabs the moving handrail. "Personally, I've never been convinced but here goooooees." Eric inhales that distinctly Underground smell – rubber, rust, soot-blackened tunnels, and the friction of wheels on track combining with the pheromones of four hundred thousand anxious commuters.

A sudden jolt just before the train draws into Liverpool Street, and Eric begins to describe for his attentive audience the man in white overalls who's regularly spotted by night workers as they patrol deserted platforms. "One employee who went to investigate an unusual noise saw nothing, but his colleague who was manning the CCTV monitor insists the pair were standing side by side. Another worker found an abandoned pair of white overalls. They had no idea who their ghost could be, but a recent excavation found hundreds of human skeletons, as many as eight per cubic metre. Imagine eight bodies crushed into every space…what, so big." Eric spreads his arms to approximate a cubic metre. "Potential for an awful lot of ghosts."

"Mind the gap!" one of Eric's party shouts to a teenager who has hauled himself out of his seat.

"Fuck off," comes the response.

"And that's another thing about us Brits," Eric reassures his group. "We're all so terribly polite."

As the carriage rattles towards Farringdon, Eric tells his group about Anne Naylor, an eighteenth century orphan whose phantom stalks station corridors, terrifying passengers with her screams. As if on cue there comes a sound – a high pitched echo that fades into the night. One of the group gasps. Eric pauses, blinks several times then dismisses it with a shake of his head. "Only brakes. Sadly. When approached, Anne Naylor's ghost disappears into thin air. She was killed by her master at a London workhouse, who dumped her body where this station now stands, leaving her to spend eternity passing endlessly through Farringdon's corridors.

"Now we're arriving at Bank station, and I'm going to take you up to see the entrance, which was constructed out of the crypt from the adjacent church. That's right. A *crypt*. Is it any wonder the station is haunted? Keep your eyes peeled for a sinister-looking spirit. Known locally as the Black Nun, she's believed to be the ghost of Sarah Whitehead, mourning the death of her brother Philip, who was executed for the forgeries he carried out while working at the Bank of England." As his neck hairs prickle, Eric laughs at himself. If he's managed to spook himself, he must be getting good at this. "Unrelated, but equally creepy, the foul smell some passengers report when they spot her may have more to do with the fact that the station was built on top of –"

"Another plague pit!" The Japanese woman has got over her initial shock and is really getting into the spirit of things.

Eric smiles at her. "How did you guess? Here's where we get off, so do please mind –"

"Mind the gap!" they chorus.

"Oh, very good! You know, arriving here, workers and travellers often report feelings of sadness, concern, and hopelessness. And it's not just the thought of another day at the office. In October 1940, a bomb blasted through the ticket office, killing over fifty people."

"Right here?"

"Upstairs, yes. We'll pass by the exact point on our way. Then our final stop will be Old Billingsgate, converted from the fish market established by Royal Charter at the beginning of the fifteenth century."

"*Very* old Billingsgate," the Japanese lady quips.

It happens as they turn the corner. Eric is buffeted by what feels like a familiar backdraft, but then he's struck by a terrible sensation. No words in his vocabulary can describe it. The feeling of being exposed is only a small part of it. He's being watched. Cold rushes through his bones, carrying a pinching fear to his very core. He slows his step, not wanting to be the first to arrive at the steep rise of the escalator. He turns his head sharply; looks for a rational explanation.

Someone says, "You know, it *is* kind of creepy down here," but the voice is distant.

Other voices are far closer. Primeval, yet distinctly human. Beyond words, beyond language, they chorus. They're wailing, lamenting, *calling his name.* This is no cross-draught. This is not the approach of a train. This is a great mouth consuming the bodies of the damned. Eric spins and the nearest members of his group hear him say, "What do you want with me?" Later he will say that the floor fell away from under his feet. He saw himself plummeting down. Everything and everyone around him was falling, hands flailing, grasping, finding only air.

He comes to lying on cold tile, a large uniformed woman towering over him. "Hey, you're back with us! I can tell you, that's the first time I've been called to perform first aid on the Grim Reaper! Oh, no you don't. You're staying *right* where you are, mister."

But nothing can stop Eric from struggling to his elbows. The first words to leave his mouth are: "What happened here?"

"You gave your group a shock, that's what! At first, they thought it was part of your act, but when they understood you were for real…"

"No." He scrambles shakily to his feet, pushing her protestations aside. "What happened here? *Here.*" He stamps for emphasis, relieved to find that the floor beneath him is solid.

Eric clasps a mug of tea in both hands. The sickly scent rising from the steam warns him it will be undrinkable. He's heard about the fifty-eight, knew the disaster had happened somewhere near here, but in 2003 Eric was a fifteen-year-old and thoughts of London were still a long way off. He can understand why London Underground wouldn't want to advertise, but had no idea that he regularly passed the exact spot. Now, at least, the sensation of falling makes perfect sense. But there's more. He hears the name Oliver Wicker, a name so familiar it seems to come from within him.

"Wait. How old was he?"

The woman shakes her head. "School age. Coming up for sixteen."

It's as if someone's turned down the volume. As the walls of the cell-like room blur and fade, the years rewind, taking Eric back to early childhood and a truth he understood absolutely. Fast forward, bypass his first nightmare, then hit *play* the year before he reaches double figures. Eric re-lives the precise moment he stopped trusting his instincts. When he finally allowed himself to be convinced to let go of this, along with many other childish beliefs. Here is where certainty crystallises: ghosts are *real*.

One in particular is very real.

CHAPTER FOUR

Interview with Jules Roche, *London Review*,
six weeks after second inquest verdict

London Review: How does it feel to be back in London?

Jules: I think… You know? I think I do not like this question.

London Review: Then… [Fumbles with notes.] Can you tell us a little about –?

Jules. OK, OK. For me, London is the city that give me everything. It is where I meet my wife. I am only here for a wedding. I am supposed to stay for two nights, that is all. But I meet Evelyn and… *Pfff* [shakes head]. She is *very* convincing. So London is the place my son is born. And then it see I am happy, and so it take away everything. It leave me nothing. You understand why I prefer to leave it behind. But sometime [holds hands about a foot apart], like now, it call me back.

London Review: Let's talk about your forthcoming exhibition.

Jules: It is not until next summer, you know that?

London Review: We'll go to print nearer the time, of course, but thank you for talking to us first.

Jules: OK. Well, my work. It is a response – my response – to the incident.

London Review: So it's how you chose to respond.

Jules: I *choose* nothing! I have such sorrow, I cannot meet it, cannot face it. So I turn it into something else, then maybe I can bear to look at it from time to time.

London Review: You only ever refer to 'the incident', is that right?

Jules: I do not know how else to call it. I prefer to let the work tell the story.

London Review: But you're trying to make sense of what happened.

Jules: There is no *sense* to make of it. That would be a lie.

London Review: So, effectively, you're using art to express what you can't say.

Jules: I have words, but they belong only to me and my son. I do not talk to the newspaper. [Widens eyes.] I leave this country so that I do not *have* to talk to the newspaper! I use art, if that is what you want to call it –

London Review: What do *you* call it?

Jules: I call it *Objets*. And I know what I am supposed to say here. My first interview I give about my work, the journalist he ask me, 'Do you channel emotions through your hands?' And I cannot answer because I do not know the word, *channel,* like it is a verb. I know English Channel and Channel Tunnel, but *channel emotions,* what is that? So I go away and look it up and I think maybe it is what I do. I channel anger. Because, the alternative, though it seem sensible to me, it might not be acceptable to society. And I am a father. I have an eighteen-month-old son. I have responsibility.

London Review: What *was* the alternative?

Jules: At the time? [Raises his eyebrows.] I think something *violent*. You also say 'violent'?

London Review: But you seem so calm...

Jules: It is over thirteen years now. [Shakes head as if amazed.] Violent thoughts, they still come, many violent thoughts. But back then it was something like breaking down doors, smashing windows.

London Review: Because you were angry?

Jules: But of course! I lash out at anyone who come near. This is how it is. Your future is stolen from you and you are angry. The way they clean everything up, wipe out the evidence, you are angry. Life insist you carry on when all you want to do is lay down and die and you are angry. Finding yourself alone in the world with a child, this make you angry. I do not think I am ready to be a father but Evelyn she say, 'You will be ready when the time comes.' So I am angry at my dead wife for leaving me in a foreign city with a child who need everything when I have nothing left to give.

London Review: Your wife was English?

Jules: My wife, my son. But I get my revenge. I take Louis to France, bring him up as a good French boy. Actually, no. He speak very good English. We are here often, in London, to visit his English family.

London Review: So your art allowed you to work through your anger?

Jules: For small time, through the work, through my son, maybe a little peace. But you do not put something like this behind you. You cannot say it is over just because a judge rule it is over. In some way my work, it keeps it alive. It is a thing I can pick up and hold. No one can wipe that out. But I leave it in the studio at night, I go home and try to be a good father.

London Review: And these *Objets*. What do they mean to you?

Jules: It is not all anger. Sometimes it is fear, sometimes it is pain, sometimes hurt. They are a *représentation* of what it was like to have my life fall apart.

London Review: And we sense that. Some of your pieces feel almost temporary. Can you tell us about the materials you use?

Jules: I like working with things that are not made to last. I like it when they already seem to be falling apart or what do you say? *Merde,* it is not *rotting* but it is something [clicks fingers].

London Review: Decaying?

Jules: Decaying! Like frayed rope or something *plastique*, that thin thin *plastique* [rubs fingertips together], you know. When I first meet my wife I do a lot of decorating – DIY, you call it. And we go to B&Q. You know it, a huge warehouse. It was one place I know, so that is where my materials come from.

London Review: Almost like Dadaism.

Jules: Maybe, but I do not know that at the time.

London Review: Then there are your 'broken *objets*', as it were. It seems to me that you deliberately destroy your best work.

Jules: *Oui,* I think that is true. I make it, then I smash it up [shrugs]. There is something primitive about the need to destroy things. Little boys, they take great pleasure, you know. My son do this when he is younger. You take him for a walk and he see a puddle that is frozen and he has to jump in the middle of it. The same with sandcastles. I watch him build a sandcastle so he can jump on top of it. I think, *Is he doing this so he can get to it before the sea does? Does he even understand that if he does not destroy it, the sea will?* And sometimes I see him jump on the sandcastle a friend has builded and he is laughing. And I tell him off, of course I do. I say, 'That is a bad thing you do.' [Wags finger.] But then I go to my studio and I copy. It is a way to feel better. I am a professional – how you say? *Vandale.*

London Review: Vandal.

Jules: Ah, you see, I only ever get stuck on words that are the same.

London Review: Is destruction part of your process?

Jules: Often yes. Like Louis – that is my son, you know? – I want to be in control. Sometimes I want to take something beautiful and leave my mark on it. I want to show the *absurdité*, you know. I want to hear the smashing, the splintering. There is a kind of, I suppose... I do not want to say *religious* meaning. But there is the idea of sacrifice. Always the most beautiful, the thing with the most promise. That is how it seem to me with life. My wife, you know, she carry a bouquet of flowers. That is what they tell me. Yellow flowers. I do not

35

know why. I do not know who they were from. Maybe she buy them for me. [Pause.] Will you take that out of the interview, please? I just listen to all this bullshit again from a man from a newspaper. He was waiting outside to pounce, you know.

London Review: Do you need a moment?

Jules: No. But I would like some water.

London Review: Can we get some water over here?

CHAPTER FIVE

Donovan, 2016

A small backstreet café provides sanctuary from the tedium of office politics. Donovan joins the queue at the counter, shaking his head. *The things people find to complain about!* Once he would have phoned Helene to let off steam. These days he saves it up so that he has plenty to tell his wife when he gets home from work. Censored snippets, rehearsed as he cycles through grey London streets. Number one on today's list will be this petty-minded complaint.

First thing this morning he received a visit from someone who'd clearly been elected spokesperson, requesting that an item be added to the agenda for today's staff meeting. Here, in the telling, he will roll his eyes, prompting Helene to ask, 'So? What was it about?' and he'll say, 'The introduction of own-brand tea bags and toilet paper, that's what!'

'Toilet paper?'

'And tea bags. This is what it means to be a manager.'

She'll laugh. 'Don't say I didn't warn you about selling your soul.'

Had the spokesperson been a man, Donovan wouldn't have thought twice before saying, 'You think it matters whether you wipe your arse with Kleenex with a hint of Aloe

Vera or Tesco's own?' But the spokesperson was a woman, and he would never say that to a woman. He imagines Helene reassuring him, 'Stop beating yourself up. You're not sexist, no way. Would I be with you if you were sexist?'

It comes back to him, as he shuffles forwards in the queue; the first time he ever heard the word. Eight years old, he was the largest of only a handful of black kids at his primary school. He was used to standing out, and hated it, but there was nowhere to hide, especially at break times. Impossibly beautiful and graceful with it, Hayley Butler had safe-distanced her posse and waltzed right up to him. Just waltzed right up and come out with it: "Are you a sexist?"

Donovan had a radar for traps, and this was one for sure. What *type* of trap it was, he had yet to find out. He assumed (incorrectly) that he'd been singled out for a special brand of humiliation. He also assumed (incorrectly) that 'sexist' had something to do with sex. Maybe to do with being sexy. Yes, that was it. Desperate not to look dumb in her crystal blue eyes, he wanted to own that word, like he'd been forced to own so many others. "Yeah, I'm a sexist," he said.

"Then you're an idiot." With a flick of her hair, Hayley turned on her heel. He watched as she was welcomed back into her fold, congratulated for bravery or whatever it is that girls do, while he was eyed with open disdain, one in a long line of boys who fell for it.

When Sean Bentley elbowed him and laughed, what else could he do but elbow him right back and laugh along with the joke? Donovan still laughs. In company, he crams dead airtime with laughter before the silence becomes stifling. "Sexist," the two boys sneered at each other. "You're a sexist." "No, you're a sexist." Donovan did a pretty good impression of Hayley storming off and they laughed some more. He'd had to ask his mother – the woman who'd brought him up single-handedly – what the word meant.

"It's another 'ism'. We talked about isms." And when he looked at her blankly she said, "Come on, you know what racism is, don't you?"

True, he knew what it was like when someone looked down on him for the colour of his skin, but what did that have to do with sex?

She put him straight: "Whenever you suggest that a woman is less capable than a man, or not as clever as a man, or that she shouldn't earn as much as a man, based on the fact that she's a woman, then that's sexist."

Donovan stood there with his mouth open, his bottom lip trembling. *Don't say that. Say anything you like about me but not that...* His mum was both mother and father to him, and he'd never doubted her capabilities. He wanted to track Hayley down and take back what he'd said, but she would laugh at him all over again, and this time it would be for caring about what she thought of him. The irony was that the cruel trick she'd played was the first time he'd ever thought less of someone because of their sex. He would go on to marry the most capable person he'd ever met and she'd push him harder than he would ever have pushed himself. And he made sure he told his daughter there was nothing she couldn't do if she put her mind to it. He sighs.

There are now three heads in front of him in the queue. Donovan glances about. Only two spare tables and all of the seated customers hanging on tightly to their coffee cups.

Back to the office his mind wanders, the toilet rolls and the tea bags, not to mention various other supplies the staff haven't rumbled yet. "Are you sure you want to raise this at the staff meeting?" he'd asked. The fact was, this complaint was likely to provoke comments from one or two of the men. One in particular, if he was honest.

"Absolutely."

Did he use the woman by allowing her to introduce a

subject that was already on his agenda? He imagines Helene saying, 'You did nothing wrong. She insisted on being heard.' But the fact is, it suited him.

They say Donovan has a knack for delivering unpopular news, but that doesn't mean he finds it easy. Management had guessed – correctly as it turns out – that hard knocks would be more palatable coming from him, given that he's... *Well, you must have heard about his daughter and her boyfriend. And the baby, don't forget the baby. You didn't know his daughter was pregnant? Such a shame.* And then the avoidance of eye contact, the looks of deep discomfort, or, since the verdict, too much eye contact. Donovan is under no illusion. This knack of his counted for ninety per cent of the reason behind his promotion. He's one of the management team, yet he sits apart. Overlooked when invitations are dished out to the basement wine bar – the place where all major decisions are taken. "Why lose sleep?" Helene asks, and he says, "I don't." Donovan has no patience for hobnobbing. Trade-offs are what interest him.

Since joining the firm, Donovan has never taken a full week's holiday. Circumstances have forced his hand. Management reluctantly relaxed what was otherwise a strict rule: no more than ten single days off in any given year, yet each holiday slip he handed in provoked sighs. Could he be flexible on the date? "I'm afraid not," he told his manager, thinking, *By now, I shouldn't need to explain myself.* Newcomers learned the hard way not to ask if he had a good day off. *How the hell was I supposed to know?*

Just as Donovan had foreseen, Jim didn't hold back at the staff meeting. After he introduced the item, starting with, "Strictly speaking, this belongs under AOB, but let's see if we can't tick it off the list," Jim went straight for the jugular:

"Let's get this straight. I've got a two-week backlog and I've been called to a meeting to talk about *bog roll?*"

No way was Donovan going to let the meeting descend into a free-for-all. He smiled as he scanned the room. "Do any of you remember school toilet paper? That scratchy stuff they used to give us?"

"Like tracing paper, it was!" This from somewhere towards the back.

"Izal, that was the name." Nodding. "Izal. Invented by a sadist."

"Well, then." Donovan killed the nostalgia dead, just by raising his eyebrows. *Wouldn't you say this is an improvement?*

The original speaker, the elected spokesperson, raised a hand. "But –"

"If you don't mind," Donovan responded.

She closed her mouth, then said almost demurely, "Go ahead." Donovan sensed her relief. No one could accuse her of not having tried.

"I want to make it crystal clear. Management aren't going to explain every purchasing decision, but on this one occasion I'm more than happy to explain *why* we took the decision to downgrade."

Small uncomfortable glances were exchanged on the front row. It hadn't occurred to them. The possibility that this might *not* be a deliberate slight. That a decision – with a solid reason behind it – had been taken.

"When we looked closely at the accounts, we noticed something peculiar. Staff numbers, as you know, are roughly the same as this time last year, while the cost of office supplies... Well." Donovan paused. *Place your bets, people.* "They've trebled." He nodded. "Yes, you heard right. So *I* thought, our supplier must have increased his prices. If we're being ripped off we should try someone else. But, you see, I was wrong." Again, he waited until people started to look curious about *how* this had come about. "Our suppliers have actually *reduced* their prices. They found themselves up against stiff competition. We're all feeling the squeeze, right?" He nodded sympathy for each and every person in the room. Someone shifted in a seat. "You can see where I'm going with this. I don't need to spell it out." People were sitting up, facing the front, studious in the way they avoided glancing at their colleagues. "I wasn't minded to carry out a witch-hunt, so…" He shrugged and turned over a page of his notes. "Next item."

"Wait. So someone's nicking office supplies and we all have to suffer?" An insulted look.

"Oh, I don't think it's some*one*." Donovan opened his eyes as wide as they would go. His gaze was returned, not one person willing to risk anything being read into the quiet downturn of their eyes. "You'd notice if the person next to you in the lift had an industrial-sized pack of toilet rolls strapped to their back. Plus, we'd have caught them on CCTV, right?" He made eye contact with as many people in the room as possible, reassurance it was *other* people he was referring to. "Make the supplies less attractive, that's what our accountant suggested. And do you know? He was right. Consumption's way down." Donovan combatted hostility with subtle suggestion: *Good news. Unacceptable behaviour has been stamped out.* Then it struck him. These hard-done-by people might be tempted to do a little stamping of their own. "I can't imagine the kind of circumstances that make people risk their jobs for the sake of a few toilet rolls are happy ones." Sheepish glances suggested he'd scored accurately. Only one face showed resentment, as if he'd accused her of planning her own witch-hunt. "I'm willing to draw a line under it and I hope I can count on you good people for support."

Thus the reason Donovan didn't want to eat lunch in the staffroom today.

'Quite right,' Helene will say. 'Give them space to bitch behind your back and get over it.' And there's the thing. She can get away with using the word 'bitch'. Donovan would have to phrase it differently.

Though the café is by no means an everyday haunt, its pint-sized owner Gus knows Donovan well enough to greet him before he reaches the front of the queue: "Hey, Big Man! Corner table's just coming free. You want your usual?" (Donovan doesn't particularly like the *big man* but he likes the idea of having a usual.)

Gus glances over his shoulder. "A large latte for my favourite customer."

There's a new member of staff today. Olive-skinned, dark-eyed, Italian looks, but in contrast with the owner, she's tall and slender. "Coming right up." She's efficient, undaunted by the hissing stainless steel monster.

While the coffee grinder whirrs to life, Gus thumbs over his shoulder. "My niece."

'I had no idea if that was supposed to be a joke,' Donovan will tell Helene.

'So what did you do?' she'll ask him.

'I smiled, of course.'

He and Gus exchange pleasantries – "How's business?" and "What about this weather, eh?" Then his coffee arrives, a fern design in the foam. Ambushed by the way this moves him – this simple, beautiful temporary thing – Donovan opens his mouth to say something, but already the girl is busy tamping down the next measure. *How will I describe the feeling to Helene?* he wonders.

"What d'you think? You don't get that in Costa, eh?" Pride tempers Gus's voice. Perhaps she really *is* his niece.

Donovan drops a few extra coins into the tips saucer and installs himself at the corner table. Only moments later a discussion escalates behind him.

"That's totally insane!"

"You think I'm making it up? Here. Read it for yourself."

"Sixty-year-old wins court battle that may enable her to become surrogate for *dead daughter's child!*"

A fish hook tugs at Donovan's skin. If he had any sense, he'd get up and walk out right now. But he can't bring himself to abandon the perfect symmetry of the fern and his favourite panini. A furtive twist and Donovan glances over his shoulder. Kids. Dressed like adults, acting the part so well they might have convinced themselves, but just kids.

"Look," the boy says. "To begin with, it's not even here, it's in America."

"You got that wrong. The *actual* court case was *here*. Now the woman wants to go to New York for IVF treatment."

"Why New York?"

"We'd tell her she's too old, most likely," the girl scoffs, a small flicker of disgust. She clearly feels no need to mute her volume.

"Damn right!"

Oh, to be so certain! Just wait. Wait until the day you find that what you thought was solid ground is quicksand and feel yourself being sucked down. Distracted by anger, Donovan stirs his coffee, unravelling the barista's artwork, destroying the one thing in recent memory to have moved him.

"She's only won the argument about what's meant by medical consent. Step number one – and *that's* taken five years."

For these kids, this isn't a person. It's not someone's life. It's something to comment on. As Helene would say, the internet has turned everyone into an expert.

"But she's going ahead. And her husband's supporting her!"

"*What?* He should be talking some sense into her."

Donovan's chest tightens. His lungs compress. *You kids have no idea what it's like to have your wife get up in the middle of the night because she can't bear to lie in bed a moment longer steeped in despair.* But if he speaks out loud he won't be the wronged party. He'll be a large, aggressive black man having a meltdown. *Thank God they're leaving!* he thinks as the young woman slings her handbag over her shoulder and pushes herself out of her seat.

The boy puts a proprietary hand on the small of her back, but Donovan doesn't think they're together. There: she's shrugged him off. As they move towards the door, the boy says, "She'll be seventy when the kid's ten. How old's the oldest mother?" He holds the door, hoping to redeem himself, no doubt.

The girl recoils. "The mother's age is the *least* of that kid's problems. Imagine finding out that your mother's also your grandmother!"

"However you look at it, it's wr–" The self-closing door cuts the boy short. Justice of sorts. Silenced, they remain in full view, mouths moving. The girl pauses to take a Vaper from her handbag. A small piece of paper – a receipt perhaps – falls from her bag, catches a drift of air and is swept out into the traffic.

Among the careless debris the pair have left in their wake is the folded newspaper, its headline uppermost. The fish hook tugs again. Donovan feels the rise and fall of his chest. *Leave it. It's none of your business.*

But it's there. On the table.

Why must he always be the one to bear witness to others' pain? Helene would answer him straight: 'Because we've had our share of misleading headlines. The next person to read this one will judge, just as those kids judged.'

So tightly crammed are the tables that Donovan can grab the paper without getting up. He smooths it out. If he's going to do this, he must do it right.

The woman, identified as Mrs X, asked the judges to allow her to carry out her only child's dying wishes.

Donovan blinks. This child had time for dying wishes. Nobody should begrudge her that.

Because of the risk that chemotherapy would leave her

infertile, the daughter of Mrs X, identified as 'A', had her eggs frozen, intending to undergo IVF. But after she learned that her cancer was terminal, 'A' asked her mother to 'carry my babies.'

He hears the small, high ringing of the altar boy's bell. *Do this in memory of me.* He sees Mrs X at her terrible bedside vigil, watching her daughter go through this thing, making the only promise within her power. And now she believes it would be a betrayal to back out.

Mr and Mrs X launched legal action when the Human Fertilisation and Embryology Authority (HFEA) refused them permission to take the eggs to a US clinic to be used with donor sperm.

Was there no boyfriend, then? No husband? What about the child they want to create? To Donovan, the child is already a 'she'. A little girl made in the name of someone she'll never know, never be in a position to love. So much pressure on one small life. She'll be suffocated. Small dark circles grey the newspaper print. As the circles widen, Donovan realises they're tears. He knows from experience how unsettling people find the sight of a large grown man crying in public. For the sake of those around him, he shields his eyes as he reads on.

The judge explained the legal dilemma that confronted the HFEA. While 'A' consented to the use of her eggs after her death, she gave no consent for them to be taken abroad. In addition, 'A' made her request without knowing that carrying out her wishes would pose a significant threat to her mother, who had herself received treatment for breast cancer.

My God, it gets worse! 'A' gave her parents the only gift she could think of, without any idea what she was asking. And now the husband, who's already lost his daughter, risks losing his wife – for the sake of what may only be a remote possibility.

There is more, but all Donovan can think of is the way that

he and Helene said goodbye to their daughter, their unborn grandchild and their soon-to-be son-in-law. The gurneys. The unzipping of PVC body bags.

"No, that's not her." The relief of it almost making him crumple.

"You said she was pregnant."

"Eight months."

"Look again."

The cruel elimination of doubt. And then to hear their daughter and her unborn child described as property. To be told that she was theirs. It was not right, not right that they weren't allowed to hold or kiss Cassie one last time; stroke the terrible swelling along the line of her cheekbone. How dare they raise his anger in a moment that should have been reserved for grief? And all his grievous words, Helene's anguished cries, the terrible sound of her weeping… Once uttered, everything became a matter for the public record. And the memory still so raw.

Life doesn't 'go on'. Donovan will never say that to his wife because she's made a litany of the words 'We did right by them.' He offers up his agreement, because Helene cannot possibly want to hear what he actually *feels*. Getting 'justice' for Cassie has made no difference to Big Man Donovan. That's the truth.

He sniffs, stands, stares down at the now abstract foam on his cold coffee, wraps his uneaten panini in a paper napkin. The need to eat has been drummed into him, but all pleasure is gone. His time in the café isn't something he'll tell Helene about. It's not the kind of thing she needs to know. Donovan drags his bones back to the office. Perhaps there will be more quilted toilet paper dramas to distract him from the things that really matter.

But, he thinks, *there must be something more.*

CHAPTER SIX

Cassie, 22 August 2003:
Incident minus 10 hrs 3 mins

To have stopped work eleven weeks before her due date would have been way too early. Honestly, though? She should have started her maternity leave two weeks ago. The commute, in this heat, at eight months pregnant? *Last day,* Cassie tells herself. *Once you're behind your desk, you'll be fine.*

Only her second 'proper' job, and in six years she's clawed her way up to management level. A woman working in a sector where official statistics show that the percentage of Black/African/Caribbean/Black British employees sits at just three per cent. Because she grew up with both Mum and Dad working in the City, Cassie had no idea just how unusual that was. Now, she'd like proof of that three per cent demographic. She begrudges each occasion she's paraded as evidence of the firm's equal opportunities policy. *One of our rising stars.* After biting down hard when the phrase 'positive discrimination' was used with reference to her, she'd let rip at her parents. They'd had no right to insulate her from the truth.

"We hoped it might be different for you."

"Attitudes don't change that quickly. At least, not in the City."

But Mum was unrepentant. "You would have stopped studying if you didn't think there'd be anything at the end of it."

"I might have worked harder."

Now, having worked so hard, having upheld all those standards of professionalism, today she must hand over the reins to her maternity cover, Little Miss I-Forgot-to-Eat.

"Where the hell are my shoes?" Cassie says, manoeuvring so that she can get a view of the floor. *These will have to go,* she thinks as she steps into the sloppy flat pumps that have been stretched by her swollen feet. She opens the wardrobe door and stares horrified at the full-length mirror. All boobs and bump. She claws at the fabric of the outfit that had fitted perfectly a week ago – the only decent pregnancy outfit she had left. The idea that she was planning to have a nude photograph taken late in her pregnancy – something to surprise Stefan with. Can you *imagine?*

Fresh from his post-run shower, Stefan comes up behind her. At the beginning of last week she was still running alongside him – slowing him down, but still running. She'd wanted to be one of those women who exercises right up to the birth. Rather than anything bump-related, the thing that caused her to stop was a nagging pain in her shins. That, and the effort involved in getting into and out of her maternity running gear, which had become a workout in itself. This morning, feeling left out, she'd actually asked Stefan not to go.

"You know I have to," he said. "Clients expect their trainer to take his own fitness seriously."

"That's right. They're all out at this time of the morning, hiding behind trees with their binoculars."

"So were your clients out in force?" she asks him.

"I definitely spotted Scott. He was behind that really tall horse chestnut." He splays his hands over her taut stomach.

When Cassie was beginning to show, Stefan's hands would

meet in the shape of a heart, both thumbs in her belly button, his middle fingers at the line of her pubic hair. Now the comforting warmth of his palms betrays just how wide apart his hands are. "How can I go to work looking like this? I'm hideous."

"Where are you looking?" He nuzzles her neck. "I was just thinking, that's one sexy pregnant lady. I should probably get round to marrying her."

"You can marry me when I've stopped looking like a fucking whale." Cassie hadn't felt tearful, just fed up, but realising how awful that sounded, and then realising that she meant it, her vision blurs.

"Only a very small one. Oh, wait. Cassie…"

The fact is, she's completely at the mercy of this baby, and there's still another month to go. She brushes at the corners of her eyes, cross with herself. "Ignore me."

"D'you want to know what the smallest whale in the world is called?"

"What?"

He rests his chin on the top of her head. "A dwarf sperm whale."

He wants her to laugh and she is so not in the mood. "Ha, bloody, ha."

"You're going to have to mind your language when the baby arrives."

"Oh, he's arrived. Can't you *see* him?"

"Am I going to be able to say anything right today?"

"Probably not," she concedes. Her attempt at a smile almost succeeds. "Anyway, like I told you, this is pregnancy Tourette's. It'll go the minute this thing is out of me."

Stefan moves his hands to the sides of her bump. "Don't listen to the nasty lady! You're not a *thing*."

"Swearing makes you stronger."

"Who says so?"

"Stephen Fry. So it must be true."

"Smiling does the same," he reminds her.

"I can't imagine I'll be doing much in the way of –"

Stefan jerks one hand away, his face lighting up. "I think I felt a foot!"

Left gasping, Cassie manages, "Oh, that's definitely a foot." She purses her lips, breathes out slowly.

He repositions one of her hands. "Feel this."

"Stef," she objects, "I don't need my hand on my stomach to feel this baby kick!"

"Sorry." His reflected expression is wounded. "I just wanted... I can't help it, I'm excited, that's all. I can't wait to meet him!"

Cassie closes her eyes momentarily and sighs. "I'm glad you're excited." Despite herself, almost to distract herself, she laughs. "Do you know what Mum said to me on the phone last night? *Enjoy* your last month of pregnancy. *Enjoy it.*"

"She's right."

Cassie allows herself to lean back against Stefan and closes her eyes. "But I feel so needy and pathetic. Not to mention being in a permanent bad mood."

"You? In a bad mood?"

"It would be nice to just stay here." But she can't. There's a busy day ahead. With the outside world back in focus, Cassie catches sight of her reflection again and lets out another wail. "How can I leave the flat looking like this?"

"Just think of the Mothercare vouchers." His hands move to her hips and then drop. "Or stay at home. It's not as if you're planning on doing any work."

"Stef!" she balks. "I've got to do my handover."

"What? To Little Miss I-Forgot-to-Eat?"

She cannot hide her smirk. "We're supposed to call her Vanessa."

"Who actually opens their mouth and comes out with stuff like that?"

"If I don't go, it will look like sour grapes."

"What for?"

"Because they didn't go with my recommendation for who covers my job." Vanessa might look frighteningly competent but, when it comes down to it, she's way too young. But Stefan is disappearing into the hall. "Hey! Where d'you think you're going?"

"It's gone seven." Stefan about-turns, hangs off the door-frame and, as he swings, his T-shirt lifts. She remembers the first time she saw that pale, pale skin of his. Two inches of muscle above the waistband of his jeans and she'd known right away.

"I haven't finished whinging yet."

"I had this wild idea that breakfast might be a good idea. Oh wait," he hops down, "I just remembered. I got you something." He reaches into the laundry basket, pulls out his tracksuit bottoms, and rummages in a pocket, coming out with a closed fist.

"For me?" she half-jokes.

"Close your eyes."

She closes them.

"Hands out."

Something cool and smooth drops onto her palm. She smiles, opens her eyes. Still shiny, it has a rich chestnut hue.

"First conker of the season."

She rewards Stefan's expectant gaze with childish delight. "Newly hatched!"

He leaves her to it. She runs her thumb over its grain, removing a fleck of white. *Like a baby's skull.*

Sounds of domesticity. The radio is switched on. The kettle is filled. Cassie turns the conker over and over. By this time tomorrow, the sheen will have dulled and with it, some of its magic. Last autumn, she and Stefan filled their pockets when they paused to stretch. She tries to balance what she's missing out on against what she's about to gain. Her eyes prick with tears once more. It's ridiculous. She's never been sentimental.

A six-month-old conversation begins to rerun.

"My parents are going to love you."

"You haven't told them, have you?"

"Told them what?"

"You're going to make me say it?" She folded her arms. "You haven't told them I'm black."

"You're black?" Stefan acted shocked. "Why didn't you say something?"

She cuffed him lightly then stared out of the window of the train, supposedly sulking, but distracted, nervous. While Stefan Googled *What to eat during pregnancy,* she'd been Googling *Bringing a mixed race child into the world.* Nothing she read reassured her. In fact, topping the list was advice about discussing the issue *before* thinking about getting pregnant. She and Stefan hadn't given any thought to getting pregnant – and in this day and age how stupid does that make them sound?

Stefan squeezed her hand. "They can't get over the fact that they're going to be grandparents. Mum was so happy on the phone."

Cassie loves Stefan George and wants to be with him, she has no doubt about that. And at some point – some future point – she'd always assumed she'd have a child. But if she'd thought about it, really thought about it…

The closer they got to her future in-laws' home, the more Cassie convinced herself that the Georges wouldn't like her. She studied Stefan side on, picking at the scab of a wound dating back to the time a primary school teacher was casting the role of Mary for the nativity play. Cassie shot her hand up, only to be told, "Oh no, I'm afraid you wouldn't be suitable."

Now, unmarried and pregnant (*but hardly a kid,* she reminds herself), she might again find herself judged unsuitable.

She turned bodily in her seat. "Have you or have you not warned your parents that their grandchild probably won't look like them?"

"I don't know how many ways I can say this –"

But, you see, Cassie can imagine Stefan's parents looking at their grandchild and thinking, *This child is a stranger.* "Are *you* worried that our baby might not look like you?" she asked Stefan.

"Have you *seen* me? Believe me, I'm counting on him looking like you."

She doesn't want Stefan to say that he doesn't see race, because their son may – and the chances are he'll identify as black. But it's wrong to pretend the problem – Cassie doesn't know how else to refer to it – will be one-sided. She's heard the story about the boy who, when his black grandfather put a plate of rice and beans in front of him, immediately burst into tears and said he didn't like them. Upset, the grandfather said, 'This is our people's food! Of course you like it.'

When Stefan says he can't wait to meet their son, part of Cassie can't help imagining a boy who constantly comes up against other people's opinion of who they think he is, based on hair type and skin tone. The child they have created will grow up with demands that he pledges his loyalty to one side or the other.

There are no 'sides'. Pull yourself together, Cassandra. It's her grandmother speaking. (Now, there was a woman with skin like an old conker.) *The boy will be himself, is what he'll be.*

She raises the conker to her lips, kisses it. *You'll be yourself.* A few deep breaths. In through the nose, out through the mouth. In on the *re*, out on the *lax*. There's no room for deep breaths. This baby has taken up residency in her ribcage, shoving everything else aside. Her body couldn't feel any less like a miracle.

A shout: "Am I safe to scramble these eggs?"

"Yes!" She sets the conker down on the dressing table. "Our last day of commuting," she promises the baby. Perhaps she doesn't look so horrendous. It's just that she'd been dreaming of herself as a girl with a flat stomach. Stop looking at yourself from the side, for fuck's sake. (Now she's *thinking* in swear words.) In fact, close the wardrobe door and stop looking.

"Yes!" She hears Stefan's shout and the volume of the radio is turned up.

Bom, bom, bom. Bom, bom, bo-bom, bom.

In spite of herself, Cassie smiles. "Daddy's favourite song," she tells the bump.

According to his mother (very welcoming, very complimentary, laughter just a notch too loud), one day, at the age of six, Stefan demanded 'the chicken song'. Nothing else would pacify him. The Georges scoured their music collection but the best they could come up with was *The Funky Chicken,* which had Stefan yelling, "Not that one! The one with the *chickens!*"

"He was a late speaker," his mother confided, mouthing the words in an exaggerated way, as if this was something a grown man might find embarrassing. "Not being able to make himself understood was like being a toddler all over again."

Bewildered, the Georges shrugged at each other.

"Something from *Sesame Street?*" his father suggested.

The demands went on for weeks. Every time there was music, it was, "I don't want this, I want the chicken song!" Then one day on the school run the intro to *Lust for Life* came on the car radio, and Stefan was jumping up and down on the back seat, yelling, "The chicken song!" It's still known as The Chicken Song in the George's household.

The story will pass into their family history now, the first of many. *And we'll be a family, not like either of our families, but something new.* She pats her stomach in time with the intro. Bom, bom, bom. Bom, bom, bo-bom bom. *Don't you worry. We'll make it work.*

CHAPTER SEVEN

Maggie, 2016

The body keeps score, Maggie's grief counsellor has told her. It's unhelpful – not to mention unhealthy – for her to expose herself to situations that trigger flashbacks. Instead, she should try writing Rosie a letter.

What Maggie knows is this: these were Rosie's streets; this was Rosie's walk to work. This is the journey Maggie makes once or twice a week, from outside All Hallows church in the shadow of the Tower of London, then along Great Tower Street in the direction of St Botolph station. It is both pilgrimage and penance. She cannot *not* walk Rosie's route, no matter how much she would prefer never to take it again.

It is not, she feels, unreasonable to hope for a sense of her daughter, something she can reach out and touch, if only for the briefest instant. Imagine not being there to capture that fleeting trace in the diesel-fumed air. But so often hope turns to betrayal. At a loss, Maggie will pretend she's one of the great unwashed, hurrying to her next appointment. This is where her routine ceases to make sense. And when her routine no longer makes sense, nothing makes sense.

Alan can't understand. Slowly but surely, she's pushing him away – and yet she's powerless to do anything about it. Only this morning, after Maggie stooped to pick up the envelope off the doormat, after she said, "Have a good day," Alan reached for her arm.

"Surely you can stop putting yourself through this now. I can't stand to see you like this, Marg."

As his eyes pleaded, hers pooled and she looked away. "You're the only person outside Northumberland who calls me Marg."

"And *you're* changing the subject."

"I'm trying. I'll keep on trying." What else could she offer?

"Well then." He nodded to the envelope in her hand. "Anyone we know?"

She turned it over. *Mr and Mrs Chapple.* "I don't recognise the handwriting."

"I'd better get my skates on. You go ahead and open it."

Several letters have arrived since the verdict, awkwardly-worded, well-meaning, all of them suggesting that grief has an expiry date. As she ripped open the seal, Maggie assumed it was going to be one of those, not the hateful, hate-fuelled words that confronted her. *Rosemary shouldn't be named Victim 59. You make me sick, saying she was the same as our daughter. She doesn't come close. It was her fault, what happened. She killed our daughter you bastards...* She let go, the sheet of paper drifting to the oak floor, where it will stay until she can find the courage to pick it up and hide it from Alan. But right now, she must get as far away from it as possible. And people think she can simply give herself permission to move on!

All sacred routines have their rules. A strict order governs Maggie's. She will skirt the solid stone walls of the Tower of London to look back at Tower Bridge, and if the bridge is up – which is rarely – then she must stand and watch until the ship, or whatever else it is, has passed through.

If Maggie gets as far as London Bridge – if, on the

approach, she doesn't experience what she's come to recognise as the beginnings of a desire to jump – she'll walk beyond
the red plastic casing, so similar in shape to the London
Underground logo, with its instructions on *How to Save a
Life*. Rosie didn't want to be saved, even if someone had had
the presence of mind. Maggie will stand close to the centre of
the bridge where she can take in the long view and greet the
Thames, an enemy so old she's grown to admire it. She will
squint towards Tower Bridge, the galvanised shadow of *HMS
Belfast* in the foreground, surprised by variations in what is
now so familiar. The gothic silhouette turning from ghostly
grey to sandstone to rose.

Maggie has a photograph of Rosie's last act on this
stubborn, unforgiving planet. An American tourist, holding
her cell phone up to the sunrise captured Rosie's freefalling
silhouette. It was, she admitted, a total fluke. She hadn't
planned on being up and about so early, but the hotel manager
insisted on sticking her in a room next to the elevator, and
seeing as she was awake she'd said to herself, *Oh, what the
hell.* This sunrise photo should have been the first of many
she took that day. She was rather proud of the fact that she'd
plucked up the courage to visit London on her own, and
she intended to do plenty of boasting. The American's first
thought was that a gull had ruined her shot, but then it struck
her: the blur was human-shaped. When the weight hit the
water, there was no room for doubt. Though she thoroughly
disapproved of pranksters, she felt compelled to look over the
parapet. Whoever it was, was floating face down; whatever
they wore on their top half puffed up like a life-jacket. *You
might not drown today,* she thought, *but next time, my friend,
could be a different story.*

The American glanced about, expecting to see a clutch of
conspiring teenagers waving over the side of the bridge. Girls
in low-rise jeans with those stupid diamante butt-logos you

saw. Boys wearing sneakers that cost half a month's salary. But not quite six in the morning was the wrong time for teens – unless they'd stayed up all night. Few people were about. Just a homeless guy who'd camped out and a lone pin-striped worker who refused to catch her eye. *Honestly, Londoners deserve their reputation for being unfriendly.* Another glance at the water below. The damned fool hadn't come up laughing, hadn't started swimming. For a second, she slipped outside reality. Zooming back in, all self-righteousness melted. This was no prank. What's more, there was no way of reaching whoever it was. It took a moment before she remembered. The shape in her hand – the reason her hand wasn't a fist – was a phone. She dialled 911. *You're not at home now, you fool. 999.* That was it. 999.

Occasionally, Maggie will stand to attention at the sight of the orange RNLI boat, its nose lifting from the water, slapping the small waves. She may raise one reverential hand to salute the crew. More often than not, she'll simply grip the rail and experience the full impact of her gnawing, aching loneliness.

The American said she'd have seen Rosie if she'd climbed up on the railing. She could have tried to talk her round. "But I was busy lining up my shot when she came out of nowhere, that's the truth. She must have vaulted."

Maggie, who'd spent the best part of a decade driving her daughter to and from gymnastics competitions, agreed. While still at middle school, Rosie had progressed from high jump to vaulting. Her natural ability was what precipitated the family's move from Northumberland to London. To Maggie, it always felt as though she was in exile – Berwick-upon-Tweed had been city enough for her – but Rosie embraced London the way she embraced everything. Her high school coach described her as fearless.

Rosie's fearlessness terrified Maggie. Her daughter's fierce concentration, the way she lifted her weight onto the balls of her feet, then attacked the run-up, elbows pumping. Sometimes Maggie couldn't bear to watch Rosie somersault towards the vault, springing from her hands, twisting and turning. Only at the commentator's excited, *'And it's a good landing!'* would she open her eyes and leap from her unforgiving plastic seat, just in time to watch her daughter's display of showmanship; a tiny adjustment of feet, arms raised high, chest jutting out.

Though Rosie worked in an Underground station, it was water she chose. And Maggie wondered, did she mean to do it? Didn't water leave an element of chance?

"She was a fine vaulter," Maggie told the American. Immediately, a barrier of disapproval came down. She stood accused of encouraging her daughter. The rest of what Maggie learned about Rosie's final moments came from expert witnesses.

'It's a matter of how you fall into the water that accounts for the amount of deceleration from the impact depth. Rosemary was unlucky enough to fall perfectly horizontally. The force of impact would have caused her body to decelerate to half the velocity in about a foot of distance.'

A gaping hole opened up in Maggie's core. One thing Rosie knew was how to land. She meant to. Of course she meant to.

It was equally clear from the possessions Rosie left behind on the bridge that she wished to spare those who found her any doubt about her identity. Her uniform, folded with military precision. A few bills, the kind of things banks demand as proof of ID, plus the keys to her flat. Left in the care of the homeless man so that he might decide what best to do with them.

He hadn't realised, he said. She didn't look distressed. People gave him things sometimes. Clothes and stuff. He hadn't stolen them.

"No one's suggesting you did."

"You don't ask questions. They don't always want to stop and chat."

"Did Rosie say anything? Anything at all?"

"I can't remember. Maybe…"

"What?"

He scratched at the inside of his wrist in a way that must have hurt. "No, it's gone. She seemed nice, though. Kind."

She was more than nice, more than kind; more than anything you'll ever know. Such an apologetic exit. If only Rosie hadn't been given this natural talent, if Maggie hadn't been so ambitious on her daughter's behalf, they might have lived out their lives in Berwick.

You carry this thing inside, always. It has such bulk, such weight, that Maggie can't believe it isn't visible. The blur of a reflection she catches in the window of a passing car is always hunched, as if she's clutching at a stomach ache.

But it's not a stomach ache. This thing fills her up until it feels as if it will burst from her ribcage. It stagnates, pooling in thoughts she'd never have thought herself capable of. *Why are you here, you with your secret smile as you whisper into your pink plastic phone, and you clasping your medium skinny latte? Why are you here when my daughter is not?*

Along Great Tower Street the assault of diesel fumes combines with all the smells you'd associate with rapid city expansion – wet concrete, solvents, sawdust and the various foods on offer. The sky has been artificially raised, pushed upwards by fortresses of glass and steel, but some buildings bear down, foreshortening the crowds, hemming them in. Here, it's impossible to feel your place in the world. Not like walking along the beach at Seahouses, feet imprinting negatives on the white sand, seawater seeping in where only a moment earlier a heel has trodden. Something so precious about the ability to duplicate an essential part of yourself, something unique, and then simply walk away from it taking in the uninterrupted horizon. Billowing white cloud as far as the eye can see.

She remembers, and the memory is so vivid it replaces the paving stones beneath her feet. A peal of Rosie's laughter rings out as she launches herself from one of Alan's great size ten footprints to another. "Now you, Mummy!" The three of them leaving a single set of prints...

A sneeze – such a small intimate sound – reels Maggie back to street level. A man who has paused dispels two more short sneezes into the palm of his hand. Before she is aware of herself, manners compel Maggie to say, "Bless you." She receives surprised eye contact, a "Thank you," but she's back among strangers. City people sharing jokes as they suck greedily on last cigarettes before entering smoke-free zones. Maggie's demon strains at its leash. *Would you look at them?* Stray tourists block the pavement, pointing cameras towards 20 Fenchurch Street, nicknamed the Walkie-Talkie, waiting for the sun to strike its concave glass. Anything that Rosie never saw has no right being here. Maggie charts alterations that have taken place since her daughter vaulted cleanly over the side of the bridge and landed perfectly horizontally. The functional sixties office block that stood here had to go because it was incapable of delivering an occupational density of one person per eight square metres. In the life that should have been Maggie's, the one in which she's a doting grand-mother, she would neither know nor care about occupational density. It would be of no concern to her that, in a building technology study, in a simulated panic, five persons were capable of developing a force of 3430N (766 pounds). Not that Maggie ever learned what the 'N' stands for.

Looking away, she finds herself eye to eye with the wool-len-hatted, blanketed young man, who positions himself against the red telephone box opposite Tesco Express. (She's close, then.) With the feeling that each of her uncharitable thoughts has been piped over a tannoy, she fumbles for a pound or two, compensation for those uninvited thoughts that thought themselves. But God she is dead, her precious Rosie is dead, and for fuck's sake why are these imbeciles slowing down?

It has crept up on her, and Maggie is never sure what to do when she gets to this point.

They wanted a scapegoat, and Rosie was dispensable.

Here, to the left, is Catfish Hill – the name that had so amused Rosie, before the very end when she felt the Thames's tidal pull. Despite the history of Old Billingsgate's arches, her daughter thought fish references were more suited to the coastal villages of her childhood. Blue-bottomed tug boats nestling against the harbour wall. Stacks of nets, blue-green and brown. Images her daughter only half-remembered, fading like an aging Polaroid, while they remain hard-wired into Maggie's DNA. In London, Maggie will always be an outsider, but how can she leave now?

An infestation of hoardings (more building works) has narrowed Catfish Hill to the width of an alley. But still the same number of commuters and tourists squeeze through, unmindful and unhindered, accepting that city life means constantly brushing up against someone. Maggie can't see the entrance to St Botolph Underground station or the elderly vendor who used to hand Rosie her copy of the *Evening Standard.* A blonde woman-child pushes past, oblivious to danger, and panic lodges in Maggie's throat. Alan's right. It could happen again. It could happen right now. And where, she looks about wildly, would the emergency services find a place to stop?

Suddenly she knows why she's here. She turns herself into a barrier; blocks the narrow walkway.

CHAPTER EIGHT

Eric, 2008

Eric's hearing slowly comes back into focus.

"I get it. When a person you love dies, you want someone to blame." The London Underground employee who administered first aid and heaped sugar into his tea shakes her head. "But what happened on the escalators? People panicked, pure and simple."

Eric doesn't contradict her comforting narrative. Deeply ingrained, no doubt it feels true. But *he* has a reference point that says it isn't: the crush at Bethnal Green.

He couldn't research the information needed for his ghost tour and ignore the case law. In terms of body count, what happened at St Botolph and Old Billingsgate wasn't on the same scale. But it happened within his lifetime, which makes it more personal somehow. Every choice Eric ever made, whether he knew it or not, has led him to this moment. It's difficult to explain, but little more than an hour ago, while dressed as the Grim Reaper, he stared into the face of death. Though he doesn't yet know what his task will be, he's been chosen.

"Thank you." He hands over the mug, pushes himself to his feet, keen to discover.

"Take it easy."

Eric stumbles back to his flat on the edge of Zone 4. His blood seems to be flowing in the wrong direction, but he can't remember when he's ever felt more clear-headed. The official story put out after the Bethnal Green incident was that the station had suffered a direct hit. But it was *just* that – a story. (It's easy to speculate that there was a cover-up, but war-time news reporting was a creative business.) Results of the official investigation were suppressed until Herbert Morrison, Minister of Home Security, quoted from the secret report. "On hearing a discharge of anti-aircraft rockets taking place at nearby Victoria Park, passengers panicked."

The Shoreditch Coroner couldn't have been more forceful. "Nothing suggested anything of the kind! There was no panic and certainly no stampede."

Doubt left the door ajar, wide enough to make it worth the while of a bereaved widow to bring a lawsuit. The steps down to the station were known to be unsafe. They were wide and had no protective railings. What's more, it was known that risks increased when a large flow of people used them. Surely, then, it must have been foreseeable that dangerous conditions would arise at the start of an air raid?

London Civil Defence maintained its stance. There was no negligence. It hadn't even altered the station, and besides, this was an injury of war, exempt under the 1939 Act.

But it turned out that London Civil Defence *had* been warned that the staircase was in need of a crush barrier. Sling your hook, came their response. Waste of money. Money, consideration number one, always at the expense of lives. And how exactly were these war injuries?

The judge's hammer came down with a crack. Bethnal Green Corporation were liable. Nearly £60,000 in damages was awarded.

"I know him," Eric says out loud as he stares at the photograph of Oliver Wicker. It's him, he's sure. He crops the photo so that it is magnified on his computer screen. He has looked into this face before. Some inter-schools competition. Sports. Chess. A mock-up of University Challenge. Eric's thing had been chess, but the rules said you had to take part in two events, and one of them had to be a sport. What's more, you couldn't win at one thing – your thing – without a passable result in the other. Oliver Wicker was the player he'd taken out on the football pitch, a place where a boy from chess club should never have been. A minor defensive offence, missed by the ref (himself a chess man strayed outside his comfort zone). Horrified at what he'd done, Eric was open-mouthed as he looked into his opponent's face, thinking, *Well, this is it. He'll grass me up, I'll be sent off. What's more, I'll be outed as a cheat. I can say goodbye to the chess trophy.* But Oliver said nothing. In fact, after he'd brushed himself down, he winked. Eric breathed out. *I've got away with it.* It was only later, when he moved his queen to H4 that he realised: he was in the boy's debt. With the name of Oliver's school and the position he'd played in, it was easy to track down his name, but that was as far as Eric took it. Now Oliver Wicker is calling in the debt.

Already thinking like a solicitor, Eric ransacks the internet. Newspaper coverage. The transcript of the original inquest (its main function was for the Coroner to identify the deceased, relinquish control of the bodies and issue interim death certificates, enabling the families to bury their dead). The public inquiry, intended to restore confidence in the transport system – a conflict, if ever he's heard one! And not forgetting London Underground's own investigation.

Treat it like detective work. A few late nights should kick-start the process. Cereal, Red Bull, black coffee – and there's always the ProPlus he bought to get through a hard night's clubbing. On second thoughts, keep that in reserve.

Eric opens his mouth, gives each side of his face three energising slaps. He reaches for his coffee without taking his eyes off the screen. He has tasked himself with looking for something, anything that's been missed, any question he can't find an answer to, evidence of foreknowledge, incriminating information. One new discovery every night, that's his goal. Not only does he have a debt to repay, not only does this feel like a calling, but he means to impress his girlfriend – yes, girlfriend!

His flatmate called him a lucky ugly bastard the morning Sorrel first padded into the kitchen and asked where they kept the coffee mugs. Andy bet Eric it wouldn't last the month. "You're on," he said, with considerably more confidence than he felt. Sorrel doesn't understand how single-minded he can be. But she will. Staying the course, sticking with the programme, that's what is going to make the difference.

His knee starts its automatic up and down rhythm as he reads how London Underground was quick to start its own investigation. An incident on this scale? Of course it was. However callous it may sound, investigation is what the law demands. But treating family members who phoned the Casualty Bureau as part of that investigation? Asking the same scripted questions to each person who showed up at the reception centre, desperate to locate their loved ones? The question is, were *those* actions in step with guidelines?

Guidelines, guidelines. Eric scratches his head. He Googles 'accident investigation'. Recommendations from the Health and Safety Executive seem as good a reference point as any. They refer to the workplace, but the Underground is both workplace and public space. *There is no such thing as being in the wrong place at the wrong time.* At least they're agreed on that! *Rather than allocate blame, the goal of any accident investigation is to understand the precise chain of actions that resulted in the adverse event. Each failing or error combined with other failings or errors has a domino effect. Only by identifying each link in the chain can a similar occurrence be prevented.* Here it is: *When a major incident occurs, it is vital to start your investigation immediately, before the accident scene can be altered...*

How long, realistically, can you preserve a scene at an Underground station with pressure mounting to get the service back up and running?

...before items are moved, repairs carried out and witnesses' memories become diluted.

Involve everybody. Question everything. Dig deep. Include opinions, experiences, observations, sketches, measurements, photographs, work permits and details of the environmental conditions at the time. Root out the root causes. Eric mustn't let himself flinch from the truth. Each lead must be followed, even if the path leads down a shadowy cul-de-sac. To be unflinching is the commitment he makes.

Eric's eyes return to hover over a single word: *photographs.* CCTV footage might be lacking but of course! Official photographers would have been on the scene while the rescue was underway. What might they tell him about the location?

He lifts himself out of his seat to refer to the 3D diagram of St Botolph and Old Billingsgate stations that he's tacked above his desk. It's difficult not to think of Dante's Divine Comedy. This too is an abyss of Hell, an engineering feat Hieronymus Bosch would have admired. Staircases corkscrew past subways, a lift shaft plunges into a deep pit. There are pipes, interchanges, flying junctions, crossover junctions. Already, Eric's bank balance reminds him he's missing his generous American tourists, but continuing with guiding was impossible. Even the thought of using an escalator makes him shudder. Dr Cumming's prophecy wasn't misplaced. If the devil's domain is under ground, then the Underground is Hell. With an index finger, he traces the route the majority of the fifty-eight took, from the entrance at St Botolph, through the subway, towards Old Billingsgate. Here they are: the lower concourse, the escalators.

Vertigo strikes just as surely as if Eric's missed his footing, then it's gone, leaving a queasy feeling in its wake. Someone stood just about here and took photographs of the dead and the dying. At the very same moment, unflinching, Eric is wondering whose strings he can pull to get his hands on them. Will what he sees mirror the images in his head?

You're getting ahead of yourself. He takes off his glasses, pinches the skin between his eyebrows and rubs at his forehead. At the moment all he has is chaos. His job is to bring order. He slots his glasses back on. What he needs is a system.

It is unlikely that any conclusion identifying human error as the cause of an accident is unbiased. That same safe narrative told to him by the woman who gave him first aid. Scapegoat number one was the poor station supervisor, with much inferred from the fact that she removed herself from the equation before her formal statement could be taken. Apparently not one of her colleagues stuck up for her – afraid of being labelled guilty by association, perhaps. Instead, their evidence led to the courtroom commentary about a critical and gaping hole in the instructions given to staff.

Then there were the passengers themselves. The crowd who wouldn't be held back. But survivors complained of being 'herded like cattle', forced out of the station in a 'stampede'. This will be the difficulty. If Eric is to get to the core of the truth, he must rid himself of every preconception he has. That has to be rule number two.

Maybe ProPlus will help after all. He reads the label. No more than two in three hours, no more than eight in any twenty-four-hour period. He pops two tablets from the blister pack; knocks them back with a slug of cold coffee.

Consider the root causes that created the environment in

which human error was possible. Inadequate training and/or supervision; poor equipment, premises or work process design; lack of management commitment and poor attitude to health and safety are all examples of factors that, arguably, make human error inevitable.

Not possible but *inevitable* – 'arguably'.

A sound basis for an argument.

"OK," Eric says and opens a new Excel spreadsheet, which he titles *Checklist for Analysis of Findings*. What he's looking for are blind spots within the system. Things that have 'always been done this way'.

As he types number 1, Eric acknowledges another problem. Fatalities meant that the police were involved, the Coroner was involved, the fire brigade, the team from Her Majesty's Railway Inspectorate... He won't be talking about a single investigation, but any number of independent investigations, the results of which may or may not already have been combined. That's fine. He can set up tabs on his spreadsheet.

But what if the investigations came to different conclusions? The idea fires him up. *Wouldn't that be something?*

He splays his fingers, then curves them over the keyboard.

1. Was the investigation (examine each in turn) objective and unbiased? (Were all staff/witnesses/relatives asked the same questions? And by whom?)

2. Did the investigation correctly identify the conditions and the sequence of actions and that led to the adverse event?

3. Did it identify the immediate cause of the accident? (May be more than one, in which case did it identify them all)?

4. Did it identify any underlying causes, any past actions that may have allowed – or even caused – undetected unsafe conditions or practices? (Bethnal Green, King's Cross fire, check other major accident details and near misses.)

5. Did it identify root causes, (organisational and management health and safety arrangements, supervision, monitoring, training, resources allocated to health and safety, etc.)?

6. What risks/risk control measures were identified?

7. Were any of those controls missing, unused or ineffective?

8. Did practices comply with legal requirements, codes of practice, general guidance, etc.?

He reads his list back to himself. There will be much more, he's sure of it, but it's a starting point.

"OK, that's me." Eric drains his mug of tea, puts it down on the coffee table in Sorrel's living room and goes to push himself to standing. "I have to go."

"Go?" Sorrel gives a sharp laugh. "You've only just got here."

Not quite true. As planned, he walked her home after their afternoon lecture. Invited in for a cuppa, an anxious feeling grabbed him but a quick mental calculation reassured. Twenty minutes to drink a cup of tea and he could still be home by half past five. That doesn't mean he hasn't been on edge, waiting until Sorrel looked the other way to check his watch. "I have work I need to get on with."

Now he's given up guiding, Sorrel assumes he'll have more time for her. She pulls him towards her. "Not due in until Tuesday."

Normally, the downturn of her eyes, her coy smile, would be all the convincing Eric needs. "Not that kind of work," Eric insists, trying to extract himself before Sorrel's lips meet his.

"Half an hour," she purrs, refusing to entertain his resistance.

Eric takes both of Sorrel's hands in his and, at the same time, pushes himself up from the sofa. This must somehow give the impression that she's convinced him. Sorrel swings round, puts her feet up and lays herself down on the couch, pillowing her head on the armrest. Eric groans inwardly. She's no less alluring than she was last Wednesday when, subjected to the drone of a university band in The Brown Fox, she'd said, "Are you enjoying this or is there something else you'd prefer to be doing?" then stuck her tongue in his ear.

"Tomorrow," Eric says – a stupid promise. Tomorrow will be the same. The thing now is to sustain the momentum.

Up on one elbow, Sorrel is no longer purring. "Explain to me. How have you come by the conviction that this has anything to do with you?"

Eric sighs. "If I had time to explain…"

But Sorrel turns her back on him, an imitation of his mother's cat when singularly unimpressed. Many things she will tolerate, but not this.

CHAPTER NINE

Interview with Jules Roche,
London Review, part 2

London Review: Are you ready for a few more questions?

Jules: [Puts down glass of water.] Do your worst, as you say.

London Review: The destroyed image can be very powerful. Why do you think that is?

Jules: I think it is a release. I don't know if I release the thing or I try to release myself, but it feels like something I have to do. It is a way of saying that I am no longer whole. I am damaged. I am... how you say? Like a mark on the skin. Scarred.

London Review: [Nods.] You often use pieces from the things you have destroyed to create something new.

Jules: The first thing I make from something else, it was a protest. I did not want to collect my wife's death certificate because it suggest she play a part in what happen, but I pick it up because I think there is something I can do with it. I think I will change the verdict to something that is more... more true. I can honour her like this.

London Review: Isn't it an offence to deface a death certificate?

Jules: Is it? Perhaps I will find out. Good.

London Review: So that was the first *Objet*, effectively?

Jules: It was a series. I make a number of certificates, each with a different cause of death. I worry because it look like she die not once but any number of times, and so I say, 'Sorry, my Evelyn.' But, for me, that is how it is. Every time I wake up she die again. I do not always want to wake up.

London Review: And the later pieces. Is there the idea of resurrection in your work, perhaps?

Jules: I like to think maybe at some time I will see resurrection, it will be possible, but not now. Maybe someone else they see resurrection. [Shrugs.] I do not mind that.

London Review: What do *you* see?

Jules: Now? Now is difficult because the verdict is so... I cannot think the word. You know, every day someone from the newspaper, they arrive at my hotel and say, 'You won, you must be delighted.' I cannot call being changed by something, when you were happy the way you were before, being *delighted.* But we have to make something new out of the thing that is destroyed. If you have a child there is no choice. None of us have any idea how we would be if this does not happen. We say we know, but that is bullshit. We only have what we have. It is the same with *Objets* I make from broken pieces. You have the original thing, then you wipe it out. New things made from imperfect things will always be imperfect, but they are I suppose like a monument.

London Review: [Nods.] To those who died.

Jules: No. To those who survive.

London Review: What do you say to people who find your work disturbing?

Jules: I say good. Who says it is my job to make something beautiful? I give them truth. Maybe they like it, maybe they do not. What I hope is that it will begin a conversation. You know, here in England talking about the dead, it is like a taboo. I see shock in people's faces when I talk about Evelyn. They do not talk to me about her in case it upset me. Upset. It is a strange idea, don't you think, when my world is already upside down?

London Review: You don't seem to like the label *art*.

Jules: *Pfff.* I love art! But to have the label *artist* pinned on me, not so much. I have no background.

London Review: You didn't study art?

Jules: I am completely untrained. To begin with, I do not know what I am doing, I just know that I must do something with my hands. I remember how I like to take things apart to see how they work, then I put them back together. Working with my hands, it is a way to stop feeling like I must smash all the windows. It is something private. I do not have something I feel I must share with the world. But later, when I have no money, when I need to feed my son, I sell a piece, and I start to be compared to sculptors whose work I love. People knock at my door. I think, *I am a fraud, I am going to be found out.* I think, *I must hurry up and find out something about art.* And so what do I read? That the people I admire, they take their anger and their pain and make something with it. So now I know what is behind their work, I know why it get me here [strikes chest]. I know why, even when I did not know their story, the work they make, it speak to me.

London Review: So you no longer feel like a fraud?

Jules: I do not know. It is crazy that Tate Modern want my work. Evelyn and me, we go there on Sunday afternoons. She like the South Bank very much. It is her favourite place.

London Review: Can I ask, whose work do you admire?

Jules: I like something big, like a gesture. *Break Down* by Michael Landy was very *passionnant.* You know, how he destroy everything he own? I see that. All the shredding. All the saws. The yellow crates going down the conveyor belt, like a construction line but backwards. I mean, that is not fake. That is everything he has. Gone. And I like Tracey Emin, the bed. Because, again, you know, it is everything you are told you must not do. Do not show the most private thing. But of course, for me, because I am a Frenchman, if you want to talk about influence, it is Louise Bourgeois, how she make everything personal. The thing make you look twice, but the story behind the thing is more *intéressant* than the piece itself. We can take terrible things in life and make art to, how you say? Understand them better.

London Review: Will the Tate Modern show differ from your Paris and New York shows?

Jules: I would like it to. I have an idea that involve the other families, but first I have to find them! Like me, they do not all stay in the same place.

London Review: Are you talking about a collaboration of sorts?

Jules: As I say, I do not talk to them yet. We will see. It is possible that they want no part of this.

CHAPTER TEN

Gina, 2016

Gina wakes to velvet blackness. Her mind picks up exactly where it left off, as if it's been patiently waiting for her eyelashes to flicker. *'Even if someone's held accountable, it won't change a thing. Ollie and all of the others. They'll still be dead.'* Bill was right. The ruling has changed nothing, that's the fact of it. Her life will not move on in the way that other lives move on. It is stuck. She has come unstuck.

That day destroyed everything Gina held dear. Not only her son, but every precious idea of who he was. Compelled to look for clues in other people's tragedies – though, doubtless, to do so is hypocritical – she scans newspapers for lovingly-crafted obituaries. 'Beautiful angels'. 'One in a million'. Yardsticks by which she measures her own grief.

All those smiles that lit up rooms, those unique senses of humour, those happy outlooks. At the dinner table last night, Gina read about a boy who'd overdosed on his first night at Glastonbury. 'A kind, innocent young man, who would never harm anyone.' No one in their right mind could blame his family for gunning for whoever sold their son the drugs. Of course, Gina's mind immediately turned to Ollie – how could it not? He could never have been described as a saint. From the moment he'd developed his own personality, she'd delighted in his wilfulness. By the time Ollie's body was released for burial, though her grief was unstoppable, these joyous memories were tainted. She'd been denied any comfort she might have had from Ollie's headmaster mourning her son's lost potential.

Gina turns to face what she still thinks of as Bill's side of the bed – not because she misses him, never that. She allows one hand to stray across the invisible divide. Bill said that drugs would have been a short-lived phase. He spoke as if it were some adolescent craze, like the time Ollie tried to learn the electric guitar. But how could he know? The hand explores, understanding that Bill was never really present even when he was there. All his absence means is a smooth cold sheet.

Last night she downed two of the prescription sleeping tablets that Dr Fellgate had repeatedly stressed shouldn't be taken for more than a week. (No, she hasn't had a drink. Yes, she's been tempted.) She'd hoped to be cast adrift from reality, but has slept for a couple of hours, no more. Early morning is the loneliest; the hours when Gina imagines she's the only soul awake. Time slows deliberately, taunting, *You were a bad mother.* Because it's not only her idea of Ollie that has been destroyed. It's her idea of herself.

She has been sentenced to a lifetime of constantly regurgitating the past, retracing her steps, except that this isn't a set of house keys she's mislaid. No use praying to St Anthony, as her grandmother would have recommended. It is her son, her Ollie. Could she have done *this* better, *that* better? Bill isn't here to shoulder his share of blame and memory offers little in the way of reassurance. Invariably, the answer that presents itself is *yes, yes, yes.*

Why, oh, why were you somewhere you shouldn't have been? God knows, she's tried to find a way back. She retracts the hand that has strayed. Tears dried up long ago, abandoning her to the terrible weight of exhaustion, the slow burning behind her eyes, a heavy-liddedness that, come daylight, will refuse to be shrugged off. Her hand has absorbed the cold from Bill's empty side of the bed, and it is this soothing cold she presses to her eyelids.

When Gina first heard the breaking news it had been Friday, after work. She was in the car, on her way to do the weekly shop. There was no detail to speak of. An incident in a Tube subway. *St Botolph* and *Old Billingsgate...* Not places Gina knew. *Avoid the City...* The only place she was going right then was home. *Reports of multiple casualties... Emergency services already at the scene...* Gina's chest may have heaved, her eyes fixed on the number plate of the car in front. *Concern that London hospitals will be overwhelmed... St Thomas's hospital has appealed for off-duty doctors and nurses...* She may have even murmured, 'Poor souls.' *The weekend of the Notting Hill Carnival... Service suspended... Check before you travel.* Whatever her response had been, it would have been detached – this was someone else's tragedy. She may have drummed distractedly to whatever song Radio 1 played after the newsflash, hands idly slapping the steering wheel, mind flicking to the groceries she'd forgotten to jot down on her shopping list.

An hour later and £129 poorer (she'd once paid less for a weekend in Paris), Gina was again installed behind the wheel of her Vauxhall Nova, elbow on the back of her seat, tentatively reversing. Incomers had a tendency to speed in their panic to bag a parking space. Her pulse was still racing from the effort of manhandling an overladen trolley, using her foot as a brake to stop the cart rolling into the neighbouring Mini while she unloaded. (She'd like to give a piece of her mind to the idiot who thought of putting a supermarket car park on a slope.) *We're getting reports of thirty-eight dead.* 'Dead,' she may have repeated, her subconscious acknowledging the change from *casualties.* The lack of any distinct memory turns her insides cold and she pulls the duvet up around her shoulders. At the time, Gina knows darned well, she was fretting about running late, mentally replacing her planned dinner menu with pizza and salad.

Three trips from car to porch. She opened the door and yelled in the direction of the staircase, "Ollie! Tamsin! Any chance of a hand?" She knew better than to expect the thunder of competing feet. They would both claim to have been wearing headphones. "Ollie! Tamsin! Don't both rush at once."

"Coming!" Her daughter appeared on the small landing three-quarters of the way up the stairs. A put-out expression was so commonplace that it gave no clue as to Tamsin's mood, but the way she clung to the bannister suggested reluctance.

Gina's tactic was to treat her daughter like a perfectly normal human being, so she launched straight in. "Hello, love. I'm running a bit late. Would you mind helping me unpack?" Of course, when conversing with an ordinary human being, there was no need to mull over possible interpretations before individual words left your mouth. If she'd said, 'Would you mind helping me with the bags?', Tamsin would have done that, but only that, then plonked herself in front of the television until dinner was served, preferably on a silver tray.

Tamsin took her time dragging her attitude downstairs. (She could pout for England, that girl!) *Great. A bank holiday weekend, trapped in a house with a hormonal teenager.* Gina fixed a smile in place and held out two bulging carrier bags. *Short tight top (too short, too tight) but baggy grey tracksuit bottoms and stripy bed socks. Dressed for comfort, then.* Her daughter took the shopping gracelessly and with no attempt at eye contact. On the other hand, she didn't demand, 'Why me?' A success of sorts, then. Following Tamsin up the hall, Gina decided to tempt fate. "Did you have a good day?"

"Look, Mum, I've just come on. And I don't want to talk about it, alright?"

That had Gina stumped. On the one hand you couldn't say that telling everyone was unnecessary (especially when she wasn't 'everyone') and then complain when something was kept from her that she felt entitled to know. As she hefted the final two bags onto the work surface, Gina stole a sideways glance. There were *ways* of saying these things. Perhaps she should have responded, 'Fine, let's talk about something else. Did you hear about that awful accident up in town?' But Tamsin's hair had fallen across her face, and she seemed happy to hide behind it. Unless she was after something, she rarely initiated anything that fell under the heading of conversation these days. Instead, Tamsin made a meal of decanting items onto the worktop, then slammed each item in turn into its destination. Agitation crept through the marrow of Gina's arms, branching off to the bones of her fingers. She couldn't stand it a moment longer, neither the attitude nor the blame being laid at her door (that age-old adage of not having asked to be born). She shoved a bag destined for the bathroom along the worktop. "Here. Tampons and pads. Why don't you take that upstairs? I'll call you when dinner's ready." Amazed by her own ability to appear unemotional when, inside, she was seething, it was an afterthought when Gina called after Tamsin, "Is Ollie in his room?"

"How should I know?"

"Oh, I don't know. I thought you might have heard him breathing." Sarcasm. She remembers feeling entitled to that.

Tamsin paused on the bottom step long enough to dispense a shrug, for a moment looking almost vulnerable.

"Oh, never mind! Apparently it's too much to expect a brother and sister to look out for each other." Make each other the occasional cup of tea, especially if one was feeling poorly. Not that Tamsin would say, 'I've just come on' to Ollie. At least, she assumed not.

Putting away the tinned goods, Gina had a memory of the first time her brother Mark brought a girl home to their parents' house. Gina had looked up from the television, fascinated by the way the girl managed to say hello as if she owned the place and Gina was the visitor. Then the girlfriend said, "I just need to use the loo."

And while she skipped upstairs, Mark lowered his voice: "You're on look-out duty. If Mum or Dad come home, come up and knock on the door. But otherwise, make sure you stay down here."

'Or what?' she'd wanted to yell after his retreating footsteps, as she heard a giggle and the bedroom door slam as if something heavy had fallen against it.

Tamsin's covering for him... Ollie's got a girl up there. Gina stayed her hand on the handle of the cupboard door and listened. *What do you expect?* she asked herself. *Creaking bedsprings? Strains of Barry White?* There was only the buzz of the fridge. Lying in bed, thirteen years later, Gina can still hear it. Not the same fridge, but the same buzz. If Bill were here, he would correct her and say *similar*. Even now she fights the urge to yell at the memory of him, 'You think it matters? You actually think it matters? We failed, dammit, we fucked up!'

It had been impossible to sit there every day of the second inquest listening to experts dissect each stage of Eric's sequence and not insert another stage or two. When she heard new questions about negligence, how could she ignore her own?

If Ollie had found his way home, if he'd been arrested, if Gina had answered a knock on the front door to find a policeman with one large hand on her son's shoulder, and Ollie wearing that sheepish expression of his. *Then* there would have been a way back, no matter how painful. She and Bill could have sat him down and had it out. He wasn't a child, they would have said. Let's be honest, Gina would have been the one to lay it on the line. Bill was all for turning a blind eye in return for an easy life. 'You'll have to earn our trust all over again,' she'd have said. Today they would start again from a position of no trust. Phone calls to ensure he'd arrived at school as scheduled. Strict control over pocket money and spending. There'd be no hiding place in his bedroom she wouldn't check. There would be homework checks too. Yes, homework checks. 'And there's no need to look at me like that. While we're at it, since money appears to be the issue, get a weekend job. It's time you learned what earning an honest wage feels like.'

Stop. Rewind. Stop. Rewind. Thirteen years and counting, these imaginary fleshed-out conversations still gnaw away at Gina. Oh, for that second chance to be the mother she should have been!

'No one's going to give me a job now!' It was possible to convince herself that Ollie had said just that; she saw the disbelief in his hard-done-by expression.

'You should have thought of that before you got yourself into this mess.' Gina wouldn't have referred directly to drugs; she wouldn't have known how to. Constantly surprised by the way her kids recycled old slang, she couldn't have faced Ollie's scorn when she used the wrong term. *Mum, you can't say that. Don't you know anything?* 'Tell me, what *was* your big plan?'

Barely a shrug.

'And that's the problem. You don't *think*. So if you're lucky enough that they decide not to make an example of you,' that would draw his gaze, 'we'll do things our way.'

But Ollie didn't find his way home on that firmly-fixed Friday. Gina is ashamed that she thinks these thoughts, although she has little control over them. She uses these fantasies to fend off reality. And reality is impossible to face when you're lying awake in the dark, knowing that you're utterly alone.

Gina thought she had wanted truth. She went in search of it. "I need to know," she heard herself repeat. "I gave birth to him. It's my right." Then, every day, a new and terrible fact.

"Wait. There was CCTV footage?"

"Not of the incident itself. As you know, the cameras in the station were down."

"But before the incident?"

"Depending on who you choose to believe, the average Londoner is caught on CCTV between seventy and three hundred times a day, but –"

"You've found something? There's footage of Ollie's journey?"

"Most agencies have a policy of deleting footage after fourteen days."

Long gone, then.

"But occasionally it's overlooked."

They showed her a video of a boy who looked like Ollie.

They brought him back to life in front of her eyes.

But he wasn't on his way to an Underground station. He was in the front seat of a car.

Something was taken from the glove compartment.

Handed over.

He was wearing the grey hoodie she'd bought him at the beginning of the school holidays.

Except that he couldn't have been her son *smile which lit up every room he walked into.*

Her Ollie was at home *bright young man with everything to look forward to.* He'd have been… He'd have been… *Come on, you should know this. You're his mother.* But Ollie was fifteen, still in bed when she left for work and difficult to tie down at the best of times. "What do you think it was? In the glove compartment?"

A pause. "This other character? He's known to us. He's a dealer."

"Drugs?" There it was, the word that features high on every mother's list of fears. "We'd have known if our son was taking drugs!" *Would you? You didn't even know where he was.*

"He may not have taken them himself, Mrs Wicker. This other chap doesn't do his own dirty work. We suspect he was using Oliver as a runner."

She wasn't familiar with the term, but it wasn't something you needed to ask. Ollie was the delivery boy. And with irrefutable proof, what option did Gina have but to revise her image of him? What option did she have but to superimpose this new knowledge over remembered conversations? Ollie wasn't just a risk-taker, he was a liar. Time and time again he'd pulled the wool over their eyes. She'd thought his untidy bedroom was the worst of it. He had them fooled because they'd *wanted* to be fooled. They refused to see him for who – and what – he was, because that's what you do. You can't risk driving your own child away. You have to offer a way back.

Piled in her arms, the facts. One on top of the other, until her shoulders ached and her back felt like it was breaking. The son she knew was edged out of the picture, and with him went the person – the parent – Gina had thought herself to be.

The next through the door on that Friday evening was Bill. About to yell, "Is that you?" Gina heard low swearing. She set the oven to 220 degrees and breathed in a muted kind of way so she couldn't be accused of sighing. "Oven's on. Tea or a glass of wine?"

Bill walked into the kitchen, throwing the local paper down on the same worktop Gina had just that moment finished clearing. He clunked his keys on the table she was about to lay and said, "Wine." Nothing more.

This time, making no effort to stifle a sigh, Gina moved the newspaper to the recycling, then rattled open the fridge. She stared, bristling, forgetting for an instant what she was looking for. *This is the man you used to burn for.* Semi-skimmed, tomato ketchup… Her eyes fell on the bottle of Chilean Sauvignon. Just within the periphery of her vision, Bill sat down, removed his glasses, closed his eyes and pinched the bridge of his nose.

Never mind that *she* was exhausted. Never mind that there was nothing Gina would have liked to do more than lay her head on the table and sleep. She assumed her husband's mood wasn't *entirely* down to the fact that they'd asked the local newspaper to stop delivering.

To ask or not to ask… *Not,* she decided, pouring two generous glasses, then upending a bag of salad leaves into the crystal bowl she had never really liked (a wedding present from Sean and Emma). She set a glass of wine down in front of her husband and, when no word of thanks followed, deliberately plonked the salad bowl in the centre of the table. After his shoulders jumped him out of his stupor, she said, "I don't know whether to put the pizza in or wait for Ollie. How hungry are you?"

"Hm."

Gina took her glass of wine for a brisk walk over to the cork board. No clues on the family calendar. Nothing to suggest she'd forgotten to pick him up from somewhere or other (because let's face it, this, too, was usually down to Gina). "I don't suppose he mentioned anything about being late?"

"Who?"

"How many sons do you have?"

"You think he'd tell me? I'm just his dad." Bill loosened his tie, undid the top button of his shirt, ran his fingers around the inside of his collar. "Have you tried calling his mobile?"

"I'll check his room. Tamsin said she hadn't seen him, but that doesn't mean he isn't hiding up there."

No response. Bill had picked up a single rocket leaf and was rolling its stalk between a finger and thumb as if mesmerised by what he saw.

Is this my life? Gina remembers thinking to herself as she stomped upstairs. *Everyone retreating inside their shells, and me constantly trying to coax them out.* With no small amount of exasperation, she rapped on her son's bedroom door: "Ollie! Are you in there?"

No reply.

"Are you alone?"

Nothing.

Tentatively, she turned the handle. The smell hit her, a toxic greenhouse implosion. Hormones, angst and socks, plus some other, less identifiable smell. No wonder Tamsin didn't want to venture into her brother's room. And to think she'd imagined... The room would need fumigating before he invited a girl up here. As if avoiding landmines, she high-stepped over discarded clothes and flung the window wide. Any lecture on male hygiene would have to come from Bill. The thought of her husband cringing his way through a father/son talk was enough to summon a smile. Though it wasn't as if Ollie didn't shower. He spent longer in the bathroom than Tamsin and her put together.

Look! Underpants, inside out on the floor by the bed. She snatched them up. Ollie knew how to work the washing machine. On a number of occasions, she'd caught him stuffing a balled-up sheet into it. She hadn't asked; hadn't offered to help. He'd proved himself perfectly capable of pouring liquid into the drawer, turning the dial and pushing the 'on' button. She'd saved it all up for an occasion like this one, and, later tonight, she would deploy it.

'*What are you doing in my room?*' She imagined Ollie arriving; stopping as if he'd hit some invisible barrier. Her natural expression always made her look as though she'd been caught red-handed. Back at middle school, a week didn't go by without her mother marching up to the headmaster's office to complain that Gina had been punished for something someone else had done, but there was blame in her eyes when she warned, "One day, my girl, you'll be singled out of a line of suspects." She'd been right. Television cameras had captured that same expression as Gina had left courtrooms, pausing at the top of the steps outside them. She wondered if people didn't imagine *she* was a criminal.

Not a criminal, just a bad mother.

But Ollie didn't walk through the bedroom door. Instead, Gina berated herself as she grabbed stray T-shirts from the floor. *Why are you acting as if you're afraid of your own son?* She headed for the door, checking the room was tightly sealed before dumping the bundle of soiled clothes into the laundry basket. She paused outside Tamsin's room. Silence from within; a sense that its occupant was holding her breath, listening, hoping to escape detection. Gina circled to make it sound as if she'd just arrived, selected a voice from the repertoire labelled *Mum* and called out: "Tamsin! Dinner in ten minutes!"

And now, in the predawn loneliness, hip bones aching, there is still an hour to go before the outlines of rooftops and chimneypots and the tall London Plane tree on the corner of Shorts Road will define themselves. Gina's senses tune to a different frequency: *Who's there?* Her heartbeat accelerates. She swallows, feels the change of pressure in her ears, hears saliva go all the way down. It would be wrong to say, 'Ollie?' "Tamsin?" she ventures.

She has no expectation of a reply. The night plays cruel tricks, unleashing unhealthy thoughts. Thoughts, she acknowledges, she'll need to adapt. Because the second inquest *has* changed something. She has her son back. Not as he was before, but damaged. In need of rescue.

"I didn't mean to wake you." A voice from the present summons Gina from the morass of guilt that she's made of her past.

Relief floods through her. She isn't alone. "You didn't. I was awake."

"The house of insomniacs," Tamsin quips, then quickly adds, "Mind if I get in with you?"

"Plenty of room." Gina's night-amplified reply sounds forced.

Bare padding feet, soft on the floorboards. From the shadows, a form takes shape. "I don't know why. I just couldn't face being on my own."

Preoccupied, Gina pulls the duvet aside, offering her daughter the empty comfort of Bill's cold side of the bed. "We all get like that sometimes." Ollie made bad decisions, but when push came to shove, his instinct was to help. She rewinds to what her daughter has just said, thinks, *Do any of us really want to be alone? We all want some space, but space without boundaries is just…emptiness.* She puts out an arm and cradles her daughter's head to her shoulder. *Shhh, go back to sleep now.* But, even as she slips inside the tide of her daughter's breathing, it's damaged Ollie she's speaking to. *Hush Ollie, hush Ollie, hush Ollie.*

CHAPTER ELEVEN

Rosie, 22 August 2003:
Incident minus 10 mins

"CCTV's down, boss," Sam says the minute Rose walks through the office door.

The way he says 'boss' jars. Maybe she'd have been better off sticking with Rosie. But Rose seemed more adult, more professional. She became Rose, slipping into character the minute she put on her uniform. Not that it's made any difference to Sam. To him she'll always be a young upstart, promoted from station assistant to station supervisor in less than two years. Only twenty mind-numbing months of manning ticket barriers and having half the population of London pissed off with her. Several times a day, she reminds herself that management had warned her she'd need to grow a hide like a rhino. *Hind of a rhino,* she thinks as an idiot tries to wave half a dozen mates through the gates with a child's Travelcard. *Hind of a rhino,* as the ancient homeless guy makes his daily appearance, wanting to beg in the ticket hall, and she knows she must tell him she can't allow it. *Hind of a rhino,* as she's sneered at by the prat who produces his annual season ticket when she stops him for sauntering past the barrier as though he's bunking the fare.

"Damn." Sam hits a button on the keyboard. "Nothing! Thirty years of so-called efficiency savings. What do they expect?"

Rose refuses to buy this line. Everyone knows the system's bursting at the seams but, comparatively speaking, the CCTV is shiny and new. "Have you reported the fault to central control?" she asks, squinting at the monitors.

"Give us a chance! It's just this minute happened." As Sam jabs more keys, Rose senses waves of pure frustration rising off him. He kicks his heels, rolling his chair away from the desk on its castors.

Through the itch of impatience, Rose reminds herself, *You need him on your side.* "Have you tried turning it off and turning it on again?" she quips.

One hand clasped to his forehead, he says, "Ha bloody ha."

Let Sam enjoy his token resistance, but they don't have much time. "What do you think? Breakdown or power failure?"

"If I knew that I'd be an engineer, wouldn't I?"

Options flash through her mind. "Well, is it all of the cameras or just one?" She positions her hands over Sam's keyboard.

"I'll do it!" The idea of someone else touching his controls tempts him back to investigate. "Not all of them." Newly alert now he's realised that not all of the cameras are kaput, Sam tucks his chair under the desk. Hallelujah! "From what I can see, it's just escalators five and six."

Four different views of the out-of-order escalator appear on the monitors. *This is so not what I need.* Rose had tried telling the Powers That Be she wasn't ready for management. "Trust us," was what they said. "We need an injection of new blood. You're exactly what we're looking for." Who wouldn't be flattered by the thought that someone had recognised in her a certain quality? And of course, she has a track record of rising to a challenge when someone puts their faith in her. On-the-job training would be provided, they assured her, and until then she would be shadowed.

"Got yourself a babysitter?" Sam had asked. But only this morning her babysitter had called in sick.

Rose imagines her 'shadow' hovering, holding back advice, but responding to her every move with a singular critical expression. *Risk assessment.* She grabs a ring-binder from an eye-level shelf and scans the index. *Reporting arrangements for different types of incident.* Here we are: *Safety alerts that require urgent communication.* OK, what she has on her hands seems to fall under the category of a local emergency, which means it's *her* emergency. A chance to prove she's up to the job. *Think!* When her kitchen light blows, it only takes out half the electricity in the flat. Scale it up, but how much more complicated can this be? "Could the cameras on five and six be on a different power circuit?" she suggests.

"Could be." Sam shrugs unenthusiastically, but then acknowledges the possibility and nods. "Could be just that one circuit down."

Rose focuses on the monitor. "So let's get this straight. We've got CCTV on the escalators that aren't working, and no CCTV on the escalators we're diverting passengers to?" Half an hour ago, she imagined that congestion control would be her main challenge. Let's face it, it doesn't take too many extra passengers to take them from the usual Friday-night sardines to an all-out emergency.

"That's the long and short of it. Oh, and it looks like the visuals on the platforms for the Northern Line are down. Nothing doing, see?"

For a moment she wonders if she's out of her depth. Sam clearly thinks so. "Perfect. Just before five o'clock kick-off." Any staff who could be spared are already redirecting passengers at Catfish Hill. There's nothing else for it, she'll have to go down there herself. But first she radios Skip.

"Skip, how's it going?"

"It's going. God knows where they're coming from but they keep on coming."

She mouths to Sam, "Can you get me a visual?" The view on the monitor changes. They see Skip and Selena positioned behind the ticket barriers, Selena looking fierce as she points the way.

Sam gives a short laugh. "I wouldn't argue with that!"

"More good news for you, Skip. The CCTV's out on the escalators *and* the Northern Line platforms. I'm heading down to see what's what. I don't want to close altogether, not unless we really have to. Do whatever you need to do to filter the flow until I get back to you."

A reluctant affirmative and Rose raises her eyebrows as she thumbs the end of the call. "I'd be pissed off as well," she admits. "They'll have to fight their way out to the entrance."

"Kicking out time," Sam scoffs. *"And* the start of a bank holiday weekend? Good luck to them."

It isn't difficult to picture the backlash. Every passenger will imagine the decision to make them wait has been taken to piss them off. The tourist who looks out of place manhandling luggage through the City. The commuters who operate on autopilot until someone gets in their way. Earlier today, she'd had her own run-in when one lady (middle-aged, impeccably dressed) who'd been unable to get through the automatic barrier thrust her ticket at Rose. All she did was ask to see the front.

"I'm showing it to you, you silly cunt."

A c-bomb, coming from another woman, and over a ticket! "I need to see the side with the date."

The woman sighed as if this was a huge inconvenience. No admission that she was wrong. No apology.

Skip and Selena will be exposed to a baying crowd, but what are Rose's options? She's hardly spoilt for choice. "Have we ever had escalators and CCTV down at the same time before?"

"Oh, you want my advice now."

"Please, Sam. You know I didn't ask for this promotion."

"I'm saying nothing."

"So that's a no." She tries to sound decisive. "In that case, I'd better get down there pronto. Will you make that call to central control? Tell them everything we know and say I'll check in with them as soon as I know what's what."

Sam tosses the telephone receiver from one hand to the other. "Am I requesting assistance?"

"If any staff are sitting around twiddling their thumbs, we could certainly use them."

Later, she will wish she'd given him a definite yes.

CHAPTER TWELVE

Cassie, 22 August 2003:
Incident minus 1hr 17 mins

Quarter to four and the handover is complete. If Cassie goes to see her director within the next ten minutes or so, she should still be able to get away before the mass exodus. A decision then. She'll start packing up. Her feet explore the space under her desk in search of discarded shoes. The first is easily located, less easily persuaded. The second proves elusive. It turns out to be facing the wrong direction. Now for her desk. Cassie untacks cut-outs of babies' heads from the edge of her computer screen and rolls the Blu-tack into a neat ball. She sweeps foil sprinkles in the shapes of nappy pins and feeding bottles into the bin, shuffling her palms together to dislodge those that have stuck.

"Can I take that?" Little Miss I-Forgot-to-Eat nods greedily at Cassie's pen tidy. No, it really *is* Cassie's, bought with her own money from W H Smith.

What's the point? She doesn't want to carry home any more than she has to and, if she leaves it on her desk, it will only disappear. "Knock yourself out," she says with an insincere smile as she peels the plastic banner from the edge of her desk.

"Cool." Vanessa slides the pen tidy onto her desk – simply slides it across the divide, Sharpies and all.

Cassie gives her replacement's triumphant face a sideways glare. *Don't get too comfortable.* She takes no small amount of pleasure in setting up an automated email, redirecting all those hundreds of daily interruptions to Vanessa's inbox, then shuts down her computer. There is something final about the way the screen blanks out. *Well, this is it.*

Sue's office isn't known as the Goldfish Bowl for nothing. When dealing with her boss of six years, timing is everything. If the blinds are open, it's supposed to signal that she's available, but it's always best to check she's alone. Sue won't think twice about deliberately leaving someone in full view while she tears into them if she thinks they need taking down a peg or two.

Deep breath.

Before Cassie's knuckles make contact with the door, Sue calls out, "Come in!" By the time Cassie has the door open, Sue is edging around her desk, heels towering, designer suit pristine. "Is it that time already?"

A wave of guilt. Ridiculous. *Why feel as if you've let the side down? They employed you on merit (they had to, it's the law), identified you (correctly) as a career woman, promoted you because you were the best person for the job.* Cassie smiles. "Vanessa's up to speed and I've filled in most of my Exit Checklist. I've just come to hand in my security pass."

Sue fails to close her hand around the plastic pass at the anticipated moment, and it sails under her desk. She also fails to grasp that crawling around on the floor is beyond someone who's eight months pregnant.

"I don't suppose…?" Cassie smiles through the humiliation of being so clumsy and uncoordinated. She can feel her bump begin to twitch rhythmically. *And now's the moment you choose to get hiccups!*

Sue's eyes pass over her stomach in a look of silent horror. "Sorry, I should have thought!" Before attempting to crouch she hitches up her skirt slightly, saying, "Bit tight."

"Oh, I know *all* about tight!"

The security pass is retrieved and Sue reinstalls herself in her executive leather chair. Though uninvited, Cassie feels it's acceptable to take a seat, if only to lean on the desk to tick the final box on the obligatory checklist.

"So..." Sue scans the form as if it's an inconvenience. Cassie waits to be told how much she'll be missed. But Sue doesn't lead with, 'I don't know how we'll cope without you.' What she says is, "You know the score?"

A word of thanks, a *good luck,* an acknowledgment of all the support Cassie's given her over the years wouldn't go amiss. She fixes her expression and matches her boss's brisk delivery. "Eighteen weeks paid, twenty-nine weeks unpaid, and I have to give twenty-eight days' notice if I want to come back before my time's up."

There's a stiffness about the way Sue looks at Cassie, as if it's an effort for her to keep her eyes on her face. "You won't."

Sue hasn't asked if she'd planned to get pregnant. If she had, Cassie might not have answered truthfully. An accidental pregnancy, in this day and age, with all of the options. From tomorrow onwards, the idea of the birth will start to get frighteningly real. "I'll go stir crazy at home."

"You'll be a great mum."

That's how Cassie will be seen from now on. Another watcher of clocks, someone who says apologetically at the time meetings were scheduled to end, 'Do you mind if I scoot?' or when asked if anyone can do overtime, 'I'm so sorry, but...' Never mind that, in the past, Cassie has volunteered for more than her fair share. *I don't have anything to rush off for.* Again, she fixes a smile in place. "I'm already looking into childcare options."

Sue's expression suggests she's heard it all before. She no longer recognises Cassie as an exception. "Let me know about your keeping in touch days."

Perhaps she's right. Priorities change. Maybe she won't *want* to come back. This could actually be the last time she sits opposite Sue. What would she miss about this place? "Will do, boss."

"And if you move house, or anything."

Although it's a joke, Cassie feels affronted by the assumption that she'll be afflicted by nappy-brain. She ventures as close to sarcasm as she dares, replying, "I'll try not to forget."

"Anyway," Sue nods through the double glazed walls, "I think you're wanted."

Well and truly beached, Cassie has no option but to kick her feet to spin the chair. There they are, mostly women, because the unwritten rules of office rituals dictate that it's their responsibility to see someone off on maternity leave. Helium balloons and flowers and – would you look at that? – Vanessa holding one end of a banner. She puts one hand over her heart only to find the still-surprising swell of her breasts. Though she tries her best to look delighted, Cassie spins back towards Sue wailing, "I told them. Nothing I have to carry!"

"I couldn't stop them, so I did the next best thing." Sue is smiling lopsidedly. "Stefan's down in reception."

"Thank you, Sue. That's… that's…" Overwhelmed with what she acknowledges is gratitude, though she has no wish to feel grateful, Cassie tries scrunching her eyes and then flaps a hand in front of her face. She breathes the way she's been taught in her ante-natal classes.

Sue has a tissue at the ready. Even in this, she's efficient. "I'll buzz down and get him to come up, shall I?"

Cassie supports her bump while she levers herself out of the chair, then opens the office door and pretends to stagger. "You guys, you shouldn't have!"

The pavement is already bustling, people keen to get home and take advantage of the last couple of hours of daylight. Cassie feels irritable. Her boobs ache and there's the small matter of the baby pressing down on her bladder. "This is exactly what I wanted to avoid," she says, then louder, "Stef, wait! You're going to have to slow down."

A woman skirting around them gives an exasperated sigh and throws a sideways glance. Disapproval morphs into a smile as she catches sight of Stefan laden with flowers, a helium balloon tied to his wrist, another knotted to the strap of his rucksack. Cassie would have gladly left the balloons behind, but he'd insisted.

"Not far now." Stefan flashes a smile at the overtaker. This isn't flirting. It's endearing that he so clearly doesn't give a damn about how ridiculous he looks. "Swap sides with me," he directs. He has this thing about being closest to the pavement. Some nonsense about having his sword arm free. Cassie doesn't have the energy to object. Plus, there's sense in having a buffer-zone.

The closer they get to the Underground station, the more congested the pavement becomes.

Stefan cranes to look over a shoulder in front. "It's not usually this bad, is it?"

Cassie shrugs dismissively. "It's Friday." Stefan hasn't appreciated what the commute's been like for her these past few weeks. His work takes him to private gyms and public parks. But the truth is, this is as bad as Cassie can remember it. Inside the crowd, unable to see out, she concedes, "Bank holiday weekend. Must be something going on."

They're herded like sheep. *Whales, cows, sheep: she's a one-woman menagerie today.* Nose to jacket – in Cassie's case, bump to jacket – of the person in front. She tries to leave a gap. She can cope with a bit of jostling, but she won't have her baby pressed up against God knows who.

"Must be something big. Are you alright?"

"At least keeping up isn't a problem any more." Baby steps. Pigeon steps, they used to call them, and with each step her heels slide out of her shoes. Barely shuffling, she rocks from side to side, but still struggles to catch her breath. She tilts backwards slightly to give her lungs a chance to take in extra air without her bump getting in the way.

"Sure you're alright?" Stefan asks. She can tell he'd like to hold on to her, but he has no free hand.

She looks up at a bobbing balloon, attempts a smile. "Another thing I don't have to worry about is losing you in this crowd."

"It'll thin out in a minute."

But it doesn't. If anything it gets worse. Cassie keeps one hand firmly on her stomach. She wraps the thumb of her free hand in her fist. A muffled announcement is being repeated over and over again, but the words are distinct. *Very busy tonight.*

"You can say that again!" someone shouts, drowning out whatever comes next.

So you'll need to...

"What did she say? Did anyone get that?"

"If you shut up a minute, we'll all be able to hear."

"Yeah, shut the fuck up, will you?"

Cassie raises her eyebrows, secretly glad not to have been the one to voice what they were all thinking. The crowd stays quiet long enough for the words *Escalator out* to reach them. *Might want to walk.*

A collective groan.

Cassie wills herself not to cry. She wants to be at home. Now. Only when she stubs her toe does she realise they've reached the station steps. As she recoils, her foot lifts clean out of its shoe. She clutches Stefan's arm for support; shovels it back on before it's trampled.

"Alright, people! It's very busy tonight and we've got an escalator out of action, so there's a diversion in place. Once you're through the barrier, just follow the signs through the subway to Old Billingsgate. It's five minutes, tops."

"Five minutes! You can double that with my waddle."

Stef lowers his arm so that pressure increases on her hand. "At least there *are* trains. I thought she was going to tell us we're stranded."

Between the bulk of unfamiliar bodies and backpacks, Cassie is buffeted, caught in the flow. Two station staff have barricaded themselves behind the ticket barriers. One is using a loudhailer, but her voice is an indistinct crackle. Cassie remembers how they scoffed at their head teacher, who installed a security keypad on his office door. Scared of the kids! People are pushing. Rammed hard against Stefan, she feels a surge of anger, the instinct to push back, kick out.

"Oi! Pregnant lady over here!" Stefan yells through a mouthful of petals.

"It's OK," she tries to reassure him, but it isn't. Her pulse is racing the way it used to at the end of a ten-mile run. Sod the Mothercare vouchers, she should have left at four on the dot. She should have turned to her bloody replacement and said, 'Here. Have everything and good luck to you.'

"Alright people! You'll have noticed by now that it's very busy tonight. Have a little patience."

Trapped in the bottleneck in front of the barriers, Cassie tries to locate a calm space inside her head. A cup of tea and a wallow in a hot bath. Heinz tomato soup. Fresh bedsheets. Once they're through, the crush will thin. Here we go. And then she is in the warren of curved-ceilinged corridors that earned the Tube its nickname. *Keep left.* No one is touching her who she doesn't want to be touching her. An echo of marching feet, and not a hope in hell that Cassie can keep pace. She shuffles forwards, Stefan by her side. Actually, she's fine. The memory of the conker makes her smile. "We should hang the mobile in the nursery tomorrow."

"I thought you didn't like it!"

"I've come round." The lazy *slap slap* of her loose-fitting shoes.

"Thank you," he says, his voice full of feeling. It was a gift from his mother.

She shrugs. It has to be a good thing that it's so easy to make him happy.

An overlap of voices, an occasional screech of brakes from the tunnels down below. People are skirting around them once more. She passes an advert for a film she had vague thoughts about seeing. "They say that going to the cinema is what you miss most when you become a parent."

"Who says?"

"The people who stop going to the cinema when they become parents." The corridor curves so she can't see how far there is to go. If it were brighter, cleaner, it might feel like a space station.

"I can't remember the last time we went to the pictures."

"We should make a point of going. Just so we can go on about how much we miss it."

A sharp right turn *help point: out of order.* Cassie is aware that the heads of her fellow travellers are falling away. They arrive at the back of the queue for the escalator. It should have been obvious this is where they've been heading, but Cassie feels unprepared. This escalator is much, much steeper than the one she normally uses. As they shuffle forwards, she feels increasingly restricted by her inability to see over the top of her bump. It's been weeks since she could look down and see her feet, and now she cannot see the step. She sets a hand on the moving rail, testing it. It tugs at her arm. Cassie stalls, everything inside her screaming *No!*

But that's the way home.

"Take your time," Stefan cautions. "People can go around you." He turns to indicate and they do. It's unnerving to have people overtake on her left. In England, overtaking is always done on the right. Why should escalators be any different?

She tries again, is pulled off-balance, feels herself begin to spin, and backs off, shaking her head. *Too fast, too steep. Too everything.*

Stefan cradles her aside, saying, "You go first," to the couple behind. "We're taking a minute out." To Cassie, he frowns. "Everything OK?"

She fights the panic; presses herself hard against the cool tiled wall. "Would you go and look for me?"

"OK," he says in a voice intended to humour. "What should I look for?"

Steep. Fluorescent lights rotate past Cassie's eyes. "See if you can see the bottom of the escalator. Count how many steps there are on the flat before they fall away."

"Don't worry. We'll go down side by side."

"That won't help," she snaps. "Not when I can't see what I'm stepping onto." Her heart is clenched like a fist. "Please."

A moment alone. Cassie fits herself into the curve of the wall. If only her insides would stop quivering. Passers-by barely glance at her. *I could be in trouble over here and not one of you would stop.* But she has a feeling that if she returned anyone's gaze, her eyes would warn: *Back off. I mean it.*

By her side again, Stefan says, "I'm not going to lie to you. It's steep."

He gets it. He actually gets it. It's not just her being a wuss. "And?"

"You only get one, maybe two steps on the flat. So here's what we're going to do. I'll go first, OK? I'll crouch down, then I'll tell you when to step. And once you're on, I'll move your feet." He looks at her, concerned. "Repeat what I just said."

"Have my eyes glazed over or something? I *was* listening," she insists.

"You'll feel better if you say it."

She sighs, exasperated, and watches the next batch of profiles blizzard past.

"Go on. Just to please me."

After pushing herself off the wall, Cassie goes to fold her arms across her chest, forgetting there's no space between her boobs and the bump.

Stefan is used to resistance, even from people who pay him to put them through punishing exercise regimes. He nods, making it clear in his calm way that no isn't an acceptable answer. In his book, talking your way through what seems impossible is the first step to nailing it.

She caves. "You'll go first. You'll crouch down, then you'll tell me when to go and you'll move my feet onto the step." Dammit, he's right. It *does* help to say it out loud. This might actually be do-able.

"Right. Now for a difficult decision. Do you mind if I leave the flowers?"

He looks so anxious that she manages a laugh. "No."

"Thank God!" He squats and props them up against a wall, then has a change of heart. "I hate to see them go to waste." He thrusts them towards the first person to pass by. "Would you like some flowers?" They carry on walking, but a woman looks longingly over her shoulder and hesitates. "What about you?" he tries again. "Would you like some flowers?"

"That's so nice." It's rather sweet, the pleasure on her face. As if Stefan's bought them especially for her.

"To be honest, you're doing us a favour. We're a little overloaded."

"You go first," the woman offers, and though Cassie doesn't feel ready, standing at the top and worrying about what she can't see won't make things any easier. She needs to be at home and this is the only way.

She hustles Stefan and the bobbing balloons in front of her. "You're on."

His head is low as he steps onto the moving tread. There's a moment when he seems to fall away, and terror rises within her. Then he turns, projecting his voice, "Wait until I say!" It's clear Stefan hadn't counted on how fast the escalator would move, but he strides back up. *You won't be able to hang about once he's crouched down to the level of your feet.* She edges as close as she dares, her eyes trained on his for the moment he gives the instruction. She may be at the mercy of this godless contraption, but she trusts Stefan George absolutely. He's going to be such a great dad.

"OK, *now!*"

No hesitation, she steps forwards, one foot and then the other. The back of one shoe flattens under her heel and she leaves it uncorrected. None too gently, Stefan grabs one of her ankles, repositions her foot. Then she's sailing down and Stefan's grinning face appears over the top of her bump.

"You were right on the edge."

It's only now that she sees his grin is one of relief. "You were properly scared!" Cassie accuses.

"I had it all under control."

"Yeah, right!" She punches one of the balloons with her spare hand and Stefan pretends to head-butt it. For one drawn-out moment the purest feeling flows through Cassie, not just happiness but something finer. A month from now they'll be a family – *a family!* Already, she's part of something beyond herself. Her husband-to-be (she's growing to like that phrase) turns to face forwards and takes one step down to avoid the collision of rucksack and baby bump. *Hello, husband-to-be.* She's still smiling when a screech of brakes announces the arrival of the next train.

A slight blow to her left shoulder, Cassie steps forward involuntarily. She doesn't see the man with the wide kitbag slung high over his right shoulder who has broken into a run. She's only vaguely aware as the rumble of a minor stampede follows. No longer in contact with anything, her left foot scrabbles for purchase. Something inside her pitches. Heat rushes up through her marrow, out through her scalp. She lunges for a handhold, the place where she expects Stefan's shoulder to be, only to find he's been forced down another step. Cassie's other foot slips from its over-stretched shoe. As she teeters, her stomach contracts into a tight ball of fear and the baby responds, fluttering then kicking out. Her bare foot slams into metal. "Stef!" she yelps a warning, but no primal or maternal instinct can protect her family as she embarks on her fledgling flight. Baby-side down – *the baby!* – she slams into Stefan. Down, down, down, her golden-haired Icarus before her, helpless.

CHAPTER THIRTEEN

Donovan, 2016

Donovan chains his bike to a lamp post outside the pub. Once again, as he tackles the lock, he falls outside time. He's deep in conversation with Cassie when, without his noticing, she crosses to the opposite side of the road, leaving him talking to himself. It might be madness, but he looks for her for a moment or two, hoping for a footstep, the sound of her voice. But large black men don't stare into the near distance for no apparent reason. Donovan has made himself conspicuous.

He sighs and glances up at the pub sign. *What am I doing here?* He has arrived at the centre of a triangle made up by St Paul's, the Bank of England and Mansion House; a cheerful beacon on the corner of an old Roman road. Rumour has it the pub was built from ships' timbers for Sir Christopher Wren's thirsty workforce. This building is a subsequent reincarnation, courtesy of the Blitz. Beneath thick layers of black gloss, its timbers are probably pine. Donovan hasn't a clue why Jules has asked him for a drink. Prior to today, you could count the number of conversations they've shared – and by this he means just the pair of them – on one hand. *What harm can a quick pint do?* he asks himself. *Helene can cope on her own for another hour.* Plus, perhaps there'll be gossip to take home.

Chatter, dark wood, chalked blackboards, and electric light make for a comforting combination. Before closing the door behind him, he takes one last look at the pavement opposite. He can't quite shake the feeling that Cassie was there. His sense of her was so real. But no.

Jules has staked out a table and is thumbing through a battered leather notebook.

"If it isn't the famous Jules Roche," he feigns cheer, sitting his cycle helmet on the tabletop.

"Donovan, my man!" Jules jumps up. He comes up to Donovan's chest. "You know, you make me feel so short!"

"And you make me feel clumsy." He points to Jules's half-empty glass. "Another beer?"

"Why not? Just a small one."

As Donovan orders at the bar, Jules scrapes a high-legged chair across the floorboards from the neighbouring table. "My baby chair," he says. And when Donovan sits, the Frenchman touches the top of his head. "You see, now we are the same height."

"Cheers." Donovan raises his glass to his lips. In his hand, the pint glass looks like a half.

"You know it is madness, this city of yours. Do you go to work by train?"

"What do you think this is?" Donovan taps his cycle helmet.

"Huoui?" Jules inhales.

Donovan marvels at how different a sound a Frenchman makes to an Englishman. He's tempted to experiment, to suck in a mouthful of air and feel the sound take shape. But Jules is indicating over his shoulder with a thumb.

"You know, me and my son. Last week we try your Boris bikes."

"Boris!" Donovan scoffs and, following the direction of the thumb, finds himself looking at champagne glasses hanging upside down above the bar. "And?"

"*Pfff.*" The extent of Jules's review.

"It's not so bad once you get to know a few shortcuts."

"I know shortcuts! You forget, I live here." How could Donovan forget? Of course, back then, there was no reason for their paths to cross. "For a while," Jules continues, "I am a motorcycle courier."

He nods, on the one hand feeling he's being invited to be impressed, on the other conscious that Jules is buying time. "I didn't know that."

Then Jules ventures: "So. The verdict. It is still sinking in, *n'est-ce pas?*"

Donovan scratches at the skin underneath his eye with a pristine white nail, a gesture observers might think surprisingly delicate for a man of his size. "It's going to take time."

"Well, time is something we *do* have. We do not know how much, but…" Jules makes a sweeping motion with one arm.

From the back of Donovan's throat comes a sound, neither agreement nor disagreement. With the sense of his daughter so real and so close, it comes back to him: the podcast he listened to while lying in bed last night. Side by side, he and his wife find their own separate ways to make it through the dark hours. He wouldn't say this to just anyone, but Donovan decides to risk saying it now, to Jules. "Have you heard of the Many Worlds theory?"

Jules nods enthusiastically, but the skin between his eyebrows creases. "What is it? Science fiction?"

A straightforward 'yes' would have been nice. Then Donovan wouldn't be struggling for words to explain a theory that feels like sorcery. "I have to tell you, quite a lot of it went straight over my head." Certainty isn't a luxury Donovan can afford. He'll grab the faintest glimmer of hope, even though the rational part of his mind does everything in its power to buck him off. "But the general idea is this. Every time you're given a choice, every time you make a decision," he can't help but pause here, "you basically split in two. There's the you who made the decision and the other you, the one who said, 'No, that's a bad, bad idea.' You peel off in opposite directions, and from that moment you're completely unaware of one another. The guy on the radio said there might be any number of different versions of us walking around in parallel worlds." He takes a sip of beer. There are the Cassie and Stefan who walked into the Underground station and there are the Cassie and Stefan who saw the hordes and thought, *Why don't we walk over London Bridge? Let's wander through Borough Market, along the South Bank. Take in the sights for the last time before the baby arrives.* And in that parallel world, he and his wife boast to the friends they invite to dinner about their grandchildren. Helene is happy. *They* are happy.

"I *know* this! Well, I do not know it, but," Jules dismisses the limits of his understanding with a shrug. "But the name you call it? Um…"

"The Many Worlds theory." Even as Donovan repeats it, Helene's face floats through his mind, forlorn. He wants so much to comfort her: *Imagine another Cassie. Imagine an infinity of other Cassies. That only this world has abandoned her.*

"You mention parallel worlds. I know it as 'Parallel Universe.'"

"What do you think?"

"I think it make my head hurt! But, I do not know…" Jules smiles distantly, secretively. "Maybe somewhere."

Resigned to the knowledge that they must inhabit the world beyond the fault-line, Donovan hopes he's given Jules the merest glimpse of a smiling Evelyn. Something intimate. A reflection in a mirror as she struggles with the clasp of a necklace. The sight of her elegant neck. Somewhere for the painful accumulation of wasted love to go.

But Jules goes on. "This theory, it is like the lies they tell about the incident. Every time they lie, they make another reality, and when the lie it get repeated by someone who believe it to be true, it take on a life of its own, while the facts live on in the shadow, *non?* Like the negative of a photograph."

Donovan blows out his cheeks. "Put like that, it starts to sound a lot less like mad science."

"I write this here for later." Jules makes a note in his pad. *Many worlds/lies.* "I am thinking if I explain to Louis, he will say 'What is a negative?' And then, when I explain him, he will say, 'Papa, you are so old.'"

Donovan won't try to explain the Many Worlds theory to Helene. Journeys inward don't end well for his wife. It pains Donovan to know that the things that comfort him – the thought of another Cassie they cannot see, a grandchild they'll never meet – would cause her untold grief. He sticks to what's safe. And meanwhile, all the lives go on inside his head.

"And now, my friend." Jules winces. "You are not going to be happy with me."

"How so?" Donovan sets down his pint.

"I agree to something – and it is not that I do not think before I say yes. But I wonder now if you think I have any right to make a decision that affect all the family."

Jules is clearly laying foundations for a heavyweight subject. Donovan frowns. "Straight to the point, Frenchman."

"I am a little bit bullied into it and – I will not lie to you – I allow myself to be flattered. Yes, I admit it, I am vain."

"Before you start on the excuses, let's have the facts."

"OK, OK. Maybe you know Tate Modern buy one of my *Objets?*"

Donovan knows little of Jules's work, but he remembers someone – he forgets who – describing it as 'a minority taste'. "They bought one of your sculptures? I didn't know."

"Last year, maybe the year before. Something small." Jules shrugs, and Donovan understands he's aware he's being long-winded.

The one time Donovan went to the Tate Modern, he narrowly avoided tripping over a pile of bricks. Thrown off-balance, he grabbed at the nearest thing, which happened to be a cordon. When a member of staff pulled him back, saying, "Sir, please stand back from the exhibit!" Donovan replied unthinkingly, "That's an *exhibit?*" But when he read what was printed on the white card, he thought, *You've really got to be kidding me.* Now he says, "Don't take this the wrong way, Jules, but I don't really get modern art." For some reason, the perfect symmetry of the barista's fern comes to mind. Art should move you instinctively. You shouldn't have to work at it. "All the same, I can see why you'd be flattered." He gives a lopsided smile of his own. "But for the love of sweet Jesus, spit it out. Why am I going to be upset?"

"Because now they give me an exhibition." His expression asks, *What can I do?*

"Uh-uh. Still not getting it."

"You do not know?" Jules sighs, at once absolutely serious. "My work. It is about the incident."

One of Donovan's eyebrows moves. It's as if someone has pulled a string. This could be big. He waits to see how the thought makes him feel. Whatever his emotion might be, it doesn't qualify as being 'upset'.

"They *tell* me what I make is art, but I do not think I am making art. You and I both know, we cannot expect happiness. All I do is try to create meaning." Jules seems to have finished but his Gallic temper flares: "Here is what is *not* flattering. I can tell you this because you will not bullshit me." Donovan's mouth falls open, but before he can offer a lame protest, Jules insists, "No it is fine. This is a good thing! That is why Tate Modern want it. Not for the work, but…" He tapers off. *"Pfff."*

Donovan nods. "It's newsworthy."

"By next summer, the verdict slip from the front page. That is when they schedule the exhibition. But, still, they get very excited when they talk about *dialogue* and *staging*." He slows down.

"An exhibition will keep it alive in people's minds." Even as Donovan says this, his thoughts begin to travel. Slowly but surely, Donovan has been raising funds for a monument. The occasional hefty donation arrives, but mainly it's a slow trickle of fivers and tenners. What if this is an opportunity? "People only really die when they're forgotten, isn't that what they say?" He's already thinking bigger. The Monument, that single column of Portland Stone built to commemorate the Fire of London. Like headlines, higher structures now compete for attention, but it's still magnificent.

"Yes, I am afraid that for you and your wife – and all the others – it will rake it all up again."

"You know as well as I do, it's always thoroughly raked." Although, as Donovan reflects, it would be more accurate to say that his thoughts are like autumn leaves, tidied into a pile, then rearranging themselves at the slightest gust.

"*Huoui.*" Jules sucks the word through his teeth.

"Let *me* worry about Helene." If he can commission something worthy, then surely she'd want to see it. She'd *have* to leave the house! "How many visitors do you think you'll get?"

"*Bof.*" Jules shakes his head. It's clear he wasn't expecting to dish out facts and figures. "The popular exhibitions – the ones by the *real* artists – get tens of thousands, but I do not know. Who in England know who I am?"

It could almost be true. Who here would have heard of Jules Roche if the papers hadn't printed the photograph of him cradling Louis' head, as if he could protect him from the surrounding horror? If they hadn't tracked him down and invaded his grief, demanding his story as if they were *entitled.*

Who could blame him for lashing out? Assuming Jules will be thinking more or less the same thoughts, Donovan leaves a respectful silence before asking, "The Tate. They'll ask people to stump up an entrance fee?"

"That is the idea."

"Ask if they'll donate ten per cent of the ticket price to our monument fund."

Surprise flickers across Jules's face and then just as quickly disappears. "That is what I like about you. Always the businessman. You know, there is something else I want to ask."

Donovan recognises a sheepish tone when he hears one. An echo of Cassie asking permission for something she'd already done. And when she needed that particular kind of permission, it was him she would go to, never her mother. "Don't tell me. I'm not going to like it."

CHAPTER FOURTEEN

Eric, 2009-2010

Another late-night session. Eric rests an elbow on his desk in the blue-tinged laptop glow. The fingers of one hand cover his mouth, his thumb acts as a prop for his chin. This is what he does now. Jeopardising his degree isn't an option. Only when his lectures are over, his coursework complete, can Eric sit down to what he now considers his mission. When he reluctantly takes a five-minute break, Eric checks every fact he used to spout as a tour guide. Compare a map of the Underground (a geographically accurate map, that is) with a street map and the evidence is clear. Forget plague pits, there's an alternative explanation for the reason the tunnels curve. Fear that buildings might collapse led to a law being pushed through parliament forcing the railway companies to buy any buildings they planned to tunnel underneath. To avoid adding to what were already massively expensive estimates, blueprints were altered. Most of the digging took place under public roads. Disappointingly, the majority of Eric's plague pit references prove to be urban myths.

Break time over, he pulls the tab on another can of Monster (he prefers it to Red Bull, plus it was buy one get one free) and takes a slug. This work demands razor-sharp wits.

Even before the Coroner recorded a verdict of accidental death, the press had reported the so-called 'facts'. The tabloids blamed herd mentality (that and the action, or inaction, of one individual whose memory was apparently disposable). It was Bethnal Green all over again. This, as Eric knows, wasn't an appropriate finding.

He centres himself, Googles 'crowd mentality' and works his way down the top five results. Some of what he reads his grandfather would call *Stating the bleeding obvious.* Before the incident, the Tube was Eric's preferred way to get about town. Even with his face pressed into the armpit of the person standing next to him, he never considered himself part of a crowd. The idea of a body with a single mentality feels instinctively wrong.

Eric skims Allport's treatise on how a common stimulus will prepare people to respond in the same way. He imagines commuters shoving aside those who stand in their paths as they attempt to run up the down escalator. Here's the appropriate classification: 'escapist', someone who is trying to remove themselves from danger.

Some of the theory Eric finds unhelpful. Some he takes an active dislike to, but he nods as he reads about *Deindividuation;* how the loss of self and the abrogation of individual responsibility might have been a contributing factor. Pockets of insight reveal themselves, but one question continues to nag. *When is a crowd a crowd?* Take this example: Norris Johnson concluded that, when a crush occurred at a 1979 Who concert, the crowd was made up of many small groups of people, mostly trying to help each other. This is one of several articles that suggests that a crowd *doesn't* always act as a single organism. He copies and pastes the detail into his control document. Eric's crowd didn't come together out of choice. They were forced into their situation. Save for the fact that they all wanted to get home on a Friday evening,

117

nothing united the fifty-eight. So that's a missing classification. Whether a crowd is voluntary or involuntary.

With no way to vent his frustration, Eric is pondering this, rubbing one eyebrow the wrong way, when someone comes stumbling through the front door and clumps unevenly up the staircase. *Pissed,* he thinks. The absence of shushing sounds and barely-suppressed laughter suggests his housemate Andy is alone.

A knock at his bedroom door, followed by a mock falsetto: "Are you decent?"

Eric pushes back against the edge of his desk, tipping the kitchen chair he's assumed stewardship of onto its spindly hind legs. "There's no Sorrel, if that's what you mean."

Andy enters the room. "More's the pity."

"How was your night?"

"We didn't miss you – if that's what you mean."

Eric takes this on the chin. He's aware that friends have stopped turning to each other in the pub and asking, 'What, no Viking?' If he's mentioned, it's only in relation to his 'obsession'.

"Still," Andy continues. "Brought you a new bookshelf. Happy Christmas." He ambles unsteadily to the stack of plastic milk crates Eric calls a bookcase, though it mainly houses scuffed notebooks and A4 ring binders. Books are skyscrapered on the floor. Neat as a Lego brick, the new addition slots into place.

"Ah, you shouldn't have. What's its pedigree?"

"Only the best. Brighton Road." Satisfied it's stable and he's the thing that's off-kilter, Andy leers over Eric's shoulder, exhaling a Jägerbomb vapour. He blinks unfocused at the screen. "Still at it?"

At least he doesn't ask *why? Why?* is all that Eric hears from his soon-to-be-ex-girlfriend. His hope to impress Sorrel was ill-founded. Last night after he resisted her none-too-subtle attempts to distract him, she turned on him. "I don't get what's so urgent. We won't be qualified for another five years at least."

He didn't tell her, not in so many words. Whatever he encountered on the Underground – and it was not the Oliver Wicker of the photograph – whatever summoned him there now stalks him. It lurks outside lecture halls, sits in the empty chair opposite him in the library, haunts the canteen. "You know why."

"Oh, that's right. You've been *chosen*." *Chosen* was sarcasm enough. Sorrel didn't need to deploy the word 'ghost'. She stormed out, leaving Eric to regret the way he'd pushed her hand away from his crotch. A quarter of an hour and she might have gone away happy.

If anything Oliver Wicker, with his ready wink, seems to side with Sorrel. He understands that Eric's debt will take time to repay, but time is something he has no shortage of. It's not that Eric is incapable of seeing things from Sorrel's point of view. They're in their second year of a law degree and there's a minimum pass mark for each foundation subject. After he graduates, he'll have to take a course in Legal Practice and then there's vocational training (he doesn't like to think about how he's going to fund himself) before he can apply for his first practising certificate. Then there's the small matter of finding a job. He's looking at a minimum of five years. So why this agony of impatience? It's a question even he struggles to answer. Who knows? Andy's drunken logic may be just the thing he needs.

He tries his nagging question out on his flatmate. "When is a crowd a crowd?"

"I don't know. When is a crowd a crowd?"

"It's not a joke. I'm serious."

"Trouble is, Viking, these days you always are."

Eric opens his mouth to say that he knows, he *knows* it's

been an age since he cooked one of his famous chilis, he knows he's becoming a world-class bore ('Becoming?' Andy would say), but his flatmate beckons. "Run that by me again."

"When does a bunch of individuals become a crowd?"

Andy looks blank. "Nope. Search me." He barely stifles a yawn. "Anyways, I need my beauty sleep. You should try some yourself. Give those bloodshot eyes a break."

"What time is it?"

"Gone one thirty."

A rough calculation. Four hours' sleep should see Eric through his morning lecture. His brain will happily tick over until three thirty, given a couple of ProPlus. Maybe three for good measure. As student vices go, this one's fairly tame. He rarely drinks these days, which must give him a little leeway in the caffeine department.

The aging plumbing clanks as Andy brushes his teeth then flushes the toilet. Eric hears him blunder across the landing and collapse into bed before the house quietens down again. He Googles 'maximum capacity on London Underground'. Topping the search results is an interesting-looking enquiry on a web forum called *WhatDoTheyKnow*:

I am writing to request information about the capacity of each London Underground station which forms part of the Tube network.

In particular I wish to know:

1) The official maximum capacity of each station, or alternatively the available standing space at each station platform along with the guideline maximum passenger density (persons per square metre).

2) The method used to monitor passenger numbers and the practice followed when capacity is approached or exceeded. For example, are the entry gates closed when a certain number of travellers enter within a given timeframe? (If this is the case please provide the numbers for each station, unless they are the same as for (1).

Almost word for word the questions Eric has been trying to phrase! Disappointingly, there's no reply, just confirmation that the request will be processed in accordance with Transport for London's Freedom of Information policy. Eric replicates the enquiry. He stares at the screen for a few moments. Should he reword the questions so that they relate to 2003? He phrases them so that they relate to both then and now, and presses 'submit'.

His small success hits home like a shot of caffeine. Eric tops it up with another slug of energy drink. Further down the page, he locates a gap analysis report from January 2003 – just months before the incident! – not surprisingly called *Mind the Gap*. He can almost hear his tourists' enthusiastic shouts. Bingo! Written in preparation for London Underground becoming a subsidiary of Transport for London (technically a private company, but government-owned), the report was compiled by an All-party Investigative Committee. There's an excited fluttering in Eric's chest. Seventy-eight pages of what was known at the time of the incident. Was the change in ownership a factor? He may be about to find out.

His eyes track downwards. Here we are. Page five: reference to passengers *already having to endure crush levels in carriages*. Though conditions in stations don't get a mention, this statement could cause embarrassment in a court of law. The recommendation is to reduce overcrowding to the *Paris Metro* standard of 0.25 square metres minimum standing space per passenger. Eric recalls days when the idea of sharing a square metre with only three other commuters would have felt like luxury.

He's on a roll, he can feel it. He opens a new window and Googles 'crush levels on London Underground'. Up pops a link to an independent review by the Transport Committee called *Sardines*. Honestly, these titles! The report highlights the effects of overcrowding, research that London

Underground hadn't outsourced or undertaken themselves
– another potential cause for red faces. Seven hundred commuters shared their experiences. But this report is brand new,
dated December 2009. Momentarily deflated, Eric cautions
himself, *Don't reject it out of hand. It might describe a worsening situation.*

Eric skim-reads. He'll print everything off when his
cheap clunky printer won't wake Andy. Impact on health
is discussed in general terms (stress leading to poor heart
health; poor work productivity, because commuters arriving
at their desks take up to two hours to destress). The coping
mechanisms described in the report certainly don't suggest
that commuters see themselves as part of a crowd. It's each
man for himself, going after a space or a seat regardless of
who else might need it, doing things they wouldn't consider
acceptable in any other situation – pushing, shoving, crush-
ing against another body just to be on time for a meeting.
Normally placid people describe experiencing uncontrollable
rage, hearing themselves use language they'll blush at the
memory of. Eric can almost feel a gathering in his chest, the
tightening of muscles in his throat. What's astonishing is the
operator's attitude. *No one is obliged to use the system if they
don't want to.* "That's right!" Eric slams down his hands on the
desk. "They can go by bus!"

"Oi, Ugly Bastard! Some of us are trying to sleep!"

"Sorry!" he yells.

No one is obliged to use the system! One of the key com-
ponents of the Mayor's strategy to combat climate change is
encouraging people off the roads and onto public transport, a
system that's already stretched beyond all reason. The Mayor
has come under fire on several recent occasions. Eric recalls
reading somewhere – he thinks it was in the 2007 budget
plans – that planned improvements would result in a ten per
cent increase in capacity. London Underground took pains

to point out that even if proposals were adjusted to increase capacity by thirty per cent, this would still produce a worsening situation because population and employment growth over the same period was estimated at forty per cent. Time and time again, increased capacity has been proposed *after* the need has arisen, and Eric honestly can't find evidence that the situation was any different prior to 2003. It's been said many times, the Underground is a victim of its own success.

He searches out the 2007 budget plan and reassures himself. His recollection was correct. Scrolling down, a headline comes into Eric's line of vision. Savings and Efficiencies. An overlooked segment, sandwiched between unpromising headlines. A committee established in 2002 (the year before Transport for London assumed ownership of London Underground *and* the disaster) with the goal of saving a billion pounds by the end of 2009-2010. By 2007 they were already ahead of target. Except for the introduction of the contactless smartcards some bright spark called Oyster cards (the world is your oyster, perhaps?) the explanation of where those savings came from is vague. But what's clear is that substantial savings were made at a time when the system was under enormous pressure. And the squeeze seemed to have come from the Greater London Authority. Perhaps London Underground really *is* a victim, and not just of its own success. After all, what hope do they have of meeting demand?

Frustratingly, the 2009 report says sweet F.A. about congestion build-up when passengers can't cram themselves into available train carriages. But here's something. *The lack of information at station entrances about the level of overcrowding potential passengers are likely to encounter once they enter is remarkable. We recommend the adoption of a simple traffic light system.*

So now we're only calling people who arrive at stations, *potential* passengers, giving them information and leaving them to make their own decisions. What if they're season ticket holders, or if they've bought advance tickets, perhaps as part of a longer journey? Eric's inner voice is insistent as he adds to his growing list of questions. Does London Underground owe a greater duty of care to season ticket or Travelcard holders than to those who haven't bought advance tickets? Is it really reasonable to expect ticket holders to look for alternative modes of transport? Thoughts trigger each other and that's good. Keep those question marks coming, baby. Should ULR/TFL be selling season tickets when they know the system is already beyond capacity? Is a maximum placed on the number of season tickets that are sold? What about self-service ticket machines? If tickets are dispensed automatically, how can numbers entering a station be limited? Unless there's a computer somewhere that counts the tickets sold and then refuses to issue any more until the crush subsides? But Eric has never found a self-service ticket machine that wouldn't dispatch a ticket, and he's been in plenty of overcrowded stations.

Back to this proposed traffic light system: how is this any different from Londoners not having to use the system if they don't want to? *Eric Carwood is on sixteen thousand pounds but this next question is worth thirty-two thousand pounds.* Is this really the execution of a duty of care or just a way of passing the blame onto passengers? *There are four possible answers. One of those answers, the right answer, is worth thirty-two thousand pounds.* Besides, with open admissions of cattle truck conditions, wouldn't the traffic light always be red during rush hour? (And let's face it, since when has the crush only lasted an hour?) *OK, Eric, thirty seconds, your time starts now. Good luck.* And how do you police such a system? If you believe what crowd theory says, one person who sees another walk straight past a red light would think, Well, if they're going to risk it, so am I. *I'm going to have to press you. Is that your final answer?*

Eric experiences his own squeeze. It's as if a golf ball's lodged in his oesophagus, that awful sensation you get after you've wolfed a sandwich. He tries to help it on its way with a gulp of energy drink. *You need to chew more thoroughly, young man.* Be serious. The only thing he's eaten since he got home is a bowl of cornflakes. No meal for a growing boy, as his grandmother would say. Perhaps he should eat something. The only thing to hand is a Twix. He peels back the wrapper. Right. Let's get on with it. Answers.

CHAPTER FIFTEEN

Tamsin, 2016

Tamsin lies very still, listening to her mother's slow, regular breathing. Tomorrow will be soon enough. In snippets and slivers she remembers.

Her mother's frustration: "He's not answering his mobile."

Tamsin, under her breath: "He'll have lost it – again!"

Dad scoffing: "This wouldn't be the first time one of us has forgotten what he told us."

There it was, dredged up. Reference to the time, only a couple of weeks earlier, when Ollie stayed out overnight. No one had a clue where he was. Their parents exhausted themselves firing blame at each other before starting on Tamsin.

"Think! He must have mentioned something."

"Why *must* he? Do you think he tells me everything?" But Mum had trailed Tamsin all the way to her bedroom, in case she should let slip the thing she was hiding. Tamsin had to say, "Are you actually going to stand there and watch me undress?" to shrug her off the case. Aside from annoyance at the idea that Ollie's disappearance might somehow be her fault, there was the hurt. The truth was that Ollie told her the opposite of 'everything'. Ever since they'd got back from the week in Swanage – which had been OK, actually – he had either barricaded himself in his room or gone out without saying where he was going.

And then the following day, Ollie breezed through the door, the total scumbag acting as if he didn't know he'd been the subject of the great How Long Should You Leave It Before Reporting Your Teenage Son Missing debate. But it *was* an act, that much was obvious. He was too full of it. Of himself. An *I know something you don't*.

"But I *did* tell you!" he shot back when Mum challenged him.

Detecting less discomfort coming from Ollie's direction than she would have liked, Tamsin lolled against the kitchen doorframe, transmitting: *Liar, liar, liar*.

Mum's brow creased in disbelief. "No you didn't."

"You were standing right there, your back turned. Making the packed lunches." It was his insistence. And, of course, 'right there' was the spot where Mum always stood to make sandwiches for the four of them, even during the school holidays. (If left to their own devices they used the filling they wanted rather than the one that needed using next.) And it was always the night before, because her mornings were rushed enough as it was.

Momentarily flummoxed, she shot back, "What did I say? Come on, tell me! What did I say when you asked if you could stay out all night at the house of a friend whose name I've never heard before?"

That's right, dipstick.

"You said…Oh." He rapped his forehead with his knuckles. *And the nomination for Worst Actor Ever goes to…*

"You said, 'OK, but make sure you write it on the calendar.'"

"I wouldn't have –"

Here's where Dad saw fit to intervene. Maybe he believed Ollie, maybe he just wanted to bring things to a head. "And did you write it on the calendar?"

Yes, plankton. Did you?

Open-mouthed, Ollie had sense enough to look sheepish. "Mystery solved."

Tamsin glared at her brother for being let off the hook too easily. If it had been her –

"But I wouldn't have said it was OK!" Mum looked fit to explode.

"You see!" Ollie flapped his arms. "That's what *I* thought. I thought you'd just tell –"

Dad raised his hands: "Zip it, Ollie. Your mother must have been distracted."

Mum opened her mouth to retaliate, but no. She let out an exasperated cry and shook her head in that *I've had it with the lot of you* way of hers.

The floor was Dad's. "The part I don't get is *why* you asked your mother if you thought the answer would be no. You're not a child. I thought we'd got beyond house rules but, obviously, I was wrong."

Reassured that Ollie wasn't going to get off scot-free, Tamsin made as if to exit stage right.

"Stay right where you are. This applies to you too."

Her mouth fell open. "How come I'm being dragged into this? I haven't done anything wrong."

"Number one. The pair of you have three more weeks of holiday to go. We can't have you continually phoning us at work, so if you want to do something on the spur of the moment, you have to take responsibility. You *know* what we'd say yes to if we were here. So go to your friends' houses," here, he pointed at Ollie, "and by that I mean the friends we know. Go for a walk by all means, go swimming, go to the shops, but let the other person know where you are, and make sure you're home for dinner. And that means on time!" Mum was standing upright, paying attention, beginning to look a little smug. "*Unless* you've had permission in advance *and* one of us has written it on the kitchen calendar – yes, Ollie, I do mean 'us', because you clearly can't be trusted to remember."

Tamsin heard the air leave her own mouth.

"Number two. We've relaxed bedtimes during the school holidays, but Ollie, you're heading into your GCSE year. Don't ask if you can stay out late on a school night. The answer will be no."

"What about weekends?"

"We'll talk about weekends once we see how the weeks go. Number three. We're never going to say, 'Of course you can stay out all night.' Not unless we've spoken to your friends' parents to make sure they'll be there.

"And finally. There's a reason we bought the pair of you mobile phones. They're not for your convenience, they're for ours. Keep them switched on or we'll have them back." Tamsin bristled. "And don't think I don't mean that!"

As soon as they were out of their parents' earshot, Tamsin hissed: "Classic, Ollie Wicker! Well done, Shit-for-Brains. If you get my phone taken off me –"

But he slammed his bedroom door in her face.

She opened it again. "Excuse me! You don't just get to –"

"Out!" He started pushing at the door so that she had to wrestle with the handle, leaning in with her full weight. "I mean it. Stay out of my room."

"Have it your way." She stepped away without warning, knowing full well that he'd fall against the door.

"Whoever is slamming doors, stop that right now!"

The next time wasn't only a weekend, it was during the school holiday. It was just possible that Ollie *might* have got a yes out of Mum, and *she'd* forgotten to write it on the calendar. At least, this seemed to be what Dad was implying.

"His phone's switched off," Mum said.

You are so losing that. Wait, does that mean I lose mine?

"We may as well eat." Dad scraped his chair across the

floor and sat, as if Friday night pizza was something to get out of the way.

No need to rehash the debate about whether to report Ollie missing. Mum and Dad chewed silently, eyes fixed on the contents of their plates. That summer was one big game of happy families, with mealtimes a regular endurance sport. At the time, Tamsin thought it was all Ollie's fault. With hindsight, it's easier to see the part they'd each played. Many later meals would be eaten in silence, at first stunned, then awkward, because Mum only seemed to know how to cook for four, plus Ollie's absence took up more elbow room than his increasingly begrudging presence ever had.

On that notable Friday, Dad switched on the radio to drown out all the things that weren't being said. Misplaced blame, countless contradictions. But music met with Mum's displeasure. "Turn that down a bit, could you?"

The minute Dad sat back down, a newsflash. A doctor saying, *Thirty-one people have been brought here by ambulance and another seven arrived on foot. We've seen a full spectrum of injuries, everything from minor to major. Our staff have behaved with absolute professionalism but we still have a challenging night ahead.* Tamsin paid scant attention. Occupied with the kind of hateful thoughts a thirteen-year-old thinks about her rogue teenage brother, she plotted what she'd say when he could be arsed to show his face. When he said, 'What's up with you?' she'd reply, 'I'm not ignoring you, fart-face. I'm just not that excited about your existence.'

Her throat catches for the millionth time. And when her mother's leg twitches Tamsin repeats to herself, *Tomorrow.*

The day emerges teasingly. Low light, infused with that particular something that distinguishes dawn from dusk. Calm, guard-lowered moments before the alarm clock will usher in a frenzied hour of preparations.

Mum lies sleeping, her lips slightly parted. The movement of an eye under a delicate lid. What must it have been like, being on the receiving end of that phone call?

"I'm sorry if this sounds a little strange, but do you know an Oliver Wicker?"

"Yes, he's my son."

Tamsin's thirteen-year-old radar tuned to the first signs of trouble. The change in the line of her mother's body yanked her attention away from some game show or other. The way Mum grabbed hold of the doorframe. The way her head trembled precariously on her neck. Tamsin remembers how, looking at the trembling, she thought of Anne Boleyn preparing for her execution. *I have a little neck.* She felt sick to her stomach.

Imagine that terrible journey up to the City, hoping against hope that there'd been some kind of mistake. *"None of his friends live in the City. He had no reason to be there."* The makeshift mortuary in an empty office block Tamsin later read about, because those details weren't things you could ask stricken parents. *"Take your time."* So much would remain untold. So much to feed a teenage imagination, then to hold inside.

She recalls perching on the second step of the staircase, teasing off flakes of turquoise nail varnish, then using her front teeth to scrape away what remained. The sick feeling wouldn't go, but she rocked a little, as if that might soothe it. Hours passed before she heard a key in the lock. Up on her feet, she was ready with, 'So you thought you'd show up, did you? You are so in the shit.' She has never lost the sense that Ollie will show up. Though Tamsin has tried to rewind the clock, the last thing she said to him won't come. Everyone else remembers, but Tamsin only remembers the lines she'd *intended* to say.

It wasn't Ollie at the front door. Wordless, blinking, her ashen-faced parents filed through the hallway into the kitchen. Tamsin filed behind, watching as they sat side by side, united at last, but in a way that had her hoping one of them might start an argument.

"Come and sit down, Tamsin. We need to talk to you."

She sat.

She stared at her mother's hand on the tabletop.

She listened.

But she couldn't take in what was unacceptable. *No. Not Ollie.* The grey hoodie meant nothing. Thousands of kids owned ones exactly like it. He was going to walk through the door any minute, they'd see. *I'm not ignoring you, fart-face. I'm just not that excited about your existence.*

Only as Tamsin pounded upstairs did she realise she was about to throw up. She made it to the bathroom before she started gagging. She ducked her head and vomited in the sink before moving to the toilet bowl, where she doubled over, bunching her hair at the nape of her neck, spitting sour strands of saliva.

Back in her room, every item she'd chosen and arranged, everything that was supposed to say something about who she was, offended her. The fairy lights that decorated her dressing table mirror: she ripped those away. The photograph from her last sleepover in the heart-shaped frame. Shredded strip by strip.

It grew dark. It grew light. Dark. Light. Dark. Light. Her world had come to an end, yet this pattern persisted, undisturbed. Radio appeals were made for donations of O negative blood. London cabbies lined roads that ran parallel to the South Bank. "Put your purse away, love. No charge tonight." Exhausted surgeons announced times of death, removed facemasks. The tally grew and grew. In an effort to identify the victims, attempts were made to reunite briefcases with hands, glasses with faces, stray shoes with feet. Foreign embassies were notified. Solemn minutes' silences were observed in offices and coffee shops. An impromptu candlelit vigil led by the Mayor of London and the Archbishop of Canterbury was held in Trafalgar Square, as no outdoor venue in the City had sufficient capacity. Names, nationalities, ages, and occupations of the dead were published under smiling photographs on front pages. Shots of ambulances and open-doored police cars abandoned, positioned diagonally across city streets. An eyewitness account from the first medic to arrive on the scene. Details of survivors' injuries. Multiple fractures to hands and legs. Head wounds. Complications with lungs. But mainly crush injuries, and crush injuries are notorious, as medical experts employed by tabloids to comment on such things pointed out. The Prime Minister toured hospitals to visit the injured, criticised because some were clearly fighting for their lives. The Leader of the Opposition, wanting to be seen taking a different approach, visited the families of the deceased and was photographed holding the hands of parents, husbands, wives, lovers.

Stray moments that come to Tamsin meld with murkier images borrowed from nightmares. Reality crashing into unreality, unreality crashing into reality, with no way of distinguishing the two.

The feeling of straining against her father's grip while, mouth cobwebby and misshapen, she yelled, "Go away!" at a family liaison officer.

Strips of images: the door of her parents' bedroom left ajar, her mother's feet and ankles, occasionally a view of her head. Doubled over, weeping.

Snippets of conversation, overheard. "Give her time. She won't miss her own brother's funeral."

She refused to engage. No, she didn't want to choose a reading. And how the hell should she know what music Ollie would have wanted? The last time she ventured into his room, when he actually yelled, "Come in!" after she knocked (could *that* have been their final conversation?), she found him ogling a picture of Britney about to kiss Madonna, mouth open, eyes down, looking as if she was really into it. When Tamsin called him a perv, Ollie tried to fob her off, telling her he was interested in how a photograph can blow an isolated moment out of all proportion.

"If you watch the video, the kiss was such a minor thing," Ollie had said.

She often thinks of that when she sees smiling photographs of the four of them. Family holidays, birthdays: it's like looking at another family. Newer, darker memories have crowded out the old ones. There are no videos of the Wicker family, nothing to lend any context to the smiling faces.

"Come on, Tamsin," Mum persisted. "There must be a song he liked."

She wouldn't give up, so Tamsin supplied an answer. *"Like a Virgin."* Mum got up and left the room without a word.

"Oh, well done," Dad said with the kind of disbelief that caused him to turn several times towards the empty doorway and then back again. "Well done, Tamsin!"

Tamsin isn't that same thankless daughter. She must deliver this next blow, but she can choose the moment, set the scene. It doesn't have to be rejection. Gareth had wanted to be with her when she made the announcement, but Tamsin resisted. Her instinct was – still is – that she must do this alone. It feels do-able. And then, perhaps looking for distraction, any distraction, Tamsin sees that the tired-looking duvet cover is the same cover she remembers from the last time she asked to get into her parents' bed. Twenty years ago. It alone has survived from a time when the worst thing to happen was her first filling at the dentist's, when Mum said, "Squeeze my hand as hard as you like." She gives the pattern her full attention. If she stares hard enough, a memory will come. Something to back up Mum's insistence of how close she was to Ollie, how much she adored and looked up to him.

And then Mum opens her eyes, her face creasing into an amused frown. "Good morning." She props herself up on one elbow. "If I'm waking up, I must have got some sleep." She seems happy. Actually happy.

Tamsin feels renewed horror at the thought of what she must do. "A good couple of hours, I'd say." She places her mum at the kitchen table and imagines how her expression will change when she hears what Tamsin has to say.

"If only I'd known it was so easy." She rummages on the bedside table for her glasses, then straightens Ollie's framed photograph (the same photograph she took to court), touches her fingers to her lips, touches the glass just above his cheek.

Everything in the bedroom darkens. Just a fraction, but perceptibly so. It's wrong, she knows it is, but to Tamsin's eternal shame, she can't help thinking of her dead brother as a rival for Mum's affection. If nothing else, it is this jealous self she needs to escape from. Why even try to emulate Ollie when he was who – and what – he was? So much is seared on Tamsin's conscience, things Mum can't possibly guess at, things that are now impossible to say. Besides, what if she spoke out and it turned out that her memory of so many unreal days and nights was false? Reality crashing into unreality crashing into reality.

Her mother turns to her. "What about you? Did you sleep?"

"Enough," she lies.

"Do you want to use the bathroom first?"

"No, you go. I'll put the kettle on." Tamsin wants to make her mother a cup of coffee. Something to occupy her hands. An excuse to pause as she sips from the oversized cup before she needs to say anything. "My first meeting isn't until ten. I thought we could have breakfast together."

The sound of her mother turning off the tap in the bathroom clunks through pipework, arriving amplified in the kitchen. The creak of a floorboard, the tick of a light switch: this is how they keep track of each other. When she's gone, who'll check that Mum's arrived home? Who'll sniff the glasses and mugs before loading the dishwasher? Scooping ground coffee into the *cafétière,* Tamsin acknowledges the need to compose herself. These aren't just any old words she has to say. They'll have consequences. What if her mother starts drinking again? Because when she drinks, she can't feed herself properly, let alone hold down a job. Can Tamsin cope with that on her conscience?

Gareth says she over-thinks everything but he hasn't had to live through the terrible run of anniversaries. The first birthday, the first Christmas, what would have been Ollie's eighteenth birthday – his coming of age. Then there was her sixteenth birthday, when she opened the first of her cards and, as her thumb traced the embossed number six – sweet sixteen – words tumbled out: "I'm older than Ollie ever got to be."

The moment she said it, she was horrified. How could she have slipped up so badly? And then, after Dad walked out on them, she'd had to be everything to her mum. (Even now, her eyes move to the ceiling which is showing signs of a slow leak. *I must do something about that,* she thinks. *Maybe at the weekend.*) But the anniversary Tamsin dreads the most still looms. The day when Ollie will have been dead for longer than he was alive. Unlike the others, it isn't an anniversary that will repeat. Once that moment arrives, the scales will tip, introducing a new imbalance in their already imbalanced lives.

"It's still two years away," Gareth said. "Are you going to wait until then?"

For a moment, Tamsin thought he was offering another lifeline. On several occasions now, she has begged for more time, which has stretched out to four years. Four years of keeping a foot in both camps. Gareth has been more than patient.

Without realising, Tamsin has been scratching at the silvery trackmarks on her arms, scars she's had to explain away over the years. *Those? Caused by a rescue cat who turned out to be so traumatised, we took her back to the animal shelter after a week.* She yanks down her sleeves, puts orange juice and muesli, milk and sugar on the kitchen table. Thumps down cereal bowls. Spoons. Too much. Move things around – this here and that over there – so they look deliberately unarranged. No, that doesn't work. Here, then. Better.

"Bathroom's free," Mum calls down from the landing, releasing in Tamsin a small animal panic.

When her mother walks into the kitchen wearing a dress and a pair of heels Tamsin stops herself from saying, 'You look nice.' Afterwards, when the debris of their conversation is picked through, it would seem as if Tamsin was trying to butter her up. "Coffee?" Tamsin hates the exaggerated brightness in her voice. She feels miscast, as if she's only playing at being an adult.

"Please." Her mother pulls back a chair and seats herself. Automatically, she slides yesterday's newspaper in from the sidelines, skims already-devoured headlines for reports of dead teenagers, licks one finger and deftly scoops up a page.

I'm here, if only you'd look up. Tamsin hasn't just been through one bereavement. She lost her brother, then both parents, not all at once, but fragment by fragment.

When they made an effort not to argue, all that was left to Mum and Dad was trying to be civil, which proved too painful. Her father removed himself physically, but strung out his removal of moral support. To begin with, he called once a week, but it was embarrassing how awkward they were with each other. Whenever he asked, "How's your mother?" Tamsin translated, "How's your mother's drinking?" as a suggestion that she was culpable, whatever the answer might be. "Fine," she answered defiantly, even if that same afternoon she'd arrived home from school to find Mum passed out, face down in a pool of her own vomit. "No thanks to you." Since then, Dad has only played brief walk-on parts in her life, and he has hardly distinguished himself in those.

"Also," she says to her mother, fresh resolve displacing guilt. "I have some news."

"You got the promotion!" Mum gives the appearance of setting the newspaper aside, but two reluctant fingers book-mark her place.

Tamsin doesn't repeat that the interview wasn't for a promotion. That she's a freelancer and freelancers have to line up the next job before the current contract expires. "Not the contract, no. I'm still waiting to hear." Actually, she's investigating alternative projects because she suspects that the funding for her first choice has fallen through.

Now her mother frowns. "Wasn't the interview over a week ago?"

The conversation is running away from her. She must steer it back on course. "It was, but that's not what I wanted to tell you."

"Oh?"

Tamsin makes an effort to smile. The script demands she make her announcement as if it's good news. Correction. It *is* good news. She must make it without apology. *For God's sake, just say it.* "Gareth's asked me to move in with him. And I've said yes."

That wasn't so difficult, was it? says the devil on her shoulder. But she's barely able to breathe. Something inside her bleeds a response: *What do you know? What do you really know about us?*

"Oh." Gina takes a moment to sip her coffee. She doesn't trust herself to look at Tamsin just yet. Illogical though it may seem, it feels like she's being robbed of something else. As if she's looking down a long corridor at an empty future. *This was always going to happen,* she tells herself. By rights, it should have happened long ago. Tamsin thinks Gina doesn't know that her previous boyfriend broke up with her because she wouldn't move in with him. To her shame, Gina overheard their row and did nothing. "Mum needs me," Tamsin said to him, and Gina was glad, yes *glad,* when she heard the door slam.

She hadn't knowingly been a bad mother to Ollie. She tried so hard, exhausting herself in the process, but it wasn't enough. After Ollie, and then Bill, something in Gina gave up. It was almost as if that final acknowledgment of her failings turned her into a bad mother. Aware she must rally, she prays that her expression isn't as transparent as her daughter's. Up until this moment, Tamsin has only told her the careful measure of what she judges Gina can bear, and in turn Gina has done nothing to upset this delicate balance, avoiding the questions that might lead to potentially upsetting detail. But there's a build-up of all the unasked questions, all the unsaid answers. Now she asks, "Will you move into Gareth's flat, or find somewhere new?"

Tamsin colours. "I'll move into Gareth's."

Gina pictures the property. On her first visit she remarked on his taste: "You have quite an eye."

"Not me. That's all Tamsin."

She was exercising her good eye because she was *making a home for herself.*

Oh, Tamsin, Tamsin! The least penance Gina can perform is to offer a way out of her obvious discomfort. "Well, it sounds as if you have it all sorted out," she says, then, worrying that her choice of words could be interpreted as criticism, she lifts herself out of her chair to kiss the top of Tamsin's head. "I'm so pleased for you. You know how fond I am of Gareth. When do you think that you'll –?"

"Soon." Tamsin jumps straight in. "But I wanted to make sure you can manage. I know my rent wasn't exactly the going rate…"

What will I be able to afford on my own? Not that it matters where I live. "Oh, darling, that's sweet of you, but it's not as if I didn't know this day was coming." *I must phone Bill, let him know.*

"Well, in that case, I should probably get dressed for work."

Tamsin can't escape quickly enough. Her goodbye as she leaves the house is cringingly cheerful. That's fine. To be alone is what Gina needs right now. If she'd thought that her cravings were consigned to the past, this moment would prove that the itch is still very much present. Perhaps if she can just sit here. Sit, clutching herself tightly, one hand gripping the bicep of her opposite arm, the other grabbing a handful of flesh just above her waist. She feeds off words – a gentle giant… absolute heart of gold… would do anything for anybody – that same vicarious emotion she so deplores when the tables are turned; when it feels as if a journalist is tapping her lifeblood. If there were gin in the house, Gina would fill a tumbler to the brim.

CHAPTER SIXTEEN

Ollie, 22 August 2003:
Incident minus 7 mins

As the Tube train rattles through darkened tunnels, Ollie and his fellow passengers rattle along inside it. The Northern Line goes on for ever with no sense of the places they pass under, how far or how fast they're travelling, let alone whether it's night or day in the outside world. At each stop, Ollie checks the overhead map: seven stations to go.

Cramped together, elbows or shoulders touching, no one makes eye contact. Headphones. Eyes focused on phones. Each in their own little world. Ollie passes the time by inventing backstories for his fellow passengers. The white kid who's growing his hair out in an attempt to cover up his acne. He's kidding himself that he's going to get lucky. *Not wearing that lumberjack shirt, you won't!* A gorgeous Asian woman, her lipstick a perfect match for her red tights. She's on the way to a cool independent cinema to see a foreign film. That shaven-headed man whose neck has a thick fold of skin where the bottom of his hairline should be – he might look tough, but he runs an inner city youth club.

One thing Ollie knows is that he's not like any of them.

What's more, he has no intention of becoming like his parents. Thirty to fifty prime customers. That's all you need. Thirty to fifty customers who'll spend ten to twenty thousand a year. Do the maths.

A girl gets on. To Ollie, everything she does seems designed to draw attention to herself. Her startling red hair, her green cardigan, the way she dumps her large black hand-bag on the seat next to hers (the last free seat in the carriage): it all screams *look at me.* When she catches him staring, it's daggers.

Squirming inwardly, he shuffles in his seat. She seems to see right through him, overdressed for August, a denim jacket over his hoodie. She knows exactly why he needs all those pockets. A single bead of sweat makes its way down Ollie's spine. *"No one suspects a schoolboy."* In term-time, wearing uniform that labelled him a child had worked a treat. Just as they said it would.

"Our customers don't want a Moroccan brother turning up at their offices in some sleek gold BMW. No amount of discretion's going to disguise the fact that that's a dealer. You, on the other hand." They shrugged.

It has paid dividends to look nervous as he asked for directions. He *was* nervous. Nerves make him appear less conspicuous, which make him less nervous. You could laugh at the irony. Here's how it works. On Ollie's first visit to meet a new client, he's always come to see where his dad works. And when those navy-blue-uniformed security guards behind their big front desks get to recognise him, he acts embarrassed. "Lost my house keys."

"What? Again?"

"I know. He's going to kill me."

He's never been searched. Security staff shake their heads, wave him past the visitors book and go back to flicking through the pages of their magazines against the background mumble of a twenty-four hour news channel. Sometimes they even give him bundles of letters or small brown paper packages and say, "Do us a favour and drop this at reception on the third floor."

It's not that he isn't who he says he is. He's two things at once. The schoolboy *and* the apprentice. That's what they call him. Never Ollie. Just the apprentice.

Yes, the red-haired girl definitely sees straight through him. Ollie pretends to be looking at something beyond her but instead he finds her reflection. That same face seen from a different angle, against a shifting backdrop of black struck through with flashes of yellow cable. In his periphery, he can still see the way she takes a notebook from her bag and flicks to a fresh page. The way she holds her pen above the blank page, indicating that, right this minute, she's having an important thought, something no one else could begin to imagine. She writes a couple of lines, a few words on each. Ollie itches to look at the notepad. She could be a poet, or a songwriter. Is that it? He knows for sure he doesn't fool her. She's written him into her song.

When he next risks a look, she's leaning over the armrest, reaching into her handbag for a tub of fruit salad. She peels back the cellophane and proceeds to eat the fruit piece by piece, taking each segment of pineapple, each halved grape, between a finger and thumb, then wiping her fingers on the underside of her short skirt, as if this was a discreet thing when, really, all it does is draw attention to her thighs. Ollie is very aware of her thighs. *Oh, God, don't let her catch me looking again.* He pretends to concentrate on the overhead map.

Next out of the bag comes her phone. (The notebook is still on her lap, in case something poignant or witty comes to her.) She uses just one finger to text (something urgent to communicate), then drops it into her handbag and looks directly at Ollie. In a Tube carriage, where any eye contact is taboo, it's startling.

Another stop (only one more to go) and standing space in the carriage fills up. Newspapers are folded away. Arms snake around bodies, hands grip poles. Look up and you might just be guilted into giving up your seat. Guilt-free, the poet/rock-star girl happily takes up her two seats.

A squeal of brakes as the train pulls into Old Billingsgate. Already up on his feet (aware that the girl is watching, he can't risk a backward glance), Ollie can see he's going to have to fight his way out. He makes a play of frowning at his watch. (She's still looking.) Rush hour's started early tonight. Inches from his own face on the other side of the glass, faces, waiting. A solid wall of bodies. The double doors whoosh apart. Unmoved by the request to *allow passengers to get off the train before you board,* no one budges, each in their commuter-zombie trance. *Must. Get. On. The. Train.* Elbows high and tight, Ollie steps into the mosh pit. The crush is several people deep and presses hard against him. A sharp jolt, he sees what the problem is and yanks his trapped jacket free. His left hand goes instinctively to his right-hand breast pocket. There they are: the outline of the foil blister pack, several torpedo-shaped pills, the small vial, still upright. Then he checks the large marsupial pocket in his hoodie: sheets of paper tabs, textures of paper and foil. White for the high, Valium and Xanax for the comedown. All present and correct. On an ordinary weekend, Londoners consume enough white to show up in the water supply on a Tuesday, but this is Carnival weekend. Business is good.

Rounding the corner, Ollie's chin is low, but shouts coming from high above jerk it upwards. At first, the pile at the bottom of the down escalator appears solid, then he recoils: *Christ!* It's like that time Mum made him take the potato peelings down to the garden composter, pulling off the lid and finding that the surface layer was a writhing mass of skinny orange worms. Ollie's hands angle backwards. He can't take it in. He would hold back the world if he could. Behind him, several passengers who have made it through the crush turn back the way they came. Others wait for a signal, or an announcement, something.

Louder now, shouts – the thing that first drew his attention – come from higher up. People are falling. Nothing as neat or quiet as a game of dominoes. One shoe on, one shoe off, people don't simply topple. They lurch, they pitch, they are felled. They hurtle headfirst, crying out, grabbing at anything, not caring who they pull with them, and they bounce off surfaces on the way down. The sounds they make are impossible to escape. And they land, God how they land.

Ollie's eyes lock onto the surreal pile of limbs and shoes and heads and clothing. Humanity is camouflaged, pin-striped, booted and suited, slow to reveal itself. There's an abstract quality about it, everything broken down, disconnected. When a pair of bulging eyes meet his, Ollie catches a horrified breath. He feels like he did when he saw photos of prisoners in concentration camps. The full impact of the situation registers. Ollie's arrival has ignited hope where it had no right to. This person is going to die here. It may happen right in front of him and nothing he can do will prevent it. Should he hunker down, make some kind of physical contact? But he's rooted to the spot, transfixed. This is desperate. And he can't see a single hi-vis jacket.

He finds his voice: "Can anyone see any staff?" In the periphery of his gaze, he locates a CCTV camera, thinks, *That's where they'll be, safe behind a desk.* Moving towards it, he waves his arms above his head, communicating in his own pathetic semaphore: "Help! We're at Old Billingsgate." Then he stands with his hands on top of his head, open-mouthed.

High above Ollie, a woman lets go of a large yellow bouquet.

Must be her birthday or something. What a birthday! She turns, yelling at people, "Go back up!", grabbing the person on the step behind her by the shoulders, physically twisting him until he too is facing upwards. "Move!" The rippling motion of people turning is almost a Mexican wave, but she hasn't grasped a basic fact: people are never so determined as when stepping onto a downwards-moving escalator at the start of a party weekend. Ollie can see what's happening ten feet below her, but the incomers assume some kind of fuckery's going on. They'll work round it, because that's what commuters are programmed to do.

Swimming against the tide, people come up against resistance. There's nowhere to go. Forced back down towards the growing pile of bodies, realisation takes grip and with it comes fear. From where Ollie's standing, it seems to be a collective thing. They won't be able to climb over the top of the pile. Even if they arrive on their feet, they'll be crushed against its walls. They grab and they clamour, pushing backwards, sitting down – though what good that will do, he doesn't know. Now he sees: they've decided to arrive feet first, like a battering ram. This really is each for their own. But, in their place, what would he do?

Some prefer their chances with the central reservation. They use the divide as a springboard, landing haphazardly on the up escalator, scrabbling and scrambling to their feet. One lad doesn't make it. Uncontrolled, he slides down the aluminium divide, slamming into something – Ollie can't see what, exactly – with a sickening crunch and an inhuman yell.

Christ, this is insane!

Ollie shouts a second time – or is it a third? – "Can anyone see any staff? Are there any doctors?" His voice an uncertain octave, he is so clearly not the person who's needed.

Responsibility almost paralyses him. Chances are, the lads who make it onto the up escalator will raise the alarm. But right now, at this precise moment, he, Ollie Wicker, sixteen next month, trying to work out how he's going to juggle his GCSE year and his job, is the only help there is. He makes fists. *Think, you fucker.* The escalator must have a kill switch. Now that he looks, he sees red triangles everywhere. *Press here in the event of emergency.* He heads towards the closest one but second thoughts cluster. His hand hovers. If the escalator comes to a sudden stop, will more people fall? Imagine he's the cause... *But even more will fall if you do nothing.* He watches yet another skydiver belly flop into the pile. Another unearthly echo rises around him. Who the fuck made this his decision?

"Push it, for God's sake!" someone behind him shouts, propelling him from his stupor.

"Grab hold of anything you can!" he yells, the authority in his voice coming as a surprise. The fact that they're grabbing hold suggests he's been heard. He goes to jab the –

CHAPTER SEVENTEEN

Donovan, 2016

Donovan's phone vibrates. He reaches into his pocket, moving stealthily from the kitchen to the downstairs cloakroom, where he reads Jules's incoming text: *Parked down the road.*

See you in a moment, his big fingers tap the keyboard.

He flushes the toilet, because Helene's always telling him off for not flushing, and washes his hands conscientiously. Back in the hallway, as he so often does, he finds himself observing his wife. Dressed in a shirt Donovan recognises as one of his cast-offs, Helene gives the bin liner she's manhandling a look of disgust. As she knots the handle, Donovan slips the keys from the hook on back of the front door into a pocket.

"I see you." She doesn't actually look in his direction as she says this. "Loitering with intent."

"Hand it over!" He approaches, beckoning. "I was just on my way out to the garage to look for something." Donovan is in the habit of inventing excuses to make sure Helene never needs to ask for help, but this is an invention of a different kind.

"Only if you insist." She raises an eyebrow, fixing him with her stare.

Something in Donovan's chest responds as the old Helene surfaces for an instant. "Oh, I do. I absolutely insist." He wills himself not to over-react as she loops the yellow plastic tie over two of his clumsy fingers.

"Be careful. The bag's got a hole in it. I don't want it leaking all over the patio."

"Right you are." He so wants Helene to be the girl with the attitude, the girl who used to say *I've got your number* with a single glance.

In her slippers, Helene stands on the threshold of the outside world. "Anyway, what are you looking for?"

He pauses but can't think for the life of him what she means.

"I'm the one who's menopausal!" She uses the roll of bin liners in her hand to point. "In. The. Garage," she enunciates as if addressing a small child. (Donovan swallows at the thought of who that child might be.) "You spent most of yesterday evening out there, so whatever you're looking for must be good and lost."

"Right!" he says, as if it's just come to him. "It's not so much looking as having a clear-out." He thinks of the bulky analogue television that finally gave up the ghost late last Christmas Eve and is sitting crookedly in the orange wheelbarrow, awaiting deportation.

"Good." She flaps a new bin liner. "It could do with one."

Donovan conceals a smirk. How does Helene know what state the garage is in? She must be imagining it as it was: sawdust, wood shavings, turps. Perhaps she ventures out there when no one's watching. No, he'd be able to tell.

When Donovan brought lobster home for Helene's birthday in 2004, she couldn't bring herself to look at it. "This is what we used to do," she said, drawing a line, a clear demarcation. He'd assumed he would be her only window to the world, but that's not how it is at all. Had Facebook not arrived shortly after his wife made her retreat, she'd have been cut off without a lifeline. But 'Lady Agoraphobic' has collected new friends both at home and abroad. When they sit down to their evening meal and Donovan relates how he bumped into a neighbour, or that idiotic thing someone said at the office, he finds himself competing with news and opinions, not to mention details of other people's love lives. Helene makes two things abundantly clear. She is not some creature who's to be pitied, but living vicariously is all she's capable of. Now that the light of her life has gone out.

Her Facebook handle doesn't paint an accurate picture. Helene hasn't suffered a single panic attack. It isn't a question of building a list of safe places or coping techniques. There was a time when Donovan tried to tempt his wife out into the garden, when he'd have settled for the sight of Helene tilting her face to get a little sun. It's too frightening a prospect to ask if the line is drawn in permanent marker. Is this what their lives will be from now on? What if the answer's yes?

His nostrils flare as a hit of rotting vegetation registers. Helene was right about one thing. The bin liner's leaking. Donovan walks towards the wheelie bins holding it at arm's length. Something repellent and slimy drips onto the crazy paving. He drops the lid on the trash, rubs his palms together, fishes for his keys. She's going to punish herself for the rest of her life. It is a possibility. It's beneath him to think that she's punishing *him*. It's also beneath him to imagine she's unaware of the affect that her 'choice' has on him. The garage door screeches up and over and he pushes these uninvited thoughts aside.

Helene is occupied as he edges past his car to the top of the drive. To the right, a car door swings open and Jules gets out. He has that effortless look that seems to come naturally to French men. A peaked cap, a casual jacket, enviably-fitting drainpipe trousers, polished leather ankle boots. After raising one hand in greeting, Donovan sidles past the car, back towards the open garage door.

Like many garages, this one rarely houses a car. Detached, it sits behind the house, and the drive is narrow enough to make him nervous about reversing any distance. Damp earth, grass cuttings, a hint of methylated spirits, these are the things it smells of. A glorified shed-cum-workshop. He works his way past a spade with dried soil clinging to its edges, a rake with a crisp brown leaf skewered on one of its prongs. Sparing a thought for Jules's polished boots, he trundles the lawnmower out of the way. To the rear of the brick structure is Donovan's workbench and, stacked on its surface are the pieces he spent yesterday evening wiping down with a damp cloth. The grain isn't as rich as the grain in his memory, the wood he agonised over before making his selection, but considering how severely bloom had dulled the surface, it has come up better than he had any right to expect.

Am I doing the right thing? But Helene would never part with family photographs, Cassie's school reports, her childhood scrapbooks. This is the only contribution Donovan can make to Jules's exhibition, and he can only make it because his project was secret. Well, almost secret. He'd confided in Stefan. "Just so you don't go out and buy one," and when the boy had looked so touched, he'd added, "Don't get too excited. The last thing I attempted to make was in woodwork class." It wasn't quite true, but whatever he produced couldn't possibly match the perfect image in his head.

"Don't tell me," Stefan said. "It was a bird box for Mother's Day."

"Nothing changes."

A sigh surges through him. Nothing changes. Until it does. Then everything changes.

Donovan did all the research. Bought all the kit. Actually, he bought the wrong kit and, too embarrassed to take it back, went out and bought more. He spent the cost of a ready-made item several times over.

The gentle scuffing of leather soles on concrete screed reaches Donovan, but he doesn't turn. Jules arrives beside him, a little below shoulder-height. They stand side by side.

After a few moments, Donovan speaks. "I Googled you. I read that you sometimes destroy the original thing and create something new out of what's left."

"True." Jules nods. "Is that what you do here?"

Donovan likes that he doesn't reach out and help himself. "Not me, no." Though he can see why it might look like that. He feels as self-conscious now as he did when talking to Stefan. "I was making something. From scratch." Donovan opens the door of a repurposed kitchen cabinet that houses tins and tubes. Brilliant White Gloss, Polyfilla, WD40. Tacked on the back of the MDF door is a yellowing piece of graph paper. The drawing pins securing it have rusted. Sketched on it is what Donovan admits looks a little like a shopping trolley.

"It is a crib." The Frenchman's use of present tense provides a direct link between the now and then. He looks from the graph paper to the lengths of wood with fresh eyes. "You make a crib for your grandchild!"

Donovan covers his mouth, re-moulds his cheek with a thumb. People occasionally speak of Cassie, of Stefan, but not of the little prince whose arrival he had so looked forward to. Whose death Donovan was denied mourning because it was somehow considered unseemly for a big man. Unmanly.

"My grandson." Donovan doesn't have a name he can use, but he can say *my grandson* with pride. Aware of his own hypocrisy, Donovan concedes there have been times – not many, admittedly. Who would make the same mistake twice? – when someone else used that word, and it seemed like a violation; when they transformed it from prayer to personal slight; when, the one time, horrified by the thought that

Helene might hear, he brandished the carving fork he was holding: *"What could you possibly know about it?"*

"Your measurements. One by three by ten. Everything down to the last screw!"

"I had it all worked out." But more seems to be expected. "Here's the end I assembled." He lifts it up, stands it on the rough concrete floor. Two uprights, a solid end panel, and, at right angles, the rail.

"And these are the other uprights." With a nod of his head, Jules indicates two struts. "You cut them yourself?"

"Cut them, sanded them, oiled them."

Jules puts his well-thumbed leather notebook down on the workbench and holds out his hands. "May I?"

Donovan gives a gravelly cough. Jules's gesture reminds him so much of Cassie holding out her hands for inspection before sitting down to dinner. He can almost hear himself say, 'Show me the backs.'

Jules picks up the two remaining uprights and holds them, flat sides together. "You make a good job of it. You cut one then draw around it?"

"I clamped it to another piece, then I traced around the shape."

"Exactement. You are very precise." Jules refers to the diagram, performs a mental calculation, repositions himself and, with a small scraping noise, stands the uprights in approximately the right place. "The wood. It is walnut, *n'est-ce pas?"*

"That's right." Walnut was the closest colour match Donovan could find to Cassie's beloved conkers. He remembers her joy at finding them newly-hatched and gleaming. Crouched down in wellington boots, knees locked, methodically working her way around the trunk of a horse chestnut. Her pleasure in helping free them when she found them still housed in the waxy pith of their armoured shells, then passing a small thumb over their damp sheen. Polishing each one in turn, filling her pockets. "Leave some for the squirrels!" Donovan would say. Stupid though it might sound (not that it's something he'd ever say out loud), he thought of his grandson as a conker, safe inside his protective casing, waiting to hatch. This precious jewel he keeps for himself.

"This is your first attempt?"

Hauled back from what seems like yesterday, Donovan agrees. "Beginner's luck. The timber yard suggested I made a mock-up in something cheap, but I've fallen into that trap before." His laughter sounds misplaced. He resolves not to turn something sacred into a joke.

"Oh yes, the mock-up is perfect and then, *pfff!* I make a crib for my Louis, only it is IKEA, and you know what? There is a piece missing. My God." Jules sucks the words in. Only two words, but filled with admiration.

Pleased he has something of value to contribute – *if* that's what he decides to do – Donovan considers. From what he's read, Jules's critics appear to agree that his work is brave, but there's no consensus on whether or not it's 'good'. He swallows. "Do you have any idea what you'd do with it?"

"I do nothing but display it. This is your story, not mine."

A wave washes over Donovan. Is it relief? Disappointment? Perhaps it's a little of each. Given planks of wood, he thought Jules might hammer them into some kind of crucifix, perhaps a makeshift coffin. But now his mind is free to turn to the bricks on the floor of Tate Modern. Ordinary household bricks, stacked in a rectangle. "I don't want anyone to mistake it for building materials."

"Non." Jules is fierce. "I will not allow that." He takes a moment and, with his head on one side, continues: "I am thinking of your Many Worlds theory. I have a feeling maybe I suspend these pieces." Still gripping the two struts, he raises them up. "We make it look like they are about to fall into place." Jules lays the pieces down, opens his notebook to a

new page and begins to sketch. "Or maybe even that they explode."

As the lines take shape, Donovan feels that he may learn something about himself. This is how someone else sees his aching accumulation of love.

"Maybe something like…" Jules finishes his rough sketch and hands Donovan the notebook.

A lump comes to his throat as he understands the strength of Jules's desire for purity. Whether or not Jules is 'good' at what he does shrinks in significance. "You could do that?" he asks.

"Oh, maybe not me, but you know, I have strong wire, plus some very clever people who work with me. You think you might be happy with something like that, my friend?"

By inviting Jules here, Donovan had thought he was only exploring a possibility, but when he opens his mouth the words that come out are: "Will you take it with you now?"

Jules looks at him very directly. "You do not want to think it over? We have time."

"I don't need time." He hands Jules his notebook. "Do you have somewhere to store it?"

"*Oui.* I hire one of those Big Yellow places, only it is on the South Circular road. The middle of nowhere." Jules grips his arm. "But very safe. There is no need for you to worry."

"OK."

"Although –" Jules stops before he has barely got started. "I do not know, maybe you do not want it back." His gaze is thoughtful, and Donovan understands that Jules is taking measure. "For some people, I think maybe the exhibition will be a way to let go."

Though this feels like an ambush, though the shock forces the air from his lungs, Donovan makes no attempt to fight it. "I think maybe you're right." He unpins his diagram from the door.

"OK." Hands on hips, Jules turns once again to the workbench. He is preparing to become custodian. "Then what we do, we label all the parts so that they line up with your diagram."

"Done." Donovan turns a piece of wood towards Jules.

"You carve the number into the wood? Every piece?"

Donovan gives a smile. It was to have been a private joke. When he drove Cassie to Birmingham for her university interview, she'd been amused how instructions for the construction team had been worked into the paving of a roundabout.

"Then we just need something to put all the pieces in."

"No shortage of these." He pulls an empty cardboard box from the top of a pile, upends it in case of spiders, places it on the workbench.

"Your wife, she will notice us carrying the boxes out to the car, *non?*"

"I'll tell her you turned up to collect something I sold you on eBay."

"She will not recognise me?"

"Not unless you spend all your time on Facebook, she won't."

"Bof," Jules dismisses the idea. "And I almost forget." He tweaks the peak of his cap. "I come in disguise."

"It suits you."

"The truth is I go a little bald."

As they duck under the garage door, each carrying a box, Helene is watching from the kitchen window. Jules nods politely in her direction.

It doesn't take long to load the car with pieces that were to have made a crib for a newborn prince. The hardest part is manhandling the boxes to make them fit in the boot. Donovan's eyes linger on his handiwork until the moment Jules slams the door.

The two men turn to each other at the kerbside. Both speak at once: "Drive safely." "It would have been beautiful."

They pause.

"Maybe somewhere in another world," Jules says.

CHAPTER EIGHTEEN

Rosie, 22 August 2003:
Incident minus 2 mins

What good are bloody risk assessments?

"How's the crowd, Skip?"

"Tempers building nicely."

Roughly translated as earthy language combined with the odd threat of violence.

"I'm letting twenty through the barrier every few minutes, but I need something definite to tell them."

"Try the truth. We've got an escalator out, plus unusually high levels of crowding. Suggest that anyone who can might like to try Monument or walk to London Bridge."

"That'll go down like a ton of bricks, but you're the boss."

Don't I know it!

Hurrying through subterranean passages, rounding a bend, Rose comes face to face with her ten-year-old self as surely as if she were looking in a mirror. They used to say this ten-year-old was fearless. It wasn't true, but she trained herself to put the fear in a box and keep it there. There are things she needs from this girl, things forgotten by the adult Rose.

In the plastic seating of the stands, her coach is watching, his confidence in her intact. Alright then. So be it. She tips forwards onto the balls of her feet, feels the return of that old sense of balance, of pure single-mindedness, and pushes off into a run. Regulation footwear is no substitute for trainers. Every step jolts. Her destination isn't a mere twenty feet in front of her. She can't see it. Passengers hurrying from the opposite direction huddle, looking distressed. In any emergency, ten per cent of witnesses will leave, either with self-preservation in mind, or thinking about getting help. These are Rose's ten per cent, and she doesn't know which category they fall into. Some raise hands at the sight of her uniform, opening their mouths to speak.

"We're evacuating," she cuts them short. Better to suggest she's in control. *Clear instructions.* "Turn back anyone you see coming this way!" she shouts, aware they are gape-mouthed, their heads twisting after her. Still on the move, she pages Sam. "Have you contacted control?"

"Just this minute put the phone down."

"Who's on their way?"

"They didn't know who was available. Any details I can give them yet?"

Nothing but the panic in the faces of people she's passed, and now something else: the inescapable sound of pain. Rose's sense of urgency accelerates. "Call control back. Say it's a major emergency. We're evacuating. Tell them we need people."

She reminds herself: she's done things before that she'd thought impossible. Ignore the whistles in the stadium, the sounds, the advice shouted by self-proclaimed experts. This is no time to allow yourself to be distracted. Stray as little from the straight line as you can. She trusts that people will move out of her way as she hares towards them shouting, "Coming through!" and they do.

And then they don't. Facing in the opposite direction they

are stationary, dodging sideways as they crane over shoulders and in the spaces between heads. Who would just stand by and watch? The image of the crowd as spectators at a Roman arena is hard to shift.

"Station supervisor! Move aside, please!" she yells, as yet unable to see what they're trying so hard to get a look at. There is no option but to stop when she reaches the bank of backs, a rugby scrum; a strategic battle manoeuvre. She drops the 'please', but when her requests go unheeded Rose pulls at arms, prising people apart one by one. Some kind of belief seems to have taken hold. They cannot abandon their posts until help arrives. Until then, it's their sacred duty to bear witness.

"*I'm* the help," Rose insists, but her age, height and weight do her no favours. Her uniform offers little reassurance when they were expecting the cavalry. "Go!" she shouts, trying to break the inertia. Surely if enough people break away, others will follow. "Unless you evacuate, *more* help won't be able to get through. If you really want to do something useful, the minute you get a signal, dial 999." A last desperate attempt. She tries yelling, "Fire!" having heard it's the word that's most likely to get through to people. Damn them! She needs to see and for that she needs height. "OK, don't move," she raises her voice in frustration, "but I *am* coming through." Her lack of weight is an advantage. She knows how to vault and she can land lightly on a beam that's little wider than one of her feet.

She backs up, identifies a sturdy-looking shoulder that will give her the alignment she needs. As good a springboard as any. As she begins her run-up, her coach's chin juts out. He whips off his glasses to watch her ascent.

How suddenly her view lurches. The echo of her unvoiced *'No!'* reverberates. What should be everyday becomes horrific. She is at the top of a steep, fast-moving waterfall looking down. There is only her. It's all down to her. And all she can think is that she must stop the escalator.

CHAPTER NINETEEN

Maggie, 2016

Ridiculous to be so afraid of the prospect of living alone, especially since Maggie spends so much time in her own company anyway. But without the promise of Alan coming home for dinner, without his filter on the world, her fear is that she will retreat further inwards.

She needs to talk to someone, someone she doesn't need to explain herself to. Maggie thumbs through her options on speed dial. Family's out. They already think she's off her rocker, her sister especially. Given that Maggie held back from telling Alan about the latest episode outside the Tube station, she can't explain what possessed her to confide in Lizzie.

It was only the British Transport Police this time, but she was recognised. They had watched the news, seen her standing tall and silent by Alan's side. *"We received hate mail. Hate mail. After losing our daughter."* She has stood tall and silent for so long, displaying such level-headedness, the general family consensus is that 'now it's all over' (how she detests that phrase), she's having a breakdown. The Transport Police clearly thought she needed to consider that possibility. They gave her strong tea and made her agree that she'd visit her doctor. But what Maggie couldn't let on was that she felt as if she was the only sane person in the small out-of-the-way office. No one else recognised any need for urgency.

"Do you need a lift home?" an officer asked, implying that he thought she should be accompanied.

"No! No, I'll just go and sit in the church for a while. Calm myself down." Maggie had an idea that if she continued along Lower Thames Street, she would come to the church that stood at the foot of what was the old London Bridge, but it was just something to say. She had no real intention of doing it.

"St Magnus's?" one asked.

"Oh, you know it?"

She looks at the phone in her hand and blinks at the name of her so-called best friend in London. Claire belongs to the school of thought that thinks all life's woes will evaporate if you put on your favourite underwear before going out into the world. Before you know it, she'll be recommending yoga, drinking green juice, taking up knitting and acupuncture. It will only be minutes before Maggie finds herself wanting to scream.

Her therapist's number puts in an appearance. She imagines her asking, 'Do you think that pushing people away is one of your coping mechanisms?' Plus, therapy is one of the expenses Alan assumes will taper off.

No, there's really only one person. They said they'd phone each other, but it was one of those embarrassed partings. Will Gina really want to hear from her?

Only one way to find out.

The answerphone kicks in. It's a Tuesday afternoon. She'll be at work. "Gina? Gina, are you there? If you're there, please pick up."

Nothing.

"I just… It's not an emergency but…" She thinks of city streets. How, despite the constant press of bodies and the bump of elbows, they are the loneliest of places. "I'd really appreciate a call when you have a moment. There's something I –"

"Maggie. I'm here. Out of breath, but here."

"And you caught me rambling. I can't stand answerphones."

"Sorry. I got into the habit of screening my calls. Too many years of having to deal with journalists. How are you?"

"Oh, I'm fine." Maggie pauses. "Actually, that's a lie. You're … You're sure you don't have somewhere you need to be?"

"No, I have nowhere I need to be." Maggie hears what she hopes is a laugh. "Actually, I was supposed to be working, but I cancelled."

"Not ill, I hope?"

"No, not ill. *And* I could have done with the money! But you go first. You called me."

Maggie closes her eyes and lets her mouth fall into a sigh. "Alan's applied for a job in Northumberland." The word brings to mind a single tuft of wool snagged on a fence, the urge to pull at it, nurse it; scaling sand dunes whose only anchor is sharp marram grass.

"That's where you're from originally, isn't it?"

It's not only where Maggie's from: deep down she knows it's where she belongs. Which is what makes her reluctance so difficult to comprehend. "We're the only members of our families who've ever left," she says.

"There's a long way to go between a job application and an offer."

"There is, but he's been invited back for a second interview." Maggie pauses and likes it that Gina doesn't leap in with advice. "He's told them that if he's offered the job, he can start immediately."

"Without asking you?"

She cradles the back of her head with one hand, feels the coarseness of her hair, a texture she'll never get used to. "Honestly? I think he thought I'd jump at the chance, if all the arrangements were made." *'How else can I be sure you don't carry on exposing yourself to situations that trigger panic attacks?'* "'How can you hate being here and not want to leave?' he said to me. And there's no answer I can give him."

"But you can't leave."

"I can't." She sighs. Admitting this provides release. Suddenly Maggie feels drained. "I've told him I won't go. It's not just... In many ways I'd love to. Northumberland's in my blood." It is the tide, the pull, the call, the ebb and flow of her. In Maggie's mind, she's already wading barefoot in the shallows; curving the sandy crescent of Emberton Bay; scavenging through tidewrack in search of hidden treasure.

"Have you talked about what that means?"

'We could get a dog again, Marg,' Alan had said. And Maggie pictured the dog tearing up a stretch of empty beach, its fur sleek and wet, nose sniffing around the skeleton of an upturned boat.

"We've talked," she tells Gina. As for arriving at any answers, well..." A wave rolls away from her, leaving a fine lace of foam. Once she'd have chased it, but that time has passed. "Alan thinks it's time we put all this behind us, but I can't go back to my old life. My old life was Rosie and..."

"Too painful."

"But for the sake of argument, say my old life was waiting, not exactly the same as it was before, but..."

"Yes."

"I'm not the same. I'm a different person." Her childhood accent has become citified. And you can't say the old words – claggy and scaddit and sandylowper – with even a hint of London.

"Of course you are. We all are."

Her husband's voice hasn't lost its music, not to the extent that it can't be summoned back with a twenty-minute phone call. "And Alan can't be here anymore. I can see that."

"So he can't stay and you can't go."

"And yet we love each other." Maggie tries to laugh, but the sound she makes is a helpless whimper. "Who wants a long-distance relationship with their own husband?" They will walk from the Ship Inn, heading through tilted fields edged with yellow gorse bushes which release the scent of coconut, angling down to where the land suddenly tips away into the whinstone columns of St Margaret's cove. ('Your cove,' Alan tells her. 'Hardly a saint,' she says.) Then the dark ruin of Dunstanburgh Castle. "And that's the other thing. Alan doesn't believe me when I say no. He thinks that if I go on weekend visits, I'll be persuaded."

"Are you afraid that you might?"

Alan will have Maggie stand on the Gull Crag cliffs when the tide is at its highest. He will hand her his binoculars and breathe, 'Look, Marg!' and she'll watch as birds whir in a frenzied cloud.

"My family will think I'm throwing away my marriage. And I'm scared." She sees Alan now, holding a gate closed, pointing to his cheek, insisting on a kiss before he lets her through.

"Scared you're making the wrong decision?"

"That's the thing. I don't see it as a decision. I don't *see* that I have a choice. But I rely on him so much. All the day-to-day stuff. How would you manage without Tamsin?"

"Tamsin was only sixteen when her father left."

Maggie could kick herself. "Of course. She must have been." Gina may *say* that Bill left, but did she feel abandoned, or did she suspect – as Maggie now feels about Alan – that she drove him away?

"She grew up fast. But I won't have her with me much longer."

"Oh?"

"She's moving in with her boyfriend. She told me over

165

breakfast. I've been sitting here, hardly knowing what to do with myself."

Someone else who thinks it's time to move on. "You'll miss her."

"She *should* have her own life. I want that for her, I really do. But, yes, I'll miss her terribly."

Their situations are more similar than Maggie had imagined. A solution presents itself but she pushes it away. Two dead children in one household? Far too much to bear. No, what they both need is a project. "I almost forgot. When did you last check your emails?"

"Yesterday, I think."

"Then you won't have read the one from Jules. He's had some news. Tate Modern's going to put on an exhibition of his work."

"The Tate? He told me there might be something but that's huge! I know he's had individual pieces displayed here and there. But I had no idea he's that well-known."

"I got the impression it came as a total surprise. But it's hardly the kind of thing you say no to."

"Why would he want to?"

Maggie is hesitant. "He realises it's going to be difficult for the families. To have it all on show." Here, especially. On the bank of the Thames.

"His *Objets? That's* the exhibition?"

"Actually, it's more than that. He'd like to create some new works. Using our mementos." Silence. Her lip trembles with the memory of that hateful letter, not something she can easily cast aside.

"You'd trust Jules with something of Rosie's?"

"I've thought it through, and if it's going to happen – which it is – I want something of hers to be part of it. We fought so hard, I couldn't bear for her to be excluded again." All of Rosie's things. Each item sealed in a plastic bag, just as they were when the police returned them. Her London Underground uniform, folded with military precision. A few official documents, utility bills, the kind of things banks demand as proof of ID. Plus the keys to her flat. "If it becomes part of something else, if he gives it meaning…"

"I'm not sure I'd be able to let any of Ollie's things go."

"There isn't something small?"

Breathing.

Just breathing.

It's up to Maggie to unravel the silence. "What?" she coaxes.

"It's all one thing as far as I'm concerned. Ollie's room. It's exactly as it was when we heard the news."

Maggie pictures Gina drawing the curtains, changing the sheets once a week, checking that it's not too hot or too cold. "Exactly as it was?"

"It's not a shrine, not that. It's just that none of us could face… And it would be strange for something to be removed now." Gina's laughter is mirthless, the kind you give when something has just struck you. "But it will have to go. All of it. I can't afford to keep the house, not on my own."

"Don't answer this if you don't want to, Gina, but when's the last time you went into Ollie's room?"

Another elongated pause.

"I'm sorry, I've overstepped the mark –"

"No, I'm trying to think, that's all. You see, no one goes in there."

Because his absence would become all too apparent, Maggie supposes. It's not something she's ever had to address. Rosie left home two years before the incident, taking the majority of what she owned with her. Within six months, Alan had requisitioned her room as an office. Is it a source of guilt for him, how quickly he redecorated?

"The door's locked. I found Tamsin in there and I blew my

top. I can't explain why. I know Ollie was her brother, but I couldn't bear the thought of anyone being in his room."

It's Maggie's turn to remain silent.

"Do you find that? That you just can't remember why something seemed so significant? But you don't undo the damage, you don't even apologise, because you assume you must have had your reasons."

All Maggie can think of is the book she was in the middle of reading when they got the call about Rosie. The dog-ear that marks the page she was up to. A page she cannot go back to because, when she read it, her daughter was still alive. She repeats something her therapist told her. "When you're in shock, memories tend to behave strangely."

"That's just the thing. I've done so many things. *So* many things I can't find an excuse for."

CHAPTER TWENTY

Eric, 2010

Apparently the escalators on the Northern Line are between seventy and eighty years old. *At any one time, some will be out of service for maintenance.* Eric bunches the hair at the back of his head into his fists. The vagueness of the language! 'Some' could mean any number above one. Plus do they mean preventative maintenance or repairs? He scrolls up and down, up and down. Really, it's unacceptable how little guidance there is on what should happen when escalators are taken out of action.

Think. Eric closes his eyes. If it was so common for escalators to be out of use, his focus needs to shift. The overcrowding issue becomes key.

Try again, prompts Oliver Wicker. One more search using a slight variation of words he's typed dozens of times before. And there it is, the number one result: a House of Commons report on overcrowding on public transport, dated 2002.

"Alright!" he says out loud.

The committee began by stating that overcrowding on public transport – described as 'chronic' – must be taken more seriously. Management that views overcrowding as unavoidable are not only short-changing passengers but are *failing to run the system properly.* The House of Commons passing the buck back to management, who, in turn, pass the buck back to *potential* passengers.

Several useful reminders highlight the state of play as it was in December 2002. The introduction of the Congestion Charge had increased the cost of car journeys, forcing more and more people onto the Tube. Respondents to the survey described the conditions they regularly found themselves subjected to as 'positively frightening'. And here's something interesting: The Corporation of London had been so concerned about the transport system's inefficiencies that it sponsored research to quantify what it was costing businesses. The conclusion was £230 million per year, *without* taking into account difficulties in recruiting and retaining staff.

Then Eric comes to something he was beginning to lose hope of ever finding – an entire chapter dedicated to capacity. *Unlike buses, boats and planes, all of which have maximum loading limits, trains are designed to run at full capacity.* So management *want* a high volume of passengers. It's the difference between 'full' and 'overcrowded' that's the difficulty, neither of which are neatly defined.

For the first time, Eric uncovers written policy on how Underground staff are expected to relieve station overcrowding. Best practice to reduce platform overcrowding is to wait for the next train to clear the congestion – assuming, of course, it has capacity. *It is commonplace for carriages to be so tightly packed that when passengers arrive at their stop, they can't get to an exit to disembark.* But elsewhere the report states that *Faced with such limited choices, passengers will try to get onto an overcrowded train rather than wait for the next scheduled train, when there is no guarantee it will be any less crowded.*

Closing a station should be a last resort. *Until congestion is cleared, attempts are made to slow down the flow of passengers entering the station. Before consideration is given to closing individual entrances, automatic barriers are changed from entries to exits, an escalator may be taken out of use, or the direction of an escalator might be reversed.* So much for the complaints from station staff about lack of instructions. This is what should have been understood by Rose's instruction to 'filter the flow'.

The report admits that these measures aren't always effective. *Preventative action should be taken so that front line staff are not routinely required to restrict access to trains or stations to relieve overcrowding.* But what this *preventative action* might be, the report doesn't specify.

Eric bites his lip and ponders, "Was the level of crowding on that Friday evening exceptional or was it foreseeable?"

"Why does someone have to be responsible?"

Eric glances up. He had been so shuttered, he'd completely forgotten that Sorrel was sprawled on his bed, the duvet rumpled underneath her, a journal lying open in front of her. She promised not to disturb him and, until now, she's been true to her word. Part of him wants to reply, 'You're studying the law; you understand Tort.' Instead, he rubs at the corners of his overworked eyes. "Too many people using an antiquated system equals foreseeability."

She shakes her head. "There were too many factors. It wasn't foreseeable that they'd all come together at the exact same moment on the exact same day, and it's unlikely that they ever will again. Plus, you only have to look at the number of agencies that were involved – hospitals, the emergency services and so on – most with budgets imposed by outside authorities, all reacting to a crisis in the only way possible at the time."

Eric already knows that an investigation that blames human error, rather than the systems that made human error possible (some would say 'inevitable'), cannot be objective.

"The idea behind a second inquest wouldn't be to prove that an individual was responsible. It would be to prove that the crowd and the station supervisor *weren't* responsible."

"And then what?" challenges Sorrel.

"Then?" Eric shakes his head as if to rid himself of the idea that something has to come next. "That'll be someone else's business."

Irritation buzzes as he returns his focus to the screen and pastes the list of experts from the House of Commons report into his control document. But Sorrel's right. Of course she's right. If there's a next, there's no way in hell he'll let this thing drop. And here's something else. *There is no mention of safety in London Underground's published list of Customer Service Delivery Standards...*

Wait. Can that be right?

The authors of the House of Commons report were astounded by the lack of emphasis on overcrowding. Yes, each station had its own evacuation plan to be employed when levels were considered dangerous. He had the terms 'full capacity', 'overcrowded' and 'dangerous' with no definitions. Now it seems that safety itself has been overlooked. A strung-out feeling has Eric questioning his own judgement. "Hey, what do you think of this?"

"Oh." Sorrel feigns disinterest. "So now you want my opinion?"

He ploughs on: "'There is no mention of safety in London Underground's published list of Customer Service Delivery Standards.'" Sorrel props herself up on an elbow, giving his words her full attention. "'Passengers are entitled to expect not only that the system is safe to use, but that the operators place their safety before every other consideration.'"

"Before every other consideration..." Sorrel muses. "All you'd have to prove is that they didn't."

Satisfied that she's confirmed his line of thought, Eric copies and pastes this section of the report. "If safety is an entitlement, then every injury represents a failing in the execution of duty."

Sorrel swings her legs around and sits up. "They're almost describing a strict liability scenario. If we can establish that…"

Take note of her use of the word 'we'. Take note but don't comment on it. "Then there's no need to prove negligence."

She nods. "The fact that the accident occurred would be enough."

Sorrel tips Eric's clothes off the only other chair in the room and drags it the short distance to the desk. Immediately Eric feels cagey. She has a habit of picking holes in arguments with no sympathy for the person on the receiving end of her critique. 'They need to get over themselves,' she'll say. 'Life will be one hell of a lot tougher in a courtroom.' And something – something is missing from his argument.

Sorrel positions the chair facing away from the computer and straddles it, resting her chin on her hands which are flattened onto the chair back.

"We have to remember." *Listen to yourself, Eric. Since when did the pair of you become a team?* But she has reached out to various objects on his desk and is busy lining them up, turning them around so that the labels face her: a can of Monster; the ProPlus box, its familiar chunky red text cut through with an approving blue tick. Though she doesn't say, 'No wonder you can't wind down,' she stands his box of over-the-counter sleeping tablets at the end of her line-up. Distracted and irritated, Eric snaps, "We only want to argue the case for a second inquest. There *is* no civil lawsuit."

"Yeah, yeah." Her neat row abandoned, Sorrel points to Eric's much-annotated 3D diagram. His personal vision of Hell. "This is the escalator where it happened?"

"No, that's the one that broke down. Staff diverted passengers along this corridor in the direction of Old Billingsgate" – he traces the route along the curving subway – "to this one."

"What about the lift?" She peels a Post-it note from the wall and sticks it next to one below.

His hands shake as they hover over the keyboard. "Don't move my notes!"

"Wow!" Her eyes wide and disapproving, Sorrel pulls the note off the wall. "We *are* jumpy tonight."

What just happened? His heartbeat accelerated in a way that even Eric has to agree is disproportionate. "I'm trying to nail the sequence." He almost feels the need to justify flying off the handle to himself. "You have no idea how long it took me to put those stages in order."

"Actually, I'm the one person who does have a fairly good idea. And I *was* going to put it back. I just find it easier to look at ideas side by side. So the lift…" Sorrel prompts.

Eric gladly goes along with what is obviously a distraction technique. "The current guide to step-free access says you have to ask if you want to use it, so I'm not sure it would have been available, or what its capacity would have been. Plus, once people were inside the station entrance, they weren't given a choice which way to go."

They exhaust a search for case law.

"Brick wall," Sorrel concurs, momentarily jaded. Then she frowns. "That simulation of a terrorist attack was held at Old Billingsgate, wasn't it? I seem to remember it was only a week or two after the incident."

"If it hadn't already been planned, you'd be forgiven for thinking it was designed to reassure the public that the emergency services could cope."

"How much information do we have about it?"

"Considering it was carried out publicly, not much. But

we *do* know that none of the radio systems worked properly, something that was supposed to have been fixed after the King's Cross fire."

"So we can assume that comms wouldn't have been working at our incident either."

"The next real test was the Seven-Seven terrorist attack. I've been through the inquest transcripts and they're full of criticism. Only one person taking emergency calls, controllers struggling to work out where the free ambulances were, how slowly the emergency services reacted, a lack of medical supplies when ambulances arrived, staff with no knowledge of major accident protocols." He pauses. Saying all this out loud seems to be helping. "Actually, I did find something interesting."

"What?"

"It was a quote from a radio interview. I copied it somewhere." He types the words, 'thinking time' into the search bar in Word. "Here. This is it. *The crisis team was to practise switching from what's called 'slow-time thinking' to the 'quick-time thinking' that's so vital in an emergency.* The idea is that, if you practise emergency scenarios often enough, you'll make the switch automatically when it comes to the real thing. But if you haven't practised often enough…"

She responds to his shrug: "And, going back to what I said earlier, you're only prepared for one thing to go wrong at a time."

"Plus, Rosemary Chapple was new to her job. If she *had* practised simulated emergencies, it wouldn't have been in her capacity as supervisor. She'd have been acting under instruction."

Sorrel gives a slow nod. "If she *did* make the automatic jump to quick thinking, her training would have prepared her to wait for instructions."

He shakes his head. "There's an argument in there some-where. It's how to frame it…" He tails off. It's like a word that's on the tip of your tongue. Pay it too much attention and he'll chase it from his mind.

And then Sorrel says something that genuinely floors Eric: "Stick at it, Viking. You'll get there."

CHAPTER TWENTY-ONE

Rosie, 22 August 2003, 9.49pm

The blood that has spotted Rose's shirt is not her own. She's refused all offers of medical attention but the phrase *trembling like a leaf* doesn't come close to describing the way she's begun to shake. On the go for fourteen hours solid, the adrenalin that sustained her has worn off.

"When you were advised that the CCTV cameras were down, why didn't you reopen the barriers at Catfish Hill?"

Her original decision is clear in her mind. Risks increase when passengers are asked to use an escalator as a staircase. Even those who happily walk down moving escalators can be thrown off balance. "The escalator was broken," she says through chattering teeth.

"Which was the right course of action when the alternative route was the safer option." As far as Rose is concerned, her interrogator might as well be faceless. He is management. A uniform. He may even be one of those who persuaded her to take the job. Other more insistent images flood her exhausted mind, washing everything else aside. "But the *minute* circumstances changed," he says in a way that suggests her decision should have been both instantaneous and obvious, "the *minute* Sam advised you that the CCTV was out, you should have reassessed."

"Right," she manages, remembering how, in the absence of visuals, she'd decided she needed to see things for herself. In the quest for that perfect ten on the scorecards, for the look of pride in your trainer's eyes, there is always a better way of doing things. Humility in the face of success. *Think of all the sacrifices that have been made to get you here.* Humility in the face of abject failure.

"Agreed." He stops his pacing and points directly at Rose. She flinches. *There will be no next time.* Never before has failing had such catastrophic consequences. "Using an out-of-order escalator as a staircase isn't ideal, but when it's better than the alternatives, that's what you do."

Huddled inside the utility blanket someone has draped around her shoulders, Rose must attempt to stop herself from shaking apart. *If only he'd stop talking.*

But he pulls up a chair, sits. Rose watches the hand that brings the mug of tea to his mouth; feels revulsion as he slurps. She'll be sick if she so much as tries to drink.

"So." He seems to take a very long time to breathe out. Time has fallen out of sync. One minute it speeds up. The next it slows down. "Walk me through what you did."

Rose's attempts to mentally retrace her steps falter. It's impossible once you've been told what the obvious course of action should have been. All she can see are close-ups of ragged openings. She can barely admit to herself that they're mouths. All she can hear are layer upon layer of low cries of pain. They've wormed their way inside her head and, already, she has a feeling that they'll never leave.

Rose was caught by a camera lens, on repeat shutter release: looking over her shoulder as she walked backwards; stepping over the lip of the station entrance; her hands under the arms of a young woman who was clearly unconscious.

(She couldn't bring herself to look at her face.) Someone else – nobody she knew, though by then, they'd learned the way the other moved – grasped the woman's ankles. They laid her on the cobbles, made sure a paramedic knew there was another one, then ran back inside for more, until they were told that non-medical staff weren't supposed to move casualties. But the men and the women and the children she'd been unable to save, she'll never stop dreaming and thinking about them.

Now, as Rose sits in a small side room, emergency telephone lines jam with increasingly desperate callers. *Why don't you know? How can you not know?* Rose cannot blank the answer out of her mind. Those same callers are hanging up and saying to husbands, wives, lovers, brothers, sisters, '*I can't just sit around doing nothing. Let's just go and see what we can find out.*' Disaster victim identification teams from all over the country are on their way. They will work alongside local forensic specialists. Slow, meticulous, scientific. Elsewhere, exhausted doctors work in appalling conditions. And it is *her* fault. All her fault. What possible answer is there to the question, 'Why didn't you do the obvious?' How can she explain why she didn't stand in the control room barking concise orders? Why she took it on herself to 'wade in'? People are dead. It doesn't occur to Rose to defend herself, let alone blame other staff.

"Look," he says eventually. His voice is that of a frustrated parent, not without empathy, wondering if he's pushed her too hard, too tired to push her harder. "I know how difficult this is, but I want you to go home and think very carefully. Tomorrow it won't just be me who wants answers." He seems to be suggesting that he's done his best to protect her. What happens tomorrow will be out of his hands.

She pushes the chair back, stands. The grey blanket slips from her shoulders.

"Oh," he says, an afterthought. "Before I forget, your

mother's left several messages for you. She's been watching the news. You should ring and let her know you're safe."

She swallows hard. "I'll go and do that now." But Rose won't ring. She's already arrived at her decision.

CHAPTER TWENTY-TWO

Donovan, 2016

For the past few days Donovan has been unable to face returning to the garage, knowing what is gone from it. But he returns to it now, screeching the door up and over, ducking his head, inhaling damp earth and methylated spirits. Something fell out of one of the cardboard boxes when he upended it, and he saw that something fall down the back of his workbench. He has an idea what it was, but that idea isn't yet a certainty. Down on his knees, hands gritty, he moves aside boxes; shunts his shoulder against the workbench and reaches. The tips of his fingers brush against something brittle. It might be, it might be. He reels in his catch.

Lobster and champagne for Helene's birthday. Donovan always made the trip to Billingsgate, taking his time, weaving between stalls, tracking down the finest. Bright vermilion with the tail tightly curled. Cassie had been frightened the first time she saw a lobster. It wasn't the claws, but its antenna and walking legs, eight of them, like a spider, but 'meaner looking'.

This year, being far more sophisticated at five years old, she turned her nose up. "Yuk, I'm not eating that!"

"Just as well, because it's not for you."

After he produced the champagne, she yelled, "Wait! Don't open it yet!" She pounded upstairs, the noise sounding as if it was made by a far heavier child.

"Is that a herd of elephants I hear?"

Helene grinning: "Don't you think I'd remember letting a herd of elephants in the front door?"

Moments later, Cassie reappeared wearing a serious expression and her new swimming goggles. "OK, I'm ready."

Helene blinked, her expression heightened with suppressed laughter. "I'm glad we raised such a safety-conscious daughter."

Safety-conscious.

In his hands, resting, the goggles look so small. Was Cassie ever this small? But Donovan remembers the weight of her when she was no longer than the length of his forearm, her head resting in the palm of his hand.

Twenty-two plus thirteen. Thirty-five years the swimming goggles have lain undisturbed, hidden. Tenderly, gently, Donovan wipes them down with the hem of his T-shirt. They are pink. (Of course they are. Didn't everything have to be pink?) He goes to clean the lenses, but, through the cotton, his fingertips meet. One plastic lens is missing. For several minutes he remains kneeling, the goggles swaddled inside his large hands. He's afraid they might disintegrate, or that he's imagined them, but no. This is Cassie's way of letting him know it's OK that he's given away her son's crib, that she's watching, and somewhere, in another world, she is still a five-year-old.

He sniffs. He must go to Helene.

She is seated on the sofa, the television tuned to some early evening magazine-style programme, and she's busy typing into the iPad on her lap. Her eyes flit between the television and the iPad. Always a proficient touch typist, this is how Helene spends most evenings. It's probably how she spends most days.

He sits beside her and waits for her hands to stop moving.

"The state of your jeans!" she says, brushing at grit that has come from the concrete screed of the garage floor.

"I found something." He uses words she will understand immediately. Helene looks him in the eye, and while she is focused on his face, her lips slightly parted, he finds one of her hands and wraps it around the pair of pink goggles, then wraps his hand tight around hers.

He sees her throat move, nods, *It's OK*. As he gently takes his hand away, Helene's unfurls, her palm facing upwards.

Her eyelashes flicker. "Oh," she breathes, nothing more. But she looks at him, and in that shared moment, beyond language, beyond words, her dark eyes mirror his own unspoken memories.

CHAPTER TWENTY-THREE

Gina, 2016

"I am thinking about absence. The absence of things. You know, like, uh, cave art."

Gina invited Jules into her home knowing she must make a decision, and soon. Estate agents can't value a house while one of the bedrooms is padlocked. It might give the impression of a hostage situation. Ollie's things have to go, it's simply a matter of how. She makes what she hopes will be interpreted as a neutral sound.

"So here is one thing." Jules sips from a mug of coffee. He opens a battered leather notebook to a fresh page and draws around his own hand.

Gina can't tell if it's the instant decaff that makes him frown or if he's simply on the trail of another thought. Not that it matters. This is his audition, not hers.

"The cavemen in my country make hands on the walls of caves by *putting* the hand on the rock and then *blowing* paint through a tube."

He's a restless man, one who seizes upon words, using expressions as subtitles and hand movements as sign language. To be seated at her own kitchen table at close quarters to such undiluted intensity is unsettling and energising in equal measures.

"Then they take the hand away but, you know, the outline, it remain."

Her heart twists. There is a hand, and you take it away; its absence is what creates the picture. *If he understands this, he won't judge you.*

"Then here is another. I watch a documentary with Louis. Something to do with his school work. It is about the excavation at Pompeii. You know, the lava and the ash from the volcano, they *bury* the town, and the rock set *very* fast around the bodies." He raps on the surface of the table. "Like a hard shell."

Gina can't imagine being able to express herself so clearly. But then Jules has been offered an exhibition at Tate Modern while she's a temp with a very specific-sounding job title, but no idea how the small task she carries out (far better than the last person the agency sent) contributes to the process as a whole. No one considers she might be interested. After all, she'll only be there for six weeks.

"This is the position they die in. Not neatly laid out, like in a coffin." Gina quivers at the word and all it implies. "When the body it decay, we are left with the hollow in the shape of the person. There it is, under the ground. The absent person."

He begins to sketch an illustration of what Gina has already pictured. She doesn't say that she's been to Pompeii in sweltering June heat, seen the rigid plaster casts bleached white by the sun. She remembers the cast of a young boy found sleeping in his mother's arms, and she remembers the cast of a dog, horribly contorted.

"When they find the first hollows, they do not say, 'We must preserve them.' They still think the skeleton is the important thing. But then somebody has an idea. If they can drill into the ground and find a body-shaped hollow that is undisturbed, then get some plaster that is the right… texture, is that what you call it?" He rubs his fingertips together.

"Consistency?" Gina suggests, a term for cake mix and pancake batter. She sees his thought process now. The plaster casts are something else that have been created out of absence.

"Yes, that is the thing!"

Though his enthusiasm thrills her, welcomed into Jules's world of imagery and ideas, Gina can't help the feeling that she's a phoney. The word might not have come to her if they weren't here, in the kitchen.

"When they pour plaster through the hole, they do not know if it is a boy, a girl, a man, a woman, how old, how rich." His voice see-saws through possibilities. "Now they wait. The plaster must set, then, very carefully, they chip away the rock, because it is harder than the plaster, yes? Inside, they have a complete body. You can see the eyes, the nose, sometimes the hair. It is how the person look on the day they die. It is the opposite of sculpture, I think."

An image of Anthony Gormley's sculptures comes to Gina. She saw a documentary about how he gave himself up to being wrapped in cling film then encased in plaster so that a cast could be made of his body. She found the footage of when his wife covered his nose and mouth – the idea of suffocation – slightly disturbing.

"We can see these people from all that time ago. It is *very* moving. I like to think that people who come to Tate Modern, they will be moved in this way. I want them to feel the absence." Jules clutches a fist to his chest. "But you know, I look Pompeii up on-line. I do my research. It is not for Louis' school work, it is for me! I read the comment people type. They think to have the cast on display, it is disrespectful. They say the dead should be put to rest in the ground; that prayers must be said. They do not stop to think that these people did not pray in the way they do, *or* to the same gods.

"Some people think the work I do is disrespectful. I do not think so. Pick any one of my *Objets* and I will give you the story behind it, the thought that go into it, how I construct it. It is not always comfortable, you know. The important thing – to me – is that I am true to the memory of my Evelyn. And also…" He shrugs. "I hear about Ollie."

At the sound of her son's name, Gina's throat constricts. Conversation has moved from generalities to specifics.

"I read about him. I see the photograph you bring to the inquest day after day. I have him in my head all the time I work with his things. But it must be *your* choice. I know what I ask and for some people it is too much. So far, I think you are the most *réticente,* but you are also the first person who say to me, 'Make sure you bring a bolt cutter.'"

The red-handled tool lies between them on the table. She picks it up, gets a feel for its weight, turns it over. *High Carbon Steel Blade.* She knows nothing about bolt cutters, but this looks as if it should do the job. She purses her lips slightly. The idea doesn't feel as wrong as she'd assumed it would. Without realising, she has begun to take it seriously. At least this way, she'll be in control. *It's not just down to you,* she reminds herself. *Tamsin may not agree. And as for Bill…* "All you want to do today is look?"

"You have not told me what I look *at* yet. But, yes, that is what we agree."

"So it's possible you might say no to me?"

He blows out his cheeks. "It is unlikely. Think of it like Eric's sequence."

Is his mention of Eric calculated? But perhaps that's unfair. Jules may be totally unaware of their relationship and how this might influence Gina.

"All of those dominoes. If any one of the family does not want to be involved, then our sequence – the art we create – will be incomplete. It can still be good art, but it will be first inquest art. It will not be the full story. By the way." He leans towards Gina, his tone confiding as he points out a stain in the corner of the kitchen ceiling. "I notice while I sit here. You have a little damp, maybe a slow leak. The bathroom is above, I think? If you want, afterwards, I take a look."

Gina feels herself colour. "I've been meaning to get round to it." The fact is, the first plumber she called wanted a call-out fee of £95.

"I am the same. I work all day and the weekend I just want to sleep. You do not have to worry. The journalist, they ask me, 'Which art school do you go to? *École des Beaux-arts*, Paris College of Art?' I say, 'I come to art via plumbing.'" He shrugs. "Also a little decorating. They do not like the truth very much."

"It's a little more than plumbing that got you here," Gina says gently.

"*Oui*." For a brief moment he is completely still, as if someone has hit his pause button.

In the quiet it comes to Gina: "What about Victim Thirty-four?"

"What about him?"

"He'll be missing from the exhibition."

Jules acknowledges this with a frown. "We need to do something about that. And I do not know what. We do not even know what he look like." His eyes brighten. "You have an idea." He points at her. "I can see you have an idea!"

"Oh, I don't know." Gina looks up and immediately her eyes drift to the stain on the ceiling. Should she take Jules up on his offer? If she's to put the house on the market, all sorts of little jobs will need doing.

"You worry it sound a little crazy? *I* am the mad sculptor, you tell me your crazy idea."

Gina begins carefully. "While you were talking, I was thinking about Facebook." The corners of her mouth twitch as she taps into her guilty secret. Sometimes, after Gina has read an obituary, she waits for Tamsin to go out, then logs on and tries to track down the victim. She types in a name and, from the list that pops up on her screen, matches the photograph with the one in the newspaper. "You know when someone doesn't post a profile photo on their page?"

"I stay away from social media, but you tell me. I will imagine for myself."

"There's just an outline of the head and shoulders. A blank silhouette."

Jules moves to the edge of his seat. "Go on."

Quite often, security isn't set to 'private', and Gina reads outpourings of grief from friends, family, former colleagues, people who remember the dead person from primary school; messages for which there is no other outlet. "They often have T-shirts for exhibitions. Maybe you could have one with a mock-up of a blank profile picture and the words *Victim Thirty-four* underneath. If you could get visitors to buy the T-shirts beforehand and wear them while they're at the exhibition…" It is Gina's turn to shrug. "It's what people do when they go to gigs."

"Oh!" Jules holds out both hands, palms up. "Is there any more in that head of yours?"

Gina understands now. Jules hasn't lifted a latch and invited her into *his* world. He has lifted the latch to let her out of *her own*. "Maybe we could cordon off a space and invite people to leave something for him. So they become part of the exhibition too."

"You are very good. For that I fix your leak *and* I paint your kitchen." He pushes back his chair and stands.

What has just happened? Gina regrets that she never had a teacher like Jules. What might she have done with a little encouragement? But now he's reaching out a hand towards her and nodding. Realising she still has hold of the bolt cutter, Gina relinquishes it. "Left at the top of the stairs," she says. "It's the second door on the right." Not that he can possibly miss it. With the weight gone, her hand feels as if it could float.

At the kitchen doorway, Jules hesitates. "You are not coming with me?"

"I don't need to." She smiles. "I have it all in my head."

As Jules looks at her, she realises that he sees right into her, but still he asks, "You are sure?"

Gina holds up a hand and splays her fingers slightly, mimicking his explanation of the cave paintings. "Absence," she says.

CHAPTER TWENTY-FOUR

Tamsin, 2016

The moment she slots her key into the lock, Tamsin senses it. Something about the house is different. She pushes the door open, and slides tonight's bedtime reading – a manuscript – onto the table in the hall. The title page pulls her attention from that initial intuitive thought. Work has always provided refuge. Tamsin creates designs that lend the appearance of reality to unreality, unreality to reality. Truth is a frequently-crossed line. All that matters is that, while the house lights are dimmed, the audience believes. She is only considering this project and already the director's vision is drawing her in. Minimalistic to the point of bleakness, any prop Tamsin can imagine placing on the stage seems over the top.

"I'm in the kitchen." Her mother's voice summons her back to reality.

"Won't be a minute!" She gives the title a final glance. The trick will be to make the design elements invisible, the kind of staging that will have audience members reaching for the programme notes and asking themselves, 'They used a set-designer?'

Seated at the kitchen table, her mum looks as if she has sat there unmoving the entire day, except to turn a page of the newspaper. Without consciously thinking what she's doing, Tamsin sniffs the air, but her mother seems strangely calm as she nods towards a chair.

"Sit down. There's something I want to talk to you about."

As she takes a seat, Tamsin's blood sings resistance. This is going to be about Gareth. Objections disguised as motherly concern. There's another unspoken bereavement, one Tamsin usually feels selfish dwelling on, but she gives herself permission to think of it now. The loss of herself aged thirteen to eighteen. The withdrawal of freedoms when she expected them to be extended. And when she did go out, prearranged check-ins, not quite on the hour every hour, but so regular they might as well have been. *I'm going to the cinema. I am not coming out in the middle of the film to call home!* In the end, it was easier to say she didn't feel like going out. Repeated often enough, invitations stopped coming. Gareth thinks it's odd, how few friends Tamsin has from high school, but that was never her intention. She only ever wanted to be normal.

Mum lays one hand on hers. "The Tate Modern's putting on an exhibition of Jules's work."

Tamsin feels her eyebrows twitch. "Tate Modern?" This isn't what she expected. "Wow!"

The throaty noise her mother makes cautions against enthusiasm. "It's *Objets*."

Tamsin's heartbeat accelerates. *Objets* will mean renewed interest from the press, just when they might have expected it to cool down. "For Jules's sake, I hope they've asked him because of his art."

"The thing is." Her mother hasn't finished. Her eyes are searching. "He's asking each of the families to contribute something."

"What kind of thing?"

"Something important. Something that means something. I wanted to ask…" Tamsin dreads what is coming. "How would you feel if I let Jules have all of it?"

"All of it?" It isn't so much an echo as a demand for clarification.

"What he'd like to do is recreate your brother's room."

This is her mother speaking. Her mother who was so incensed to find Tamsin in Ollie's bed that she had Dad go straight to B&Q in the dark grey suit he'd worn to Ollie's funeral, buy the most industrial-looking padlock he could find and drill it into the doorframe. "In Tate Modern?" she hears herself ask. It's extraordinary that Mum is even entertaining the idea.

"He sketched out a couple of ideas. "Obviously, your dad would have to agree as w–"

"Wait." Tamsin's hand is a stop sign. "Let me get this straight." She squeezes her eyes closed momentarily. "Someone we don't even know that well… has been allowed –" She wants to say 'inside the mausoleum' but cannot, so she points at the kitchen ceiling. (It doesn't matter that the room directly above is the bathroom.) "He's actually *seen* Ollie's room?" Blood coursing, coursing madly. Tamsin doesn't care that she's used her brother's name, something she'd ordinarily avoid doing, like swearing in front of her grandmother at the dinner table.

"This afternoon, yes."

"Is the padlock still off?" She knows that her mother can see her shaking, the outward sign of barely-contained fury.

Mum nods, though she doesn't appear to understand the need for outrage.

Torn, Tamsin pushes herself to standing. One urgent part of her wants to grab her things and slam the door on the way out. But for so long, her mind has been a museum and she's curious. What kind of a curator she has been?

She doesn't ask permission. She takes the stairs one by one, her hand sliding up the bannister. This moment, like many before it, feels dreamlike, unreal. She was a child, and in shock. At best, her memories are fragmentary. She may be about to discover that some are false.

Over the years, various people have told Tamsin they dreamt about discovering secret rooms in their houses. Their own private Narnias, hidden behind bookcases and wardrobes. To her, that sounds like a luxury. Her house has had that extra room, unmentionable, yet in plain sight. Can you imagine sleeping next door to Netherworld? Because, when she was denied access, that's what Ollie's room became. *Perhaps Dad was talking sense after all. We should have left this house.* Now, the door to her brother's room stands open, an insult to all the years in between.

"Just come and look at the flowers. They've made a lovely job of them."

But Tamsin had a sense of the sheer number of the wreaths, the shapes the florist had teased and manipulated them into, and could not. Next to them, the sight of a plain wooden coffin would be nothing.

"You may not feel like coming with us, love, but if you don't, I really think you'll regret it. Perhaps for the rest of your life."

Unmoved by Mum's pleas, Tamsin lay facing the wall that separated her room from her brother's, his bed the mirror image of her own. Part of Tamsin felt as if she was acting up, but she clung to the part that seemed certain that what she felt was very real.

Her father's frustration was palpable as he paced the landing and paused to fidget in the doorway. "Gina," he said eventually. "There's another service booked straight after ours. We can't keep them waiting."

Her mother's voice was gentle. "Just a minute, Bill."

"No, not just a minute. We have to go!"

"Last chance, Tamsin." Her mother's weight lifted from the

mattress, then there was a pause. "Alright, then. But don't you ever say I didn't try."

Slow even thuds, dignified footfalls on the staircase. Momentarily, Tamsin felt as if she'd got her own way, but by the time the front door slammed any sense of triumph had evaporated. A spasm moved across her face. Who would have wanted *this*? On the wall that separated her room from Ollie's, she tapped out an urgent message in their private Morse code. .-- .... -.-- / -.. --- -. - - / -.-- --- ..- / .- -. .... .-- . .-. / -- . --..-- / .- .-. .... . .-- .. .--. . Silence. Tamsin's face contorted. She stuffed her mouth with duvet before realising. She could howl if she wanted. No one would hear. With this new knowledge, a strange numbness took over. Almost as if she'd forgotten how to be. She was as empty as the house. Convinced she'd be able to un-numb the numbness if she could just lie down on her brother's bed, she ventured out onto the landing and twisted the handle of his bedroom door. Nothing. Twisted and pushed. *How dare they!* She rattled and rattled it, her need accelerating to the point of desperation until she sank to the floor, furious in defeat, kicking out at the bannisters and laddering the heels of her new black tights.

The sharp *bring* of the doorbell robbed her of breath. Whoever was there must have heard her tantrum. Not her parents. It was still several hours before they would return, stiff from sitting in an unfamiliar church pew, standing in the cold grey damp, followed by forced niceties. Voices drifted to the top of the stairs, muffled, male. Friends of Ollie's perhaps? Tamsin walked her hands down to the small three-quarter-way landing, where, tipped headfirst, it was just possible to make out two grey heads through the frosted oval glass. The heads blurred. They were leaving! Overcome by an urgent desire not to be alone, Tamsin forgot that less than an hour earlier she'd insisted that was precisely what she wanted.

Her feet translated yearning into thunder. She didn't give a thought to how she might look. As she swung the front door inwards, something – a boy – crashed through the opening and landed at her feet. She shrieked with the unexpectedness of it. With nothing to break his fall, the boy hit the floor, fists in front of his sternum, hissing like something punctured. This was no one Tamsin knew. By her estimate, he was nineteen, twenty.

Her heart pounding, Tamsin looked from the boy at her feet (she didn't think of him as a man) to a second boy who was leaning against the side of the porch. In his posture she recognised all the arrogance of someone who knows he can capture a young girl's gaze. Even so, Tamsin was unable to stop herself from gawping. She took in the zip of his leather jacket worn over a grey hoodie (another grey hoodie), hands in pockets, blue jeans, white trainers.

He replied with a question of his own. "Is this Ollie's house?" As if nothing out of the ordinary was happening.

"He's dead." Tamsin's grief counsellor had suggested she use straightforward words, and this one topped the list, but releasing it in the hall felt as if she was killing Ollie all over again.

The good-looking boy tightened his lips as if it pained him to plough on with whatever he had to say. "We saw the car leave." He half-turned to indicate a space outside the Grants' the length of two ordinary-sized cars. Tamsin supposed the hearse must have been parked there. "We didn't think anyone would be home."

They weren't here to pay their respects, that much was obvious. So why *were* they here?

"You must be his sister. Tamsin, isn't it?" Not only did he know Ollie; he knew who *she* was. It was difficult to know whether to feel threatened. Before Tamsin could form a breathless reply, he had dropped his gaze and was nudging the boy at her feet with the toe of his trainer. An angry-looking carpet burn highlighted his cheekbone. "Are you just going to lie there?" Then he stepped over him, a wide exaggerated step.

Tamsin found herself closing the front door behind them.

"Two years younger than him. That makes you, what? Thirteen?"

She winced, newly conscious of her red eyes, mussed-up hair, the creases down the front of her demure black dress, bought for a single purpose and newly redundant.

He nodded, giving no indication of having noticed any of these things. "Straight up, Ollie had something that belongs to us."

"The police haven't given us his things back yet."

"All he'd have had on him was Friday's deliveries. And like I say, it's ours." Whatever 'it' was, this was why they'd washed up at her door on the day of Ollie's funeral. "Mind if we take a quick look?" The second boy wasted no time and began to edge past.

Tamsin circled, keeping the distance between them, making sure she didn't turn her back on him. Both powerful and powerless, she had already broken any number of rules. "His room's locked. I've got no idea where the key is."

"Not to worry," he said pleasantly, then he was on the staircase taking two steps at a time.

Looking at the first boy take a run-up, Tamsin twigged. The grey head in the frosted glass, it hadn't been moving *away*. If she hadn't opened the front door – if she'd stayed in her room – they would have broken it down. And if not the door, then a window.

A series of loud thuds. All she could do was stand by and let whatever was going to happen, happen. Because that was the thing. When your time was up it was up; she knew that now.

A moment later, they were in. Unexpectedly, a surge of weightless exhilaration displaced any residue of fear.

"Ollie, you messy bugger!" the first boy scoffed, clutching his shoulder, the only words Tamsin heard him speak.

The good-looking one strolled to the centre of the floor and surveyed the chaos. "No one will ever know we were here."

That was the thing about not knowing you weren't coming home. You left your underpants inside out on the floor. But what Tamsin noticed – what stopped her in her tracks – was that Ollie had rearranged his furniture. His bed was no longer against the wall. She'd been blithely tapping Morse code into the back of his wardrobe.

Thirteen and a half years later, the room is a time capsule, opaque with dust so dense it resembles that iron-on stuff costume departments use to take up hems. *Will Jules bottle the dust? Or will he manufacture some kind of fake replacement dust?* She catches herself in the act of surveying the scene as if it were a job. A rough sketch showing the placement of furniture and props, detailed floor plans, front elevations marking up window and door openings. A 3D model. Everything will need to be photographed in situ and catalogued before it's packed away. And the unpacking and installation will have to be carefully supervised. She could help… If Jules happens to ask. Callously, dispassionately, from a purely professional point of view, it would look good on her CV.

Back then, Tamsin watched with a kind of helpless rapture as the two boys ripped open drawers, upended them onto the bed and rummaged ruthlessly through the fall-out. She remembers being acutely embarrassed for Ollie, not that they showed the slightest interest in his Teenage Mutant Ninja Turtle figurines. They were more interested in feeling around the insides of the drawers.

Emboldened, Tamsin asked, "What are you looking for?" While her mother was throwing a handful of earth on top of Ollie's coffin, she stepped over the threshold, the first time in at least a year that she'd entered her brother's room without an invitation. He'd had secrets, perhaps a whole secret life, and she wanted to know everything there was to know.

In places, the surface layer of dust has been flattened into footprints. Only one set. Jules's, Tamsin assumes, judging by the pointed shapes that mirror his ankle boots. She navigates carefully, standing inside the footprints, an awkward game of Twister. What caught Jules's eye as he stood here? What would he have been thinking?

"You really don't know?" the good-looking boy had asked, in a way that implied that she was naive.

She didn't want him to think that. "Of course I know!" Tamsin watched as the pair unshelved books, casting them aside or shoving them back into slots they'd pulled them from. Looked in the bottom of the wardrobe, grabbed at a shoe box. Shook pillows out of their cases. Lifted the mattress from several angles, letting it flop back down. They worked fast and were thorough. It was as much as Tamsin could do to remember exactly where everything came from so she'd be able to put it back again afterwards. There was too much, too much going on; a surreal version of Kim's game.

From time to time one of the boys pocketed a find. *Should I say something?* she wondered, but they were too quick and she struggled to see what those things were. Not so the cigar-sized roll of bank notes. Ollie would *never* have been able to save all that, not even from his birthday and Christmas money! Then, a stash of money bags, the kind the Post Office use for pound coins.

A gasp snagged in Tamsin's throat. Ollie was pretty dumb but surely he wasn't so dumb as to have brought drugs into the…? Had *she* been so dumb as to let *dealers* into the house? Is that what they were? As she took an involuntary step backwards, the good-looking one turned his head and grinned. *Got it now, have we?* Tamsin had been let in on a terrible secret. One she would never be able to tell.

She reassessed the boys. Her main knowledge of drugs came from soap operas and crime dramas that painted dealers with a grungy kind of glamour. How far up (or down) the chain were these two? More importantly, how far in had Ollie been? Perhaps he'd been blackmailed into working for them. But the money, the roll of money, said not.

It struck her then: maintaining the appearance of a bomb site had been Ollie's insurance. Mum was reluctant to venture into his room. Even now, all these years later, it might still contain secrets. The single bed, its pillow still crushed, its sheets wrinkled, draws Tamsin to it. The Sleeping Beauty she finds there isn't Ollie. It is her thirteen-year-old self.

Finally, after putting everything back in its rightful place, careful not to tidy anything away that hadn't been put away before, Tamsin lifted the duvet and climbed into her brother's bed. "Gross," she said, a typical thirteen-year-old but weighed down by things no thirteen-year-old should know.

Startled awake by the sound of her name, every muscle in Tamsin's body tensed. Even as she felt the vibrations of footsteps on the stairs, she knew she had to stay lying on Ollie's mattress, exactly as she'd planned before her discovery that the door was locked.

"What are you doing?" Mum's voice was appalled. "Get up! Get out of your brother's room."

Tamsin got up. In recent months she'd had to learn the real meaning of words she thought she already knew. Now she must learn how to put on a performance. She walked silently past her shaking mother, past the damage to the doorframe, so slight it might have gone unnoticed. With little proof anyone had been there, even if Tamsin told the truth, she wouldn't be believed. In any case, there was no way to admit that she'd let a pair of drug dealers into the house, then stood by and let them steal money from her dead brother. There had been no need for the boys to warn her to keep her mouth shut. Before leaving, the good-looking one had simply put one hand in his pocket and said, "Sometimes it's good to feel numb. Are you sure you won't...? No, of course you won't, a good girl like you."

"Tamsin!" her mother yelled.

"What?"

"Don't you have *anything* to say for yourself?"

Better to say, "I broke down the door." I broke down the door so that I could lie in my dead brother's bed. *I'm not doing this for you, arsewipe. I'm doing it for them. They don't need to know.* That's what she told herself as she listened to her mother's stifled weeping and, later, to the dentists-chair vibrations as her father drilled screws deep into the doorframe (how she wished she and Ollie hadn't clubbed together to buy that cordless drill for his fortieth).

I made a pretty good job of it, Tamsin thinks as she looks about her, although her professional eye detects subtle signs of staging. All said and done, over the years, I've made a pretty good liar. But as Tamsin learned first-hand from a newspaper headline – at her local newsagent's – her parents *had* known. They'd thought they were protecting her from the knowledge that Ollie died with drugs on him – probably why they'd locked the door in the first place.

"I'm sorry you had to find out like that," her mother said. That's all.

It would have been the perfect opportunity to come clean, but something inside Tamsin cried out, *Why? Why didn't you tell me?* Because then she wouldn't have had to keep her silence. All the time the grief counsellor was telling her to let her feelings out. And she might have done if she hadn't been so afraid of what else she would let loose. But by the time she became known as the girl who'd had a drug dealer for a brother, it was too late. Her parents had told her one time too many how they would learn to cope *as a family*. When she discovered how hollow those words had been, Tamsin turned inwards. The things they have protected each other from over the years! They don't bear thinking about.

With a great heave of her chest, Tamsin's anger disperses. The sight of Ollie's sagging, curling, fading things depresses her. Tamsin, who studied ancient history at A-Level, used to obsess about the rituals that surrounded death. No gilded figures here. No Fayum portrait never intended to see the light of day. Nothing is 'beautifully preserved'. Certainly nothing that would be of any use in whatever life comes after this one. Not Ollie's Nerf Gun. Not even his iPod. There will be no eternal resurrection for the boy king. This, after all, was her gobshite of a brother.

There's no way to admit what really happened on the day of Ollie's funeral, she thinks, as she pockets the padlock, its metal loop sheared through. The gesture has the feel of an ending. Whatever Jules creates from this wreckage will mean totally different things to her and Mum. There will always be this wall between them.

Tamsin retraces her steps, pausing once to look at the oval glass in the front door and again to put on her coat, pick up the manuscript and sling the strap of her handbag over one shoulder. She cannot be under the same roof as Mum tonight.

She makes her way to the kitchen doorway. "I think you should do it."

"You do?" And her mother's face looks so hopeful.

Tamsin tightens her mouth, then turns and leaves.

CHAPTER TWENTY-FIVE

Maggie, 2016

Maggie smooths the slim plastic bag on top of the pile.

"You know these things." Jules rubs the stubble of his chin. "What they represent. They are very precious."

"I think that's important. Don't you?"

He blows out air. "The idea, since Picasso, it is *as* important as the art. But, uh." He opens his mouth and now seems cautious about the way he exhales. "I don't know." He puts one hand over his mouth.

First the hate mail continuing after the verdict and now Rosie is going to be excluded all over again. Maggie can bear many things, but not this. "Does it make any difference that I want you to have her things?" She pushes at the pile. It slides so easily, the action has a desperate quality. Close to begging, Maggie is painfully aware of her own outsider status.

She has another lesser concern. Jules's exhibition – and her essential involvement in it (something she'd taken for granted) – is one of the few legitimate reasons she has to remain in London. Until she's given Alan what he calls her 'final decision', he's taken a room above a pub. She knows the place well; pictures him seated at the bar. In stilted telephone conversations, Maggie has found herself defending London. Its quiet corners, alleys where tarmac gives way to sudden cobble, the ruin-turned-garden of St Duncan's in the East, ivy creeping over lichened stone. Through glassless Gothic windows it is possible to frame the City, to hold its greed at bay. The mystery of a bricked-in doorway, of gravestones buried up to their midriffs.

After her first unscheduled foray, Maggie has returned several times to St Magnus's church. There, she sits with her aching emptiness and feels the silence. She has studied the stained glass. *This would be a place where I would like something small. A brass plaque.* Words with which she might pray evade her, but 20p buys a candle, and she can be still with thoughts of her daughter. In the past they followed a pattern. *If only she'd come home, we could have protected her.* Since Rosie has been numbered among the victims, there has been a divergence. Last week, as she watched the flame flicker orange in the dim light, a new thought came to Maggie. It didn't feel like betrayal or heresy. The thought was this: she was glad that Rosie made the decision to do what she did *when* she did. Because, even though a court ruled that she hadn't been responsible, Rosie would have *felt* responsible. And those who cannot find a way to move beyond their anger would have posted hate-fuelled letters through Rosie's front door, not hers and Alan's. Thirteen years of guilt would have worn her down until, one way or another, it destroyed her. Like Eric's sequence, the outcome would have been inevitable. It was simply a question of timing. This wasn't something she could imagine saying out loud, certainly not to Alan, and with that acceptance came a willingness to allow herself to weep, there in the shadows, where no one would see.

And so Maggie watches in agony as Jules considers her proposition, reluctance in every gesture. He sucks on his bottom lip; taps two fingers on the table. *Ba-boom. Ba-boom.*

Until this moment she hasn't considered the possibility that one of the letters might have been from him. No, perhaps not him, but his parents-in-law. It is entirely possible that Jules blames Rosie for his wife's death. Evelyn would still be here but for...

At length, Jules nods. *"Oui.* Yes, it matters that you trust me with Rosie's things." But he doesn't go as far as giving her the yes she craves, nor does he enthuse about her offering. Isn't it big enough, is that the problem?

Unable to endure the torture any longer, Maggie prompts, "What are you thinking?"

"Well," Jules says, as if he's been caught out. "I. Am. Thinking." He separates the words. "What I am actually thinking is of the Great Escape."

Unable to make this leap with him, Maggie's head shakes involuntarily. "The prisoners of war?"

"The film, actually. You know it? The scrounger, the tailor, the forger."

"Donald Pleasance?"

"Oui!"

"I have no idea where you're going with this." Maggie thinks she may cry again. She's going to cry.

"That is because my thoughts, they are a work in progress. Thoughts in progress, you can call them. I have some concerns, you see. For one, we have this London Underground uniform. Do you mind?" He gestures to the pile.

"Help yourself."

The uniform is in what is the largest of the plastic bags by a long way. Jules pulls it from the pile and lays his hands on it. Not for the first time, Maggie wonders if he can take an object and divine the history of those who owned it. There's a name for what she's thinking of, but she doesn't know what it is.

"I do not think that London Underground will be very happy if we put it on display," he says. "And I do not want anybody to march in and say, 'Give this back, it is ours!' So what I think is we make a replica."

It's not a no. He needed a solution, that was all. "You could do that?"

"The tailor, he do it with blankets and boot polish. We have technology on our side. You know, I will have to take the jacket apart to make a pattern, but I can sew it back together exactly as it is." He's frowning at the uniform jacket again. "I think maybe I change the logo."

Maggie can see the sense in what he proposes. "And the other things?"

"There is something very personal about a passport, n'est-ce pas?" He looks up. "We have the photograph, the next-of-kin, the record of where that person go. I also have a forger. He call himself an artist, but we both know the truth. And you know, the advantage is that this way we do not just display the item. We are entitled to call it art. The question I do not know the answer to is *how* we display it. For everything else, I have an idea, I recreate an Underground station, so what I ask myself is, where does it fit?"

Maggie closes her eyes momentarily. She doesn't want to openly disagree, but what he's said isn't right. "But Ollie's room…" she says. "That doesn't belong in an Underground station."

"Oh yes, you are right. And Unfinished Crib."

"A crib?"

"The crib Donovan make for his grandchild."

"Oh." This demands respect. "I didn't know."

"Nobody know. It is a secret. And he trust me with it. This half-made – well, not even half-made thing. It is very powerful. It is like art, because you pick up the pieces and you *sense* his emotion as he cut them." Jules leafs through a leather-bound notebook to a sketch. He slides the book across the table in a way that forces Maggie to take it. "It is my job to show all that love and that hope, so this is what I do."

On one page is a pencil drawing of a child's crib and on the opposite page is a sketch where individual pieces of wood are suspended. They are not simply floating. There is a sense of movement, of violence. The sketch shows a lightbulb hanging at the very centre of the piece, how shadows will be thrown onto the ceiling, the floor and the walls. As she studies the notations, Maggie is pricked with jealousy. By comparison her offering seems humble. Except that these were the items Rosie chose to be identified by. The promise she made to herself to go through with it. Surely it must be of equal value?

"I like what you've done," she says.

"Does it remind you of anything?"

"In a way. It's a kind of nightmarish children's mobile." When Jules looks blank, she adds, "You know, the thing you hang above a crib. For the baby to look at."

"I wonder…" Jules looks as if he's seeing his own sketch for the first time. "I wonder if we can make it rotate." He scribbles a note and at the same time says, "You know, Donovan is very keen for a monument. It is more important to him than the verdict. I do not think he has any idea how much it cost, the thing he has in mind. But if anyone can raise the money…"

Maggie can't return to what she wants to say without pause, and so she nods and waits a moment, possibly not quite long enough, before saying, "Do you mind if I make a suggestion?"

"No, I do not mind." He makes a hand gesture as if to say, *Go ahead.*

"It's like your great escape. It's a thought in progress."

"Then it is best to say it out loud."

"The only thing is, what I'm thinking of. It's been done before."

"*All* the best ideas are taken. The thing is to make it just different enough."

"If the exhibition space isn't going to be exactly like an Underground station, then maybe you need something to tie what's there together. What about a fake Tube map with the names of the fifty-nine in the place of the stations?"

"It all form part of a vocabulary, yes." He makes another note. "But I am also thinking how we create a sense of *désorientation,* you know. I want people to *feel* the panic, the claustrophobia. I need something that change the visitor's perspective."

"Will there be an escalator in the exhibition space? I mean, actually within it?"

"Within it? I do not know. Why?"

"I was just wondering if people could go down into the exhibition by escalator."

He gives a slow nod. "We make a tunnel over it. I have all the posters, the advertisements down the sides. We send noises up it maybe, like a wind."

Maggie picks up the *cafétière.* "Will you have another coffee?"

Jules checks his watch. *"Merde!* I am late to meet Eric. He is coming with me to look at the space. How long will it take to walk to Tate Modern?"

"From here? Forty minutes?" Maggie shrugs, and before she can stop herself she adds, "I didn't know Eric would be part of it."

"Well, you know, the only reason we are news is Eric's sequence and now his blog and the report he make into the book. Without him there is no exhibition. And." He shrugs and pushes back his chair. "The way I look at it, Eric is another victim. This thing, it almost destroy him."

She frowns. "I heard he has his ups and downs."

"More down than up, I think, but still he donate half his earnings from the book to our legal fund."

"I had no idea," Maggie falters.

"He is Eric. He does not shout about it. But it is not just him. Look at what the survivors go through. Look at Crisanto.

Even *he* is not numbered as a victim. Can that be right? You know, four people need hospital treatment for each person who die. Not even those who spend months in hospital are given a number; not even those who have their leg amputated. Excuse me for saying this, but it seem to me that in court you only matter if you die. That is *bullshit!* You know how many of the injured die since? There are not just fifty-nine victims. *You* are a victim, *I* am a victim, *my son* is a victim. And if your Rosie is a victim, then every other person who work at London Underground, they are also a victim. The police, the paramedic, the ambulance men…"

Maggie can do nothing but nod. Has she been so blinkered by sorrow that she hasn't considered the wider picture? Or was the wider picture more than she could bear?

"Come with me."

"Me?"

"You have some very good idea. In fact, maybe you want to help. Do you have a notepad and something you can write with?"

"I can lay my hands on them." She pulls opens a drawer in the console in the hall. "Yes."

When she looks up, Jules is studying the reproduction of William Holman Hunt's *The Scapegoat*. He recognises it, she is sure, and he recognises why it's hanging there. The red cloth wrapped around its horns represents the sins of the community and the animal has been driven into the wilderness. *A land not inhabited.* Alan has never commented on it, but she isn't sure Alan understands what it is. "Good." He jerks his gaze away, looks at what she has in her hands. "You will want to make some notes."

CHAPTER TWENTY-SIX

Tamsin, 2016

Moving out day. At the flat, Gareth is standing in the kitchen doorway. "Come here." He holds out his arms.

Tamsin goes to him, glad as he cocoons her, as she feels the scratch of lambswool on her cheek, that he refrains from saying more. At the same time part of her dares him to say, 'That wasn't so bad, was it?'

After a while has passed, he asks, "Want to tell me about it?" She feels the movement of his lower jaw through the top of her head.

"It felt so strange, leaving Mum behind." Her voice is muffled. If only she didn't feel so in-betweeny and out of tune with herself. Part of her will always remain in the house where she lived with, imitated, envied, and – according to Mum – adored, Ollie. That's to be expected. She imagines her mother on her way to the off licence, and feels the inevitable pull of guilt.

"She'll be fine." Gareth's answer to the question she's thinking grates. Instead of feeling cocooned, Tamsin is suddenly suffocating. *How can you possibly know that? How can you even say what 'fine' means?* Because it doesn't matter that she's seen what her mother is capable of on her good days. The period of furious activity immediately after Eric walked into their lives. The fierce highlighting and margin-scribbling as Mum strained her eyes over words that finally explained what had happened on that fateful Friday and why. How Mum helped Sorrel nurse Eric back to health after his breakdown. Tamsin's done her research. An alcoholic is never cured.

If he detects her tension, Gareth doesn't address it. Instead he asks, "So, is it official? Do you live here now?"

"I suppose I must do." She looks about her – at the mirror she sourced on-line, the hatstand she found in a Marylebone vintage shop – and has the odd sensation that she's standing in a set design. Something flimsy and insubstantial to be broken down and loaded onto a lorry immediately after curtain call, perhaps before the last member of the audience has even left the theatre. But life can be snatched away without warning, so the marbling effects on MDF and clever lighting that provides depth to what is shallow are justifiable. Just as it's justifiable to say something positive while reflecting on the truly awful thing you've just done. She both does and doesn't want Gareth to scoop her up and carry her into the bedroom, the action demanded by stage directions for happy endings.

"Good." The proprietary something that has entered Gareth's voice snaps Tamsin out of her reverie. Does she like it?

Suppose he hadn't said 'good'. Suppose he'd said nothing. If only she could be present in the moment; appreciate the feeling of the back of her head being cupped, set aside thoughts of Ollie's room, the padlock that's already weighing her down, something she has no idea what to do with and yet will never be able to discard; the kitchen that needs painting and will go unpainted unless she does it.

"OK?" he asks.

Caught in the act of thinking private thoughts, Tamsin nods, bumping his chin, and steps backwards, newly self-conscious. She's only just arrived and already she's craving her own space. There is one reception room and one bedroom. Where will she find privacy to read scripts, to store her notebooks and materials? The option of going to 'her room' no longer exists. Here, not even the bathroom door has a lock.

"Shall I crack open the bubbly or would you like a cup of tea?"

"Tea first. I'll just go and…" She indicates towards the suitcase and hold-all.

"Is there more in the car?"

"Some." Knowing this day was coming, she has been decanting things from house to flat. Her out-of-season clothes are already shrunk into vacuum bags under the bed, her favourite paperbacks have been shelved on the living room's single bookcase. The last-minute things are mainly creative projects; models she's spent her spare time working on this week, plus her laptop.

"I'll come down with you."

"I can manage," her voice erupts, harsher than she intended.

Gareth holds up his hands, palms showing, and backs into the kitchen. "I'll put the kettle on."

Gareth points the remote control and the image on the flat screen television shrinks to a small black rectangle. "Don't tell me you were watching that."

Tamsin, who is hugging a cushion to her chest, deadpans: "I was watching that." They have drunk the last of the prosecco, but the evening has been distinctly uncelebratory.

He slides the remote onto the coffee table, a careful movement and a dead giveaway that he's about to broach an uncomfortable subject. "I could actually hear your brain ticking over," Gareth says.

Tamsin smiles wryly at this prelude.

"This evening isn't just any other evening. It's the start of our new life!" He turns to face her. "Did I say something wrong?"

"No!" she insists. "I'm feeling a little weird, that's all."

"At the thought of living with me?"

"Of course not. The whole…" Why stop here? It would be easy to admit she finds change difficult. She delayed it long enough.

"Tell me one thing. Just one thing." It's a phrase Gareth employs so often that you might go as far as saying it's one of 'their' phrases.

Perhaps on this evening of all evenings, this new beginning, part of the reason Tamsin's so tense is that she's been expecting it. It seems that Gareth wants to possess not only everything she is, but all she has ever been. For someone who's worked so hard at holding everything inside, being picked apart one stitch at a time is agonising. She sighs. "Just one?"

He holds up an index finger, then swaps it for his little finger. "I won't even say anything."

He's so certain that whatever she is keeping from him has a neat beginning, middle and end. In Tamsin's experience, memories are far more slippery than that. Those she retains are indistinct, indistinguishable from nightmares. *If* she could have found her way back to the Ollie Mum talks about, she would have done. Not for Gareth's sake (though she wouldn't have excluded him), but for her own.

Where do you start when no subject is safe? Only one thing comes to mind, but it offers no guarantee of safety. "Remember Jules Roche, the sculptor?" She waits for his nod. "Tate Modern is going to put on an exhibition of his work."

"Wow!" Gareth mouths. His eyebrows remain raised as she continues.

"Maybe. The whole thing's about…" She tails off, then starts afresh. "You know how he's into recycled art?" Another

213

nod. "The families are being asked to contribute things he can make new pieces out of." Instinctively, Tamsin's hand feels for the cold solid outline of the sheared-through padlock. "The thing is, Mum wants to contribute Ollie's room."

No obvious reaction.

Every time Gareth used the bathroom at their home – Mum's house, she corrects herself – every time he stayed over, he passed her brother's padlocked door. If he thought the whole thing macabre, Gareth never actually came out and said it. Perhaps she needs to be clearer. "All of it," she adds.

"Hmm."

With no way to interpret the sound, Tamsin recreates it in her own throat, testing how it feels. Even then, she's undecided. "His room's been opened," she continues. "I saw inside, for the first time in years." She tightens her mouth. She decides to change tack. "I thought I might offer to help Jules."

"You should definitely do it. That would be great for your CV."

'Should' has always made Tamsin want to rebel. The fact that the exact same thing crossed her mind doesn't stop it from rankling. "That's what you think my priority should be? Beefing up my CV?" Saying this sets her heart thumping. Confrontation is something she normally goes out of her way to avoid. Tamsin can't understand how people say terrible things and expect to be forgiven. You say terrible things, people die, and the things you've said can never be taken back.

"Obviously not your *priority*. But that's no reason to ignore the fact that it'll give you an edge. I can't imagine that many set-designers can say they've helped stage an exhibition at the Tate."

"Tate Modern," she corrects him. "And I wouldn't be staging it." Even though that's precisely where her imagination has taken her. She already has several suggestions for how Jules might tweak his ideas. Exhausted, she leans forwards and puts down her empty glass. "Anyway, that's your one thing. I'm going to call it a night."

"Fine, but I *am* going to break through that wall you've built around yourself." Even though it's said in good humour, Tamsin tenses. "Preferably in a way that involves me not being afraid to ask how you are and you not jumping down my throat whenever I make a suggestion."

Tamsin has grown used to the idea that Gareth sees her as a damaged thing in need of fixing. Now she stands accused not only of blocking his efforts, but of punishing him for making them. She waits for the shouting, the lightning strike but nothing comes. "Is that it?" she asks.

He looks bemused. "For now."

She hadn't necessarily imagined sex – she's too tired for that. But curling up next to Gareth, stretching an arm across his chest, a leg across his legs… Now, he's taken that possibility from her. She pads to the bathroom and closes the door. Her eyes brim. *What have I done?* All this time she has been hoping for liberation. But this is not it. This is not it.

CHAPTER TWENTY-SEVEN

Donovan, early October 2003

"Pete." Donovan takes the hand Stefan's father offers and squeezes it. His mouth is a tight line. It is the first time they have seen each other since the funeral, a joint service, which meant sidelining personal preferences. In total, it's the fourth time they've met. "Sorry I'm so late."

"Well, you're here now. That's all that matters." Sadie displays no confusion about the nature of their relationship. She kisses Donovan's cheeks, then stands for a moment holding his forearms before looking about as if she's mislaid something. "No Helene?"

The corners of Donovan's mouth twitch. He's torn between anger at his wife's absence and the loyalty he owes her. Perhaps it's not 'anger'. That's the wrong word.

"Why didn't you say something earlier?"

"It's not that I won't go. I can't," Helene said, completely calm, completely measured.

"Well, it's too late to cancel. The Georges will already be on their way. They have further to travel than us."

"I'm not suggesting you cancel. I said that I won't be going. Not today and not on any other day."

This wasn't a spur of the moment reaction. It had been carefully thought through, and – the part that Donovan finds hardest to accept – the decision to delay the announcement calculated so that he had no option but to go without her.

"She's not feeling up to it, I'm afraid." He hopes to God his voice doesn't betray his inner turmoil, but Sadie appears to take him at face value.

Still holding his arms, she looks up at him. "You should have said! We could have rearranged."

How pinched Sadie's eyes look, how dark the circles underneath them are. *See! You're not the only one!* "I have to be honest with you," *and this is going to sound awful given that you've been through the exact same thing,* "I don't think she'll be feeling up to it anytime soon."

The Georges exchange furtive glances.

"I'm sorry to hear that." Pete doesn't sound sorry. If he's at all sorry it's because things are not as prearranged, as expected.

"But we have to start the probate process. There are important decisions to take..."

"You're not listening. I don't want to talk about money. Not now and not in the future."

With every one of her gestures, Donovan sensed that Helene was turning away from him, turning inwards. And what could he do? *"Alright."* He flapped his arms. *"Alright."*

Compelled to offer the Georges assurances, Donovan addresses what he hopes is Pete's chief concern. "It won't slow us down. I can speak for Helene."

But can he? His wife of thirty years has often surprised him, but never so much as when she said, "I can't." Used to having her at his side, *on* his side, he's rattled by her absence. With hindsight, Donovan can almost pinpoint the moment she reached her decision. It was on the day of the funeral. She hasn't left the house since.

"In that case." Sadie rallies and fishes in her handbag for her keyring.

The flat Cassie and Stefan called home is on the second floor. Far grander than Donovan's first home after he moved out of his mother's place, though there are certain similarities. Whitewashed walls. Identical front doors, each painted navy blue. Stairways that bring to mind his high school. A modern flat is a modern flat.

Except that as soon as Sadie has the door open, and the hallway offers what should have been a glimpse of Cassie and Stefan's lives, it is not. It isn't the same at all. Post, strewn on the doormat and beyond, a scattering of brown and white envelopes of varied sizes, and they are addressed, they are addressed to... He draws relief down into his lungs. *Thank goodness Helene isn't here.* But he doesn't need to imagine her reaction. It is mirrored in Sadie's face.

"I'll just..." As discreetly as he can, Donovan edges past, stooping to pull the envelopes towards him, squaring them into a pile. Official logos among the junk mail. Some of the very companies he notified so that no one should find them- selves in this unforgivable situation. *Why didn't you think of store cards?* Tesco. Boots. And this won't be the last of it. While arranging to have Cassie's post redirected, Donovan learned that an average of eighty items of post are addressed to deceased people in the year following their deaths. Eighty insults per person. One hundred and sixty cuts to the heart. Some will land on their own doormat for Helene to find. Some, no doubt, will land on the Georges'.

He moves further down the hallway, allowing Sadie and Pete some space. On entering the kitchen he calls over his shoulder, "I'll put the kettle on. I brought a pint of milk."

The dishwasher, he knows, has been emptied, as has the fridge. The rubbish has been taken out but nothing else has been moved. That was their agreement. From the doorway, he can see the postcards and photographs on the front of the fridge. He will be brave. He must. While still clutching the pile of envelopes printed with Cassie and Stefan's names, he looks at the grainy black and white ultrasound image. The profile of a boy-in-waiting. A boy made entirely of light and stardust and shadows. His nose, his lips, his tight little fists. Biding his time.

Footsteps behind him. Irrational though it may be, he sidesteps as if in fear of being caught red-handed. He stacks the envelopes on the work surface, then shrugs off his ruck-sack and unloads the milk, bin liners, three A4 pads, half a dozen biros wound up in a rubber band. Only once he's sure the Georges are seated in the living room does he remove the fridge magnet and turn the ultrasound image over so that he can read the words: *Holy shit, it's actually happening!* Cassie's handwriting. And underneath, Stefan's response, *I love you both so very, very much,* followed by enough kisses to embarrass a man like Donovan into putting the image back where he found it.

As he takes three mugs from an eye-level cupboard, his hands shake. *Holy shit.* He can hear his daughter saying the words, see her overjoyed face, zoom in on her eyes, her smile. He remembers how Stefan held fast to her hand, so proud, so confident, while she made the announcement: "We're going to have a baby." Excitement overflowing into laughter. Helene shrieked and jumped up to hug Cassie. And while she asked, "How many weeks?" he went to take Stefan's hand, but Stefan pulled him into a hug, and he felt himself go tense before he slapped Stefan's back, trying to think of something to say other than the obvious, 'Do I call you Son?' There must have been similar moments with his own parents, with Helene's, but he has no memory of them.

The tea made, he carries a tray into the living room – on the one hand a perfectly ordinary living room, on the other, a stale-aired frozen space where nothing is acceptable. Pete is sitting with one hand high on Sadie's back. She seems to be holding it together. They have sat in what Donovan knows as 'the visitors' chairs'. He scoots a coaster across the table and sets down a mug in front of Sadie. She stares at the pale brown liquid.

Pete speaks for her. "My wife doesn't take milk."

"I'm so sorry, I didn't think to ask…"

"No, I feel like milk today." Sadie picks up the mug and sips. "Mm. Much appreciated." Effort-filled words.

He returns to the kitchen for the paperwork (he could kick himself). There he scrunches his eyes shut. *Which chair should he take? How will Sadie feel if he sits in Stefan's chair?* On his return, he doesn't allow himself pause. He seats himself in what was Cassie's chair. "I hope you don't mind, but we made a list of questions and printed off some information about probate." Another thing that feels calculated. Helene's insistence that they made a checklist. Using the word *we* makes him all the more conscious of the empty chair next to him. "Oh, and I also made you copies."

Pete frowns at the paperwork but doesn't seem displeased. "It's a good job one of us is organised."

Donovan doesn't credit Helene in case the Georges reach the same conclusion he's arrived at. *She never had any intention of turning up.* "I don't expect two young people would have made a will," he says. It seems a terrible word to air.

"I wouldn't have thought so," Sadie agrees and glances sideways at Pete.

"We might find a trust deed with the mortgage," he offers.

Donovan adds *trust deed?* to his checklist and risks a wary smile. "Knowing my daughter, she'll have a comprehensive filing system." But where? He scans the room. Somewhere discreet, but not hidden.

Sadie picks up a biro. "Apart from the three of us, plus Helene, are there any other next-of-kin?"

This is the next question on Donovan's list. "Our parents are still alive, but I don't think they'd want to… You?"

"No."

The end of two family lines, two blood lines. He makes a note in the blank space he has left for the reply. "And do you think you'll administer Stefan's estate yourselves or appoint someone?"

Pete fields this. "We thought we'd wait until after today."

Donovan wonders if he should be wary of Pete. The hand-shake. The holding back. *But I'm the one who turned this into a business meeting.*

"It depends how complicated it looks," Sadie says, then shakes her head. "I know we have to, but it almost feels inde-cent to be talking about money."

"I don't care about the money. I don't want to talk about the money."

Donovan swallows. "Are we certain that we don't want to keep the flat and rent it out?"

"Positive." This from Sadie.

Pete gives what looks like a reluctant nod, but a nod it is. "So we're all agreed on that." Another note. "I assume Cassie and Stefan had equal shares."

"Maybe not." Pete tucks his chair under the table. *Pete cares about the money.*

"You're right. But do you have any idea about their other finances?"

"Salaries, savings…" says Pete.

"And debts, potentially."

Sadie's face registers alarm. "Oh, I don't think they were in debt."

"I only meant credit cards and unpaid bills."

Pete turns to his wife. "We loaned Stefan money for the deposit."

"Won't the proceeds from the flat take care of that?" she asks.

"I suppose my question is," Donovan steers the conversation, knowing what answer he'd like, "do we treat them as if they were married and split everything fifty-fifty? Or do we look at who paid for what, and who owed what?" He turns, quite deliberately, to Sadie.

She's ready with her reply. "Assuming we don't find a will, we should do what we think they would have wanted."

Pete shakes his head. "I'm playing devil's advocate here, but what if we discover they had separate bank accounts? Do we assume they wanted to keep everything separate?"

The fact is, Stefan and Cassie were not engaged. Helene had speculated that they might make an announcement when they introduced both sets of future grandparents to each other at what was effectively a celebration of the pregnancy. She mulled at length over the fact that it hadn't happened. It's possible it wasn't a priority. But it is also perfectly possible that they had no intention of getting married.

"All I'm saying is that we should try and put ourselves in their shoes." Sadie lays one hand on her husband's arm. "If they knew what was going to happen…"

From Pete: "There are going to be an awful lot of ifs, that's the problem."

Pete isn't being provocative, he's stating facts. There is potential for this to become tricky. It might be simpler to let solicitors handle the whole thing.

"I'm sorry, I'm sorry." Sadie shields her face. "This is another one of those things I never imagined finding myself doing."

Donovan shakes his head. "Me neither." Helene has made the choice not to, while others whose suffering is equal weren't aware they could exercise that option. "You take your time. I'm going to see if I can't find that filing system."

"You don't mind if we make a start in the bedroom?"

There are only so many places to look. In the sideboard, Donovan locates an expanding document holder with concertina-ed, alphabetised sections. One is labelled 'mortgage'. There, in chronological order, is everything from the estate agent's details, the mortgage application, correspondence with solicitors, title deeds and the trust deed that Pete spoke about. The mortgage application clarifies a number of previous unknowns. Cassie earned more than Stefan, but so what? He skims the trust deed. *Unequal shares.* Even with the Georges' loan, she'd stumped up more of the deposit. He's proud that his daughter was smart about protecting her investment. But that was before… And on the basis that they seem to have gone fifty-fifty on repayments and household expenses, Stefan contributed the greater portion of his salary. Plus, who knows how they planned to fund Cassie's maternity leave? Everything evens out. But what, he wonders, would Pete do with this information?

"Hey, stop it! Why are you pointing that thing at me?"

Donovan's heart stammers. The flow of his blood reverses. As Cassie's voice spools through his mind, paperwork flutters from his hand. He is here in his daughter's flat. Half an hour ago her voice was inside his head, but this isn't imagined. It is Cassie speaking.

"It's a video camera."

"I can see what it is. My question was why are you pointing it at me?"

Donovan listens intently. Again, he has a deep sense of doing something he shouldn't. He's eavesdropping, and if he so much as breathes, he'll be caught out.

"What have you got there?" he hears Pete ask.

"What does it look like? It's a camcorder."

"Wait a minute, Sadie. Pause it."

Every emotion Donovan has tried to tamp down is on the rise. Unsteadily, he clambers to his feet. It feels like a long way up.

Sadie gives a sharp laugh. "Why?"

"Number one, we need to ask Donovan. But think about it… Think about where you found it."

He's only aware that he has arrived outside the bedroom when Sadie looks up at him. "Donovan," she says, flustered. She's sitting on the bed and has in her lap a silver camcorder, the screen sticking out like a wing mirror. "Pete thinks I've just found a sex tape."

Pete, who is standing, folds his arms across his chest. "That is *not* what I said!" At this correction, Sadie colours dramatically and hangs her head. "But think before we wade in. This might be private."

Pete could be right, Donovan cautions himself. Already, he's seen details Cassie didn't choose to share with him. That was a legitimate invasion of privacy, but this? This is different.

"What do you think, Donovan?" Though Sadie's voice is defiant, her eyes plead as if he alone holds the answer.

His will be the deciding vote. He tries to think what Helene would say, but knowing this thing exists… "Is there anything to suggest…?" He censors himself.

"It's just Cassie sitting cross-legged on the living room floor. From what she's wearing, I'd say she was doing yoga."

"She's your daughter." Pete spreads his hands, clearly exasperated. "I'll be in the living room."

As he walks down the hall, Sadie leans to one side and calls after him. "What would you have us do? Delete what's on the tape?"

This idea so appals Donovan that it leaves only one alternative.

"I'm sorry," Sadie says. "I shouldn't. Not in front of you."

He dismisses her apology with a shake of his head and sits down next to her. "Could you rewind to the beginning?" he says and covers his mouth with one hand. He cannot breathe for wondering what he will see.

"Hey, stop it! Why are you pointing that thing at me?"

"It's a camcorder."

"I can see what it is. My question was why are you pointing it at me?"

Tears gather in his eyes. Cassie is brought back to life and, my God she's so like her mother.

"I bought it to record our pregnancy journey."

"Please tell me that's some kind of joke."

It feels like a gift. It feels like a fresh loss. Such a terrible waste. Beside him, Sadie mutes a laugh. She looks almost girlish.

"I thought it would be nice."

"Nice? Is that something you read?"

"No."

"Is it something all the expectant fathers are doing these days?"

"No."

"No? Then turn that thing –"

The segment ends with a shot of the ceiling. Sadie looks at him, silently asking for permission to continue. These young people, so full of life, such energy. The idea that they are gone, and with such suddenness, such permanence. He nods his consent.

"Today we have just got back from shopping." The camera is less steady this time. Either Cassie has come round to the pregnancy journey idea or is out for revenge. *"Remind me what we were shopping for, Stefan."*

"A cuddly toy."

"And why did we go shopping for a cuddly toy?"

"Because you have a phobia about plastic dolls."

"Because we have to take a toy to our first NCT class and pretend it's a baby."

"I offered you Action Man, but you turned him down."

"Yeah, on that point, viewers, whoever you may be..."

Donovan holds his breath. Cassie is no longer speaking to the camcorder. She is speaking to him. *"I don't know why, but there's something very wrong with the idea of pretending I've given birth to Action Man. In fact there's something wrong about pretending I've given birth to a teddy bear. So in my wisdom I thought I'd let Stefan choose. Go on. Show them what you chose."*

On the small-scale screen, Stefan holds up an unidentifiable animal. Blue with large violet-coloured ears. A tuft of blue hair on its head.

"What *is* that?" Donovan asks.

Mesmerised by the image of her son, Sadie gives a small shake of her head. She wouldn't care what she found on the film. She would carry on watching, just to have this piece of him. *Could Helene have been persuaded?* he wonders. *If he'd been in a position to tell her there was a video.* And in the next instant, *Does she even deserve to know?* He flinches from the unworthy thought.

"It's only one of two options."

"You didn't choose Lilo, who is a human child. You chose Stitch. Who I think is supposed to be a dog."

"As I say, one of two options."

"And what is the other option?"

Slowly, grinning, Stefan brings his second choice into view. It's an ET doll. *"Twentieth anniversary edition. Complete with removable blanket."*

Sadie pauses the tape and sniffs. "It's all fine," she calls out to Pete, then as an aside to Donovan, says, "We'll make you a copy," before pressing play again. It hits him hard. He will not be taking Cassie home with him today. This head-spinning knowledge is unbearable. But you heard Stefan. *He* bought the camera. Donovan resolves to hoard every word, absorb each expression.

"Changed my mind!"

Stefan turns the camera on himself. *"They just showed us the birth video."*

"Not doing it. No way."

He lowers his voice. *"I have to be honest. Bit squeamish. I just looked in the general direction of the screen. The noises were bad enough."*

"This is your fault."

"That's very kind, but I can't take all the credit. I think it was fifty-fifty."

"They gave me a homoeopathy kit for the pain! A fucking homoeopathy kit!"

Donovan winces at his daughter's language, but beside him, though her eyes are brimming, Sadie is laughing.

"I'll just go and make some tea," Stefan confides to the camera.

Both parents swipe away tears.

"I can't quite believe it," Sadie raises her eyes to meet his. "I think I need to ration myself, if that makes sense."

"Perfect sense," Donovan says, powerfully wanting more.

"Our wonderful, wonderful children."

"They made quite a double act," Donovan concedes, hating the intrusion of the past tense. "Stefan had his work cut out for him."

"Oh, he gave as good as he got. He adored Cassie. That much is obvious." She lowers her head and takes a minute. "Did you find the paperwork you were looking for?"

"I didn't find a will, but everything else, yes. I'll take copies so you can see what's what, but you heard him. I say fifty-fifty on everything."

A slight noise from outside the door makes them both jolt and look up. Pete.

"You'll have no arguments from me."

CHAPTER TWENTY-EIGHT

Eric, 2010

By studying time-lapse photography of foot-traffic flow on walkways and stairs, we can see just how severely human space requirements have been underestimated. Environments created without proper appreciation of the relationship between traffic-flow and the space requirements of pedestrians will be inherently hazardous. Tube stations date from 1863, so that must be true of them. In some instances, overcrowding has resulted in loss of life. Eric writes Underestimation of human space requirements on a Post-it note.

For the few short hours each night when he sleeps, Eric dreams the sequence. It has passed from his conscious to his subconscious. What at first seemed complex, he now understands to be a mathematical equation, pure and simple: a + b + c = inevitable outcome.

It's instinctive, but he knows exactly where in the sequence this new sticker belongs. He stands and moves several dozen Post-it notes along the busy wall to create a space. "I'm hurrying," he answers, automatically.

Deeper and deeper into the morass Eric wades. He comes to articles about crowd forces. This is where he'll find Oliver Wicker and all the unignorable others whose images tumble and writhe behind his eyelids. For the first time, he has nothing left to give. "Not tonight," he says. He cannot face reading another word. For once, the fifty-eight skulk away, shoulders hunched.

It is his own face he sees in the bathroom mirror. *How do you process this stuff if you were actually there?* Eric asks his reflection, but the question is rhetorical. He knows that your mind protects you from the worst, then releases it over time, like a slow-release caffeine pill. The living aren't haunted by the dead, but by the images their eyes have refused to process. Eric processes images on behalf of the dead.

Away from the work, he feels on edge. Fretful he'll forget something, he constantly jots things down as soon as they occur to him. The margins of his lecture notes fill with scribbled messages. He's never entirely present. Like competing children, the wraiths tug at his sleeves. They refuse to play second fiddle to anything or anyone. He's been known to dig out pen and paper while friends are mid-sentence, confiding disappointing exam results or raw details of a break-up. Where they might reasonably expect him to commiserate, he props a notebook against his chest or rests it against his thigh, saying, "Carry on. I'm listening," not even pausing when he hears their exhalation of disbelief and the "Fuck you, Eric." More than deserved but he can do nothing about it. After he's nailed the sequence, then he'll make it up to them.

With Sorrel off visiting her mother who's come down with a nasty strain of flu, and Andy staying over at his girlfriend's, there is no one to tell Eric it's time to stop working. Later, as arranged, he meets Sorrel from the Sunday evening train. Clammy, jittery and in a manic mood, he hasn't slept since Friday.

"Give me your bag. How was your mother? Did she like the chicken soup?"

She frowns. "You're twitchy."

"No I'm not. I'm just pleased to see you. How was your journey? Was the train OK?"

"Mum was much better. Have you eaten?"

"I thought I'd wait and treat you to fish and chips."

"I don't mean tonight. I *mean* since Friday."

"Of course I've eaten!" he dismisses her, but the truth is he has no recollection of whether he has or not. No matter. He'll eat now.

Back in front of the keyboard, Eric steels himself. The cause of almost all the deaths was compressive asphyxia, what happens when people are stacked on top of each other. At the 1971 Ibrox football disaster, bodies were piled ten feet high. This has been Eric's vision these past two years. He's raised corpses from the dead, and stacked them back into the piles they died in, and they're none too pleased about it. People at the bottom of the pile would have experienced chest pressures of 3600-4000N (800-900lbs), assuming half the weight of those above was concentrated in the upper body area. Assuming the piles were neat, in other words. But his visions tell him they weren't. There it is then. How the majority of the fifty-eight, Oliver Wicker among them, met their ends. He closes his eyes and counts a minute's silence, making no attempt to silence the sound of weeping.

"You look like death."

"Hello to you, too."

A closer look and Sorrel revises her opinion. "Actually, you look worse than death."

"Well, that goes a long way towards explaining why, out

of a large number of applicants, I was chosen to be the Grim Reaper."

"What you need is an evening away from all this." She gestures at the notes, the statements, the report, his screen.

It is Sorrel's concern, the lack of accusation that he's been neglecting her, that makes Eric agree. If he's honest, he's also swayed by the results of his annual eye test, shaken by confirmation of something he'd suspected. Significant deterioration in the space of a year. After he reported headaches, the optician showed far too much interest in his general health for Eric's liking. Then came questions about screen time. "Heavy use," she said as she wrote his answer on the card. "I know it's difficult. Study, exams; I was the same. But eyes are like any other muscles. If you don't exercise them, they get weak. And if you only train them to look at things that are a foot in front of your face… well." Another inevitable outcome, apparently.

He looks up from his screen and says to Sorrel: "Why not? Let's go to the pictures."

"Really?" She sidles onto his lap; drapes her arms around his neck. "You'll take a whole evening off?"

"What are you doing right now?"

"I'm going to get ready," she jumps up, "before you change your mind."

If Eric had anticipated how watching a film about something completely unrelated would free the trapped connections in his mind, he would have suggested it earlier. They file out through the cinema foyer, bypassing popcorn dispensers and the queue for the late-night show. Eric is about to suggest a pint but Sorrel gets there first. "I've been thinking." Never a good prelude, guilt sets Eric's warning bells ringing. Sorrel's best friend at uni has just moved in with her boyfriend. It's not as if the subject of co-habiting hasn't come up, but with Eric's unreasonable hours and Sorrel's unashamed need for sleep, a solution has evaded them. The fact is, Eric has never quite understood what's in their arrangement for Sorrel and he's afraid to ask. His flatmate Andy, on the other hand, hasn't held back.

"I still don't get it. You could have me. What do you see in the ugly bastard?" he has asked while cramming Marmite on toast into his mouth at the kitchen table, when he passes Sorrel on the narrow staircase, when he emerges from the bathroom with a thin yellow towel draped around his waist. And depending on her mood, and whether or not she thinks Eric can hear, Sorrel's answer has varied.

"Let me think. Oh, yeah. He's passionate, and you're an arse."

Once she stumped him by saying, "His enormous knob."

"He sees past this." Eric had to imagine which part of her anatomy she was pointing to; whether or not she flashed Andy. "And thinks of me as a person."

Eric wonders if she chose him, at least initially, to make the point that she doesn't prize looks highly. Eric used to be fun – he used to be *funny.* Now, he must accept that he's neither. As for Sorrel, her relationship with looks (her own and other people's) is complicated. She hates the fact that people – and by 'people' she means men – can't see beyond her blonde hair and tits (her word, not Eric's). But she's not the type to uglify herself.

"Did you know? Women who wear make-up to work get paid significantly more than those who don't?" she's told him. "*You* could roll out of bed and rock up looking like *that.*" And when he's responded to her gesture with a mildly offended *thanks*, she hasn't been in the least apologetic. "That's the world we live in. People might not notice me unless I'm wearing lippy. When they *do* notice me, they make assumptions. But if I *don't* draw attention to myself, then they won't discover there's a brain in here."

Though he wouldn't dream of saying so, Eric, who never

doubted Sorrel's intellect, thinks she enjoys the power the attention she receives lends her.

But this isn't going to be one of those conversations. To his surprise, Sorrel asks, "When are you going to contact the families? You can't carry on with your research indefinitely, not without checking they're on board."

He feigns incredulity. "I thought I was having a night off." They are just outside the main exit, at the top of faux-marble steps.

She elbows his ribs, a gesture full of knowing. "Don't give me that."

"Am I that obvious?"

"Your eyes drift when your mind wanders, and tonight they were all over the place." She finishes her reply with what she may have intended to be a quick kiss, but Eric grabs the lapels of her long black winter coat and reels her in. Through the kiss, he feels Sorrel's mouth widen into a smile. *She can't be too unhappy then.* It's probably because they're kissing in public, and spontaneous displays of affection aren't something Eric's given to. If he's honest, he's become an 'OK, I can spare half an hour, get your kit off' kind of guy. Judging by the sound of faltering footsteps, people are having to skirt around them. The thought of disapproving looks brings a smile to his own lips. When eventually they come apart, Eric surprises himself by not pulling away. "I couldn't do this without you, you know."

"I know," she says simply. "And no one else would put up with you."

"You're not wrong there. Should we get out of the way, do you think?"

"You're going nowhere. Kiss me again."

CHAPTER TWENTY-NINE

Gina, 2010

Walking home from the latest in a succession of unstimulating temp jobs, Gina encounters a memory so vivid it's like bumping into her former self. The muted black and white of barely-alive days is transformed into uproarious colour. She is marching her children along the pavement, one small salty hand in each of hers, her mind several feet ahead. Her schedule has slipped, all because she stopped to admire a pair of Adidas trainers.

There they were. Three perfect turquoise suede stripes contrasting with the navy blue. "Tamsin, can Mummy have a quick look at something?"

"Fetch Ollie now." At three years old, her daughter finds it unacceptable to be parted from her brother for longer than is absolutely necessary. She wants to be everything he is, do everything he does. Tamsin's protests almost broke Gina's heart when her daughter learned she wouldn't be allowed to go to school with Ollie; when Gina explained that she wouldn't be allowed to go to school for another two years. The suggestion of a compromise – a nursery – met with angry protest. Either Ollie should be allowed to stay at home with her or she must be allowed to go to school with him.

Unfinished Sympathy lured Gina inside. "Mummy will only be a minute, I promise."

"I'm just looking," she announced before the shop assistant, more Madchester than Croydon, had the chance to ask if he could help. But the fact was she'd already picked the trainers up.

"May as well try them on. I bet you're a size six. Am I right?"

Gina studied her feet from every angle, remembering something about the person she used to be. In retrospect, her life seemed like a blur of gigs, open mic nights and comedy clubs (she'd never been one for clubbing).

The shop assistant stood by, head cocked, arms folded. "You know when you've been tangoed, right?"

But how could Gina justify spending such a huge amount of money on herself? Those few short years when she wasn't contributing to the family coffers were such an enormous source of self-imposed guilt, she felt bad about spending *any* money on herself.

"What do you think, Tamsin?" But her daughter was down on hands and knees, investigating a circular porthole in the side of the wooden cube that served as a seat.

There was *some* justification. Next to the blue suede trainers, her sneakers looked scuffed and muddied, the laces grey.

"Try them at home. You can always bring them back."

Home! Checking her watch created sufficient panic to force a decision. "I'll take them. In fact, I'll keep them on."

And the result of this extravagance is that there's a machine-load of washing to hang out, the kids' tea to prepare – it will have to be fish fingers – tomorrow's sandwiches to make, then the beginning of the bedtime routine.

They're about to pass the alley that leads to the children's playground when Ollie pulls up sharply and stamps down a regulation school shoe. "No, Mummy, no!" Cheeks flush with righteous indignation, he struggles free of her grip.

Here come the demands for swings and slides. *Pleeease,* the battle will begin, intensifying sharply. Perhaps it's the Adidas trainers reminding Gina of life before kids, but suddenly the demands of motherhood seem overwhelming. The ups and downs, the mood swings, the meltdowns, the Oscar-winning sodding drama of it all. "What have I done now?" she asks, trying to sweep exasperation from her voice.

But instead of pleas, Ollie shrugs. "You're standing on a crack in the pavement. That's ten years' bad luck."

'Stand on a crack and you'll be eaten by bears' is the line Gina's grandma used to trot out. It didn't matter that the nearest bear was safely behind bars at Chessington Zoo, Tamsin did as she was told. "*Ten* years?" she protests. "You only get seven for breaking a mirror."

"Well…" Ollie has that intense look of concentration, the one he wears when he's run out of fingers and the sum moves inside his head. "It's just gone up!"

"That can't be right." As Gina pretends she's about to step on another crack, Tamsin shrieks loudly enough to vibrate eardrums. A proper grown-up woman wearing a black business suit, ten denier tights (without a single ladder), and four-inch heels throws her a look of pure disgust, recoiling from the sight of Tamsin in Ollie's cast-off anorak, orange, not ugly in itself but ugly on a girl. Gina pulls on her daughter's hand. What she wants to say to the towering woman is, 'I didn't make her wear it. She insisted.' Before they left the house, rather than slot them into the sleeves of her pink jacket, Tamsin folded her arms across her chest. Nothing could persuade her. With wilful toddlers, you pick your battles carefully.

Oblivious to the looks she's attracting, Tamsin points to Gina's feet. "Oh no, 'nother crack!" she says dramatically and does a little run on the spot.

"Eleven years!" Ollie pronounces his verdict.

"What do you think I should do?" Gina looks down in mock dismay but all she sees is the trainers (secretly, she's delighted by them, and will continue to be delighted, even after the Barclaycard bill betrays her extravagance).

Ollie takes control. "Jump off it. Quick!"

She obliges, light on her feet. "You'd better warn me when there's another one. I can't afford *twelve* years of bad luck."

If Gina anticipated a warning that wouldn't scare passing dogs, she's proved wrong.

"Crack!" shouts Ollie and she hops onto one foot, lifting the other behind her. Not to be outdone, Tamsin yells, "CRACK!"

A neck turns. *Why can't mothers discipline their children?* On another day, Gina might have hushed her brood: 'Quiet! You're hurting my ears.' Today, she lands on both feet, her knees bent, awaiting her next instruction. "CRACK!" comes in unison. She hopscotches home flanked by small feral children. It's a deliciously rebellious feeling. "CRACK!" is Gina's new definition of freedom.

"Evening," a voice says.

"Evening," Gina says on autopilot. As her children's hands slip from hers, her head jerks up in dismay to see which neighbour has summoned her back to the present. Those blue suede trainers she was secretly thrilled with have been replaced by easy-fit black pumps. There are no paving slabs beneath her feet. Tarmac is more practical for kids haring around on scooters. Once again, Gina is her strung-out weary self.

The itch returns, the creeping itch for that first drink of the day. The weight of a litre of Gordon's has tightened the handles of the plastic bag, bunching the skin of her fingers into ugly welts. She drinks to escape the voice in her head that reminds her what a bad mother she was for not knowing what a monster her son had become, for failing to keep him off the streets and under control. She failed Tamsin too, that's the truth. Everything from the way she broke the news onwards. How are you supposed to tell a child her adored brother is dead? (How it pains her when Tamsin insists she can't remember the long hours she and Ollie played together.) Be clear and direct was the advice. Don't avoid words like 'dead' and 'killed'. No words can make the news any worse. But my God, the sound of those words, spoken aloud. And then Tamsin's wailing!

She will make amends. Gina will share this story with Tamsin in the hope that she can add it to the small store of older memories that haven't been crowded out by the new. Gina attempts to slot herself back inside the memory so that she can cement the detail in place, but it isn't something she can conjure at will.

Damn her neighbour!

Eleven years' bad luck. Here's a summary of the interven-ing years in mental arithmetic. It was ten years later that Ollie went out and didn't come back home, ten years later that they told her Ollie was a stranger and she lost him a second time; eleven years before the newspapers outed him as a small-time drug dealer (as if his lack of success made his choice worse). And of course Tamsin had to find out by reading it on the front page of a newspaper, so Gina lost her daughter's trust as well. It was there, according to Ollie, that Gina's run of bad luck should have ended. High time too, because what could anyone take that hadn't already been taken? But the very next year, the Coroner declared that Ollie had not only contributed to his own death but to those of others, and two years further down the line, having allowed themselves to be convinced that a civil court would see things differently, the families' class action failed.

Logic should dictate that Gina's run of bad luck didn't start with an extravagant purchase, but since unimaginable things started to happen, logic has loosened its grip on her life. Perhaps she should have been more superstitious. She carelessly trod on cracks in the pavement, when even a five-year-old knew this was foolhardy.

Gina is on the garden path before she notices the two people standing in her porch. She sags inwardly. Had she seen them, she might have walked past the gate and kept on walking. The couple turn, a young man with a laptop bag slung across his body and a young woman. Gina had hoped the days of newspaper reporters, those self-appointed judges, showing up uninvited were over. "Can I help you?" she asks sarcastically. What she wants is this and only this: to see Tamsin, who'll be upstairs working on her latest 3D model, and tell her the story about the cracks in the pavement. Then, after she has told Tamsin once more how much she missed Ollie while he was at school, she'll pour her first gin, and will drink steadily until she can avoid going to bed no longer.

"We rang the doorbell but no one answered," the girl says. There's an awkwardness about the way she holds herself – just a little too straight – but it's nothing compared to the nervous energy her companion gives off.

"So you thought you'd wait, did you?" Without checking to see if her sarcasm hits its mark, Gina fishes in her handbag for her keys, annoyed when the pair don't take the hint.

"We'd very much like to talk to you, Mrs Wicker."

Gina flinches. Worn these past twenty years, 'Mrs Wicker' has always felt like an ill-fitting dress, part of the pretence of being a grown-up. She doesn't object when it's attached to her children's names, names she chose with great care, repeating them many times until she was satisfied that they paired well with her husband's surname. Ex-husband, as he'll soon be.

"But there aren't any Olivers in the family," her mother-in-law said. And later, bewildered, "We don't even know any Tamsins." Which gave Gina a great deal of satisfaction.

She turns on the young man and points the sharp end of her front door key at him. This is her house and she wants them to leave. "Look, if you're from the papers –"

"We're not!" Abrupt in denial, this boy captures her attention. He has ginger colouring, skin that looks as if it sees little daylight, dark shadows under bloodshot eyes. *You look almost as appalling as I feel.* He pulls at one earlobe and repeats, "But we'd very much like to talk to you, Mrs Wicker."

Conscious of the bottle of gin suspended in the plastic bag, of its weight and of wanting to crack open the seal, Gina says, "You know my name. You know where I live. I seem to be very much on the back foot."

"I'm sorry." The young man shakes his head, but his attitude suggests relief. "Eric. Eric Carwood. And this is Sorrel Malloy. We thought it might be easier to speak to you in person."

"You mean you thought it would be trickier for me to be rude to your faces. So tell me," she demands. "What do you want?"

"We've – at least Eric." The girl is humble, apologetic. "Eric's spent every spare moment of the past three years studying your son's case. Not just your son's case. The whole fifty-eight." She tucks a loose strand of hair behind her ear. "He thinks the result of the first inquest was wrong."

"Then he's wasted his time." Gina's voice runs flat. "We've known that all along."

But the boy at her elbow seems determined to be heard. "Is that a gut feeling or do you understand why?" He lifts the flap of his bag, thumbs through papers. "Because I can demonstrate that crucial arguments were missed."

Gina closes her eyes momentarily, but the view behind them is far, far worse. "And who are you? Who do you represent?"

"Ourselves." Eric's voice is quizzical, as if it's peculiar she feels this question is necessary. His face is as open as any Gina has ever seen, it's true.

Bill always complained she was taken in too easily. Now she must police her own borders. "But who made my son your business? You see, we've been bled dry by ambulance chasers." There was enough blame to go around, the families were told. Some felt they deserved their pain to be measured in pound signs, but all Gina ever wanted was assurance that no one else would ever have to go through what she went through. Not that she'd have been in any position to turn down compensation if it was offered. "Their promises came to nothing." She doesn't feel bitter, just very, very tired.

Eric opens his mouth as if to speak but then pauses. The corners of his mouth quiver and he looks down at his feet.

Gina follows his gaze. He's wearing black plimsolls, the type she remembers from school gym, shoes that became all the rage for students in the eighties. He is pale, exhausted and wearing cheap fabric shoes and he's spent three years researching the fifty-eight. Why? It strikes her. "You knew Ollie?" Compelled to reach for his arm, Gina's fingers wrap around his thin wrist.

"No." He shuffles his feet, then glances at the girl – Sorrel, wasn't it? "I'm sorry, Mrs Wicker. We shouldn't have turned up on your doorstep."

The young man removes his arm from her grip, nods to the girl and they turn away. Who *are* they? Suddenly it's imperative that Gina keeps them here. She calls after them. "If you'd phoned I would have said no."

The pair turn again. In the girl's eyes she sees both hope and acknowledgment of her own hope. "You said he's been studying the case for three years."

"Every spare minute." Behind Sorrel's ready gaze, something burns. Pride.

Gina looks from one face to the other. If they're together, they're as mismatched a couple as she's ever seen. "If that's the case you deserve five minutes of my time." She turns the key in the lock. "Come in, both of you." She beckons, then shouts up the stairs, "Tamsin, I'm home!"

Eighteen. It is eighteen years since Ollie and Tamsin yelled "CRACK!" all the way home, but only today that she remembered it.

A muffled reply could either be hello or I know. Satisfied, she answers an unasked question. "Twenty-one. She's studying set-design."

"For the cinema?" Sorrel asks.

"The theatre." Gina nods towards the living room door. "Go through. I'll put the kettle on."

The boy calls after her. "Is Mr Wicker home?"

She pauses, fixes a smile in place and then turns. "We're separated. Soon to be divorced."

"Oh, I'm sorry," the girl says and glances at the boy. "We didn't know."

"Why would you?" Gina shrugs, not yet understanding that Eric has made it his business, as far as is humanly possible, to find out what has happened to each member of the families. Any lack of knowledge he sees as a personal failing.

Five minutes later they are seated around the low coffee table, though none of them is sitting comfortably. Eric retrieves a stapled sheaf of papers from his bag. "This is just to give you an idea."

Gina takes his offering, a numbered list. She puts on her reading glasses and frowns. About half of the items are highlighted in yellow. "What am I looking at?"

"The sequence." He pulls on an earlobe again, a habit she'll come to know. When sitting opposite him, Gina will occasionally catch herself mirroring this gesture. "Every factor I could identify that led to the accident."

This isn't the hard sell Gina was expecting. Her hands are shaking and the papers are rustling. (When she and Tamsin eat dinner together, Tamsin only needs to lower her gaze to the cutlery in Gina's hands for her to know she's been caught out. Unable to control the shaking, just as she's unable to control the itch.) "This is three years' work?"

"There's a full report backing up every point and cross-referencing all the information I sourced."

"And the items you've highlighted?"

He shifts forwards in his seat. "Those are points that weren't included in the initial investigations."

Gina takes a sip of tea, nothing like the crisp cool hit she craves. "All of these, they're new?" It's a struggle to process what she sees in front of her. "So they weren't put to the Coroner?"

"And they didn't come up in the public inquiry."

Sorrel is quick to add, "Or the class action."

"Maybe information wasn't as easy to access at the time." Eric takes the lead again. "I found most of this stuff by following trails on the internet. Maybe they didn't think it was relevant. Or," he shrugs, "Maybe it was inconvenient."

Deliberately excluded! Gina flips to the final item, numbered 248. "Who else has seen this?"

Eric shakes his head. "You're the first." That open boyish expression returns. "I wanted it to be you. I've always... I felt a connection with Oliver. I'm not much older than him, an ordinary lad, no saint." His pale skin colours.

"We should have hired you!"

Eric grimaces. "Oh, we're not for hire. I'm still a year off being able to get a job as a trainee solicitor."

"You're a student?" It seems so obvious now he has said it. His nervousness, the shoes, how thin his wrist is.

Eric defers to Sorrel. "We're both law students."

"And this is what? A joint dissertation project?"

"No, no, it wasn't study." Keen to correct misunderstandings, Eric still seems reluctant to explain what's actually happening here.

"Then what?" Gina coaxes.

He lets go of the breath he's been holding in. "In my first couple of years at uni, I worked for a company that specialised in ghost tours. My tour was called Ghosts on the Underground. Let's just say I developed… an interest."

"An obsession, more like!" The change in Sorrel's expression suggests she'd like to take back what she's just said. From this, Gina understands that the project has become the thread of Eric's existence. He will follow it through to the end. "What I *mean* is that this is real – the first time we weren't just studying case law. This is an injustice and, what's more, it's ongoing."

"It was resolved." Gina points this out as if breaking bad news. Already, she senses the toll this project has taken on the boy sitting in front of her. "We took it as far as we possibly could, and we lost."

Gina is surprised when Eric matches her tone. "We think it's worth another shot."

"No. You need to understand. We're not looking for someone to blame. We've exhausted that route." It was done in anger. And anger, as Gina knows, is the second stage of grief. Some will never work past that. Some, like Bill, embraced defeat more readily than others. The fight had been too exhausting for him. Either that, or he'd had insufficient appetite for it in the first place.

But Sorrel sits forward, as if she's seen a way in. "That's what Eric's *always* said. It's not about blame. It's about clearing the names of those who've been turned into scapegoats."

Gina heaves a sigh. "Most of the individuals we've met along the way were just ordinary people trying to do their jobs." She thinks she's finished, but realises she has more to say. "There was one woman whose job it was to co-ordinate ambulances, she was singled out for criticism. Imagine finding that more than half of the fleet was out dealing with other emergencies! Then there were ambulance drivers who couldn't make it through the gridlock. Paramedics who had to improvise because their equipment didn't work…" She presses a fist to her mouth. *We did that. We forced those poor people to stand up in court and defend themselves.* She remembers how a twenty-two year old police officer, one of the first on the scene, wept as she said she'd been unable to do her job because she was rigid with shock. *We forced them to say things about their colleagues they might never have said unless they'd been brainwashed into thinking that one person had to be responsible.* A moment passes before Gina is able to resume. "Some… some of them were heroic. There was an off-duty junior doctor. He turned up to help, even though he heard the radio announcement on his way home from a double shift."

"You can add your son to the list of heroes."

Gina looks at Eric, stunned. "My –" Her hand moves to her throat.

"There's a thing I read about. It's called the bystander effect. Basically – ironically," he widens his eyes, nodding all the while, "the more witnesses there are to an accident, the less likely it is that anyone will do anything to help." Distaste passes across Eric's face.

"What were you about to say?" She wants to hear that it hasn't all been wasted. The money. The fact that she had to leave a good job. The breakdown of her marriage.

"Oh, it's not from this case."

"Tell me."

He shakes his head. "A New York photographer. He saw a man being pushed onto the tracks at a subway station. Instead of helping, he took a photo." Eric's lip curls.

No fan of press photographers, Gina finds herself looking for excuses. "Taking a photo of something newsworthy, it might have been his natural instinct."

"I don't accept that. There are *rape* cases where people have stood by and watched." Eric seems to pull himself together and looks Gina in the eye. "From everything I've read, Oliver was the first person who made a decision to help other people. Up until then, people were only trying to help themselves."

Gina's eyes brim. "It didn't work," she says through a quivering mouth. He'd be here today if he hadn't gone for the emergency button at the exact same time as Rosie. Ollie was directly in the path of those who were thrown off the escalator when it came to a sudden stop. A simple question of timing.

"He broke the inertia. That was crucial. What he did helped save lives."

After her vision clears, Gina spends several moments staring at the list in her lap. *Ollie saved lives.* Eric believes this absolutely, she has no doubt. *Poor Rosie,* she thinks as she skims the section about the overcrowding, the risk assessments. *Maggie needs to see this.*

"It won't be easy to persuade the government to fund a second inquest. *If* they agree –"

Sorrel blows out her cheeks but says nothing.

"I admit, it's a fairly big if – but we only intend to apply to firms who are willing to take on the case."

"You as well?" Gina asks Sorrel.

"I'm the back-up plan. In case one of us finds work before the other. Timing might be critical."

"I need to be absolutely clear on something," Gina says. "We won't be talked into another class action."

"We understand that. But even if we exhaust the official channels," Sorrel nods, anticipating what Eric is about to say, "There's enough new information to undo the damage that was done by everything people read in the papers. And if you're not looking to hold an individual responsible, changing public opinion might be enough."

"How?"

"I'd publish my report. Blog about it, put it out on social

media, turn it into a book – provided none of the families object. Maybe even get some of the papers on our side."

Gina raises her eyebrows. "There are some papers we *won't* talk to."

"We'd do all of that," Sorrel says.

"Let me put it another way. There are some newspapers the families won't *want* you to talk to."

"Of course. We totally understand."

Gina had thought herself defeated, but the pair's conviction makes her realise she might have a little fight in her yet. "Your report? Do you have it with you?"

"Right here." Eric reaches into his bag.

"Who was –?" Tamsin cuts herself off with a small exasperated breath and stops in the kitchen doorway. "This place reeks."

Sitting at the table with Eric's report open in front of her, Gina watches her daughter scan the room, disapproving eyes lingering on the row of empty bottles. "It's not me," she says and holds up her mug in a mock toast. They both know she's offering it for inspection.

Sceptical – rightly so – Tamsin strides across the room, takes the mug, holds it under her nose and sniffs.

"It's tea. Just tea."

Tamsin sips; winces. "I don't get it." She looks defeated.

"Try the sink." Gina turns a page.

Her daughter opens the cupboard under the sink then slams it shut.

"The plug hole," she prompts. "But go easy. It'll make your eyes water."

Tamsin scoops back her hair, lowers her face and looks as if she's walked through a spider's web.

"That's all of it, gone. Even the stuff from the hiding places you didn't know about."

"Which places?"

"Oh, the top of my wardrobe, the back of the garden shed, just to the right of the loft hatch."

"The… But there's an off licence at the end of the road!" After Tamsin straightens up, she stands with her back turned to Gina. "So that's it?" she says when she finds her voice. "You've given up drinking?"

"I'm not going to insult you by making a promise I have no business making. But I think I might have found some motivation."

CHAPTER THIRTY

Maggie, 2016

"I think maybe we can still make it to Tate Modern on time if we take the riverside path. There will be fewer people to slow us down." Jules pauses at the top of the steps. "You are OK with that?"

The Thames's currents are particularly fierce and the temperature is cold enough to prevent anyone from swimming. "Yes," Maggie says quickly before anxiety has a chance to take hold.

"It is OK to say no, I just make a call to Eric. You know, I have a tendency to take London personally. I would not blame you if you did too."

Even somebody who wants to drown – sorry – can't resist the urge to breathe, so they draw water into their lungs.

"Did I say it wrong?"

"No," she manages. "You said it perfectly."

Though the Thames is murky green, though its surface is a rippling mass, Maggie reminds herself that the path can't possibly feel more threatening than the chaos of Great Tower Street. She breathes in her old enemy. Salty, briny, sweet and rotten.

"All of this here..." Jules throws out an arm and Maggie follows its line to a tug which tows a heavy cargo of yellow crates in its wake. "All of this, it remind me how I search for my Evelyn. I do not think for one moment she is dead, not at first. I go from hospital to hospital – these terrible places – and I cannot always find the emergency department. Maybe I find a sign that say Major Catastrophe and I follow the arrow, and each time I queue because there are injured people who need help, and everyone who is not injured is looking for someone. When finally I arrive at the desk, I say who I am and who I am looking for. Each time it get harder to repeat. I am begging and Louis is crying, because he is so tired. And I wait while they go away and check."

Maggie doesn't feel as if she's being asked to comment. Instead she shoulders the weight of what is being piled on top of her. For a moment Jules appears distant, then he continues, "All the time I run from place to place Louis is strapped to my front. By then he cry himself to sleep. His head it slump to one side and I worry he get a stiff neck, but I have to keep moving, so I press my chin down on top of his head, I try to keep him upright. His head it is hot and his hair is like feather, and I say, I tell him, 'We are going to find *Maman*'." Jules throws a look across the expanse of Thames to London Bridge Hospital and repeats, "We are going to find *Maman*. You know London Bridge Hospital, it is private. They do not have an emergency department. 'You should be ashamed you do not open your doors,' I tell them."

Maggie nods.

"I say I take it personally! After I have been to several hospital I realise, there are two lists that they check. The living and the dead. So I am not sure I want the nurse at the desk to tell me they have my Evelyn. Another no means she might be somewhere else, safe. Sometime they offer to call another hospital for me, but they say it is quicker if I go. And only when I have been to every hospital, only then do I think I will go to the Underground station. When I get there I see many people having the first aid. I did not know there would be so many injured, so again I think, OK, maybe…"

They walk. Hair whips Maggie's face. She hopes Jules interprets her silence as solidarity, that he understands she is listening as intently as she's ever listened.

"I lose hope when I get to the Family Centre and I see all the priests with their white –" He touches his neck.

"Dog collars," Maggie says, though she cannot say why she should have chosen to break his flow for such an unimportant detail. She didn't comment as they passed the brick arches of Old Billingsgate.

"I think, I think, *My God, how the hell am I going to get through this?*"

Maggie's chest rises and falls. Orange buoys, the shape and size of hay bales, move to the same rhythm. There is something bovine about them, but also something desperately sad. At any other time she wouldn't feel foolish mentioning this to Jules who, she thinks, would dismiss nothing. Perhaps, even now, Northumberland and Alan are summoning her.

"I like the place names," Jules offers at last, a more usual version of himself, though still not quite the face he normally presents. "Dark House Walk. Old Waterman's Walk. Names that say something about the history."

Maggie licks her lips and tastes salt. She agrees, certain that agreement is all he wants. To her right, a man in a long dark coat paces the same square of paving stone, flicking ash from a cigarette as if he has some kind of nervous tic. Two men are scaling a blue glass building in which a reflection of the Shard is distorted. Buckets clipped to their belays, they are cleaning windows. Yes, that's the word. Belays. It's amazing what she's stored away.

"You like that job?" says Jules, and she sees that he's watching her as she watches the window cleaners.

"I've done a bit of abseiling in my time." Somehow she

doesn't object to the Shard. She has a feeling Rosie would have liked it.

"Then you are braver than me."

Not you, she thinks. *Never you.* "I doubt I could do it now. It was before I had Rosie." Long before. "But actually, I was looking at how the Shard is reflected in the glass."

"I read there are eleven thousand glass panels in the Shard."

"That's a lot of cleaning."

"Do you know what it make me think when I hear that? I think that I could smash every one of them and still it would not be enough. It would not be enough to show how I feel." Maggie's mouth opens, but Jules's pause isn't long enough for her to reflect on her reaction. "What do you think of the word 'detritus'? Do you think it is better for London than *Objets?*"

Shaken by the unexpected subject change, Maggie finds herself asking, "For the exhibition?"

"The material I use, but also the detritus of life. The pain of making something meaningful from the scraps we are left with. I do it for Louis. Perhaps it is a little more obvious with me, but you too, I think."

Maggie's response is resistance. She has actively avoided *doing* because she assumed that focusing her efforts on something else would mean forgetting Rosie. But if it's all for Rosie…

"I have a belief that the parents they pass trauma down to their children," Jules is saying. "And Louis has trauma of his own, so I do not want him to end up with mine as well. So, you like it?"

The key ingredient in Jules's sculptures is grief. His masterstroke is to transform that grief into energy, but it's also a handicap. His apparent surplus of energy gives the impression that he's suffering less. But from what Maggie's learned today, that isn't true.

She channels thoughts of home. Could Jules link the title

of the exhibition to the river? Flotsam, jetsam, mudlarks, tidewrack.

"I cannot hear. You will have to think a little louder."

She laughs. "Sometimes I forget I haven't spoken out loud. Growing up by the sea, having all that sky, we don't seem to need so many words." Most people would consider that she and Alan don't communicate. Daily telephone calls force conversation, making it seem stilted and mechanical. Email would be easier, but it offers no substitute for companionable silence. "There's a word from where I come from. Tidewrack."

"What is this?"

"It's like detritus, but more specific. It's the rubbish the sea deposits along a shoreline."

He looks at the opposite bank of the river and experiments with the word. "Tidewrack."

Embarrassed by her contribution, she adds, "But London was a Roman city and detritus is from the Latin…"

"*Latin?* I will have you know it is French! In French it is *détritus,* from *deterere,* 'to wear away'."

"I didn't know that."

"So we have the scraps we are left with and how life it wear us down."

Worn down. It's almost a perfect reflection of how Maggie feels. She may yet be worn down by Alan's persistence. But there's more. Sorrel wore away at the courts until they overturned the original verdict. The trauma of the accident has worn away marriages, relationships, love. "It's perfect," she says.

They make their way up the steel steps to London Bridge and it is then that Maggie sees it. The red plastic casing. *To save a life.* She doesn't stop, but she must falter in some small way because Jules gently takes her elbow. Perhaps, seeing the life saver, it has struck him where they are. As they reach the second landing, there is time to contemplate the height difference between the water, the riverside path and the street level of London Bridge. Maggie has an image of Rosie clenching her hands into fists and then releasing them, the tension pointing downwards through her arms as she shifts her weight onto the balls of her feet. In this vision, Rosie is wearing the red, white and navy leotard she used to compete in. Maggie's knees react. Her stomach reacts. Both she and Jules come to a halt. A black bird with an iridescent green chest is sitting on the rail, chirruping and teasing, its song urgent and out of place. *There was a moment when I felt as if I was flying. There was a moment when it felt like release.* Then a bus rumbles past and, with a flurry of feathers, the spell is broken. The bird is gone.

"A starling," Jules says. "They are as common as pigeons in Paris."

CHAPTER THIRTY-ONE

Eric, 2013

Eric comes to with a start. Sorrel is hurling a flurry of words at him. Pure gibberish.

"Youhaven'tbeenpickingupthephoneandtheysaidyouweren'tatwork."

Nothing he can make sense of. If it was a poem it would be *The Ning Nang Nong*.

His room is in semi-darkness. Early morning, then. Any minute now the alarm will go off. It would be good to pre-empt it because his head's pounding violently from all of the shouting (if only it would stop). Eric tries to raise his head, just an inch or so off the pillow. It won't co-operate. His neck feels peculiar and he seems to be lying in a pool of sweat.

Wait. Sorrel has paused. He should say something. "What are you doing here so early? Did you forget something?"

"Where have you been?" At last. Words arranged in rows. "Two days ago, you said you'd call!"

Two days! He laughs. That's a good one.

Sorrel looks the part, dressed in her new black suit. His own is dark grey. "Do you even know what day it is?" Her arms are folded across her chest.

In front of Eric, stuck to the back of his bedroom door, are yellow Post-it notes numbered 212-248 (he has long since run out of wall space). Everything is exactly where it should be. "Of course I do," he protests.

"It's Thursday."

This is a cruel trick she's playing. And during his first week on the job. "Right. I've missed two days' work."

"That's what I've been trying to tell you." Sorrel marches to the window and yanks the black-out curtains apart. Daylight floods every corner of his chaotic room. "It really is Thursday."

She's serious. He throws out a hand for his glasses, grimaces at his alarm clock. Numbers blink. The thing is to catch them before they disappear. The first is a 12. Realisation shadows his face.

"Finally!" she says. "I'm on my lunchbreak. And I haven't got long."

"I've got to –" Eric swings his legs out of bed but that's as far as he gets. He tries to bridge the two-day gap. Neurons spark, but fail to ignite. There is nothing.

"Did you go out drinking?"

"No, I was here. Working!" He sits swaying, holding on to the mattress as if it's a life raft. Has he suffered some kind of stroke?

"OK, Viking, I'm not checking up on you. I'm just wondering if this is a two-day hangover or something more. Are you sure they didn't take you for a drink after work?"

"No!" he insists. "It isn't a –" But he stops himself. A pint-of-vodka hangover would be preferable to the alternative. What if he *had* gone for a drink? What if someone spiked it? He has no memory of getting home. "Was I unconscious? When you arrived, I mean –"

"Calm down. You were out of it, but you were asleep, that's all."

"I don't remember." With this admission, his eyes brim. Through the blur Eric sees Sorrel rearranging the cans and bottles on his desk. He wants to yell, 'Leave them alone, stop touching my stuff.' He also wants to yell, 'Give me that!' Words ring loud inside his head but he can't remember how to get them out.

Sorrel has the ProPlus box in her hand and is opening it, checking the foil pack. "How much of this stuff have you been taking?" She hasn't found the Tesco own brand, which Eric prefers because they also contain glucose.

"Stop that," he manages, swiping the air with one arm.

Sorrel steps back, real alarm on her face. "Did you mean to hit me?"

He slumps to the left. "No." From there it's only a short drop to the floor. He stays down, shaking, the mechanics of sitting beyond him.

"OK, that's it," says Sorrel, although all he can see of her is her serious black court shoes. Court shoes. At any other time, he'd turn that into a joke. "I'm calling a doctor."

"Don't!" Eric is as miserable as he has ever been. "I'll be fine."

"No you won't. And you don't get a choice in this."

"Extreme stress over an extended period. How long, I don't know, but I have my suspicions. All I can say is I'm surprised it hasn't happened before now."

Eric struggles to process this. *What* hasn't happened before now?

"I asked your girlfriend if she's noticed anything strange about your behaviour over the past few months."

"Strange?"

"Out of character. She told me how, when you've been working non-stop, you're either totally non-communicative or you talk crazily for hours on end. On its own that wouldn't be cause for concern. Letting off steam can be an effective coping strategy. But then she mentioned this project of yours.

From what I understand, for several hours a day, you've been putting yourself in an extremely damaging mindset. You've become far too emotionally involved." Eric breathes heavily, feeling betrayed. "She also tells me you haven't been eating or sleeping and that she can't get through to you that this might be a problem." Each sentence ends with an upward inflection, as if the doctor is challenging Eric to deny what he's saying. Eric says nothing.

"My guess is that this has crept up on you. You're an intelligent guy. You've managed to explain away the tiredness, the stomach upsets, all the aches and pains. Any number of minor symptoms that barely seemed worth a paracetamol. But add them all together and…" The doctor punches the palm of his opposite hand. "Bam!"

Quietly seething, Eric does the maths.

"Let's talk about what happens when you're stressed. First, the body produces adrenaline – the fight or flight hormone. Then it floods you with cortisol. The idea of cortisol is that it slows you down, forcing you to take a break until your energy levels are back in balance. But instead of listening to your body, *you've* been downing serious quantities of caffeine to keep going." Eric looks towards his desk. Sorrel's neat line-up is gone. *Dishonest appropriation of property belonging to another.* "And because you've consistently ignored your body, your mind has taken charge. It's shut down for a while."

Is he being told that he's having a nervous breakdown? The prospect appals him. "I can't afford to take time off."

"Tough luck, I'm afraid. I've written you a prescription, but that will only target the symptoms, not the cause." He looks about the room. "I'm referring you for therapy. Meanwhile you need to make some serious changes. If your girlfriend hadn't called today, I'm not sure what state I would have found you in." The man is clearly exasperated. "Don't you know how counter-productive lack of sleep is? Your sub-conscious problem-solves for you. *If* you let it."

Tell me something I don't know. The sequence didn't just line itself up while Eric sat behind his laptop.

He doesn't watch the doctor leave.

Sorrel pads into the room. Eric detects sheepishness as she asks, "What did he say?"

"You know what he said. You were listening outside the door."

She perches on the mattress, on what they refer to as her side of the bed. The slim skirt of her business suit won't allow her to sit with one foot under her as she would ordinarily. "You frightened me, Eric, and I don't frighten easily."

Her blouse has come untucked. He takes the silky material in one hand; scrunches it into a fist. "I've fucked up." The job he's waited so long for. All the course fees, the debt – and what's more, the fifty-eight, the families, Oliver Wicker.

"Technically, you've frazzled your brain." After a crooked smile, Sorrel prises his fingers apart, tucks her blouse back in and lies down beside him. Her breath brushes his face. "But we'll un-frazzle it. I'll, uh." She frowns, blinks and cups one side of his face. "I can't promise I'll make a good nurse, but you need keeping an eye on. I'll go back to my place after work and pick up some stuff, then I'll go to the chemists'. Maybe even stock up on some fresh fruit and vegetables."

He feels the press of lips against his cheek. This is chronically bad timing, but she's doing her best to be cheerful. The problem is, Eric isn't sure he can cope with cheerful. His diagnosis makes him feel ashamed. "I need to make a few calls." He reaches his arm out towards his desk but, even fully extended, it falls short.

"I've confiscated your phone." Sorrel props herself up on an elbow. "Don't look at me like that. You'd only find a way of working on it."

Eric groans, and follows it with a childlike sobbing sound. He is not only to be monitored, he's to be dictated to.

"I've tried dropping hints but subtle doesn't work with you, so now you don't get a choice. You've turned me into a nag. Which is something I never wanted to be."

He doesn't comment. Instead, he tries another tack. "What if my mother calls? She'll worry if I don't pick up."

"I've already called her."

"She knows?" He twists his head.

"Someone in your family had to. Especially when you're in denial."

Very quickly, he's losing what little control he had. "Work, then –"

"Done."

Eric's heart is in his throat. "What did you say?"

"Don't panic. I said it was all my fault. You didn't call in sick because you thought I'd done it, and it slipped my mind because I've just started a new job. They think we live together, by the way. I'm down as your next-of-kin."

OK. OK. She's probably made a better job of it than you would have done. "What did you say is wrong with me?"

"Norovirus."

"The sickness bug?"

"I'm sorry if that was the wrong thing to say but I had to wing it. Stick to something no one wants to catch, that was my thinking. They said to tell you not to rush back, but I'm to call on Monday if you're no better."

Is it possible he'll be better by Monday? He'll stay in bed for three whole days if that's even a long shot. "Will you phone Gina? I was supposed to get back to her with the… the… the thing."

"Also done. She's coming round after work. She offered and I was in no position to say no. The earliest I'll be back here is nine o'clock."

"What if I can't get to the door?"

"I gave her the code to the key locker. She'll let herself in."

Her voice is full of disappointment. He wants to protest that there's no way she can be as disappointed with him as he is with himself. So many people are relying on him and he's jeopardised everything.

The mattress lifts as Sorrel pushes herself off it. She pauses at the bedroom door. "The doctor said you were lucky to have me." And then she's gone.

CHAPTER THIRTY-TWO

Maggie, 2016

A former power station, the Tate Modern makes no effort to disguise its industrial credentials. Odd that people campaigned to save the structure. Unlike St Paul's, it's not an easy building to love. But, then, it houses art that isn't always easy to love.

They locate Eric at the entrance to the Turbine Hall. Maggie looks at him anew, unsure of herself. Words that should be simple stutter inside her. *I never got the chance to thank you.*

"Ah!" he greets them. "The wretched and the brave."

Maggie assumes it's Shakespeare. After all, they're only a stone's throw from the Globe. "Which am I?"

"The brave, of course." In the nervous energy Eric exudes is a clear sense of sacrifice. It seems so obvious now, she can't understand how it has remained cloaked for so long.

Jules clasps him by the hand. "You see, we have a new accomplice. Maggie is going to write our wall labels."

This is news to Maggie, who has never thought herself much of a copywriter. She smiles and taps her notebook as if she knows exactly what's expected of her.

"Great." Eric holds the door open for her.

I never got the chance to... It cannot be this hard.

A carpeted floor slopes away in front of them. An adult couple roll over and over each other as if they're children playing and it's a grassy incline. People picnic, sitting cross-legged. A toddler walks in circles chewing on the ear of a toy rabbit, while another shrieks repeatedly, creating echoes in the vast space.

"Isn't that Led Zeppelin he's singing?" says Eric.

"Right!" Jules gets the joke before Maggie does. *"A Whole Lotta Love."*

Once again she's the new kid who hasn't made any friends. They walk and Maggie finds her voice. "I haven't been here since they finished the extension. It changes the way you feel about the space, doesn't it?"

"Definitely," says Eric, and points to the meandering crack on the floor, what was originally an art work. "I really like how they've made no attempt to hide the repair."

Maggie lets her eyes follow the full length of the concrete scar.

Jules stands alongside her. *"The Visible Fracture,"* he says. "You know, in Japan, they repair broken pottery with gold. The repair becomes part of the history of the *objet*. It is like us, *n'est-ce pas?*"

So complete is Maggie's sense of being damaged, and of the damage being on display for all to see, that she stifles a gasp.

Eric is striding about. "So, they're giving you the Turbine Hall."

The damage is part of my history.

"Well, you know, an overnight success like me…" Jules puts his thumbs in the small of his back and looks up with a critical eye. "We will have to see if we think it will work."

Maggie drags her gaze to the place where Jules is looking; at the building's exposed steel frame. A piece of machinery looms overhead. She is about to ask what it is when Eric says,

"You'll need to turn it into a series of claustrophobic spaces. Like a maze."

Jules holds out his hands. "A maze! And now you are going to tell me how we can get rid of all this natural light."

"Not so easy."

He purses his lips. "What I think is we go upstairs and work our way back down. That way, we arrive in the space. And I need *you,*" Jules turns to Maggie, "to study what is written about some of the other pieces."

Maggie stands in front of an exhibit. Six squares, each painted a different colour: brown, pea green, blue/grey, beige, orange and lime green. Her eyes drop. Whoever whitewashed the walls forgot to mask the floor.

Jules comes to stand behind her. "You like this?"

Caught out, she says, "No, no I don't."

"Well, that is a reaction at least. Without looking at the label on the wall, tell me what you think it is."

Maggie replies with the first thing that comes into her head. "It's like colour swatches. The kind you see for decorating."

"That is what it is, *exactement.* The artist base the colours on an old paint chart."

She reads the card for herself. No hint of irony, the description is purely factual. Her brow furrows. "I thought you said that modern art's all about ideas."

"The idea is that you can see a colour and recognise when and where in history it was used."

Flummoxed by this, Maggie says, "I can't." What's even more baffling is why it was considered important enough to put in an art gallery.

"Read the label. Write it down. Try and get a feel for the words."

This is ridiculous. What can she possibly contribute?

Someone who knew what they were doing could nail these descriptions in less than half the time she'll take to study them. But study them Maggie does. The order in which the information appears. The artist's name (will she need that for a one-person exhibition? Or will the name of the family appear?) followed by the title, followed by the media (oil paint, fabric, glue on canvas), then the measurements in centimetres and, finally, the description. She notes the use of bold typeface and italics.

There is only one exhibit in the next room and only one person looking at it. A girl in a simple black T-shirt dress stares intently. Careful not to stand too close, Maggie is aware of other people walking straight past, barely glancing at the sculpture. Who can blame them? If she's honest, it looks as if several breeze blocks have been stood on end.

Out of the corner of her eye she sees the girl's feet – she's wearing what fashion magazines call gladiator sandals. With a smile at the ready, Maggie glances sideways at the girl's face. Immediately she startles, not having anticipated such perfect skin, such exquisite cheekbones, the beauty spot just to the right of her mouth. And no make-up; not a single adornment.

Eyes front. Maggie trains her attention on the bare breeze blocks, which are punctuated with regular square holes, like windows in a building. The gladiator sandals move away and Maggie turns her head to check that her eyes weren't playing tricks. It's the girl's limp she notices. Not the kind that's caused by blisters, but a side-to-side movement, as if one of her legs is shorter than the other. She regrets immediately that she didn't say, 'My goodness but you're beautiful.' It's almost as if the girl's limp makes her more accessible.

Ugly and impersonal, the sculpture could be a multi-storey car park or the skeleton of a new block of flats. It's everything she hates about cities. OK. Time to read the label. *Monument to the Living.* She repeats this to herself and, as she repeats it,

Maggie thinks of what Jules said about only the dead being recognised as victims. The more she repeats it, the more she thinks that he's right; the more she likes the idea that it's the living and not the dead who need monuments. But why call something so ugly a monument? The wall label supplies her with an answer. The breeze-block construction is a scale model of an unfinished building in Beirut. At the outbreak of civil war, it was put to use as a sniper tower. There is a distinct shift in her attitude towards the sculpture, but she can't articulate what it is. Does knowing *why* a thing is ugly help? She catches herself in the act of being curious. Does that mean that this ugly object is *good* art?

Maggie passes into the next room and compares it with the last gallery she was in, which had walls of heritage red; confident brushstrokes within gilded frames. Here, many of the works have a hurried, almost unfinished quality.

A right turn, and Eric is standing in front of an exhibit. Maggie hesitates, then sees that this may be her only chance to catch him on his own. "I…uh," she begins, self-conscious. "I never got the chance to thank you properly after the verdict." What right does she have to use the word 'properly'? It suggests she *did* thank Eric, but only informally.

"Oh." He shrugs dismissively, something Maggie takes for modesty. "But Sorrel was fantastic, wasn't she?"

Maggie feels the need to press her point. "You obviously make an excellent team. It meant the world to us to have Rosie included."

"It was just a mathematical equation." The strain of having to engage shows on Eric's face. "Add everything together and, well, the result was inevitable."

"But *you* grasped that, no one else." She has said what she wanted to say. It can never be enough and yet it will have to be, because it's evident that Eric is uncomfortable with being dragged into the spotlight. Maggie turns to the glass case he's giving his attention to. Is the exhibit what it appears to be – a drab brown blanket hooked up to a flag pole – or a representation of something else?

"It was better coming from Sorrel," Eric says, his eyes unwavering. "I became too involved."

This would be the time to ask how he is, but that question feels too personal, somehow. "How's the book going?"

"Oh, you know. It's washed its face." With more of a grimace than a smile, Eric moves to the right and reads out loud from the wall label, "Fabric, blood, earth and other substances," and all tension is dispersed.

"It's interesting," ventures Maggie. "The word 'blood' registers as being more powerful than 'earth.'"

"Yes, but what about 'other substances'? They might be bodily fluids or they might be anything at all."

Maggie crosses to the label, takes up her notepad and begins to copy. The blood, soil, and everything else was taken from the sites of various murders on the Mexican border with America. Because the murders were drug-related, neither government did anything to intervene. The exhibit is called *What Else Can We Talk About?* "Clever title," she says, admiring how neatly it scaffolds the concept. "I only hope Jules doesn't expect me to come up with them."

"Artist's privilege. At least, I assume that's how it works."

"You don't know either? And here I was thinking you were an expert."

"Me? I just about know my Damien Hirst from my Tracey Emin."

They are laughing when Jules arrives. "It is *intéressant* that I find you both here. This is very powerful but you know, the most powerful exhibit I see in an art gallery, it is a bus stop. Something familiar. Nothing threatening. And then I read that it is the stop for the bus to Auschwitz. And the whole thing, it change in front of my eyes."

"So all I have to do," Maggie says, "is make what looks ordinary extraordinary."

"See! You are an excellent student."

Eric leans towards her and hisses, "Swot."

Jules steps onto the escalators. *"Non,"* he says, his voice sharp. "This is no good. There is no vertigo. Can you feel?" He looks over his shoulder, demanding an opinion to shore up his own.

Maggie has been watching the rubberised handrail rotate, trying to understand how it works. The only comparison she can think of is those rotating towels they use in public toilets. How you pull on the towel and another patch of damp towel is produced. Disproportionately uneasy as she steps onto the ridged metal step, Maggie then finds her balance without so much as a wobble. "Nothing." She feels foolish at having been so concerned.

"It is crazy how slow this escalator is!"

"Then switch it off," she says.

"Switch it off?"

Maggie nods. "Rosie explained it. When you step onto an out-of-order escalator, your eyes tell you it's not moving, but your body's autopilot instructs you to move as you would if it was working." She shrugs. "It throws you off-balance."

Jules laughs, but she can see he gets it. "Switch it off." His facial expressions suggest he is turning the thought over, examining its underbelly. "Why not? So the next thing you help me with," Jules gestures to the open space ahead, "We need to close the escalator in, or if we cannot close it in, like give it a ceiling, I think we suspend some advertising boards so that visitors are blinkered."

"I always say that people would never use the Underground if they weren't blinkered," Eric agrees. "When you're surrounded by people, the only way to cope is by shutting them out."

"Oh!" Jules points to the wall opposite. "Maybe we can create vertigo. What do you think if we project a film onto the wall?"

"What would be interesting," Eric ponders, "is if the height of the film was the same height as the original escalator."

Jules nods his agreement. "What I am thinking, you remember Crisanto's testimony? How he do everything to avoid the words for what he actually see." A stray memory comes to Maggie, how Crisanto always wore the plastic wristband he was given in hospital. As if he needed any other reminder. "He describe a waterfall and then he talk about buffalo. How they have eyes at the sides of their heads, and when they stampede, they do it with their heads down. They do not see where they are going."

Eric nods, frowns. "The Indians drive them over the cliff."

They move aside to make way for a school party and gather where the view from the mezzanine opens out through a lighting rig into the Turbine Hall, all the way down to the lower ground floor. An elderly woman wearing a lime green cagoule is clutching the handrail and hauling herself upstairs from the cloakrooms. Maggie experiences her old unsettling curiosity about what it would be like to jump.

"You are thinking again, Maggie. Give me your thought in progress."

Heart thumping, she reminds herself that she is safely behind a glass wall. There is a question she must answer. "I know nothing about buffalo, but there's a scene in *Far From the Madding Crowd* where a sheepdog drives a herd over the side of a cliff. You're watching helpless while they..." She cannot bring herself to finish a sentence that involves both falling and water.

Jules nods, saying, "The sacrificial lamb."

"If we're talking sacrifice," Eric suggests, "there's the opening scene of *The Mission* where the priest is tied to a crucifix and sent over the waterfall."

269

"So everybody who come they are a bystander, and after they stand and watch, we tell them how many people stand by on the day and watch."

Maggie experiences a wave of nausea. "Is it going to be too shocking?"

"No, it will be just shocking enough," Jules replies. "You cannot make art and then apologise for it."

CHAPTER THIRTY-THREE

Tamsin, 2016

They have been treading carefully, edging past each other in the bathroom, pretending not to look at the other as they dress. Tamsin takes time over her make-up and packs her bag for work. While making sure she has everything she needs for her ten o'clock meeting with the costume department, she's torn in two by an image of Mum standing at the kitchen worktop, a stack of sandwiches for the packed lunches growing taller.

She'll phone, but not for another hour. If she phones at breakfast time, it will look as if she's checking up on her.

Eventually Tamsin is ready, her bag is ready, and the kitchen table is unavoidable. Gareth's cereal bowl is empty; his mug drained. He's been waiting, rehearsing whatever it is that he's so determined to say before he leaves for work.

"What I said last night, about helping Jules," he begins. "It came out wrong."

"No, it was me." Tamsin sighs, feeling fragile, willing to contribute whatever needs to be said to negotiate a truce. Like the clash of teeth during a first kiss, her words are clumsy and awkward. "I took it the wrong way." She takes a seat. Her seat.

"Just shut up and let me apologise."

Admonished, she sits up straight like a small girl, her hands in her lap.

"I don't want you *not* to contact Jules because of what I said. I think it's a *great* idea. Not for your CV, but for both you and your mum. For most people, clearing things away is part of the grieving process."

Tamsin determines not to take offence. "It would be good for my CV too," she admits.

"Well, there is that." His smile is anxious. Perhaps she really has made him nervous to say what he thinks.

Tamsin must take a risk. This relationship won't survive on a foundation of secrets. Secrets are poisonous. All of those unsaid things, even the small misunderstandings that go uncorrected, lead to lies. And the toxic accumulation of them became another presence in Mum's house. "For years now, Mum and I, we've shared Ollie's ghost." Her brother's name summons a lump to her throat. "I'd…" *Without even asking, Mum has not only set him free but…* "I'd managed to fool myself that he was locked in his room. So when I found it empty…" Gareth places one hand over hers and she understands that he's waiting. She presses her lips tightly together and shakes her head. There is no more.

"Go easy on yourself," he says. "Give yourself a few days. I know," he holds up both of his hands. "I've got to stop telling you what to do and let you find your own way. I'm going to try, alright?"

Tamsin nods because, right now, that's all she's capable of.

"I just wanted to say I'm on your side. That's all. Actually," he looks embarrassed, "that's not quite all."

Panic flares in Tamsin's stomach. "Oh?" She swallows, the movement in her throat cumbersome.

He picks up an interior design magazine she remembers seeing lying about in the living room; opens it to a page he has earmarked. "I found a picture of a kind of desk in a cupboard arrangement. I can see you're worried about space, so I wondered if you thought it might work in the hall. It won't be like having your own office, but –"

"No, it will," she says, already seeing the 3D model she'll mock up, the measurements she'll give to Richard, the most accurate carpenter she knows. "It will be. Thank you."

Saturday morning. With a growing sense that she's stayed away too long, Tamsin takes advantage of a valid excuse. Dressed in decorating clothes (always playing a part in her own life), she makes a couple of trips from the car to the house that until last week she'd described as home. She ferries paint pots and bags containing brushes and turps. Digging in her handbag, it really strikes Tamsin: this is no longer her house key. She rings the doorbell before turning the key in the lock. "It's only me!" she shouts, but it's as if her voice crashes into a wall.

Her mother is there in the hall. She isn't dishevelled, shows no visible signs of distress. In fact, she gives the impression of having been in the middle of something. "What's all this?" Mum nods towards the bags in the porch. "Moving back in?" Her voice is good-humoured, but her expression says, *Checking up on me?*

Almost too enthusiastically, Tamsin holds up a carrier bag containing her DIY booty. "I thought I'd give the kitchen a lick of paint. I've been meaning to get round to it but what with one thing and another..."

"Oh," her mother begins, her turn now to falter. "Oh, that's sweet of you, but..."

"But?"

"Jules has done it. He fixed the leak in the bathroom, then insisted on coming back the next day to paint. I tried to stop him, but..." She shrugs.

Bloody Jules. That was my responsibility. Tamsin hadn't imagined she would be replaced quite so quickly.

"You didn't buy paint specially, did you?"

"It's white emulsion. I'm sure I can find a use for it."

"Come and have a coffee and tell me about your week. I just made a pot." Mum laughs. "Forgetting there's only one of me!"

Guilt pricks, no matter how thoroughly Tamsin reminds herself that adult children leave home.

"There's a sound I always thought was you. Quite an irritating sound actually."

"Thanks!" She follows behind. Again, no signs of disarray. The washing up has been done. The surfaces are clear.

"A ticking. It turns out that it was something to do with the central heating all along."

This period of readjustment cannot be hurried. Strange as it was for Tamsin to leave, it must be stranger still for Mum to find herself alone in the house with its noisy pipes – not to mention unfettered access to Ollie's room.

Tamsin inhales slowly, trying to camouflage what must be blatantly obvious. A lingering smell of paint blunts the aroma of fresh coffee, but that other smell, the undercurrent she dreads, is absent. Relieved, Tamsin glances up to the place on the ceiling where the water stain had been creeping outwards in concentric circles, like rings on a tree trunk. She expects to detect a trace, some kind of evidence of its existence, but there is none. "He's made a good job of it," she admits.

"Hasn't he?" The shake is absent from Mum's hand as she pours the coffee. "Now I won't have to feel embarrassed when the estate agents come round."

"Estate agents?" Tamsin parrots, without thinking what she's saying.

"Your father says we should go for the best of three valuations, but yes."

The words stop Tamsin in her tracks. "You're selling?"

"Oh, darling, you didn't really think I'd stay here on my own, did you?"

The future closes in. Within a few short sentences, a critical assumption has been turned inside out. If things don't work out with Gareth, she won't be able to make a tearful phone call and say, 'I made a mistake. Can I come back home?' There will be no bolt-hole. This is the end of the sequence she set in motion. The inevitable outcome. Tamsin feels her face begin to contort.

"Oh, you did. Oh, I'm sorry."

"But I asked you. I asked!" She tucks her chin in to her chest.

Mum's reply is gentle. "Your father and I had an arrangement. He would contribute to the mortgage for as long as you lived here."

Tamsin is shaking. He can't simply cut Mum off. It's only been a week.

"Given that he has a new family to support, he's been more than fair."

Talk of Dad's new family stings like an unexpected slap. To hear her mum make reference to his girlfriend, not to mention his teenage step-daughter and their two-year-old, and without any hint of bitterness. How can that be? "Why didn't you tell me?" she manages, her voice little more than a whisper.

"We never wanted you to feel as if you were being pushed out of your home."

This is a new *we*, a unity she'd been unaware of. Tamsin remembers how Dad sat her down and held both her hands while he explained that he loved her and Mum very much, how he would always be her father, but he couldn't cope. It seemed terribly unfair, when none of them was coping. All that talk of dealing with their grief 'as a family' had meant nothing. He had decided to remove himself and that was that. She didn't know that people could just pack their bags and walk away. Left to translate, Tamsin thought he had meant he couldn't cope with being a husband and a father.

Steered into a sitting position at the table, Tamsin feels her hands being curved around the coffee mug. Her mum begins to rub her back in small circular motions, and she is transported back to those first bleary days.

For the longest time Tamsin was terrified that she would arrive home from school to an empty house and find a note. But Mum didn't pack her bags and leave. Instead, she found ways of coping, some of them self-destructive (as were her own, though hers were under control), many of them frightening to a teenage daughter (just as hers would have been to her mum, had she known). Tamsin learned the danger signs and kept vigil, and was good at it, forcing herself to stay awake until, finally, she heard Mum go to bed.

And then Dad announced that he'd met someone else and, what's more, that someone had a daughter who wasn't a dissimilar age to Tamsin. It turned out that what he couldn't cope with was *them*.

Has the need she's felt to stay in the family home simply been the echo of her mother saying, 'Don't rush her, Bill. This is her home'? Has she been wrong about Mum? Is she relieved not to have Tamsin hovering, sniffing the air the moment she walks into a room? *She's* the one who hasn't been ready for change.

"Do you see?" Mum is saying. "That's why it makes sense for Jules to have Ollie's things."

Fresh panic flares in her chest. Her voice emerges, child-like. "He hasn't taken them yet, has he?"

"No, no. He says it all needs cataloguing first. If you feel up to it," the back rubbing continues, "we could do it together."

Yes. Together they will sort through their own broken pieces. "I'd like that."

"Drink your coffee. It will all be alright. Everything will be alright."

"Will it?" The house holds so few happy memories. Then why does the thought of it being sold leave her so afraid?

"Yes, it will. You'll see."

"I can't remember his voice."

"Oh, darling." Her mother strokes her hair. "That's because it was in the middle of breaking. I swear, one minute it was Vienna Choirboy, the next it was Pavarotti. OK, then. Think of an Ollie saying. Don't say it out loud. Just repeat it inside your head."

Yeah, right. Yeah, right. Yeah, right.

"How does that feel?"

Nothing.

"Maybe try something that isn't so Ollie, but put an Ollie spin on it. Like 'Are you planning on spending *all* day in the bathroom?'"

Are you planning on spending all *day in the bathroom? Are you planning? Are you –?*

Tamsin bites her lip.

There. There he is.

CHAPTER THIRTY-FOUR

Maggie, 2016

Two hours inside Tate Modern, and it has rained. Outside it could be a different day entirely, the sky a brilliant blue backdrop for the dome of St Paul's, which glows silver and sandy gold.

He asks, "You want that I walk you home?"

"No, no that's fine." They have already said goodbye to Eric, who is cycling upriver. Guiding, he said. Maggie volunteered that she'd like to go on one of his tours, and meant it.

"You know…" Jules frowns, inserting the slightest of pauses in his sentence. "As we walk across London Bridge, I notice how you drag your feet. And your hand, it reach out. I think you normally stop. Somewhere near the middle."

Maggie hopes it's not too obvious that she's gripping the rail, but suspects that Jules sees everything. "It's rare for me to come south of the river. I usually turn back when I reach the centre of the bridge."

He looks at her quizzically. "You confront it. That is very brave of you."

For a moment, she was afraid he would say, 'The starling. You thought it was your Rosie.' Now, when he doesn't, she's almost disappointed. Confused by her sudden yearning for intimacy, Maggie dismisses his suggestion. "I'm not brave. Not at all." Then she adds, "Some people tell me I should stop revisiting it."

"Some people! What do they know?" A spark of anger on her behalf, but it fizzles out. "You are here." In Jules's musical voice, it sounds as if this is something to be proud of.

Maggie turns her back on the river and looks beyond the slender silver birches to the rise of Tate Modern's central chimney. Trapped between an obsolete version of herself and the new her – whoever that might be – she's in need of a push. "Do you ever wonder what your life would have been like?" she asks.

It is Jules's turn to hesitate. "You know, my Evelyn, she had a brilliant mind. Brilliant. I do not exaggerate. She never look down on me because I am a plumber. In those days, you know a plumber in London earn good money. I more than pay my way. But would I be happy to be a plumber now?" His smile twists. "I say to the journalists I do not like to call myself an artist, but the journalists they make me want to lie. Being an artist, it suit me."

"You have the temperament for the job."

"You think it make an excuse for my bad temper?" How easily he laughs! "But would I have found my way here without...?"

There is no need to finish the question. Maggie nods.

"And you?" he asks.

She breathes in. Something faintly maritime; saltwater heaving in and out of the Thames estuary twice daily. "If Rosie were still here, if she was settled and happy, I wouldn't think twice about moving back home to Northumberland. But because Rosie isn't here, I feel tied to London." Maggie shakes her head. "Even *I* can see that makes no sense."

"You feel how you feel, that is all."

She smiles at the simplicity with which Jules validates her

feelings, so unlike her experience of therapy. She still doesn't know why he asked for her help when there's no guarantee that she'll do the job well enough, when it would be far easier to ask a professional, but she's grateful. "I enjoyed being your accomplice."

"Yes?" He seems genuinely pleased. "I have converted you to modern art?"

"The ideas perhaps. I felt very... present. Normally, I would have started to feel guilty."

"But why?"

She wonders how to respond. For doing something for herself. For absenting herself. For going on what she would have thought of as a jolly. She shakes her head, dismissing these options. None are true.

"It is all for Rosie, *non?* That is how we carry on."

She takes stock. "Yes." A shift in attitude so simple, she can't work out why it has never occurred to her as the answer.

"Well, there will be a lot of work between now and June. I will send you photograph of my *Objets* and you will write your little pieces. The facts. Very plain."

She taps her handbag, the place where her notebook is stowed. "Don't worry. I shan't try to be clever."

"We will make something to be proud of." He moves towards her and, as he kisses her, once on each cheek, then a third time, she experiences a kind of reflexive curiosity. Does this mean they're friends? Alan can't abide social kissing – but Alan isn't here.

South of the river isn't Maggie's London. She walks briskly through Borough Market where, with a clang of metal poles, stallholders are beginning to pack up for the day. A hit of pure sea from the fishmonger's where an octopus hangs, crusty loaves, bowls of olives, rows of chutneys. Wearing the ghosts of Jules's kisses on each cheek, she walks with purpose in the direction of promised work, as if she'll arrive home to an influx of emails with numerous attachments. Past the towers of cheeses and the punnets of strawberries. A flower stall giving off a faint scent of decay. Past Southwark Cathedral. Hot fat. Past the posh burger stands. Up Nancy's steps. Into the fray.

She crosses through the mayhem at the traffic lights, keeping a keen eye out for cyclists who don't see the need to stop. Past the fire juggler, the born again Christians thrusting their leaflets in her direction. She buys a *Big Issue,* something she's never done before, and walks the entire width of the bridge with her free hand trailing the slanted rectangular rail, displacing one thousand droplets of rainwater. She passes the red casing of the life saver. No need to stop. *It's all for Rosie now.* She passes the edge of the steel staircase where, earlier, the starling perched and sang. She can recall the reassuring touch of Jules's hand on her elbow, the precise notes of the bird's song. She decides to brave the City's streets.

Lycra cycling shorts, stop at the traffic lights, a circus trick, balancing on pedals. Maggie crosses the road, embracing her own curiosity, knowing at the same time that it won't last. But if she can find it for half an hour, she will find it again. Look up, look up! Steam, billowing from a vent. A gold weather vane, the church spire it sits atop lost between two buildings, once part of a skyline of monuments to worship of a different kind. Something at street level catches her eye: a woman dressed in black swinging a bright pink clutch bag. Hi-vis, hard helmet, takeaway coffee. A signpost for Dr Samuel Johnson's house. Maggie dares herself to glimpse into the mouth of an alley so narrow that horses and carts would have had to edge their way. Evidence of an older London suddenly revealed: just as suddenly, gone. Cigarette butts and, only a metre away, a cigarette butt holder with a face like a Cyberman. Bass booming from a blacked-out car window. A white-haired City gent towing a wheeled case; trouser legs an inch too short. Double yellow, parking meter, double-mouthed letterbox. A café door propped open, an order shouted: "Dry skinny latte extra shot no chocolate!" Tables crammed into a corner, exposed brick wall, exposed pipework. *"No fucking consideration. Driving on the wrong bloody side of the road, right in the middle of Borough High Street."* Cufflinks in the shapes of rugby balls, rowers, steering wheels, eagles. Young men with beards, furious texting, surprising eye contact as they approach. Over there, a woman magnificent in a yellow coat. Site of the Haberdashers Hall 1458-1996. Pavement dips, water pools, puffed-up pigeons crouching in a puddle. St Andrew by the Wardrobe. A row of Boris bikes. Life!

CHAPTER THIRTY-FIVE

2017

Phone in hand, Donovan pauses to watch his wife through the crack in the living room door. Flick, flick, flick goes the screen of her iPad.

Sudden laughter, a surprising raucous sound, transports Donovan to a time when the room was full and Helene was at the centre of it all, looking a million dollars. (He misses the rainbow version of his wife.)

The Christmases they used to have! Their daughter officiating the tree-lighting ceremony.

"Daddy, do the countdown!" So bossy, even at five.

"Alright, then. Ten, nine, eight, seven. Oh! Oh! You didn't wait!"

And Cassie and his wife would collapse laughing because this was the joke. Cassie never could wait. The grandchildren in his mind would have been just as impatient, just as impulsive.

Adults braving Christmas morning, shaking off the night before. Helene up earliest of all, bright-eyed, ready with the coffee pot, cooking double because Donovan and Cassie liked turkey but the older generation insisted on their glazed ham, roast chicken, and rice and peas. And still she made time to join in the fun.

He sidesteps the ghosts of Christmas future. They're too painful.

Regular open house nights when the volume of the music – African, reggae, jazz and blues, ska and not forgetting a little Aretha – was edged up, notch by notch. Wine flowed, and when new neighbours came to the front door to ask if they could please turn down the volume, Helene inveigled them inside. They ended up being the last to leave.

Evenings in front of the television. Cassie, wedged under her mother's shoulder, sucking her thumb when she was too old to be sucking her thumb, or sitting patiently on cushions on the floor between Helene's legs and having her hair braided.

Helene, taking down the hem of Cassie's white Easter dress.

Emancipation day, a new tradition, but one Helene decided they should observe. "Our girl should know about her heritage."

"And we teach her about hardship with what? A *party?*"

"Traditional food, traditional music and traditional dancing."

The argument was lost the minute Helene wrapped her arms around his waist. (In those days it was still just about possible.) He sighed. "I'd better invite the neighbours."

And of course, Carnival. The celebration that didn't happen in 2003, and hadn't any year since. For fourteen years now Donovan has been living in a limbo he has no expectation of emerging from. The phone stopped ringing. Invitations stopped arriving. Donovan understood what was happening. Rather than risk saying the wrong thing, friends said nothing. In fact, they did more than say nothing. They crossed the street or moved to another queue at the supermarket tills when they saw Donovan approach. They didn't think he saw them, but he saw them alright. If saying hello was unavoidable, they always had something urgent to rush off for. He'd imagined that grief would isolate him, but no. It was the reaction of others. His friends left him shipwrecked. Even Helene – the one person Donovan assumed he would be able to turn to – cut herself off.

I miss my wife.

Few people come to the house now. There's really only the postman, the Tesco deliveryman and the woman who braids Helene's hair every third month. How *does* a natural extrovert cope with an adjustment of such magnitude? How did she manage to shut that side of herself down? For himself, Donovan is glad to leave his house of memories: glad to have a routine that takes him out into the world – yes, even the petty office politics he tells himself he hates.

Here at home, the experience of revisiting scenes from his life – however vivid, however happy – is bittersweet. Ultimately, there is always the comparison between then and now. 22 August 2003 is a clear demarcation. Cassie existed in the world. Cassie no longer existed in the world. And neither did Stefan and the precious soul who would have been his first grandchild. Two generations wiped out in a single blow. Donovan feels the rise and fall of his chest then, remembering why he's standing here spying, exaggerates a sigh.

"Is that you?" Helene asks without a glance in his direction.

"Guilty as charged." Donovan pushes his pain aside as he nudges open the door.

She pats the cushion beside her. "Come over here and grab a pew."

He sits down heavily and sighs a second time.

"Am I going to have to ask you what's up?" Her busy hands don't pause, not even for a moment.

"It's Jules and this exhibition of his. He seems to forget I work full-time."

"What's he asked you to do now?"

"The Victim Thirty-four T-shirts are ready to go. He

thinks it would be a good idea to get a social media campaign underway. The more we sell, the more curiosity we create and the more people will turn up at the exhibition wearing them." Helene's flickering hands make him think of Louise Bourgeois, who sculpted her mother as a spider because her hands were always busy. This is what Jules has done by sending him that damned book on modern art. Now, he associates his wife's hands with spiders.

"And the profit from these T-shirts?" she asks. "Will that go into the monument fund?"

"At the rate he's spending, there may not *be* any profit. Jules sent publicity shots showing his staff wearing the T-shirts. I had no idea he has so many people on his payroll."

Helene's hands pause at last. "Show me." She reaches for his phone, expands the picture on the screen. "*He* looks a bit young to be working."

Donovan leans in. The teenager in the shot is taller than some of the adults. "He looks like Jules, don't you think? I think he must be Louis."

"Little Louis?" Helene will be thinking of the one photograph all the papers printed: Jules cradling Louis' head, as if trying to protect him from the surrounding horror. In the background, survivors sit huddled, rocking in the gutter.

"Not so little now!" Perhaps this subject is one Donovan should steer away from, but Helene moves the conversation forwards.

"Even if there's no profit," she muses, "the exhibition will raise awareness about our fund."

Donovan maintains an unenthusiastic stance. "I suppose it might."

"I could do it. That way I can make *sure* it raises awareness."

He puts one hand on her knee. "A campaign will only be the beginning. What Jules forgets to say is that this will involve processing orders, packing the T-shirts –"

"You think I can't pack a few T-shirts? I virtually *ran* the Family Support Group. I've acted as secretary for all your fundraising."

Donovan stifles a smile. He has never known anyone who can be so tender one moment and so ferocious the next. "Of course I don't think that, but –"

"You know where you can stick your objections. I'm doing it." Already in Facebook, she clicks on Add a New Page. "You'd better send me those photos."

"You're sure?" Donovan will have to keep on top of trips to the Post Office, but he counted on that. A regular, he's forever returning things Helene has ordered on-line that don't fit, or are a different shade from the colour shown in the catalogue.

"I've started, haven't I? Call Jules or text him or do whatever you have to do to tell him I'm on it."

And she is. She really is. That page is almost populating itself.

"Alright then." He stands and moves towards the door, already typing into his phone. *She'll do it!*

Without looking up, Helene points at the ceiling. "Oh, and while you're at it, ask if I have an advertising budget. I need to know how many favours to call in."

A long day hunched over the computer working on her descriptions for the pieces, Maggie's back and shoulders burn. It's surprisingly difficult to keep the words simple. She has decided to put off writing the words for Rosie until she has the knack of it. No unnecessary emotion, just the facts. Let the work speak for itself. But words come, words come, though she tries to deny them entry.

She runs a bath, the first she has run for fourteen years. Dressed in a white towelling robe she perches, mesmerised by the water pouring from the mixer tap, thinking of Jules's waterfall, trying not to think too much about the buffalo, the sheep. One of her hands trails in the water. After shrugging her bathrobe from her shoulders, she tests the temperature with her toes, then steps in. Thoughts of the images that may come prevent her from immersing herself. It is too much. She crouches, pulls the plug then stands and watches until the last of the water has drained away. Deep Heat and a large glass of wine will have to do.

Tamsin stands in the doorway of her brother's room and breathes, steeling herself for the task ahead. Though the room has been aired, something noxious and musty lingers. If the smell has seeped into the bedlinen, the curtains and the carpet, then it will become part of the exhibition. And if it doesn't, will the exhibition be a true representation?

She visualises Jules's alternative propositions. In the first, *Keep Out* will be displayed within a cordoned-off area of a gallery. People will be free to wander its circuit, looking at whatever they choose. This is the option Mum favours. Perhaps she doesn't want people to sense that the room was ever sealed. In the second, visitors entering the gallery will be confronted with a cube-like structure the exact dimensions of Ollie's room. They will peer through openings, their view restricted. It is this option Tamsin prefers. To her, it seems truer. Dad hasn't expressed an opinion. "Just clear the damn room," were his exact words. No suggestion that he might help.

Tamsin moves into and around the room, taking photographs from every angle. Despite telling herself this is a job like any other, she repeats in her head a mantra, the inscription from Tutankhamun's tomb. *Eternally and Forever.* She can't afford to dwell on how she'll feel when other people are allowed access. Tamsin has never visited Ollie's grave. After refusing to go to his funeral, it would have felt hypocritical. Sealed off but a constant presence, this room and her memory of what was in it is all she has ever had to remember her brother by. Always there, on the other side of her bedroom wall. Until she moved out, Tamsin has never had the option of leaving it behind. It's not just Ollie's ancient history in this room. It's hers too. But make a good job of this and it may also be a passport to her future.

For the last series of shots, she lies on her left side and aims her lens under Ollie's bed. Forgotten homework assignments, lost ear buds, an odd rugby sock, junk food wrappers.

"Ready with the floor diagram, Mum?"

"Right here."

She takes the laser rangefinder out of her jeans pocket and measures the room, its door and windows, plus other features that might be used as openings. An airbrick. A poster for *The Big Lebowski.* Perhaps that mirror could become a two-way mirror. She calls out numbers, while Mum stands on the landing with the diagram she mapped out on graph paper. North is marked so that Jules can make sure the exhibit points in the right direction. Mum repeats the numbers back as she makes her notations. From these details, Tamsin will program a 3D image, capable of being rotated and viewed from every angle.

She takes the measurements between every item of furniture and calls out the figures. Before they move on to the detail, Tamsin inspects the floor plan.

"Look at you." Mum brushes at dust that has attached itself to Tamsin's left side.

"Don't!" Tamsin steps out of her mother's reach. "I'm under strict instruction to bag that. Jules wants to recreate something similar."

"He's going to manufacture dust?"

"One of *his team* is going to manufacture dust. He thinks they can make something to spray over the surface of everything." Tamsin nods approvingly at the diagram, then smiles. "We make a pretty good team."

Mum looks pleased. "That's the thing about temp work. You have to be quick at picking up instructions. And yours were one hell of a lot clearer than some I'm given!"

"Ready for the precise stuff?"

Mum lays a stapled list alongside the floor plan. On it, Tamsin has itemised every object she could see in the room. It runs to three pages. "As I'll ever be." Acknowledgment of the possibility that there may be a few hidden secrets.

Not for the first time, Tamsin is grateful that certain items were removed by grave robbers. Perhaps Mum will be thrown by how little evidence there is of Ollie's short-lived career. She imagines her saying to Dad, 'Do you know, there was nothing to back up what they told us.'

"Mum?" Tamsin begins tentatively.

"Yes, love."

"Did the police ever search Ollie's room?"

"Not that I know of."

"Meaning?"

"Meaning your father had the key."

"Even after he…"

"After he left, yes. Not that I suppose he gave it much thought."

"So," Tamsin changes her tone. "After I call out each measurement and you write it on the diagram, cross the item off the other list."

Tamsin aims the rangefinder and measures the exact positioning of every object, from the homework under the bed to the Nerf Gun. "Something to add to the list. Packet of condoms. Intact, thank God."

"I wouldn't be surprised if your dad handed them over during one of his father/son talks."

"Will he be bringing her to the opening night?" The question tumbles out before Tamsin can prevent it.

"It depends which 'her' you're talking about?" Mum's tone

makes Tamsin feel like a petulant child, but then it softens. "I think we have to assume that either Jackie or Sophie will be there. Maybe both. Wouldn't it be strange if they stayed away?"

'No,' Tamsin would like to say. 'This has nothing to do with them.' But it does. She tries to banish an image of the moment they come face to face. She padlocks it in a room. *Concentrate on the job in hand.* Only when she has cross-referenced the photographs with the sketch can she move items from their positions. Only then will she code, pack and label each one, ready to be moved to storage, and from there to the workshop where Jules will base his operation. Only after everything else is labelled and boxed will Jules send someone to lift the carpet. She has an idea that the real secrets have yet to reveal themselves.

"What's this?" asks Helene, taking another individually bagged T-Shirt out of a cardboard box. Her expression is horrified as she lays it on the dining room table.

On the back of each T-shirt is a single word. *Victim* or *Bystander.* (On each plastic bag are the words *danger of death by suffocation.)*

"Are there just the two designs?" Donovan asks, wondering if there might be a third: *Survivor.*

"Two," she says, picking one up, putting it down again. "All jumbled in together."

No instructions but, where Jules is concerned nothing is random. This will have a meaning. "We'll make two piles."

After emptying the second box, it is quite apparent that the Bystander pile will be four times as high as the Victim pile.

He sighs. "I think you get to play God."

"Like hell I will!" Helene retorts, and pushes past, sweeping the bulk of them onto the dining room floor as she goes.

Why the hell didn't Jules warn me? Donovan stands looking at the strewn T-shirts, unsure what his wife expects from him. This could be one of those occasions where he should leave everything exactly where it is, or it could be one of those occasions where he should remove every trace from the house. Problem is, they've already said that Helene will fill the orders. His wife struggles with the notion that it matters whether or not she honours commitments. Every promise pales when compared with how terribly the world has betrayed her. *He* could package the T-shirts, he supposes. He could work from his bench at the back of the garage.

OK.

He bends his knees and squats, not quite decided, wondering about the word *Victim*, how suddenly life is snuffed out, and why he must be the one who goes on with all its empty routines. *Snap out of it.* Then he starts to pick up the slippery plastic bags. When he tries to pile them on his right thigh, they don't want to stay put. How much time could packaging them possibly take? More than he has at his disposal, that's for sure.

Several minutes pass before Donovan senses that he's being observed. If he's right, Helene has only stormed halfway up the stairs – to the step they used to call the naughty step – and she's sitting, looking through the bannisters. There's something almost childlike about the position he imagines her in. He thinks of all the times he has watched her and assumed she didn't know he was there and thinks, *She knew!*

And then she says, quietly, "I'm ready to come back down now," and it's so like Cassie announcing that she's ready to say she's sorry that Donovan can barely stop himself from weeping.

Emails start arriving. Orders for T-shirts. People who live outside the UK buy on-line, but still they pledge money to the monument fund. The columns on Donovan's spreadsheet begin to fill up.

"You know what I think," says Helene the minute he closes the front door behind him.

"Do I get to take my coat off?" Off comes his cycle helmet then his hi-vis outerwear. He stashes his gloves inside the helmet and lays it to rest on the floor directly below the row of coat pegs. There are no smells of cooking to suggest dinner is under way.

Helene has abandoned blouses and jumpers in favour of her Victim Thirty-four T-shirt. Unlike other family members, she isn't saving it for the opening night. Seated at the dining room table, she is packing yet more T-shirts. She doesn't look up from her stash of padded envelopes and adhesive labels. "I think you should run the London Marathon wearing Victim." They're on first-name terms, she jokes. Victim isn't the only man she's on first-name terms with. There is Eric and Bill and Stuart and any number of others. "My virtual boyfriends," she calls them, and Donovan tries to suppress an illogical pang of jealousy.

"A marathon?" He grabs a handful of stomach. "Have you seen the size of me?"

This makes her look. She responds with laughter. "If you aren't going to do it, find a younger colleague who will."

Donovan balks at the 'younger', moves into the kitchen, opens the fridge and looks for the thing with the earliest 'use by' date.

"Green Thai curry do you?" he calls to Helene.

"Mm-mm."

Maybe he should start running again. A couple of months and he might be able to manage a 10k.

"I'll put a shout out as well. I've got a few friends who do these Parkruns."

Helene always has a few friends up her sleeves. *Who do*

I have? Donovan asks himself as he reads the microwave instructions. *I have colleagues.*

Donovan has never been a fan of social media, but he monitors the Facebook group as it fills up with reports of T-shirt sightings. Eric is first, photographing two American *Da Vinci Code* fans who showed up for his City Temples tour wearing Victim Thirty-four T-shirts. *'They won't be here for the exhibition but they knew they would be exploring the City, so they bought the shirts anyway! I'm going to set up a gallery page on my website.'*

'It's out there!' Lady Agoraphobic posts back. *'Can you tweet the photo and put it up on Instagram? Make sure you use #Victim34.'*

"Go easy on Eric," Donovan cautions.

"He's fine," Helene insists.

"I'm just saying."

The following week, after someone turns up wearing a T-shirt for his tour of Wren churches, Eric announces that he's decided to start flagging down everyone he sees wearing a Victim Thirty-four T-shirt and asking if they mind if he takes a selfie with them.

Donovan notes that Sorrel posts, *'Don't overstretch yourself. I'll be home at 9.00 x.'*

Eric replies. *'I know. It's a fine line.'*

He hopes Helene takes note of this exchange.

Photos begin to appear all over social media. Typical Eric won't take any credit. He shares photos posted by tourists who have taken their own selfies at the top of the Monument or in front of Tate Modern.

'Yeah, baby!' posts Lady Agoraphobic, who is capable of being enthusiastic and flirtatious; not the Helene Donovan knows, or has ever known for that matter. Lady Agoraphobic

is not the same woman Donovan comes home to after work. *'#Victim34 is trending!'*

In fact, their hashtag rarely strays from the top of the list. Helene posts memes with 'quotables', like *If a man isn't missed, did he ever truly exist?* and *A man doesn't die while his name is still spoken.* They produce replies by the hundreds.

'I hope you've got your end of the deal covered, Jules!' Donovan texts.

Jules arrives at the docks to supervise the loading of the shipping containers. This is the kind of detail he refuses to delegate. It feels peculiar to watch crates with the names of familiar *Objets*, things he thinks of as extensions of himself, being scooped up by forklift trucks. He has brought Louis with him, telling his son he thinks he'll find it interesting, but really, what sixteen-year-old finds his father's work interesting? What sixteen-year-old in the middle of his exam year has to contend with having his baby photo – a moment he has no memory of – splashed all over the internet? Perhaps, thinks Jules, Louis wants nothing to do with Detritus.

On seeing the crate labelled Victim Thirty-four Louis gives a small shout. Jules raises a hand in a stop sign. The boy must have seen something. As the forklift truck jerks to a halt, he fears for his polyester resin and fibreglass mannequin. There is serious work to be done, possibly the most serious Jules has ever attempted, and no room for a single fuck-up. A breakage would be a disaster. *"Qu'est-ce qu'il y a?"* Jules demands.

Louis looks sheepish. *"Je veux prendre une photo."*

"Une photo? C'est pour ça que tu l'as arrêté?" He breaks into a trot, shouting an apology as he goes. "My son, he give me a heart attack. All he want is a photo of me with Victim Thirty-four."

"Kids! They're all the same," the driver says from his cabin. "You want to sit up here?"

"I do not want to get you into trouble."

"You won't, mate. Not if I turn the thing off." The man kills the engine and clambers down.

Jules grins. "Well, in that case."

Donovan digs out his running shoes. It's been a while. Scruffy but serviceable is his assessment. He Googles 'training schedule for 10k run' and scrolls down to 'Intermediates'. He imagines the advice Stefan would have given: 'The best approach would be to start slowly.' The beginners' programme is designed for people who can already walk/run three miles in less than forty minutes. Donovan only knows his cycling speed but a thirteen-minute mile sounds do-able. Then reality hits. The first week's training is based on three sessions. Fifteen-minute runs broken up with two minutes of walking. There is no need to consult his GP to know that does *not* sound do-able. Instead, he opens a new spreadsheet in Excel. Week one, he'll aim for three sessions of five five-minute runs broken up with two minutes of walking. It will be two weeks before he can embark on the beginners' schedule. And that's if all goes well.

Ten minutes later he presents himself at the dining room door. "Back in forty," he says.

"Where are you off –?" Helene looks up from her brown paper pile and sees how he's dressed. Baseball cap, T-shirt, tracksuit bottoms and trainers. "Look at you!" she says and there it is: the smile. Something her on-line boyfriends don't get to see.

Inboxes fill with emails from Tate.org.uk about the 2017 summer line-up. *Members enjoy free unlimited access to all our exhibitions.* Pre-order tickets for Detritus are snapped up. Posters are plastered outside Tate Modern on giant billboards.

Eric messages Helene a photo. She messages back that the official artwork isn't a patch on what they've been putting out in the Facebook group. More posters adorn gleaming Underground tunnels and hang framed alongside the drops of escalators. People turn their heads and make mental notes to look up details of the exhibition without realising they're passing the very spot where the disaster originated. Personal invitations go out for the opening night. Helene sees an opportunity and sets up an on-line auction for hers. She purses her lips at the first bid of over five hundred pounds. *Hold out for more.* Interviews appear in magazines and newspaper supplements. There is no doubt that Jules gives a good interview. Those who've been scathing about his work in the past clamour for their fifteen minutes with him and he says things like, "It is so long ago now that people forget. But the families, we do not forget." He says, "Detritus – it is from the French, you know? It is about life wearing you down, expecting something when you have nothing to give. And it is about trying to build a life out of the things you are left with." Occasionally he says point blank, "No. I will not answer that question," and they seem to like these soundbites the most. Pictured on the front of *Time Out,* he cradles Louis' head, hugs him to his shoulder. The only part of Louis on display is his back but, at sixteen, he's already taller than his father. We can see the passage of time.

The thing takes on a life of its own.

CHAPTER THIRTY-SIX

2017

Opening night. Tamsin teams her T-shirt with a leather jacket, skinny jeans and biker boots. The unshakeable feeling that she'll be on display reminds her of a particularly nervous first-time director who, after refusing to go to his own opening night, sneaked into the back of the circle.

"You paid for a ticket?" she'd asked.

"Restricted view – in case I couldn't bear to look."

She studies her reflection in the mirror for signs of too-careful staging. It won't just be saying hello. A full-on conversation will be unavoidable. Which will probably mean spending the entire evening with him. Correction: with *them*. Whoever *they* happen to be. She experiments with a scalding glare. "I don't think you've met Gareth."

"Charming fella." Gareth kisses the crown of her head as he sidles past to fetch the nail clippers.

"You crept up on me!"

"Practising for your dad?"

"Hmmm."

"It's about time I met him. It's been four years."

"It's not you I'm worried about."

"No, But he's still your dad. You look great, by the way."
"I don't know. My eyebrows are lopsided."
"Really?"

Opening night: Maggie and Alan walk hand-in-hand along the South Bank. Alan's idea is to stop for a pizza. He's counting on a generous quota of free booze and intends to line his stomach. Capable of shutting out the London skyline – all the warehouses converted into shopping arcades and offices, church spires wedged into the spaces in between, backed by palatial glass and steel structures, architects' lavish daydreams made a reality – he tells Maggie how work takes him up and down the coast.

"I know I'm almost home when I see Holy Island."

Home. It's a strange in-between place Maggie finds herself in. The comfort of her husband's hand and those grounding names of childhood. Berwick upon Tweed, Bamburgh, Alnwick. Beyond Newcastle, over the York border, down to Whitby, the favoured location for family holidays. Places where change is slow, where buildings don't spring up overnight and vie for attention. Guilt tugs at her, and she doesn't want to feel guilty. What she wants is for Alan to be impressed by her contribution to the exhibition. She's checked her copy, satisfied herself that each label stands up to scrutiny, discreet so as to have no discernible style. She worries – of course she does – what Alan will think about the copy for *Identification,* that single paragraph she agonised over. But foremost in Maggie's mind is concern about Alan's reaction to *Identification* itself. She has an idea what to expect – she's seen the fake uniform and forged documents, so like the originals he'll wonder what the point was. And, of course, there's no way of knowing how seeing the exhibit in a glass case will make her feel. No, pizza is the last thing Maggie wants right now.

"I went on one of Eric's tours," she volunteers, in search of distraction.

"Oh, yes?"

"Wren churches. He's extremely good at what he does. He would have made a fantastic barrister."

"Burnt himself out, poor lad."

"I was wondering if I might be able to do something like that."

"Barrister?"

"Tour guide."

"Here?" He drops her hand.

"To begin with."

He says nothing. For a few terrible moments Maggie wonders if she should have spoken out, then her mind turns to whether he'll interpret her choice of words as a sign that her resolve is weakening.

"More tourists, I suppose," he says.

Opening night: Gina frets over her choice of clothes. She thought her best black trousers and heels would do, but they make her look as if she's on her way to a job interview. Two things you can count on: Bill won't work himself up over wardrobe choices, and bloody Jackie will manage to look glamorous in whatever she throws together at the last moment.

"Fuck it." She stamps off the trousers then sits on her bed with her head in her hands. Tonight, her usual social shorthand won't cut it. She's suffering from the kind of anxiety that precedes school reunions. The thought of all those people you haven't seen for years, come to flaunt their perfect figures and perfect clothes and photographs of their perfect lives on the latest smartphone. All the small talk, the niceties, the bonhomie she'll have to extend, not only towards the man who cast her aside, but towards the woman who replaced her in his affections. Others, seeing them side by side, will be unable to avoid making a comparison.

Stop it, she rebukes herself. *You can't let Tamsin see you like this.*

Tamsin! Quickly, she dials her daughter's number. "Hello, love. I just phoned to say my cab will be here at six thirty."

"We'll see you there, then."

"What are you wearing?"

"Jeans and biker boots."

"Are jeans OK, do you think?"

"Why, do you think they won't be?"

"Honestly, I'm despairing. I think Jules thought having a uniform would make life easier for us."

"Oh, no. You can't blame Jules. The T-shirts were your idea."

"Well, right now I'm wishing I'd kept my big mouth shut!"

"Calm down, Mum. Whatever you're wearing right now will be fine."

She laughs.

"What's so funny?"

"I'm sitting here in my underwear. If I go like this I'll be arrested."

"Put on those indigo jeans of yours and your black boots, then sling a chunky cardigan over the top. And do that up-thing with your hair that makes it look as if it's falling down."

"It usually *is* falling down."

"We'll meet you outside the front entrance."

"OK. Sorry. I'm a bag of nerves." *I could do with a drink.*

"Me too."

"Why should *you* be nervous? You've done a great job. I'm so proud of you."

"*We* did a great job."

"Can't I tell my daughter I'm proud of her?"

There's a pause. "Thanks, Mum, but it's not just about the exhibit."

"Your father's the one who should be feeling nervous, not you."

"I bet he won't be."

"No, I bet he won't. And neither will bloody Jackie."

Tamsin gives a sharp laugh. "Did you just say what I think you said?"

"Yes, I did. Bloody Jackie. I used her official title."

Opening night: Donovan's knees seem determined to betray him as he plods downstairs to find Helene, arms folded, in the hall.

They stand and look at each other. He doesn't want to go alone, yet he can't ask Helene to come with him. Neither can he make her feel guilty about the fact that she can't go. "We wouldn't have got here without you," he says.

She nods. "I did OK."

"You did *more* than OK." He slots his big arms into the sleeves of his Day-Glo waterproof jacket, ducks into his cycle helmet.

"You'll send my love to Stefan's folks, won't you?" Suddenly Helene sounds anxious. "The Georges sent such a nice Christmas card."

"I will."

"Tell them I still light the three candles."

He nods, momentarily overcome.

"You got our gifts for Victim?"

He taps a bulging pocket.

"Tell Eric he did good too."

"Don't worry. I'll send your love to *all* your virtual boyfriends."

"You do that. Now get out of here."

As he swings his leg over his cycle, Donovan is aware of his wife, standing in the doorway. Not Lady Agoraphobic but

Helene, standing on the threshold of a forbidden world with her unending sorrow.

"You will come home to me, won't you?" she calls after him. It's the first time she's ever asked this.

CHAPTER THIRTY-SEVEN

2017

Another waiter halts at Gina's elbow with a tray of champagne. They're doing the rounds, offering fresh glasses to anyone without, stealthily topping up anyone who has drunk more than an inch. Again, Gina politely refuses, tucking one hand inside a knitted sleeve to scratch at her wrist. The real longing is impossible to scratch.

She smiles at Sorrel's anecdote about an impossible judge, but keeps half an eye on people milling about the mezzanine foyer, which, for the purpose of the exhibition, is Jules's ticket hall. Though they raise hands or nod when they recognise her, an atmosphere of apprehension hovers. *How did* he *worm his way onto the guest list? And over there, isn't* she *a London Underground employee?* It's the not knowing quite what to expect. The feeling that after all these years of avoiding public transport, they won't be brave enough to confront it – whatever *it* is.

Gina is only too aware of what she'll have to confront. As the lift doors open, she stifles the sigh that surges through her chest. "Bill," she says softly, touching Eric's arm, both announcement and apology.

"We'll catch up with you later," he says.

Perhaps for the best, Tamsin and Gareth are nowhere to be seen. Though this is no chance encounter, Gina senses it's going to be every bit as excruciating as the scene from *When Harry Met Sally* where Billy Crystal is singing karaoke and his ex-wife waltzes in with Ira on her arm. In Gina's case, her agony will go on for the entire evening. How she handles these first few moments will set the tone. For a moment she imagines behaving badly; latching onto someone, pretending to flirt, throwing back her head and laughing. Instead she does the thing that will make others feel comfortable. She fixes a smile on her face and strides across the shining expanse. Everyone else on the mezzanine at Tate Modern, all those blank Facebook profiles, fade into the sheen of black walls and floor. There is only Bill and Jackie, the look of solidarity that passes between them when they see her approach, the way they so obviously steel themselves.

While Gina leans in to kiss Bill's cheek, Jackie keeps a firm grip of his hand. "And Jackie." She kisses the air at either side of her ex-husband's girlfriend's face, cheering herself with a solitary thought. Once the house is sold, there will be no reason for any further contact. She'll be free. "You managed to get a babysitter!" Her cheeks squeeze upwards like a squirrel's into a fake smile.

"Sophie stepped in." Bloody Jackie. Her hair is immaculate, of course.

"Ah," Gina says (for some inexplicable reason, this will become her default for the evening. Still, it has an authority that 'Oh' lacks).

Tamsin materialises from an out of the way corner. Gina cannot quite rid herself of the notion that it's her job to broker a truce. There's a step-brother and a half-sister she should get to know. But no prompting is needed. Tamsin steps forwards.

"Dad, Jackie, I don't think you've met Gareth."

Gareth lunges for Bill's hand. It's sweet, really, how keen

he is to make a good impression. Perhaps he'll be the one to build bridges.

Close by, another waiter is hovering, angling his bottle.

"Hey, don't give my daughter any more of that," Bill says, overloud and overhearty. "She'll have it all over the floor."

Don't, Gina thinks. *Don't imagine you can sweep everything under the carpet with a joke.*

There's a ringing sound: metal on glass. "I am sorry to have to interrupt you!"

"I think Jules is about to say a few words." Rarely has Gina been more grateful to be handed an excuse to turn away. The effort of being pleasant to someone she would normally avoid is particularly trying as forms of torture go.

Another waiter is at her elbow with a tray of what looks like more champagne. Irritation sparks. She has her hand ready in a stop sign when he asks, "Some sparkling elderflower for the toast?"

"Perfect," she mouths, glad to have something in a glass that doesn't invite that awkward question, 'Aren't you drinking?' Or that slightly less awkward question, 'Are you driving?'

"I hope you will not mind giving me a moment of your time."

"A moment. Right!" Donovan laughs his booming laugh. It's infectious.

"OK, so maybe two." Jules shrugs. "You know, people ask me, 'Why is your work all about the same thing?' Sometimes I tell them, 'Artists have to make choices. We can make a small noise about a lot of things or a lot of noise about one thing.' Sometime I say like Cohen, 'I have a very poor imagination. What I am is a journalist.'" The mention of journalism raises audible booing. "But sometimes, you know, they catch me out. I am honest. I tell them, 'It is because I still look for the answer'. I tell them, 'And my kind of malady, you know, there is no cure.'

"Everyone here tonight, we are all the same. That is why I ask you all to trust me with something personal. Maybe *the* most personal thing."

Though Gina has strayed outside her comfort zone, it is a privilege to be here, in this gallery. Yes, even with Bill and Jackie. She feels lighter as she holds her head high, and her mouth broadens into something approaching a smile.

"And out of it we make something that tell our story. It is a story I would rather we did not need to tell, but it is important that we tell it, and what I hope is that we do it justice. For all of you, I hope you are proud of what we do here."

This *is* pride. Not just in Tamsin, but in herself. Gina has been part of something. She camouflages a glance in Bill's direction. If he feels pride, he has no right to. But she finds Jackie nodding at her, smiling, which leaves only confusion.

"I have many, many thank yous to make and I am afraid I miss someone off, so I say thank you to you *all.* For being here, for your wisdom, for making the noise with me, for keeping the faith." Hands palm to palm, he gives a bow that brings to mind the Dalai Lama.

"Tonight, my friends, we all go down the escalator together. It will not be easy, but you know, the inquest it is not easy. *Both* inquests are not easy. You do not need me to tell you!" Jules hugs Louis to his shoulder. "But first, let us not forget our most important guest."

In the fake ticket hall is what will become another cordoned-off space. This evening the cordons are down. Victim Thirty-four is displayed on his plinth, a blank-faced mannequin, no identifying features, no country of origin, no fixed abode. One of the hidden five per cent, thought to have arrived as part of the post-2001 surge. Perhaps smuggled in the back of a lorry. Perhaps delivered by coach to Victoria station. He may not have been fleeing war, famine or perse-cution, but one thing is certain. If he found the better life he came in search of, it didn't last.

Jules approaches the mannequin. "Maybe the most important person here, and we say tonight that we have not forgotten you, Victim Thirty-four." He drapes the puffa jacket he has brought around his naked shoulders. "You are not from this country. This is so you do not feel the cold."

Louis has brought him a pair of headphones.

Crisanto gives him the *I Love London* baseball cap he no longer has a use for. His testimony helped secure the verdict. The families have paid for his flight out of here. He's on his way home to his family – at last.

Donovan balances a pair of sunglasses with startling amber lenses in place, quite a challenge when Victim has no ears to speak of. He crouches to set down a Tupperware box. "From Helene," he says. "Rice and peas."

Alan Chapple has brought a stick of pink seaside rock. "All the way from Whitby," he says.

Maggie, who told Gina that she hadn't done any embroidery since she sewed Rosie's initials into her school sportswear, has stitched *Victim Thirty-four* on a plain handkerchief, which she tucks into his coat pocket.

Tamsin struggles to get the friendship bracelets she's made over his stiff resin hands. Gareth lets out a small cheer as she succeeds in getting them onto his wrists. He has brought a Harry Potter wand, apparently picked out in desperation after wandering for two hours around a car boot sale.

Gina bumps shoulders with Bill as they both step forward at the same time.

Bill defers to her, "You first." Nobody watching would guess she begrudges him this, not only his timing – which seems a deliberate attempt to lend a suggestion of closeness to Tamsin and Gareth – but his appearance of politeness. Of course she was first.

She had wanted to bring something significant but the more she thought about it, the more it escaped her. In the end she did what she was good at. She wrote a name on a piece of paper. Now she slips it into his inside pocket, and offers a silent prayer. *No one should be known as a number. Here's your new name.*

Bill lays an *A-Z* by his feet. Gina, who has been the recipient of many of Bill's ill-advised presents, thinks it a strange choice, and then feels guilty about being so uncharitable.

Sorrel holds up the mocked-up document she's made. She reads, "Freedom of the City of London." There are small sounds of approval as she manages to place the scroll in one of Victim's curved resin hands.

But cheers are reserved for Eric who sticks a single Post-it note on Victim's chest. It reads *A + b + c = inevitable outcome.*

Someone, somewhere is missing a husband, a son, a father. Someone, somewhere must wonder. Gina sends up a thought, like a Chinese lantern rising into the night sky. *A man does not truly die while he is remembered.* She can never forget.

Movement out of the corner of Donovan's eye, an exchange of light and shadow. The footage of the waterfall has been switched on. He looks to the couple who were to have been grandparents to his grandson. They return his weak smile. "Shall we?" he invites.

Sadie inhales slowly, carefully, and exhales in much the same way. "You first," she says.

"Perhaps I should…" Donovan glances backwards and makes eye contact with Jules.

"Go!" Jules bats the air with a raised palm as if giving the command to attack.

Now there is no option. Though his eyes tell him the escalator is static, Donovan's body insists the opposite is true. Here is the paralysis, here at the precipice. Logic tells him *This is not the same escalator, it did not happen here,* but it is the same escalator, it happened right here. He reaches for the handrail and Cassie reaches for the handrail. He steps forward and Cassie steps forward. Claustrophobia, as if everything's closing in, but it's only the proximity of the adverts that hang suspended from the ceiling – replicas of the ads that adorned Old Billingsgate in August 2003, but Jules has replaced the models' faces with those of the victims. Unsure he's ready to see Cassie staring back at him, Donovan turns his attention to the wall opposite. He isn't certain what he's looking at. That large black silhouette with its legs and cloven feet that look too small to carry its bulk. Is that some kind of bison? There is no grace in the way it somersaults through the air. Suddenly everything is real. He imagines plummeting down, everything and everyone around him falling, hands flailing, grasping, finding only air. We think we are better than beasts; that we wouldn't follow blindly. The thing he wants to do most is lean backwards, sit down on his big behind, but he looks at his feet and walks down the escalator's immobile steps, his knees bent, like a little old man.

The waterfall doesn't shock Eric. Nothing can displace his own vision of Hell. But stepping off the bottom of the escalator, he comes to a sudden stop. A bouquet of yellow flowers has been propped up against the wall onto which the waterfall is projected. This simple gesture floors him.

Impatient to point it out to his wife, he waits for Sorrel who is walking down the stationary escalator with none of her usual grace. Eric wasn't expecting the strength of her grip on his arm.

"Seven years," she says, "all of that detail, and *still* I wasn't prepared."

"Do you want me to warn you what's coming up next?" he asks. Eric holds the exhibition, each room, each corridor, inside his head. Next will be number one of two new pieces Jules has made, assembled in situ on the vast slope of the Turbine Hall, their station concourse.

"No." Sorrel is more herself now that she's back on level ground. "That would defeat the object."

"Flowers," he nods, giving her something simple to focus on.

"Jules?" More of a breath than a word. Here, all meaning is amplified.

"Perhaps. Perhaps Louis."

Together they turn the corner and are confronted by *Crowd.* It is as Eric imagined, a many-headed Hydra that comes at them like a wave, ragged mouths gasping and wailing. No doubt it's crude, but Jules's use of unfinished clay lends a raw quality that makes it so striking.

"What kind of crowd is that?" Sorrel asks.

"The mob. The one the newspapers invented." But even as he says it, individual personalities start to emerge. Here are Sergi's delinquents and criminals, the aggressive elements. Other faces simply seem to be looking for escape. Knocked about, jostled, elbowed and pushed against the cordons that run alongside the piece, the individuals who make up the crowd have no choice. They are a large number of people fighting for limited resources. "It's monstrous," he says.

"Perhaps," Sorrel agrees. "But it's also inspired."

Maggie and Alan move into the maze – the tunnels. Her nervousness for Alan overtakes anything she might have been feeling for herself, expressing itself in an outpouring of words. So much is here that ordinary visitors won't be aware of. She points out how Jules experimented with lighting until he achieved the precise quality found in Tube tunnels; the scaled-down dimensions. But it's not Rosie's belongings they come to next. It's Donovan's crib.

It's quite extraordinary, the contrast between the fluorescent glare of the tunnels and soft warm glow of the side gallery. Although the transition seems to demand silence,

Maggie can't help making the sound of an O. There is a very real sense that a child is sleeping in this intimate side chapel. She holds her breath, tiptoes, glancing back at Alan, silently communicating that the child mustn't be woken. The light and the shadows strike Maggie next. They have the same effect as the cylindrical night light Rosie loved so much, the one that rotated, its cut-out shapes projecting circus animals onto her bedroom walls. There are the end pieces of the crib, and the struts, each ready to fall into place. Or blown apart, but blown apart with such delicacy. Hanging from wires, catching the light, are the nuts, bolts and screws that would have held the whole thing together. And like Rosie's night light, everything is rotating very, very slowly.

She covers her mouth with one hand, marvelling at the miracle Jules has performed. Poetic and yet incredibly potent. And there they are, Donovan and the Georges. Transfixed, they lend form and shadow so that they, too, are part of the sculpture. No one will read her label. *Which,* she tells herself, *is exactly as it should be.*

A tug at her sleeve. "Come along, Marg," whispers Alan, nodding towards the doorway where people with reverent expressions wait, not wanting to crowd the space. Reluctant, but knowing she'll never drink her fill, she allows him to lead her by the hand.

She waits until they have moved away before speaking. "That was –" But there is no way to finish her sentence.

"Yes, it was," says Alan. "Clever bastard, your Frenchman."

Gareth frowns at the neat pile of items stacked on the plinth in their individual plastic bags. "What is it?"

Though Tamsin understands exactly what she's looking at, she's reluctant to try and put it into words. What if she chooses the wrong ones? "Let's read the card on the wall." Then her mouth falls open. If Maggie wrote the copy for all the cards, she will have written the words to go with Rosie's possessions. The sheer awfulness of this thought roots her to the spot.

Behind her, the flat footfall of shoes, and a low mutter: "I see everyone's a fucking victim now."

It's as if a pin has been stuck deep in the flesh of Tamsin's stomach. Her hand goes to the spot; her shoulders hunch. She remembers Dad grabbing Mum's arm, hissing, *"She's got a nerve showing her face."* She daren't look to confirm her suspicion of the speaker's identity for fear he wanted to provoke a reaction, and she cannot look behind her for fear that the Chapples might be close by, expecting her to jump to Rosie's defence.

Beside her once more, Gareth focuses his attention on the exhibit and she's glad of this moment's privacy. "They're all replicas," he says, taking everything in: the passport, the utility bills, the keys, the uniform. Everyday things in any other context.

"I see everyone's a fucking victim now." The words reverberate.

Tamsin only heard that one sentence, not what prompted it, nor the reply – assuming there was one. It may *not* have been about Rosie. Quite possibly, it was a reaction to the presence of London Underground staff, ambulance controllers, paramedics. Jules expects the families to be better than they are.

"It's so sad, what a life comes down to." Gareth's head jerks up, as if he's shocked himself and would take it back if he could. He reaches for Tamsin's arm. "Sorry."

She looks at him but doesn't see, not really. *"Everyone's a fucking victim now."* Something inside her, some part she's previously been unaware of, begins to unravel.

"I didn't mean to upset you."

"You haven't. Honestly." Even if the speaker was someone

other than her father, it was still her father speaking. Even if her father didn't say it, he thought it. He never wanted Mum to have anything to do with Maggie.

"I don't think I got it." Gareth's Adam's apple moves. "Until tonight."

Tamsin's eyes prickle with shame. Before tonight she didn't get it either. Before this evening, she had no idea that, on one level at least, she blamed Rosie. But not any more.

Suddenly she needs to be near her brother. "Come on," she says. "Let's go and see Ollie."

Some cruel unwritten etiquette has dictated that Gina must spend what feels like an unreasonable amount of time in the company of her ex-husband's girlfriend. Admittedly, Jackie has been more pleasant than she's ever been before. Perhaps she feels as if the baby's arrival has legitimised her relationship with Bill. Perhaps marriage is on the cards. It may be the news that someone's put in an offer on Gina's house, that an improvement in finances is on the horizon – finally! But none of this makes the situation any more bearable. Gina doesn't want to have to make one more introduction, repeating, "This is Jackie, Bill's girlfriend" and to wince at the response, "It's great how comfortable you all are with this," when the opposite is true. Perhaps Bill thinks he's giving the 'women in his life' as she heard him refer to them, space to get to know each other. Now, there's an horrific thought! What's even more galling is having to watch him shake hands with Eric and Sorrel, people he had zero confidence in, and the very people she'd prefer to be talking to.

Every few moments, Jackie's eyes flit about, as if she's reassuring herself of Bill's presence. Gina can pretend that she's simply offering a commentary on who he's talking to, but the truth is this: she is aware of Bill, wherever he is, whether or not he's standing behind or to the side of her, whoever he's talking to, even if she's pretending to studiously ignore him. Resent him all she likes, Gina can still miss and want him. She summons snapshots from the time when she and Bill couldn't keep their hands off each other, when they were still exploring each other's bodies, discovering the freckles and moles few others would see. She relishes the thrill that comes from conjuring images into being while smiling at an unsuspecting Jackie.

Even this cannot compensate for the fact that Tamsin and Gareth are keeping their distance. Not that she can blame them. It's just that she had so wanted them to see *Keep Out* together.

And then it's there. The white box with its wooden framework on the outside, small openings on each side. She had thought she wanted the open-plan option; the option you could walk up to and around. Gravity pulls Gina towards it, step by solemn step, like walking up the aisle of a church, like the careful walk through hospital corridors towards the maternity ward, like the tarmac path towards a mound of damp, cold earth marking the place where a son will be buried. Gina thinks about the words 'gravity' and 'grave'. If any two objects in the universe were to be drawn to one another, it would surely be her and this structure.

This is not a moment she wants to share with Jackie. *If she* dares *say anything now*. Gina gives herself permission to experience the moment deeply. How it feels to find herself shut out once more. How terrible Tamsin must have felt when she found herself exiled – and for that Gina must shoulder the blame. But here is an opening. Here is hope. She is about to introduce herself after an absence.

She blinkers her eyes, leans her hands lightly against the structure, and looks in through a square opening at head height. All of the Ollies are there. Ollie laid on her breast for the first time. *CRACK!* Her shoulders jump, but the memory of jumping over cracks in the pavement brings a smile to her lips. She looks again. Ollie the adored and much imitated big brother. Ollie of the outlandish excuses. Ollie, accomplice to a drug dealer. Eric's version of Ollie – the teenager turned hero. The prodigal son.

"Oh, Jackie."

Bill's voice comes from somewhere to her right, and she doesn't want to be pulled away, not now, but look she must. Jackie's head is low and she has the middle finger of one hand to her forehead so that her eyes are obscured. Her shoulders are shaking. Bill glances at Gina as he reaches Jackie and pulls her towards him. It's almost as if he's saying, 'See what a caring person she is?'

"I'll be fine in a minute," Jackie is saying, "I just need some air."

"Come on. Let me take you outside."

"There's no need. You should stay, see the rest of the exhibition."

"Of course there is."

As Bill walks away, Jackie leaning into his shoulder as she allows him to lead her out into the maze, Gina experiences an unexpected wrench. *Without him there would have been no Ollie. There would be no Tamsin.*

Then Gareth is beside her, Tamsin only a moment behind. "We just passed Jackie. Is she alright?" Gareth asks.

"Gone to get some air." *Gone. Gone,* she tries to communicate to her daughter. *Gone,* she thinks, trying to adjust to the feeling.

Gareth nods, his expression serious. "It's so powerful, really *seeing* it all for the first time. But it must be that much harder for you and Tamsin." Gina likes the way he defers to her daughter.

"I told you. Stop fussing. He keeps fussing, Mum."

Gina smiles. "Come and look, darling."

Her daughter walks towards *Keep Out,* but instead of putting her face up against the square opening, she wraps her arms around Gina. Gina strokes her daughter's hair then kisses her head, and it's almost as if she can feel goosebumps. But before she can say anything, Tamsin says, "I love you, Mum."

It is not over. It will never be over. There is an unspoken promise that there will be a continuation of what has happened here, and that it will continue on any number of levels. It comes as no surprise to Donovan when Gina stops beside him and says, "What's next?"

"The monument, of course."

"How's the fund looking?"

"It could always be better. But good. Good."

"Rumour has it you're running next year's London marathon."

He gives an exasperated cry. "A *half* marathon! And between you and me, even that's going to be a push." He scowls into Gina's amused face.

"It must be nice to have someone who believes in you."

Irritation fizzles. "You know, for a woman who hasn't left the house in the past dozen years or so, my wife gets about a bit." There. He's alluded to the fact that he's jealous. Helene has given herself permission not to go out into the world, but he must. If Gina notices anything, she doesn't react.

She shrugs. "Still."

"Was that –?" Unsure how to refer to the woman he assumes was Bill's girlfriend, he moves his mouth to the side, sniffs.

"Jackie," Gina says, as if she's both bemused and has a bad taste in her mouth. "Or Bloody Jackie, as I call her. Yup." She smiles. "I loved *Crib.*" It's a new subject. They're done with Jackie.

"*I* loved *Crib.*" Donovan is still staggered. "I can't quite…"

317

"What about Helene?"

"No." There is no question about it.

"That's a shame."

"She makes her own choices." But Donovan wonders if, had he known what it would be like to be there with the Georges, the only other people who can possibly understand, if there had been some way to bypass the escalators, he might have been able to persuade his wife to cross the threshold. Just for one night.

ACKNOWLEDGMENTS

To the many…

I drew inspiration and collated information from a number of sources, including Disasteraction.org.uk, Health and Safety Executive Website, House of Commons Transport Committee, Overcrowding on Public Transport, Seventh Report of Session Volume 1 2002-2003, The Future Tube Priorities Investigative Committee, Mind the Gap (between what customers actually want and what they get), January 2003, Too Close for Comfort (passengers' experiences of London Underground), December 2009. Any misinterpretations are my own.

A mountain of praise to my team of beta readers, especially Liz Carr who goes above and beyond, Beth Allen, Karen Begg (without whom I would have had Ollie wearing school uniform during the summer holiday), Sheila de Borde, Anne Clinton, Kath Crowley, Sheila Christie, Sue Darnell, Sarah Diss Evans, Helen Enefer, Mary Fuller, the lovely Dawn Gill (to use her official title), Sarah Hurley, Liz Lewis, Lynn Pearce, Deb McEwan, Sarah Marshall, Matthew Martin, Harry Matthews, Amanda Osborne, Delia Porter, Will Poole, Sally Salmon, Peter Snell, patron saint of indie authors and bookseller extraordinaire, Julie Spearritt, Eleanor Steele (who read the manuscript when she was soon to give birth to her second child and so generously shared her pregnancy experiences) and Clare Weiner.

Extra special thanks to my editors Dan Holloway of Rogue Interrobang https://rogueinterrobang.com/, John Hudspith (http://www.johnhudspith.co.uk), proofreader Perry Iles (contact him at chamberproof@yahoo.co.uk). Special thanks to Carol Cooper (http://pillsandpillowtalk.com) for the French translations.

And not forgetting Andrew Candy for his fabulous cover design, JD Design for typesetting, and, last but by no means least, all of the team at Clays.

ABOUT THE AUTHOR

Hailed by *The Bookseller* as 'One to Watch', Jane Davis is the author of eight novels.

Jane spent her twenties and the first part of her thirties chasing promotions at work, but when she achieved what she'd set out to do, she discovered that it wasn't what she wanted after all. It was then that she turned to writing.

Her debut, *Half-truths & White Lies*, won the Daily Mail First Novel Award 2008. Of her subsequent three novels, Compulsion Reads wrote, 'Davis is a phenomenal writer, whose ability to create well-rounded characters that are easy to relate to feels effortless'. Her 2015 novel, *An Unknown Woman*, was Writing Magazine's Self-published Book of the Year 2016 and has been shortlisted for two further awards.

Jane lives in Carshalton, Surrey with her Formula 1 obsessed, star-gazing, beer-brewing partner, surrounded by growing piles of paperbacks, CDs and general chaos. When she isn't writing, you may spot her disappearing up a mountain with a camera in hand. Her favourite description of fiction is 'made-up truth'.

A personal request from Jane: "Your opinion really matters to authors and to readers who are wondering which book to pick next. If you love a book, please tell your friends and post a review. Facebook, Amazon, Smashwords and Goodreads are all great places to start."

OTHER TITLES
BY THE AUTHOR

Half-truths & White Lies

These Fragile Things

A Funeral for an Owl

An Unchoreographed Life

An Unknown Woman

My Counterfeit Self

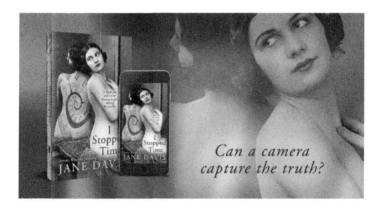

Can a camera capture the truth?

For further information, visit https://jane-davis.co.uk. Sign up today at https://jane-davis.co.uk/newsletter to be the first to hear about future projects, pre-launch specials, discounts and competitions. You'll also receive a free eBook of reader favourite *I Stopped Time*.